Cloudy Hands

Peter Trenouth

DEDICATION

For my family.

CHAPTER 1

July 2006

A low flagstone wall in exactly layered slabs bordered the trim, verdant lawn of the Douglas Funeral Home. My weary legs and back ached after the second two-hour visiting session. With suit jacket draped over an arm, I sat on the wall and faced St. Joseph's Episcopal Church. The next day I would eulogize my wife Cara while her earthly remains dissolved in a crematorium ten miles away.

My son Luke waited with me. Behind us the illuminated Douglas sign lit the large, white house. The summer night's mugginess felt better than the air-conditioned room where we had stood and greeted visitors, everyone familiar except Cara's co-workers. Luke sat on the wall. Our knees bent sharply. We had been the last to leave, right after my daughter Katelyn and her husband Gareth left to get the car. In their last view of Cara, she wore a pink Red Sox cap Gareth had given her because she hated her wig. Cara didn't want an open casket. Her sister, who had arrived from Florida, asked for one last look. I had already seen too much, from the hospital stays and outpatient treatments through the hospice weeks to the silent last breath in our bedroom, but I gave in to her sister's request. For the funeral director this was an easy maneuver, which he and an assistant quickly arranged after he asked everyone to leave the room for a moment. The pink hat atop the hairless head caught my sight as I re-entered behind my sister-in-law, her son and daughter, and her husband. When they exited to the foyer, weeping, Katelyn and Luke entered again and knelt by their mother's casket. That's when I backed deeper into the hall and stood with Gareth and the few remaining visitors.

Across the street granite boulders cut in rectangles shaped and buttressed St. Joseph's. The edifice rose from high ground retained by more granite. Though it was never Cara's spiritual home, she consented to have her memorial service there. I had finished typing her eulogy the morning before the wake, parts composed at unwritten intervals during the months of Cara's decline, her fate known since February. She endured the treatments while we lived one day at a time.

The seven-year old Mini pulled up, Katelyn driving. Gareth stepped from the passenger's side and gently offered me the front.

"You sit next to Katelyn," I said and lowered myself into the rear seat.

My legs and back still hurt. My knees drew up close again. Luke climbed in next to me. Katelyn asked how I was doing. I said okay and asked about everyone else. They each said they were fine and relieved the long day had ended.

"Yes," I said, "a long day."

CHAPTER 2

The Epiphany dinner at St. Joseph's drew about forty parishioners, a decent turnout. New England's January cold kept many people home, and some churchgoers never came to Saturday events like this. I looked forward to the company, and the food was always good. Besides, getting out of the house I had lived in the past twenty-three years had become a necessary habit.

My retirement from teaching started the month before Cara died. After the funeral Katelyn and Gareth returned to Queens, at best a four-hour drive away, and Luke flew back to Seattle. I made a point of seeing my sister Fran once a week. Twice I hosted a dinner party with Fran and her husband Dom and one other couple. I consulted Cara's cookbooks and planned carefully. I also experimented with one new dish—"jazz" was my name for it, never the same thing twice, usually a vegetable mix—and served lots of wine. Sometimes Fran would invite me over or we would see a movie together. Most of all, activities at St. Joseph's kept me involved. People there were good to me.

When the hospice weeks began, I figured daily visits from nurses and aides would keep Cara as comfortable as possible while I did whatever else needed to be done for her and around the house. Experienced caregivers at St. Joseph's knew better. They organized teams of parishioners and teacher colleagues to bring meals, clean the place, tend to Cara, and provide the restful times I often needed. When she slept, Cara breathed with labored, throaty sounds that kept me awake because the silence between each breath lasted forever. When awake, she couldn't transfer from her bed to the commode and back without help. In the final ten days she couldn't leave the bed at all.

The hospice nurses taught me to administer the morphine from the bedside dispenser that puffed an aspirated sound each time it sent the drug into Cara's I-V. The doses became stronger and more frequent as the last day drew nearer. Katelyn, Gareth, and Luke came home after hospice started. At first the strangers in the house bothered them, but once they saw how a family-only deathwatch would be unbearable, they welcomed the "angels," as I called them, all women.

By the time I walked into the parish hall, several angels had already arrived. The here-and-now often took me to the past. St. Joseph's rector, the Reverend Diane Fleming, had cautioned that haunting memories couldn't be willed away, though time reduces their frequency and eases the sorrow. She was right.

Cara had been the household treasurer with a frugality she didn't want questioned. My resentment always vanished at Christmas and birthdays, the only times Cara could spend money happily. Retired and alone, I took up financial responsibilities and worried too much, which was stupid. I was debt free. The house's thirty-year mortgage was paid off in twenty-four. Our loaded savings account awaited ready for whimsy, and my pension checks came faster than needed—all due to Cara's pinched pennies. I got through the holidays buying a ton of gifts. It was fun. Now with no long range plans for managing income or anything else, even six months after Cara's death, I at least knew my age was sixty-two, not eighty-two, and my best course was to follow whatever impulses kept me active.

Diane watched my going to the card table near the parish hall's entrance. The teenage girl whose name I couldn't remember agreed to sell tickets after she discovered she was the only person her age at this event. Diane was St. Joseph's first female rector. She wore a long wool skirt and embroidered sweater buttoned over her black blouse. As usual she wore a cleric's collar. Short red hair framed her round cherub face. It seemed all the more youthful with her petite, slim stature. Diane had wanted to be a priest since she was a teenager. She was ordained while still in her twenties. Six years ago I had been on the search committee that recommended her to the vestry. Now a thirty-four-year-old single woman living in the rectory adjacent to the church, Diane guarded her private life and her feelings, yet she projected a natural grace people trusted. We met weekly to discuss parish business. Sometimes these sessions became personal. Diane asked how I was doing and offered pastoral advice. Sometimes I asked her how she was doing. She always replied she was good and added little else.

"I want you to meet some new parishioners," Diane said.

She beckoned a man and woman and a girl who I guessed was their daughter. Parishioners, especially lay leaders, should welcome newcomers, no easy trick for many Episcopalians. The parents looked to be in their late thirties. The husband was my height and carried about twenty pounds more. His wife, six inches shorter, looked trim. His balding dark hair contrasted with her thick, auburn curls. Diane introduced the husband and wife and their eight-year old daughter who had her dad's dimpled grin. She said hello and hurried off to a corner table where Diane had stacked crayons and paper for the kids with instructions to make pictures of the Wise Men's arrival.

From the kitchen a large, buxom woman my age waved at me, her fingers flapping away. I was relieved to see she was too busy talking on the cell phone tucked under her dyed mass of yellow, frizzy hair and watching two angels take roasts from the oven to burst into the parish hall. She would make some big deal out of seeing me, a habit she developed a week after Cara's funeral. Harriet Pringle loved to cook, or so she said. Whenever a team of women took charge of St. Joseph's kitchen, she struck me as a third stringer.

"This is Stephen Pentheny, our senior warden," Diane said to the couple.

"I wish Anglican custom hadn't created that term," I said. "I'm really not an aged jail keeper."

The couple laughed, and Diane excused herself and walked to the kids' table. The couple explained they had recently moved to Scrooby and after some church shopping decided on St. Joseph's.

"We're new to the Episcopal Church," said the wife. "So what does a senior warden do? I don't think I ever heard that term before."

"Good question." I stopped myself from saying "whatever the rector tells me to do."

One of the angels, a member of the Ladies' Group who had prepared the dinner, announced people should now line up to be served at the kitchen counter. Salad, pitchers of water and punch, and bread were already on the tables. Everyone fell into line.

"I suppose every denomination has parish lay leaders," I continued. "In the Episcopal Church the rector is the parish's chief administrator as well as priest. That's typical everywhere, I guess."

I feared sounding like an arid, old bore but kept going anyway.

"The rector is hired by and answers to the vestry. We have twelve people on the vestry, what in other denominations might be called the parish council. The vestry also includes the treasurer, clerk, and the two wardens—junior and senior. The parish elects them at our annual meeting. In fact, we have one coming up the end of this month."

The couple seemed very interested. "Yes, I noticed that in the parish newsletter Diane gave us. So you're like the leader of the parish?" the husband said.

"The lay leader, one of many. Here at St. Joseph's the hardest working layperson is the junior warden, Jerry Devereaux."

I pointed to a broad shouldered man whose back was to them. "He's in charge of building and grounds. St. Joseph's custom has the junior warden handle those things. He's much more important than I am."

I lowered my voice to a whisper. "But you mustn't tell the others, and for heaven's sake don't tell him."

The couple copied my mock seriousness as they whispered this secret was safe with them.

Jerry Devereaux sat across from two Asian women whom I had not met but had seen after an eight o'clock service in early November. Two months before an angel in the choir had urged me to join. She probably concluded the Thursday night rehearsals would do me good. She wasn't the only person to think so. Sunday mornings the choir also arrived an hour before the ten o'clock service for a final run-through. Jerry, my best friend, sang in the choir and insisted that if he could come to church an hour earlier I should haul my lazy ass in at the same time. That November Sunday I had noticed the two women on my way to the choir room because St. Joseph's had very few worshippers at the eight o'clock and fewer nonwhite worshippers in the whole parish. The two had lingered after the early service. Jerry sat with them. He was the son of a Creole jazz trumpeter and like Diane knew all too well the old joke about Episcopalians being God's frozen people and hoped to change that image at St. Joseph's. The three had seemed very serious.

With my plate loaded I stepped to two containers of boxed wine and filled my small plastic cup with Merlot, then headed towards Jerry's table. Last year Diane and I had instructed vestry members to sit apart during coffee hour and church gatherings because they shouldn't seem like a clique separate from everyone else. This practice was so well established I knew it would look odd for the two wardens to eat together tonight, even if they were best friends. No doubt Harriet Pringle noticed my move. She had been studying me since I walked in. My excuse was I wanted to meet more newcomers, which was true, but I especially wanted to meet the younger of the two women, the one who most caught my attention in that quick-step moment after the eight o'clock service two months ago.

Each table sat four on each side. The new couple and their daughter followed me. I took the open seat next to Jerry across from the younger of the two Asian women, their seats the closest to the table's end. I introduced the new family to Jerry saying their first names only, Bill and Jen. I had forgotten their last names. They introduced their daughter, Becky, who sat next to her mother who sat next to the older of the two women. Bill sat next to Jerry.

"You're new to St. Joseph's then," Jerry said. He shook hands with the new family before he gestured towards the two women. "I'd like you all to meet Qiao-Yun Wang and Wen Du. They're also newcomers."

I tried to duplicate Jerry's pronunciations and spoke Qiao-Yun as "*Chow-Yoon Wong.*"

"*Chaow-Yooen,*" the younger woman said. "*Wahng.*"

I repeated what she said, hoping my obvious difficulty with foreign sounds didn't offend.

"Yes," Qiao-Yun said. "Very good."

I then said, "*When Do,*" hoping I heard the two English-sounding syllables correctly.

"Very good," Wen said.

I said their names again. Everyone chuckled and exchanged greetings. Wen's age seemed about fifty.

"Jerry say you senior warden," Qiao-Yun said.

"Yes." I extended my hand. Qiao-Yun looked no older than my daughter. She smiled. It had been a long time since I had pondered a young woman's smile. It's not my habit to make strong eye contact, but now I did. Qiao-Yun's fingers touched my palm with a warmth I hadn't expected. It delayed my taking Wen's hand.

"Qiao-Yun and Wen usually come to the eight o'clock," Jerry said.

Two tables away Diane stood and asked everyone to hold hands for grace. Jerry sat to my right. Qiao-Yun stretched her arm across the table towards me. Jerry's hand was large and calloused, though I barely felt it. The reach across the table caused Qiao-Yun to cup her right hand upwards. I cupped mine downward, and my four fingers hooked within hers. All through Diane's prayer, which I barely heard with my head lowered and eyes closed, I again felt the warmth in Qiao-Yun's fingers.

Everyone starting eating, and Bill asked if there was any significance to roast beef for an Epiphany dinner. Jerry said he couldn't think of any and went on to explain other seasonal events at St. Joseph's. Qiao-Yun ate and listened. She had no wedding ring. Wen did have one, which to my Holmesian reasoning meant married Chinese women wore wedding rings and Qiao-Yun wasn't married. The indentation on my ringless finger disappeared last fall. I sipped my Merlot.

Jen spoke Qiao-Yun's and Wen's names. "Are you both from China?"

"Taiwan," Wen said.

"We don't know each other there," Qiao-Yun said. "We meet here."

I tried to recall ever speaking with anyone from Taiwan other than a server in a Chinese restaurant back in the day when few people from mainland China could get into the United States. Americans called that country Red China and officially said its two billion residents didn't exist. At the same time we armed ourselves to the nuclear teeth to keep them and the Soviets away. There had to be a China somewhere, so for thirty years we said it was this small island a hundred miles off the mainland because it wasn't Communist. I lived through enough twentieth-century history to know Taiwan's former global status had collapsed into a pile of contradictions. The mainland had been officially recognized since the Carter Administration, and Taiwan, the Republic of China, held a vague standing with the rest of the world. It lost its seat in the United Nations to the People's Republic of China. Meanwhile the PRC said they owned Taiwan and proclaimed the Republic of China didn't exist except in the minds of the apostate Taiwanese who should keep their mouths shut if they knew what was good for them. No one outside Taiwan argued the point but traded with the island as though it were its own country. I was curious about all this geopolitics but not nearly as curious as I was about Qiao-Yun.

"How did you know I was senior warden?" I asked her.

"I see your name sometimes. Not many peoples go to the early service. Most peoples who do the things here go to the ten o'clock service. Jerry told me who you are."

I cut into my roast beef, consciously making small pieces instead of gulping through my meal as usual. I sipped my wine again and decided this single cup was enough. The table conversation shifted to the food, everyone agreeing the roast was delicious as were the Delmonico potatoes. Jen and Bill asked Jerry about new projects at the church, and he explained the kitchen needed new storage cabinets and the downstairs bathrooms needed new flooring. Bill asked him how he became junior warden. Jerry explained how past junior wardens had been architects or contractors or guys who knew something about building maintenance. I stopped listening and spoke to Qiao-Yun.

"I used to teach high school English. What do you do?"

"I teacher too. I have martial arts school, and I teach Chinese language. I also do acupressure sessions in my home."

I knew almost nothing about martial arts, had no idea what acupressure was, and wondered whether food words like *Foo Yong* were authentic.

"What kind of martial arts do you teach?"

"Tai Chi."

I pictured people in Chinese dress like the ones on television when the arrival of the new millennium was global news and cameras were positioned to catch the era's first sunrises. Scores of Chinese people had gathered on a hillside and were going through careful steps and hand motions. The announcer said this was the ancient practice of Tai Chi and many Chinese did these fluid exercises every morning. It fit none of my notions about Asian martial arts, which came from channel surfing past movies I never wanted to see.

"I don't know anything about Tai Chi," I said.

As Qiao-Yun spoke, her face suggested she was answering my question with a question of her own, but I couldn't hear her. The din of conversations and clatter enveloped her words, and her accent required careful listening. The food was delicious, though, and everyone's attention turned to eating. I was about to ask Qiao-Yun to repeat what she said when Bill's voice broke through the moment.

"How long have you been senior warden, Stephen?"

I wanted to ignore Bill and talk with Qiao-Yun. Instead his question brought memories of Cara. Three weeks after my term started it was clear the hysterectomy hadn't removed all the malignant cells. They spread to her brain and elsewhere, and the prognosis promised no cure. Cara needed all the help I could give her. After consulting Diane, I explained my resignation in the parish newsletter. My predecessor agreed to finish my term as senior warden until the fall when Diane urged me to resume the job I started and then serve another term. I had no reason to refuse but didn't want to explain all this to Bill, not now anyway.

"Both Stephen and I are finishing our first years," Jerry said.

"And you, Jerry, are you an architect or contractor?" Bill asked.

"I have a pick-up truck and many tools. I do home renovations. Grounds keeping is another specialty."

Jerry pushed his chair back from the table. "But right now I'm most interested in dessert. Becky, would you like to help me bring some to the table?"

Becky looked at her mother who nodded. The two headed toward the counter. I finished my Merlot and asked whether anyone wanted coffee.

"I know what Bill likes," Jen said. "I'll help you."

I asked Qiao-Yun and Wen how they wanted their coffee. Qiao-Yun said she would have a black decaf. She started to collect the dishes. Wen wanted nothing and helped Qiao-Yun.

People at every table were now active doing the same shuffle. Diane, with the help of a boy and girl, posted the kids' sketched and crayon colored Epiphany scenes on the bulletin board by the entrance, six in all. Jen and I returned with the coffees as Qiao-Yun carried her stack of plates into the kitchen. The jangle of dinnerware, together with the churning of the dishwasher, caused voices to rise, and I watched Qiao-Yun weave between tables and chairs on her way back. She and Wen spoke briefly.

Across the hall Diane stood and asked for everyone's attention and pointed out the kids' pictures, asking each artist to explain its contents. The kids drew babies better than they drew camels. Each had the general idea, even though nearly every Wise Man looked like Dumbledore. Becky's picture was the most original. She had perspective. She placed the Wise Men in the distance, approaching but not quite arriving at the manger scene. I whispered this appraisal to Bill who said his daughter loved to draw.

Diane then spoke about gifts, the ones from the Magi, and the gift Jesus was to all humankind. My side of the table faced Diane. Qiao-Yun had turned around. I hoped Diane would soon finish. When she did, Qiao-Yun shifted back and like everyone else delved into her dessert. I wanted to ask her what she had asked me but then thought it probably didn't matter since she hadn't raised the question again. Still, it must have been something. I wondered how old she was, certainly younger than Wen, maybe in her early thirties. People said I look no more than fifty, which I liked to believe was right.

Qiao-Yun was very pretty. Her hair was long and dark, her figure slender and curvy within brown slacks and blouse that somehow looked more exotic and alluring on her than if a Caucasian woman wore them. Her metal necklace and dangling earrings added to the foreign allure. Maybe her clothes and jewelry came from Taiwan. Although she was about seven inches shorter than my six-feet, any man would notice and remember her. It was the smile that did it, that and the touch, the warmth in her hand.

From across the room Harriet Pringle worked her ample form behind Qiao-Yun's chair.

"Stephen, I haven't spoken to you in ages. How were your holidays? Of course your family was here for Christmas."

I last saw Harriet at the choir's Christmas party a month ago which seemed a bit odd because Harriet wasn't in the choir, though she was on the vestry and friendly with the host, an alto who also served on the vestry. I remembered her refilling my eggnog cup as I contemplated the table of food people had brought. She loaded my plate with meatballs, claiming they were her secret recipe. I tasted one and didn't touch another. That was hardly ages ago.

"No, I drove down to New York, Harriet. It was good to see Katelyn and Gareth again. Luke flew in too. It was very nice."

It would be just like Harriet to offer an opinion about why the children should come to the father his first Christmas as a widower, and I didn't want to hear that or explain why getting up at four and driving down with hardly any traffic to spend my first Christmas in thirty-eight years away from my own home and with my VW Beetle loaded with presents was truly my idea of holiday fun. I could have left the day before but wanted to sing with the choir at the late Christmas Eve service. Christmas Eve at St. Joseph's, Christmas Day in Queens—that suited me very well.

"If you're ever traveling on Christmas and know you'll go through tolls," I said, "Give candy canes to the booth people. You'll make them very happy. I now have a dear friend who works the Triboro Bridge. How was your Christmas, Harriet?"

Harriet looked down at Qiao-Yun then smiled at the others.

"Oh, the usual," she said. "They all love the spread I put out, so everybody comes to my house on Christmas."

I couldn't imagine who the everybody was and wanted to change the subject because if she asked about my New Year's Eve, I didn't want to explain my spending the night alone and going to bed at ten. Nor did I want to explain how Jerry showed up the next morning with an armful of breakfast groceries and how we cooked up mounds of pancakes, omelets, home fries, and ham before sitting down to *The Twilight Zone* marathon on television we had started watching separately the night before. She of all people would never understand.

"We have some newcomers at this table, Harriet." I introduced Bill, Jen, and Becky. As I mentioned Wen and Qiao-Yun, Harriet moved to the side of the table to get a better look. Bill started to rise.

"Oh, please, enjoy your dessert," Harriet said. The eyes under her wrinkled brow examined the two Chinese women. It was a moment too long before she spoke again. "It's so good you could join us. We love preparing these dinners."

"It shows," Jerry said, holding a forkful of cake to his mouth, which became a stern, straight line. While other voices at the table praised the meal, his unyielding focus stayed on Harriet.

The parish hall clatter grew again. Chairs shifted in the mild chaos of forty-plus adults and ten children getting ready to leave one place and move on with whatever else their evening might hold.

Over the noise I said, "We all hope the new people at this table become regulars at St. Joseph's."

Harriet returned Jerry's glare and held it for what seemed like thirty seconds before she looked at me.

"Yes, I'm sure that will be very nice," she said.

When she walked away, Jerry ate his cake.

Now everyone at the table was standing and bringing dinnerware to the kitchen, scraping excess food into a fifty-gallon garbage can, and placing their things on racks atop the stainless steel counter. Two ladies arranged the racks and pushed them into the dishwasher machine. Three husbands grabbed sponges and headed towards the tables. The cleanup was in full form. A person was either a part of it or getting out of the way.

I saw Qiao-Yun by the coat rack with Wen, who already had her coat on as Qiao-Yun reached for her hanger. Exiting the kitchen was awkward, especially against a crowd determined to get to the counter. Qiao-Yun saw my intention while her arm went into a sleeve, and she started to step towards me. We met a few feet from the shuffling arms and twisting torsos near the coat rack.

"I hope you had a good time," I said.

"I driving with Wen," she said. "I liked dinner very much. Wen want to go home to her husband. I must go now. I looking for you to say good night."

"I'm glad we met. Welcome again to St. Joseph's."

"Thank you. Tell Jerry thank you too. And…" She said something lost in the commotion about Bill and Jen I didn't quite hear, but her next sentence came through. "I think the little girl, the Becky, she very good artist. Good night, Stephen."

"Goodnight, Qiao-Yun," I said. She took my outstretched hand. I hoped mine didn't feel cold compared to hers.

After walking to each table and squaring the chairs, Jerry filled two plastic cups with wine before one of the women took the boxes away. He sat at a table far from the door where I stood with Diane, saying goodnight to the exiting parishioners. Jerry and I would lock up.

"Did you enjoy your dinner?" Diane asked.

"We always eat well at St. Joseph's. The kids were cute. Nice work with them."

Diane put her coat on, her voice rising to say goodnight to Jerry who waved and said the same. We agreed to see each other in the morning as she flipped her scarf over her shoulder and left. I walked to Jerry's table and sat across from him. He passed me a cup of wine.

"Is it wickedly sinful," he asked, "for me to say here in the parish hall that Harriet Pringle is a pain in the ass?"

"Probably not." I took a deep swig.

Two elderly angels, together with their husbands, wiped down the kitchen counter and sorted the steaming silverware from the last rack out of the dishwasher.

"Did you have a good time tonight?" Jerry asked.

"Yes, I did."

"I'm glad. Did you tell Qiao-Yun about George Herbert?"

"Why would I go into all that?"

Jerry loved to goad me. "Because you and I and Diane are probably the only people at St. Joseph's who know George Herbert ever existed. And I only know because you told me about your book. Qiao-Yun likes you. Anyone could see that. It might interest her to know you're literate."

"I told you I'm writing a book about George Herbert because you're my friend, more or less."

"Which means you know I'd care that you're writing a book. It doesn't matter whether it's about a sixteenth-century Anglican priest who wrote poetry or—"

"Seventeenth century."

"Or anything else. It's what you do, along with whatever it is you do around here. You're doing something. You're productive. You're not just some drooling, old retired guy sitting around the house waiting for his next bowel movement."

"And since I didn't announce I'm writing a book that's how people assume I spend my time?"

Jerry drained his cup. "I can't say for sure. The point is writing that book is very important to you. It's an impressive thing, writing a book. And come on, you wanted to impress Qiao-Yun."

"Let's just say she impressed me. I'm way too old for her."

"Not if you're still young enough to write a book. That's what I'm trying to tell you."

"You have an odd way of figuring ages."

"It's better than yours."

"You know it was Diane's idea I should write about George Herbert."

"The point is you're doing it."

The people in the kitchen were done and bid us goodnight as they grabbed their coats and walked towards the door. We thanked them for their help.

"This wasn't the first time I saw Qiao-Yun and Wen," I said. "They were sitting with you after the eight o'clock about two months ago. What was that about?"

"Oh, you do notice a thing or two." Jerry sat back in his chair. "Qiao-Yun has a house way down off Lake Street. I fixed a leak in her roof. Wen wanted to come to St. Joseph's but didn't want to come alone. All their Chinese friends trek to a church in Lexington. Qiao-Yun had been a Quaker back in Taiwan. A middle school friend's family encouraged her to join them. When she moved to Scrooby, she wanted to go a Chinese-language, Christian church, but long drives to and from Lexington ate up her Sundays, her only free day. I said if Qiao-Yun could live with our English they should come to St. Joseph's together."

"And you just happened to be at the eight o'clock the Sunday they came?"

"More or less."

"I remember how they looked. They weren't happy."

"I have that effect on some people."

"A lot of people." I finished my wine. "Are you going to tell me what you know?"

"I don't know much. But everything I told you is true. Let's just say she was looking for someone like Diane to talk to."

I pictured the two together opposite the coffee table in the rector's office, Diane's face in the same expression she held during my sessions with her.

"I think that's true for most people, more than they know."

Jerry took the empty cups to the trash. I got the lights. On the outside steps, Jerry asked if I would talk with Qiao-Yun again.

"Of course, I'll talk with her. I'm senior warden. I talk with everyone."

"You know what I mean, Stephen."

Bright lights gleamed from across the street. The week-old snow reflected the glare around the Douglas Funeral Home's sign, making the house and lawn a shiny white island amidst the shadows of leafless trees.

"See you tomorrow," I said.

CHAPTER 3

My house was a three-bedroom Cape. Five years after Cara and I moved in with the kids, we added a two-car garage. Two years later, after her father died and left her seven thousand dollars, she wanted an in-the-ground pool. To me Cara's inheritance was hers to do with as she liked, but I wondered whether the family would ever again spend a summer's day at the beach. We didn't, and for good reasons. We never had to spend a boiling summer afternoon searching for an ocean-side parking space or a towel-width track of beach sand, and with the pool we all became excellent swimmers. Cara built most of the decking around the thirty-eight-by-eighteen foot pool herself with concrete blocks, sifting the dirt and tapping each ten-pounder into its place with a rubber mallet. Two months after Cara died, Fran's husband Dom helped me close the pool for the winter, a project that took longer than usual because Cara had known the routine better than anyone, even though I had closed the pool twenty times with her. Dom also helped me open the pool just prior to the hospice weeks.

The largest bedroom was on the first floor. I seldom went upstairs to Katelyn's and Luke's old rooms, except to do some infrequent dusting. I gave much more attention to the downstairs where adjacent to the master bedroom there was my study, which contained two desks, one with my computer, and my overloaded floor-to-ceiling bookcases. The house's combined living and dining room extended from the front to the back, and the kitchen was alongside with one door facing the front of the house and opposite a door to the back porch. Within these rooms I spent nearly all my time, especially after the cold weather came.

A kayak I bought in September, Gareth's suggestion, hung from straps in the second garage bay, what had been my parking space. I had given Cara's old station wagon to Luke, which he drove cross country after the funeral, and moved my Volkswagen Beetle to the bay nearest the house. When I left in darkness for the Epiphany dinner, I remembered to leave the outside light on for my return, which this Saturday night came at eight-thirty.

I hung my coat in the closet and switched on the light in the study with thoughts of doing some writing. I considered putting on the computer and then typing up my notes scrawled on a legal-size pad. These were jotted fragments about "Aaron" taken from my volume of

George Herbert's poetry. The poem has five stanzas and each stanza has five lines. The name "Aaron" has five letters. I had tapped out the poem's meter and found a consistent rhythm of four stressed and unstressed syllables ran in the second and fourth lines of each stanza but not the other three lines. Aaron was Israel's first high priest. He was Moses' brother-in-law. They had stood together through the challenges to Pharaoh and into the wilderness, but Aaron also ordered the making of the golden calf while Moses went off to Mount Sinai. Neither Moses nor Aaron made it to the Promised Land. Herbert began his poem with reference to Aaron's exquisite robes. In his priestly vestments, Herbert felt closer to Aaron whose faith had lapsed than to Christ whom Herbert had pledged to serve. Herbert's poetry always has tension such as the contrast between his "Defects and darkness" and the "Perfect and light" he so desired. Herbert bended toward divine light, but his own darkness always kept part of him in shadows. That was the point. Only part of the interior self, two lines within each set of five, matched the desired mold. No wonder Diane wanted me to study such poetry.

I looked at the bookcases. Some shelves contained the books I taught high school classes. Some others contained well-worn tomes, most about language and writing, and history books and biographies while other shelves held favorites I would always keep, and then there were the books I promised myself to read someday, their numbers growing. I kept all my hardbound undergraduate anthologies and the texts of criticism from my graduate classes.

I knew a lot about literature and the ways to teach it and believed writing served two functions, the second of which is communication; the first, I told my students, is to teach yourself things you don't already know, to form clarity from the vagueness and confusions of life. My last superintendent, Bob Norris, had accused me of having unrealistic priorities. He removed me as English Department Coordinator. That was almost three years ago. Every day I thought about this dismissal, the people and circumstances behind it, just as every day I thought about Cara, especially within this house. I put down the legal pad and shut off the light. Perhaps tomorrow I would return to "Aaron," and there were those other George Herbert poems too, the same tensions but in different ways.

I walked to the living room and turned on the television. A

documentary about the Second World War was on. I often watched such programs. "Dad's dreary documentaries" my kids called them. They never saw what was so appealing about these shows, but Gareth did. Despite all the carnage and destruction, the good guys finally won. I went into the kitchen and pulled the cork from a bottle of Chianti opened the night before to go with my spaghetti and sausage dinner. I filled a wine glass and returned to the living room where Allied ships steamed towards England across the grey, U-boat infested Atlantic.

In the morning I arrived at St. Joseph's a few minutes before nine o'clock. Choir members were supposed to change into their black robes and white cottas, which are like quadruple large t-shirts that we wore over the robes, and then assemble to rehearse the anthem, the hymn sung during the collection, and review the other hymns. Jerry sang bass, and I liked to stand next to him because I can't read music and tend to sing the sopranos' melody in a deep register instead of the bass line. In high school chorus I always made the same mistake until the choral director placed me next to his best bass. Only then could I get the right notes. My voice wasn't as good as Jerry's. Sometimes when the music and words moved me and my confidence was strong, I sang in a rich, round tone that landed on correct notes more often than not. Usually, though, I mumbled in a voice too cautious to make much difference.

Cara had a sweet singing voice, but she would never join St. Joseph's choir. That would mean regular church attendance and participating in a group activity, neither of which attracted her. The few times she went to St. Joseph's she would stand and hold the hymnal while the congregation sang and she silently read the words, Christmas carols the lone exception when she released her voice with the others. Once I asked her why she wouldn't sing the hymns. She stiffened and didn't explain. Thirteen years ago when I started going to St. Joseph's, she said, "If it weren't for Henry VIII's divorce, you'd be as Catholic as I was."

I once hoped we could join the choir together. If I had joined without her, she never would have come to my church because she would have to sit separated from me among congregants she considered strangers just as she regarded most people as strangers, and strangers always made her uncomfortable. After Cara died, I joined the choir to have a place to be with familiar faces one night a week. At Cara's funeral ten choir members sat in the stalls, and their singing carried the music Katelyn, Luke, and I had chosen. I owed them something for that.

My bond with the choir was stronger than my bond with the choir director, Janice Patterson, whom I respected as a competent musician. Some people saw her as the main reason why the choir's numbers dwindled over the years, barely half the thirty when Janice came ten years ago, basses and tenors the fewest in number. Although Diane recruited other musicians from the parish who brought guitars and sang an occasional contemporary song, the choir's repertoire remained traditional, and like all old church music it could be beautiful sometimes but often sounded somber and dull. At Diane's urging Jerry occasionally played his guitar and sang. Also at Diane's urging, once a month he assembled a bunch of Sunday school kids and labeled them the children's choir. Jerry taught the kids simple songs of praise, and he had a lot of fun doing this, which contrasted sharply with his displeasure for Janice. Long ago his father told him Duke Ellington kept his orchestra together after big bands became unaffordable. He paid them with the royalties from his compositions.

"Ellington used his band like a piano. He composed with them," Jerry said, interrupting me from my silent rehearsal of the biblical selection I was to read during the service. We were robed and waiting in the choir room for Janice to come and start the run-through of the anthem. "Ellington needed his musicians to challenge him so he'd keep making something new. Now here's the thing. Janice uses us like her personal instrument. But there's a huge difference. And there sure isn't anything new happening."

"Why are you telling me this again?"

"Because you've got the good sense to appreciate Ellington."

"And?"

"And you know what I'm talking about."

Throughout my career, I knew some teachers used kids in ways similar to what Janice was doing with the choir. Bob Norris was the same way, a leader who needed more than he could give so he kept taking, all in the guise of a greater cause, and he was very good at this. Bob and I started teaching English at the same high school the same year. We became friends. I was pleased when he became an assistant principal and later the principal. By the time he left to become an assistant superintendent in a posh district north of Boston, I was glad to see him go. He had changed or, to put it more accurately, his ability to disguise his priorities deteriorated as he rose up the ladder, at least to me. Two years after his departure he returned when the school committee hired him back as superintendent. School committees rarely see through people like Bob, and he didn't like my promotion to department coordinator in his absence. My status as a member of his administration would have to change, sooner or later. Something would be lost, I knew—my mind, soul, or job. I got off easy. I lost the job, and Bob let me take a position teaching Grade Eight U.S. History at one of the middle schools rather than remain in the high school English Department working with a new coordinator whose first allegiance was to the superintendent and certainly not to notions I had—what Bob called "idealistic and lofty"—about learning. Jerry and Duke Ellington had their idealistic and lofty notions about the kinds of music people could create. Janice Patterson thought differently. In Jerry's view nothing good would happen with St. Joseph's music program until Janice Patterson was fired. Knowing a thing or two about getting fired, I hoped for a different solution.

"You're personalizing what's wrong with the music program, and I'd rather fix it without getting into what you're talking about," I said to Jerry.

"That's what you've been doing with that music committee you and Diane slapped together. That's how you always approach problems, but you know as well as I do—"

Janice Patterson's entrance into the choir room stopped Jerry from finishing his sentence. I knew little about her other than she taught a business administration course part-time at a nearby college. Her undergraduate major had been music; her MBA came sometime later. How the one led to the other I didn't know. She became an investment counselor with a big firm, a job that had not ended well. She looked like the stereotypical no-nonsense career woman devoted to maintaining the right image: tall, thin, always conservatively dressed and properly accessorized. She had dark, meticulously colored hair that she parted high on the side and had cut just below the jaw line framing a face abundantly made up without looking like enamel.

The choir knew all the hymns for the service. Two run-throughs of the anthem brought them to where they had been the previous Thursday when they had rehearsed, which meant we needed more practice to be any good. This anthem was impossible, a Latin piece in complicated, mechanistic parts. For me following the bass line and pronouncing the unfamiliar words were frustrating. Besides, my mind was elsewhere until Janice focused on the basses, working the four of us through each measure. With no place to hide, I concentrated to reconcile the sounds I heard Jerry and the piano making with the printed page and the warble falling from my mouth. The third isolated run-through brought me closer to where a bass should be, although my understanding became nothing more than a series of sounds strung together.

Janice looked at her watch. "Well, that should be all right," she said. "Let's get ready for the processional."

St. Joseph's sanctuary was one of my favorite places. One aisle ran the full length dividing the nave, where the congregants sat, each side marked by fifteen oak pews. The south side widened with a second aisle bordering a side chapel with seven pews. The altar in the chapel stood before a columbarium set against the facing wall with its multiple tiers of rectangular niches, some containing urns and bearing engraved names. These vaults became part of the chapel ten years ago, someone's fundraising idea that caught on. Cara's ashes were not placed there. From the time the doctors knew her cancer would kill her, neither she nor I brought up the question about what to do with her remains. We had endured these months acting as though the chemotherapy and radiation would work. At the same time we knew the malignancy networked faster than any remedy. Diane brought up the subject during one of her pastoral visits. Cara liked Diane, who certainly knew her job. Cara said she didn't care what happened to her ashes. Diane told me, "She does care. She doesn't want to talk about it."

The wall opposite the chapel, the sanctuary's north wall, held four great arches of stained glass. Three held images of Jesus. The other showed Paul, Silas, and Barnabas facing a band of men before a hillside city marked by Greek architecture. The sanctuary's rear wall held another image of Christ, this time carrying a lamb and flanked by two other male figures. One held the Greek letter Alpha; the other held Omega.

At the sanctuary's other end four marble steps separated the nave from the chancel where four choir stalls occupied one side. The organist could face the choir from the opposite side. Years ago three other choir pews stood near the mighty pipe organ. These pews were removed to make room for the sound system console, an electric keyboard, and space for the musicians Diane brought in. On the wall over the occupied choir stalls hung a large mirror, a leftover from the days when the choir numbered over thirty, the men on one side of the chancel with women on the other. The mirror made the organist's gestures visible to both sides. With the entire choir easily seated across from Janice, the purposeless mirror remained.

As usual in Episcopal churches, the altar was placed at the very front of the sanctuary, and was elevated one step up from the chancel. Red cushioned pads lined the step, and a rail with a hinged segment to allow entrance spanned the space. Acolytes closed the gate and arranged the cushions during the Eucharistic prayers, and Communicants knelt to receive the bread and wine, their knees on the pads and their hands above the rail. Elegant wood paneling rose behind the altar leading to two magnificent woodcarvings. One was an image of Peter holding the keys to the kingdom. The other was Paul holding a sword symbolizing his spiritual struggle and a scroll representing his epistles.

The church's iconography and oak pews reminded me of the parishes I knew as a kid. St. Joseph's long, heavy beams supporting the sanctuary's roof reminded me of the first church, the one I was baptized in. My mother took Fran and me there every Sunday until my father's ever-present financial shortfalls caused him to give up the only house he ever owned and move the family to a succession of apartments farther south of Boston. St. Joseph's woodwork and stained glass windows reminded me of the second church, the one where I was confirmed. These images from my boyhood worked now as they did then. They said the universe makes sense despite whatever went on outside the church's walls.

As the choir entered the sanctuary to line up for the procession, I studied the faces in the congregation hoping to find Qiao-Yun. She was sitting next to Wen and smiled when she realized I spotted her. As the choir walked the side aisle to reach the back of the church, I looked back. She and Wen were facing forward. The organ prelude was ending, and soon the procession would start, with acolytes and choir going first, then the Eucharistic ministers, and then Diane in a white robe and green stole, the color for Epiphany. I walked and sang the processional hymn beside Jerry and took my place in the back choir stall with the other two basses and one tenor.

Although parishioners knew the drill of switching from the two hymnals to the Book of Common Prayer and back again while holding the weekly order of worship—what some old timers called Episcopal calisthenics—Diane announced what book and page were needed next in the hopes someone new was present. This Sunday I was also a reader and a Eucharistic minister, someone who helped serve the bread and wine the priest had consecrated. Once the opening hymn and prayers ended, the Biblical readings came next. One of the angels, Olivia Finch, read the Old Testament passage in her soft, almost whispering tone, and led the congregation in the responsive reading of the appointed psalm. Diane would read the Gospel selection, but before that I would read what usually came from one of the New Testament's letters, but on the first Sunday after Epiphany the passage came from Acts.

I edged my way out of the choir stall, walked towards the lectern, and found my place in the huge open book of service readings and spoke the words Peter spoke to a group in Caesarea after he had converted a Roman centurion. I read, carefully pacing my delivery:

You know the message he sent to the people of Israel, preaching peace by Jesus Christ—he is Lord of all. That message spread throughout Judea, beginning in Galilee after the baptism that John announced: how God anointed Jesus of Nazareth with the Holy Spirit and with power; how he went about doing good and healing all who were oppressed by the devil, for God was with him.

I truly believe messages like this, though not the devil stuff, not literally. I lifted my eyes from the text to say the closing words, and Qiao-Yun looked directly at me.

"The word of the Lord," I said.

Qiao-Yun and the congregation responded, "Thanks be to God."

I had two remaining roles in the service. Before Communion came the Prayers of the People, a litany of intercessions. I led those, and after each the congregation responded: "Lord, hear our prayer." During Communion Diane offered the wafers of bread. One half of the rail went to Olivia Finch who, like me, carried a chalice of wine. I had the rail's other half.

"The body of Christ, the bread of heaven," Diane said, making eye contact with each communicant.

Behind her Olivia and I offered: "The blood of Christ, the cup of salvation."

Qiao-Yun sat on the right side of the aisle and came to Olivia's side of the rail. We had connected earlier in the service, between the sermon and Communion, when worshippers offered peace to each other. While everyone shook hands and said "Peace" to the persons seated nearest to them, I quickly followed the custom with Jerry and then bolted across the chancel to where Janice Patterson sat wedged behind the organ.

"Peace, Janice," I said as she took my offered hand.

"Peace , Stephen."

I exchanged the word with the acolyte who crossed my path as she headed toward her parents, and then I darted towards Qiao-Yun to touch her hand again, to make that contact once again. I spied on her during Olivia's reading of the psalm and Diane's Gospel passage about John's baptizing Jesus. Maybe Qiao-Yun spied on me too. I hoped so and realized I was acting like a seventh-grader hung up on the gorgeous new girl who cooed he was really nice when he showed her how her locker combination worked. I would have felt silly if it weren't such fun feeling this way, a sensation that lasted well into Diane's sermon. She had been retelling the events of Epiphany and tying them to Jesus' baptism and then brought them together with her reflection about the passage I had read. Diane mentioned the Communion we would share and said Peter's account of Jesus' ministry would have no lasting purpose unless Christians since his time had striven to keep it going. The reenactment of the Last Supper is the symbolic part of how we do this, she explained.

This was all I heard, and it made me think of Cara because Anglicanism, especially St. Joseph's brand of it, contended with Catholic dogma despite the similarities in words and appearances, and Cara knew this. Over the years I wondered whether she didn't sing the hymns and take Communion because they resembled her childhood Catholicism or because they weren't exactly the same, and then I realized I was thinking about my dead wife while I longed to touch the hand of a living woman who sat three pews in front of me—a Chinese martial arts expert who spoke an English at odds with the one I had taught and who might be thirty years younger but was beautiful and seemed to think me attractive, and who went to my church. What's more she read prayers aloud with the congregation and sang hymns, and I could tell she would come to Communion. And I knew we had something more in common even though I couldn't name it but had vaguely sensed it that November morning when I first saw her. She was sad that Sunday and had brought her sorrow to St. Joseph's hoping to get rid of it just as I had done on a Christmas Eve fifteen years before. Yes, we had this church experience in common, which was nice, very nice. But it wasn't the thing I couldn't name, nor was I going to spend any more time this morning trying to figure it out.

As I plodded my way through others' hands offering peace, I took them and said the words, all the while stepping and shuffling towards the third pew, and I could see Qiao-Yun saw me coming. She smiled again. I shook the hand of the elderly man in her pew closest to the aisle. I couldn't remember his name. Wen grinned as she took my hand. We offered peace and said each other's name, and Wen looked at Qiao-Yun as though she knew something special was happening when I bent my frame past her. Qiao-Yun's arm caused Wen to lean back, almost forcing her to sit. Qiao-Yun's fingers slipped over mine, and my fingers slipped along hers until we found each other's palms. My angled stance brought my face to her level.

"Peace, Qiao-Yun."

"Peace, Stephen," Qiao-Yun said.

I hurried back to the choir stall before Diane read the weekly announcements, my mission accomplished and my face no doubt still beaming even as we droned the anthem during the collection. Qiao-Yun had done nothing extraordinary. She had a church dinner with me and took my hand. She had looked into my eyes. She had wished me peace. Yet somehow all this was extraordinary.

Diane and the congregation read the final Communion prayer: *...Send us now into the world in peace, and grant us strength and courage to love and serve you with gladness and singleness of heart; through Christ our Lord. Amen.*

A different gladness held me. During the recessional when the choir, acolytes, Eucharistic ministers, and priest parade down the center aisle, I sang the last hymn with buoyant full voice as though I too were "westward leading, still proceeding."

After the dismissal and the people responded, "Thanks be to God," and the two acolytes, one boy and one girl in their early teens, extinguished the altar candles, Diane walked towards the arched entrance to greet the exiting parishioners who did not head the opposite way towards the coffee and pastries upstairs. I followed her and stood ten feet away flashing my senior warden good cheer.

"Great sermon," I said, all the while watching for Qiao-Yun, hoping she would stay for coffee if I invited her. She and Wen moved closer towards me in the talkative line. I kept eyeing her as I shook hands and spoke with those who approached me. Qiao-Yun said something to a vestry member, Josefa Garcia, whom she apparently knew because she called her Jo. Two hand shakes later Jo stood in front of me.

"I'm sorry I missed last night's dinner," she said, "had to work. Qiao-Yun tells me it was a good time."

"It was a good time," I said, and Jo moved on to Diane. And then Qiao-Yun was in front of me.

"I'm glad I come to ten o'clock service."

"I am too. There's coffee upstairs. Please join us."

Now I had to think. If she said no, I needed a plan. I didn't have one. I couldn't ask her for her telephone number, not now, not here, not with other people milling alongside.

"Thank you," Qiao-Yun said. "We must be going. I'm sorry."

I tried to think of something else to say.

"Maybe next week," she said, ending the silence I couldn't think fast enough to break. "That would be nice."

Wen said, "My son borrow my car. Qiao-Yun drive me home. I am why we go now."

I took Wen's hand. "Well maybe next week you both can come to coffee."

Qiao-Yun looked at Wen. "Yes, next Sunday will be better."

Behind them stood a man and woman in their eighties who were the last in line. I knew the couple. They attended Cara's funeral even though they, like all of St. Joseph's parishioners, hardly knew her. As much as I wanted to speak longer with Qiao-Yun, we had said all we could about coffee, and I couldn't keep the couple waiting.

"I'll see you then," I said.

Qiao-Yun and Wen walked toward Diane who all but shouted their names. The three women broke into laughter.

CHAPTER 4

I took half a bagel from the coffee hour remnants on the parish hall's counter and munched it while I drew coffee from the near empty urn. Moments earlier as I was leaving the sanctuary, Janice Patterson gathered her sheets of music from the organ. Twice before I had invited her to join the committee Jerry spoke of. I approached Janice and asked whether she had time to attend the Music Committee meeting which would be starting after coffee hour.

"Thank you, Stephen," she said. "I still think it's best if that group works without me."

"This isn't just an empty courtesy, Janice. We could use your input."

Again Janice declined, and she walked away, excusing herself and saying she had to return the sheets in her hand to the music room. I sat in a chair across from Olivia Finch and put my coffee on the table and considered mentioning my Janice conversation and maybe telling about Qiao-Yun. Years ago Olivia must have looked like Botticelli's Venus, with her flowing ginger-colored hair. Only a few facial lines and strands of gray spoke her age. I asked about her family, her husband Ralph who rarely came to Sunday services and her grown children who, like mine, had moved to other states.

Olivia glowed. "We expect our grandson to arrive any day now."

I remembered Olivia's telling me her daughter-in-law was pregnant. "This has to be very exciting for you, Liv."

"It is, very exciting." Olivia pealed the paper from her cranberry muffin. "I'm afraid I'm still in my holiday eating mode. How was the Epiphany dinner last night?"

"Quite nice."

"Sorry I didn't go. You know how it gets sometimes." Olivia broke off a small piece from the muffin. "What with being a Eucharistic minister plus my Altar Guild work and the Music Committee and all the Christmas activities here and of course vestry."

She put a tiny muffin piece in her mouth and dabbed her lips with a paper napkin. "You know how it gets."

I knew. Olivia was very active. The Altar Guild did all the preparations for Communion and cleaned up afterwards. It was not something men did, one of those long-held traditions that never made sense. Olivia had sung in the choir. She quit last year. Jerry said she was fed up with Janice.

"Did you like the anthem this morning?" I asked.

"I like singing and hearing Christmas carols two weeks after Christmas passes. I'm glad the congregation did that. Have some of my muffin."

I took a piece. "So you didn't like the anthem?"

"Not much."

I noticed the new couple, Bill and Jen, standing by the door about to leave as Becky buttoned her coat. Jerry approached them and said something. Everyone laughed. I waved, and the couple waved back.

"I met that family last night. They're very nice."

"Yes, Jen, Bill, and Becky Forsythe. They came last week. I introduced them to Diane after the service. I bet she encouraged them to come to the Epiphany dinner."

The parish hall was near empty as people dropped their paper plates and cups in the trash barrel while others climbed into their winter coats. Diane was the last person leaving a table of women twice her age. She headed towards the barrel by way of Olivia and me.

"Let's get this meeting going, you two. The weather report says snow this afternoon."

By the time I arrived home, light snow had started. The car radio predicted anywhere from two to six inches depending where you lived in the Boston vicinity. I decided not to put the television on. The local stations reveled when snowfalls approached. They gave weather reports in increments to keep people tuned in, and they annoyed me with expressions like "the jackpot" to designate places destined for the worst accumulations. When thick clouds threatened winter days, the stations skipped nearly all other news except sports or whatever celebrity scandal was fed them. Apparently the violent perpetrators behind the usual lead stories cancelled their activities as though they too became fixated with the weather once heavy clouds gathered. Blizzard warnings sent throngs to supermarkets, and hardware stores reordered snow shovels. These events filled news gaps until the first flakes sent television crews to highway median strips. From such vantage points they reported what everyone already knew. The next day TV reporters would question people clearing their driveways: "What do you think of the snow?" Last year I found much profundity in one shoveler's philosophic "Whadahyahgonnado?"

The news wouldn't come until six anyway. Despite the cleaning I gave the house after taking down the Christmas decorations and hauling the denuded tree into the woods, the house still needed dusting and the carpet another vacuuming. Before my retirement, putting Christmas away meant the return to school was near, always too soon. Last year Cara and I knew she had cancer again. Boxing up the decorations and window candles seemed like a precursor to her fate. We pretended this wasn't so. This year I noticed almost every ornament had a story, a connection to some past Christmas and associations with family, going all the way back to my childhood. A disciplined nostalgia took hold when I decorated the tree ten days before Christmas and put on the old familiar music. Only three other persons saw the house—Fran, Dom, and Jerry—the family for whom I cooked dinner on the twenty-third and exchanged gifts. We made it work.

Cara had always vacuumed first and then dusted because she believed the carpet work-over stirred up more dust. I continued her routine and sprayed and wiped a scented polish on the woodwork too. I also watered the potted plants on the sill of the bay window overlooking the backyard. I had no idea what they were called but tended to them because they were Cara's and someone said a house should have plants. My haphazard watering kept them somewhat alive, and as I picked up a few dried, fallen leaves from the sill I stopped to watch the backyard receive the new snow's gentle layer. The yard's slope towards the walkout basement would have eroded years ago if Cara hadn't terraced it with stones. This was no easy task. Her wall's five-foot height and thirty-foot length broke into four tiers, each about two-feet wide, and built with melon-sized rocks she had gathered from the contractor's excavation on our lot and others in the neighborhood. With Katelyn in half-day kindergarten and Luke a toddler, Cara built her terrace, which she later seeded for flowers. The four tiers held up for over a quarter of a century.

After her funeral I decided what to do with Cara's ashes. Water Street in Scrooby extended over a mile along the oceanfront. Briskly walking it back and forth was Cara's favorite exercise. Occasionally I joined her. I remembered those times and Cara's fascination, like mine, with the waterfront's changing appearance. The sky's tint, the water's texture, tides, wind, clouds, and the sunlight always caused variations. To me the stark winter scenes were the most beautiful. These memories of our shared walks caused me last September to paddle my kayak a hundred yards off Water Street and continue parallel to the shore. At the time of Cara's cremation, I had bought an overpriced box from Douglas's for keeping her ashes. Twisting my upper body seaward, I spread some of Cara's white, powdery remains across the ocean and watched them sink from view. I then paddled a bit farther and repeated the dispersal until half the box was gone. The following weekend Katelyn brought some potted chrysanthemums from New York, and together we transferred the flowers to Cara's terraced garden. Into the holes we dug, Katelyn and I poured Cara's remaining ashes. Bits of bone dissolved into powder when squeezed between thumb and forefinger. We pressed everything into the dirt. Our bare hands gently swirled and merged Cara's white grains into the brown soil. The plants went on top, and everything was watered. Neither of us spoke.

I watched the new snow join old snow in covering the terraced garden Cara built, making it appear no different from the rest of the yard and the surrounding trees.

I called my sister. "What have you heard about this snow?" We hadn't spoken since my dinner two nights before Christmas.

"Not much, an inch or two, maybe just a dusting for us. North and west of Boston will get more."

"Dusting" sounded good. My house was situated below street level with steep hills on each side of a circular drive. The year before I bought a snow blower in November that went unused until February and not again the rest of that mild winter so different from the previous year of what seemed like bi-weekly northeast storms. With no kids at home to help, Cara and I agreed our reliance on shoveling had finally run its course after twenty-five seasons with the formidable driveway. I resented my snow blower's noise, and my mechanical skills awkwardly maneuvered the damn thing and often misdirected the throw shoot.

"Well, that's a relief," I said and asked about her holidays.

Fran summarized her Christmas gathering, the call she received from her son in Florida whose work schedule kept him from traveling this year, the gifts she received and her special delight in the travel books, and a mellow New Year's Eve at a neighborhood party.

"How was church today?" She knew my Sundays started at St. Joseph's.

My mind sped through multiple answers. "You know that music committee I told you about. We met today."

"That's the group Jerry says ought to do something about your music director."

"That's the one. His latest rant is about anything sung in Latin."

"I thought he was a Classics major."

"He was and still reads Cicero and all those guys even though he's a grad school drop-out. And he loves all kinds of sacred music too. What he hates is pretension. He says it's what destroyed Rome. You should have heard our anthem this morning. It proved him right."

"So what will your committee do?"

"Well, we need to get away from complaining and getting hung up on the music director. Instead, we will define just what an excellent music program should be. How we implement it comes next."

I had worked on enough curriculum development committees and had devised enough group assignments for my students to know how the committee should proceed. Fran liked my plan.

"Well, it's the start of a plan" I said. "But that's not all that's been happening in church lately."

I was sitting in my office, my eyes roaming the bookshelves and the desk piled with notes and copies of George Herbert's poetry. They almost obscured the framed photo of Cara and the kids taken sixteen years ago.

"Saturday night we had the Epiphany dinner." I noticed my left hand was nervously twirling the receiver's cord, so I abruptly stopped. "And I sat across from a woman."

"There was a fifty-fifty chance that would happen," Fran said, "unless of course the chair remained empty."

"Right. You're so insightful. Well, anyway we, I think, we kind of hit it off."

"What's she like?"

"She's younger than I am".

"Most people are. Is that a problem?"

"I don't know. She's Asian. Chinese, well, actually Taiwanese. You know that island off China we used to call Formosa. Anyway, that's where she's from. I really don't know much beyond that, except she teaches Tai Chi. Do you know anything about Tai Chi?"

"Why are you telling me about what makes her different from you? Does any of this matter? Did you like her?"

Fran's first question was her way of telling me to relax. The answer to the second question was, of course, no. The answer to the third was the reason I called her in the first place.

"Yes, I like her very much. We talked a little during the dinner, and I saw her during church this morning. I think she likes me too."

There, I said it, and hearing myself say it made it true. I knew Fran wouldn't say that six months after Cara's death was too soon to date anyone. In August she said grief was misery and I owed no one any more misery. Nor would she ever tell her brother he was acting like an old fool even if she thought he was. Fran and Diane knew that the first weeks after Cara's death I sat by the pool trying to read or write but instead watched the back porch's screen door. Once I cried out her name loud enough for the neighbors to hear. Through the autumn I would be someplace doing something when another reminder would slap me into despondency for a minute or longer, and then I would carry on until the next time. Diane called it "getting on with life."

"I'm not surprised she likes you," Fran said. "Tell me why you like her?"

"Well, she's very beautiful. I mean any man would think her nice to look at. So that's part of it. I touched her hand—four times, I think. When we were introduced and shook hands was the first time. I felt something. And then we held hands during grace, and I felt it again, and again when we touched hands as she left. And this morning during the peace I felt it. She has brown eyes, beautiful brown eyes and a smile that's so nice. I suppose everyone who's ever been near her must have felt the same. But I think she cranked it up for me."

"Well, this sounds very interesting. Have you asked her out?"

"After the service I asked her to coffee hour."

"And did she go?"

"No. She rides with a friend, another Chinese—I mean Taiwanese—woman, who always needs to get home right away. Her husband worries about her, or she worries about him. Anyway, Wen, this friend of Qiao-Yun's—oh, that's her name Qiao-Yun, Qiao-Yun Wang—had to get home, so that meant Qiao-Yun had to go too. Maybe next week she'll stay for coffee."

"Coffee?"

"Yes, coffee?"

"You're waiting week to week for her to go to coffee hour? Why don't you just pick up the phone and call her? Ask her out. Take her to dinner."

"I didn't ask for her number."

"Have you tried the phonebook or directory assistance? How many Qiao-Yun Wangs are there in Scrooby?"

When we were kids, Fran never missed a chance to tell me I was a jerk. Now when she prodded me, her attitude was a little less pointed.

"Maybe I'll do that."

"When?"

"When I'm ready."

I stopped myself from saying there were circumstances. These circumstances had to be right, and that meant I should be careful. I just needed more time. What could be taken as a church romance could get as awkward as a workplace romance. If it fell apart—if indeed it ever got built—there would be all that uneasiness. I wanted to increase church membership, not drive people out, especially minority people. It was good for the church to have folks like them, and it was good for them to have St. Joseph's. It really was a good church, and I had no business doing something that would screw that up for anybody. I had Katelyn and Luke to protect too. Their mother was dead. They were still grieving. This was delicate stuff. I couldn't go trampling on their mother's memory just because I was too weak to handle a proper waiting time and was getting all worked up over some young chick's positive energy, which probably meant I just wanted to get into her pants, and, if the truth were told, of course I wanted to get into her pants. No, there were definite circumstances here, and the instincts holding me back were correct. There was no need to rush, no need at all.

"I understand," Fran said. "When you're ready. You know best."

"It hadn't really occurred to me to seek out a situation like this. It just kind of happened."

"Are you happy it did?"

"Well, it wasn't horrible. I mean, yes. I'm glad it happened"

"I am too."

The ending of our conversation coincided with the sun's descent. I had a bottle of Cabernet Sauvignon on my counter and a bottle of Pinot Grigio in my refrigerator. Since I had defrosted a package of chicken breasts for dinner, I decided on the white wine and opened it, filling my glass to the brim. I put the oven on, peeled two large potatoes, cut them in half and then quartered each half before preparing a baking pan for the chicken and potatoes. I took a long sip of wine and then another before re-topping the glass. I took butter from the refrigerator when I returned the wine to its shelf. From Cara's spice rack I took only black pepper and set to work getting my food ready for the oven. From this dinner would come at least two others. In about fifty minutes I would boil some frozen broccoli. The phone rang. The Caller ID showed Katelyn's number. We spoke almost every week.

"I wanted to call you before we went out tonight," Katelyn said. "You know how Gareth is always busy Sunday night—it's always something—but tonight we are. He's taking me to dinner. You know that French restaurant on Austin Street?"

"What's the occasion?" I asked.

"There is none. He just wants to take me out. Maybe a movie too."

For decades I never went out on Sunday nights. I had the same kind of workload that consumed Gareth, an assistant professor of history at a small college in Queens. A Columbia Ph.D., Gareth yearned for a position at a place different from this greenless campus wedged within a block of gray office buildings. He earned a laborer's pay. Katelyn, childless and tired of her job, wanted something better for him too. The book he tried writing was to be their ticket out, and he never had enough time to work on it. He taught an evening class and summer classes too. They tried to save. At the company where she worked Katelyn was titled Events Coordinator, which she defined after her first month on the job as "the organizer of breakfasts, lunches, cocktail parties, and dinners for clients on the make who crave schmoozing with business contacts also on the make."

Katelyn wanted me to visit. I listed the weekends full of church activities. I would have a better idea after the parish's annual meeting the first Sunday in February. I ran out of things to say. The oven's bell declared it had reached 400 degrees.

I quickly explained my dinner plans. Our conversations rarely went beyond twenty minutes. We avoided awkward silences.

"Bon appetite," Katelyn said. "I'll let you get back to work."

"Bon appetite to you too. Give my best to Gareth."

That's how it ended. Luke and I spoke less often. With his job at the food co-op filling his weekdays, and his nights and weekends devoted to music, he put in longer weeks than Gareth. The three-hour time difference was inconvenient too. We made an agreement he would usually make the calls, a deal he kept about as well as I would have in his situation.

I placed my baking pan in the oven. My wine glass was almost empty. I refilled it after taking the box of frozen broccoli from the freezer, gulped more wine, and put on the outdoor light by the kitchen door just in case someone might drop by. I considered working on my commentary about George Herbert's "Aaron" and typing it into the manuscript. All that seemed like too much effort, so I turned on the six o'clock news.

The snow had ended south of Boston and would taper off within the next hour north and west of the city. A full report was coming up later in the broadcast, the weather guy said, with more snow in the extended forecast. I changed to the PBS station. It showed an aged Barry McGuire singing *Eve of Destruction*. When he finished— the world still intact—the image changed to a woman who appeared way too often on my screen. Her smile took up half her head. She told the viewing audience that such wonderful programming was only available through their generous contributions.

I thumbed the TV remote to another local station's news. A car dealership commercial ended, and the co-anchors cheerfully introduced their weather guy who now stood before the national map and, waving his arms about as though he were sending semaphore, explained how a cold front moving across the Midwest might meet another coming down from Canada and maybe join up with moist air gathering in the Gulf of Mexico, possibly moving towards the southeast coast which could then climb northward and bring a "substantial storm" by the coming weekend. "We'll be keeping an eye on that for you," he said before detailing the clear skies and moderate temperatures developing Monday morning and lasting into Tuesday.

I drained the remainder of my glass and headed to the kitchen to start boiling water for the broccoli. Another full glass came and went with dinner. I ate while watching the last half-hour of *The Maltese Falcon* during a Bogart tribute night on the commercial-free cable movie channel. I quickly rinsed my plate, knife, and fork and put them in the dishwasher and covered the pan of leftover chicken and potatoes with plastic wrap and put it in the refrigerator before watching *Casablanca* for the millionth time.

As Monday's and Tuesday's clear skies gave way to increasing cold and cloudiness and the next weekend approached, the weather forecasts grew more certain. Winter's first major storm was indeed on its way. I went through the week faithful to my routines of exercise, housework, and writing. My mind returned to Qiao-Yun a lot, but not as much as it turned to Cara. Wednesday morning Diane and I planned the parish's annual meeting. This event set the agenda for the rest of the year. I said nothing about Qiao-Yun. At Thursday's choir practice everyone anticipated the coming snow. If it were the blizzard predicted, it could cause the cancellation of Sunday's services. This possibility threatened my seeing Qiao-Yun Sunday.

By Friday morning I had completed work on "Aaron" and edited my notes about other poems. Friday I made sure the snow blower could start. I did my laundry. While ironing, I paid special care to the turtleneck and pants for Sunday. I did my weekly grocery shopping, the supermarket overrun with blizzard-crazed shoppers. Saturday morning the television weather maps showed the storm's progression through New York City and into New England. At four o'clock heavy snow started. Diane phoned at seven to say she was calling the radio stations and sending out a parish-wide e-mail. Services at St. Joseph's were cancelled.

Sunday night while the snow and wind continued, I called Katelyn, and Luke called me. We spoke mostly about the weather. Katelyn said her night out with Gareth was wonderful. Luke said his day job at the food co-op went well enough, and he hoped his father didn't have to work too hard to clear the snow. He had written two new songs. The open-mic patrons said they liked them. In Scrooby the electric power went out during the night and returned by late morning. Monday went to clearing the driveway and steps. The neighborhood shifted from pristine, white beauty and quietude to the drone of snow blowers like mine. Heavy plow trucks dumped their spillings onto driveways recently cleared, and soon cars chugged down the sanded, slushy street. By midweek my new yellow Beetle bore the same filth covering every other car.

My routine went on as usual. I returned to George Herbert, this time focusing on "The Sacrifice," a very long poem written in four-line stanzas, all in Christ's voice. Each stanza's first three lines rhymed and detailed a particular lament; the fourth was a refrain: "Was ever grief like mine?" The fifty-fourth stanza and the last, the sixty-third, ended with a variation: "Never was grief like mine?" I determined an indication of my mental health was that I never identified with these refrains. I worked on "The Sacrifice" off-and-on through Saturday, not sure if any of it would find a place in the book.

The Annual Meeting was this Sunday right after the ten o'clock. Diane and I had prepared the agenda weeks ago. During the service I didn't see Qiao-Yun, though Wen was in the same pew they shared two weeks earlier. Whenever my eyes weren't on the prayer book or music, I looked out at the congregation, hoping Qiao-Yun would arrive late. After the service, Wen met me in the center aisle. She nodded politely.

"Qiao-Yun not come to church today."

"I didn't see her with you."

"She in Taiwan. Her father very sick, cancer. She plan to go back for Chinese New Year end of month. Her mother call, and she change ticket. I will tell Diane."

Qiao-Yun was on the other side of the world with people I couldn't imagine.

"She in Taiwan two months, maybe longer," Wen said. "She will have much to do. She will call me in a few days."

"Please tell her I'm very sorry."

Wen said Qiao-Yun's father had been sick for a long time. I didn't know what else to say except that we had a group of parishioners who pray for anyone in need. "Diane will ask them to pray for Qiao-Yun and her family."

In the choir room I stashed my music folder, robe, and cotta before taking the stairs to the parish hall for coffee and the Annual Meeting that could not start without the senior warden. I barely paid attention through the whole thing.

CHAPTER 5

A month later on a Friday afternoon I was driving to New York. Thursday night I had a burger and dark ale with Jerry at Linnehan's, a pub in downtown Scrooby. As the trip entered its second hour, my mind kept replaying our conversation. Jerry made an offer, and I promised to think about it—which I did, despite my repeated efforts to think about something else.

"When I'm not singing with a groaner like you," Jerry began. "I'm singing with the Old Colony Festival Chorus—very classy. I understand you've heard of us."

I knew about the O.C.F.C. Every year they performed with the Scrooby Philharmonic at the Christmas concert in Memorial Hall, the town's turn-of-the-last-century civic auditorium. Jerry had auditioned for them the previous September, his rich voice winning a place with the bases. He sold me three tickets to the Christmas concert because he knew Fran and Dom would go along. The O.C.F.C. employed a conductor and an accompanist and hired professional soloists and musicians for their oratorios. Jerry took rehearsals very seriously. Jerry also took seriously the ballroom dancing club he joined where the women outnumbered the men four to one. When I accused him of being a song and dance man with ulterior motives, he corrected me. What was true about his dance partners was not true about the sopranos and altos in the Old Colony Festival Chorus.

"So I was wondering what you were doing the third weekend in April," Jerry continued. "It's just three weeks away."

"If you're hinting there's a concert worth attending, I probably can find the time, especially since it means I get to see you look ridiculous in a tuxedo."

"I'll hold two tickets for you. You hear that? Two. You shouldn't go alone, and you shouldn't go with your sister or brother-in-law."

I remembered Jerry's penetrating stare. After Annual Meeting, I told him about Qiao-Yun's trip to Taiwan and my self-reproach for never having considered her a person with human experiences and responsibilities. He called me an asshole who loves flagellating himself. Jerry also said Qiao-Yun had stayed in touch with Wen. He checked. Qiao-Yun would be back before the concert date, and now just before I pushed the button on the car radio to get the Red Sox spring training game, I recalled his point-by-point reasoning about the O.C.F.C.

concert and two tickets:

"First, it's Haydn's *Creation*, a great piece loaded with that King James language you and someone like George Herbert go for, and the soloists are excellent. Anyone would like it. Qiao-Yun will like it. Remember her? Second, it's a Sunday afternoon. You two could go after coffee hour. It's in the Congregational church down the street. It's practically a continuation of our own service. Third, I know if you think of it as a date, you'll get all weird and find some big heavy cross to carry around instead. So think of it as the sharing of a cultural event with someone who also shares your religious sensitivities. It's educational. You're a teacher. It's just another field trip. It's okay."

"I'll give it some thought, but you need to get your facts straight. Although the King's James Version was completed in 1611, twenty-two years before George Herbert's death, he preferred the earlier English version, the Great Bible of 1539."

Jerry told me to shut up and do what he said.

A quarter way through Connecticut I lost the ballgame's signal, and that ended the best distraction from thinking about Jerry's tickets. Okay, I would probably buy them. I would have to see. Just what I might see I didn't know, although my imagination galloped through possibilities. There was no way to know what Qiao-Yun would say. She still might not even return in time. She might not return to St. Joseph's. There was too much beyond my control. The best thing to do was remember how uneventful all this really was, one way or the other. It wasn't a date. I just happened to have an extra ticket for a local chorus concert on a Sunday afternoon. I would see. Time would tell. Soon I would be in New York.

Approaching the RFK Bridge, I remembered Robert Kennedy and my absentmindedness for again forgetting to order an E-Z pass online. When I first visited Katelyn and Gareth, the RFK was called the Triboro. Now signs along the way used both names to designate the bridge, depending on proximity. Anyone seeking the RFK would find no distant indicators of its whereabouts. People in route through the Bronx seeking the Triboro would find that once they drew within a mile of this span to Manhattan, Brooklyn, and Queens, it disappeared. I knew the Triboro and the RFK were the same because Katelyn advised me ahead of time. Now thirty-eight years after their senator's assassination, New Yorkers decided he rated a bridge. The surprise was not the tribute but that it took so long. Neither Katelyn nor Gareth had an explanation. Katelyn first learned about Robert Kennedy because photos of him and Dr. King hung in my study. My son-in-law, the historian, told Katelyn, "To understand that era you have to know someone like your father."

On the way past Shea Stadium, I remembered the pact Gareth, a Mets fan, and I made when Katelyn first brought him home: the enemy of my enemy is my friend. We reinforced this bond when our teams and the Yankees reported to Florida. Katelyn and Gareth lived in an eight-story brick building in Forest Hills near Queens Boulevard, the street running from the city's border in Long Island to the Queensboro Bridge, which crossed the East River to Manhattan. Simon and Garfunkel called it the Fifty-Ninth Street Bridge. I hated Queen's Boulevard. No motorist ever slowed down because he moved too fast and had to make the morning last. I always avoided it. From the exit off the Grand Central Parkway, I went by millionaires' grandiose homes looking like court houses, mausoleums, and stucco Beverly Hills mansions, all crammed into tiny lots. Each had the congruity of a Sumo wrestler wearing a tutu.

Four blocks of opulence gave way to rows of middle-class apartment buildings. Katelyn and Gareth lived on the sixth floor of one. My first drive to their neighborhood brought me a fifty-dollar ticket because I didn't notice the parking restrictions for street cleaning times. After two years I became much more adept at avoiding all the prohibited spots as well as mastering my Beetle into constricted spaces. Katelyn had given me keys to the building and the apartment, but I always made a phone call once the car was parked. Gareth answered.

"Hurry up," he said. "It's the bottom of the ninth. The Mets are down a run with two on and nobody out."

Pushing the elevator button for the sixth floor, I thought about the hillside park across from my car. Maybe someday my grandson or granddaughter would play there. It offered swings, slides, and a jungle gym for small children. Protective adults stood nearby watching them closely while the late afternoon sun began its exit behind the buildings. Six teenage boys on the basketball court wore baggy knee-length shorts and hoodies while everyone younger and older wore winter coats. Up the park's block-wide slope people occupied benches. Some read or just sat; others listened to music. Young people had earplugs with white wires. I liked visiting cities but knew only a few. I liked the parks most of all, which was why I couldn't love a city. Though the Parks Department maintained trees along some streets, the forest in Forest Hills had vanished long ago. One block from Queens Boulevard, a park had been inserted into the rigid urban scenery. When the seasons and skies allowed, people came to such patches for play and meditation. Suburban New England better suited me. There only tall pines obscured the sun's broad arc. Open fields and cranberry bogs appeared along back roads. The ocean bordered Scrooby's eastern edge. Neighborhoods, no matter how thick, nestled within wilderness. Silence came more often than noise. No one can say that about Queens.

Gareth opened the door the moment I inserted my key.

"Come in, come in." He took my bag, and with one arm on my shoulder ushered me towards the television. "The Phillies just changed pitchers. The Mets have one out with runners on first and second. I don't know any of these guys. They're all subs, minor leaguers."

"That's often the way this late in a spring training game." I looked around the small apartment and heard nothing but the TV announcers and the street sounds outside. "Where's Katelyn?"

"Shopping, be back any minute." Gareth's eyes fixed on the screen. "We're out of wine. She's cooking Italian tonight."

We sat side-by-side on the couch. The Mets' pinch hitter had worked the count full. He fouled off the next pitch. My interest in the game became as intense as Gareth's. We bent forward. The hitter fouled off another pitch before stepping out of the batter's box. He stared down the third base line, focused on the coach's swipes down each arm and the tugs on each ear and the glide across his cap's brim while everyone watching knew the batter should smack the ball to right field. I recognized the pitcher, a veteran of many major league clubs. Gareth said the Phillies were trying him out as a non-roster invitee. The pitcher's grim face tightened. The boyish hitter stepped back into the box, set his feet and knees into a sturdy stance. He took three practice swings before awaiting the next pitch—a breaking ball that didn't break.

It jounced from the hitter's quick, level stroke and shot two feet above the leaping second baseman's glove to the gap between center and right fields. In motion with the pitch, the lead runner now pounded third base and cut toward home as the center fielder scooped the ball from its ricochet off the wall. He fired toward the infield. In the moment it took for the relay man to catch the throw and pivot toward home, the lead runner scored, and the runner darting from first base flew passed the windmill-gyrating third base coach. Gareth and I stood when the ball bounced once before disappearing in the catcher's glove. He turned and jabbed the runner's torso too late in the spray of beige dust as the runner's lower body lacerated the base path and his foot slid into home plate.

Katelyn pulled the key from the door as she entered, her arms cradling two shopping bags while her husband and father cheered in front of the TV. Before I turned to the sounds of her entrance, the Phillies' pitcher walked toward the dugout. His head angled downward. He pulled off his glove and carried it with the webbing suspended from his throwing hand's forefinger and thumb. I watched while the camera stayed with the pitcher until he disappeared beyond the dugout's steps, probably for the last time. Then I walked with outstretched arms towards my daughter.

"Let me help you with that," I said.

Katelyn said she had everything under control and stepped from the apartment's living and dining room into the kitchen. I followed her and placed one bag on the counter while she placed the other next to it. We looked at each other. Katelyn stood an inch taller than Cara. Her fine straight hair, perfectly cut, fell to her shoulders with blonde streaks highlighting the brown that had once been my hair's color. At thirty-four Katelyn still had a cheerleader's figure. Under her open wool coat, she wore a bulky turtleneck and tight jeans tucked into high leather boots. Her pendant and earrings matched. Her makeup and rouge barely hinted she had any on at all.

"How are you, Daddy?" She put her arms around my shoulders, and we drew close, kissing each other's cheek. She pulled back so I could see her smiling face.

"I'm fine, Katelyn. How are you?"

"I'm okay and very glad to see you." She hugged me again.

Gareth entered the kitchen from the adjoining room connected to the living area. He reached from behind and drew Katelyn to his chest, his hands around her waist. He kissed her neck.

"You're better than okay," Gareth said. "You're beautiful."

Katelyn closed her eyes, tilting her head to expose more of her neck. Gareth kissed her again, and her smile widened.

"You both seem quite well to me," I said.

Katelyn turned against the counter and took two bottles of Chianti from one of the bags. "Let's have some wine. I got imported pasta, the real thing. I have sauce and meatballs simmering for hours. You two can celebrate while I get a pot boiling."

"So what's going on?" I asked. "What's the good news?"

"My husband is wonderful. That's all."

Gareth and I were close friends. I knew his story. His mother had a great name, Désiré. She descended from slaves who fled to Nova Scotia with the Loyalists who evacuated Boston in 1776. Désiré married Raymond Ross, an American sailor whose father had emigrated from Nova Scotia to Maine as part of a diaspora from the hard-luck Maritimes. Raymond's father found work at the paper factory in Millinocket. Eventual U.S. citizenship and marriage to a local girl kept him in Maine, and each of their four sons, except Raymond, worked their lives in the mill. At eighteen Raymond joined the U.S. Navy, becoming a nuclear power technician aboard submarines.

When Raymond's sub visited Halifax, he met Désiré during her internship at the Maritime Museum. She was fascinated by this soft-voiced, earnest young American, who was equally fascinated with her. His ancestors included Scottish fishermen and Micmac Indians. Hers included descendants of Arcadia's French colonists and later generations of American runaway slaves who took the Underground Railroad to the far North. Raymond came to the museum every day his duty section had liberty. His last night in port they ate at the best restaurant in Halifax Raymond could find, choosing from a French menu Désiré translated for him. When Raymond's submarine returned to New London, he was assigned shore duty. He and Désiré wrote every day. He phoned her four times a week, dropping a pocket full of quarters in the barrack's pay phone, and when leave came he drove to Portland and took the ferry to Yarmouth, Nova Scotia, and headed to Halifax. His discharge led to a civilian job at the Electric Boat Company in New London. Raymond and Désiré married and settled in Connecticut. A year passed; Gareth was born. Two years later a drunk driver hit Désiré as she crossed the street from the library where she worked. She died instantly. Raymond never remarried.

In his Millinocket days Raymond and his brothers never joined a baseball team, but he played catch with his son and cheered every Little League game Gareth played. "Even though I was an easy out and couldn't field a beach ball," Gareth said. Wrestling became Gareth's high school sport. Inspired by its intensity and ancient roots, he trained hard and developed the muscle and agility to win matches. Raymond attended every competition he could. He also went to every parent-teacher conference night at school, always hearing what a good student Gareth was.

I knew Raymond only from Gareth's stories and old photos. He died from a heart attack after Gareth's first year in college. With cutbacks in submarine construction after the Cold War, Electric Boat terminated Raymond. His savings evaporated, and he sold his modest house. The life insurance and multiple student loans put Gareth through college, which together with a fellowship got him through graduate school. He met Katelyn at a Columbia friend's party in upper Manhattan. Katelyn had come with a girlfriend who didn't want to go alone. Even after two years in New York City, Katelyn had never seen a man as striking as Gareth—cinnamon complexion, green eyes, black wavy hair, and a freight-car physique. Small wire-framed rectangular glasses bridged his straight nose. His baritone voice, barely audible above the party's din, spoke with easy cordiality: "My name is Gareth. I don't think we've met."

I wrapped my curiosity inside a joke. "Yes, Katelyn, your husband is wonderful. Is that what are we celebrating? Or did Senate Republicans follow each other over a cliff?"

Katelyn groaned. "This is serious, Dad. Gareth has finished his book. It's done, and it's bound to get published right away. Isn't that fantastic!"

I knew about Gareth's book, a project he started almost as soon as he finished his Ph.D. dissertation, which also focused on immigration. Unlike the first book, loaded with laboriously cited data about the return of penniless, exhausted Loyalists to the independent American states, the new book was more personal with a thematic account of something broader —*The Ellis Island Principle* his working title. It chronicled stories about people from all over Europe who had little in common other than their determination to make a new life in America. Differences in language and religion didn't matter as much as their eagerness to help each other.

I congratulated Gareth and assured Katelyn that this indeed rated a party. We clinked glasses before Katelyn shooed us men away so she could finish preparing dinner. She told Gareth to get their best dinnerware, the sets Cara and I had given them.

I hadn't seen the dishes and silver since their wedding, which had been a small affair. Gareth's grandparents were dead, and his American uncles and cousins rarely left Millinocket other than to hunt and fish in the woods near Mount Katahdin, and they never left Maine. Cara, deep in her second bout of breast cancer, could barely withstand the beatings from her chemotherapy. Twenty of Gareth's and Katelyn's New York friends drove to Scrooby for an outdoor civil service at our house. Katelyn had no interest in St. Joseph's. Fran got a one-day license to be a justice of the peace.

Though Cara later recovered and lived another four years before stricken the third time, our daughter's wedding remained for me a memory made bright only by my admiration for Gareth and the happiness he and Katelyn gave each other. The day smelled of mortality.

Jerry saw it all. During the ceremony when Fran read Elizabeth Barrett Browning's "How Do I Love Thee," our mother's favorite poem, I felt worse. Luke had written a song for his sister's wedding. He played his guitar and sang, and everyone cried. Jerry had brought his guitar and played backup. The remembered image of my son wearing his only suit, newly bought for the occasion, and his loosely knotted, off-centered tie almost made me cry again. Nothing terrible happened. Life went on. The caterer's food was excellent. No one got terribly drunk except a young woman who came with Katelyn's former roommate. The jazz trio played well. Jerry sang *The Best is Yet To Come*. People danced on my lawn, and the grass withstood it all. Jerry, Gareth, Luke, and I made sure Cara danced whenever her failing energy let her. The co-worker who brought Katelyn to the party where she met Gareth caught the bouquet. Luke caught the garter. Later Luke drove her back to her hotel on Scrooby's waterfront. He returned the next morning. She went back to New York. He went back to Seattle.

I helped Gareth align the linen tablecloth then took a deep drink from my goblet. "Nice wine."

I set out dishes for three, and Gareth slipped knives, forks, and spoons in place. We drank more wine, and Gareth went to the kitchen for the bottle. I took my seat and waited for Gareth's return. A multi-framed collage of photos hung on the wall. Cara was in every one. In two she stood alone: when she was twenty and when she was forty-six. Another showed her next to me. In the rest she was with her son or daughter or both kids. Over the years I had taken them all, except the picture with just the two of us, which Fran took thirty years ago, and another showing father, mother, daughter, and son taken by a stranger at an amusement park in Rhode Island that closed two years later.

"So how's everything with you, Stephen?" Gareth asked when he approached the table and refilled our goblets.

"Well enough, I have my moments. You understand." Gareth sat down across from me. I wanted to change the subject. "Look, I haven't really congratulated you for finishing that book. Do you have a publisher?"

"Not yet. Colleagues recommend someone they know who knows someone else. Katelyn says she has contacts, including an agent she met at one of her company's events. She says it will head bestseller lists and fly me into an endowed chair at some ivy university."

"I really liked the chapters you showed me a year ago."

"I would have shown you later pages—" Gareth paused as though he wanted to choose his next words very carefully. "I printed another copy of the full manuscript. Would you like to have it?"

I said that would please me very much. He slipped into the bedroom and returned with two inches of paper bound with heavy elastic bands. "Your opinions mean a lot to me, Stephen."

I placed the manuscript alongside my overnight bag. "This will be a best seller."

"If it gets published and a few academics like it, maybe I can get kicked up the ladder a little and pay off my student loans. I'd settle for that."

My daughter burst from the kitchen, her hands around a steaming bowl of linguini. "Gareth, help me bring the rest. Dad, you stay where you are."

Gareth returned to the kitchen with Katelyn, and I drank more wine. Gareth entered with a bowl of thick red sauce, its aroma reinvigorating the savory smells that had floated through the apartment since before my arrival. Katelyn followed him and carried a platter of shimmering, brown meatballs. The couple scooted out again and came back. Katelyn carried a basket of warm rolls and breads. Gareth carried the salad. He left again reappearing with a box of matches that he gave Katelyn who lit the two candles on the table and dimmed the overhead lights. Gareth crossed to the stereo, and Ben Webster's breathy saxophone seeped into the dining room's shadows.

Between the first and second helpings of Katelyn's dinner, Gareth opened the other bottle, though Katelyn had barely touched her wine. Conversation drifted from Gareth's book to hopes for Luke. Would the gigs his new band got in dungeon clubs lead anywhere? Katelyn said he seemed happy in Seattle. I called him two nights ago.

"What did you two talk about?" Katelyn asked.

"We talked about a lot of stuff." I took a roll from the basket of bread, all the while pondering whether Katelyn should hear the same story I told Luke, the one that Jerry heard the night before. It might have prompted him to push me about taking Qiao-Yun to hear the Old

Colony Festival Chorus. Jerry said I would always be the kind of man who couldn't possibly serve his own self-interest unless there was something in it for somebody else. I didn't see myself the same way but admitted he was right about my attraction to Qiao-Yun.

"A blind man could see it," Jerry told me. Fran had perceived it too over the phone weeks ago when I told her of this woman with the magic touch; and Fran, unlike Jerry, had never seen the two of us together, but she knew, and she also knew she would have to wait until something else happened. Something unrelated did happen on a Saturday morning in Boston. That was the story I told Luke and Jerry and began telling Katelyn and Gareth.

"We have this group at church called the Pastoral Care Ministry. It's a small group of women who visit shut-ins and nursing home residents or anyone in need. You met the members during the hospice weeks. They were those church angels who were so helpful."

Katelyn nodded. She remembered. Gareth nodded too. They had lived at the house during Cara's final two weeks.

"Well. They're awfully short-handed, so I thought I would help out."

My narrative started with my mother's stroke, which happened when my kids were in elementary school. After twenty years of visiting her in a nursing home, I never wanted to be inside one again, but Pastoral Care needed help. Visiting Eucharistic ministers bring Communion to folks who can't get to church. For me it was a chance to get out of myself by doing something nice for another person. I figured, what the hell, I'd get on Pastoral Care. But there was a catch. I had to go to a training session at St. Paul's Cathedral in Boston, a daylong thing that cost forty bucks. Well, okay, I could do that. It included a lunch. Besides, I didn't know anything about being a visiting Eucharistic minister. So off I went on this March morning. Whenever I go to that part of the city, I park at the garage under the Boston Common. I'd walk the length of the Common to Park Street Station and cross the street to St. Paul's.

"I can picture that garage," Katelyn said. "I think it was the first time you took me to Boston, a day in the summer. I was five or six and had never been in a huge underground place before. I was enthralled. We went up the elevator, and crossed from the Common to the Public Garden."

"Remember the Swan Boats?"

"Of course and the little statues from *Make Way for Ducklings*."

"Yes, we did all that."

It was a brilliant June day amid radiant flowers and graceful weeping willows along the pond where pedal-powered boats quietly shushed beneath the arching footbridge, and I bought her Italian ice and took her picture when she posed with the storied ducklings from the book we had read together over and over.

Over the years I walked through the Public Garden a lot, but I had walked through the Common much more often. I protested the Vietnam War there with a hundred thousand others, heard Gene McCarthy and George McGovern there. That same year George Wallace spoke to a rally of our homegrown bigots, and I came with hordes of other students to boo his rants. We were everything he hated. Cara and I went to two Joan Baez concerts there. Joan insisted the city couldn't charge more than two bucks for a ticket. Cara came with me to see *Twelfth Night* on the Common and really enjoyed it. Boston's twenty-mile walk for hunger starts and finishes there. I've done that four times. Cara came with me to protest the Bush-Cheney invasion of Iraq. My bishop was one of the speaker's.

"Boston Common is loaded with memories for me. So here I am on this blustery March Saturday walking though the Common at eight-thirty in the morning, and the place is empty except for a few chilly pigeons. The sky is overcast. The city is almost lifeless. It was like walking in a black-and-white movie."

I didn't tell the worst about that March morning, my feeling that my best years were behind me, that I was old as hell. I crossed Tremont Street and walked through the side door to St. Paul's as though ankle weights burdened every step.

"And then everything changed." I needed Katelyn to understand this next part.

"Near the basement hall where the class was, I heard all these voices chattering away, and I turned a corner and went down some steps and entered a brightly lit room and the smell of fresh coffee. And the people had to be the nicest people in the whole world, nearly all my age or older and very cheerful."

I noticed Gareth's eyes stayed on me all through this story. Katelyn's gaze shifted to her plate and returned to me only when I had finished.

"It wasn't just being among people with a religious sense of mission, though that was part of it. I was among happy, friendly people who believed they were useful."

"What was the training like?" Gareth asked.

"Oh there was a kind of manual for getting people into conversations. It explained proper ways to administer the bread and wine, the little service we do, the layout of the Communion kits. They walked us through all that. We did a lot of role playing too."

My daughter no longer had the grateful child's face. "What did Luke say?"

"Well, he asked questions and I answered them. We agreed I'm not a little old man who needs care, who's likely to leave his teeth at the corner diner or forget to zip up his fly. I exercise regularly, keep myself hygienic, and handle responsibilities without screwing up a lot. I have friends, and I might even make some more."

I almost said something about the Taiwanese woman I wanted for a particular friend. The wine pushed me towards it. I dug in. That news—if it ever became real news—would have to come later.

"And one of these new friends, I found out, will be a ninety-year-old lady in a nursing home, and I can do her some good. I'll see her Wednesday. Luke was happy for me."

Gareth's shoulders pulled him forward from the back of his chair. "Me too."

Katelyn sat motionless. "And so am I."

I expected Katelyn to say that everything available to me in Scrooby was here in New York. An Episcopal Church was close by. Queens had nursing homes with loads of lonely people I could visit. Most of all I could have her and Gareth and the grandchildren they would give me. Three months ago over Christmas dinner, she had almost said as much, and I pictured the future's tapestry she had sewn with subtle hands. It included my selling the Scrooby house, and with that money we could buy a condo or co-op together with an in-law apartment and all the fantastic things I could do in New York. I wouldn't be a father and grandfather living hundreds of miles away. The first stitch, how concerned she was for me, appeared during the Labor Day weekend, with the other strands threaded through nearly every call and visit since. From the outset I suspected what was coming tonight over goblets of wine and the kind of Italian feast Cara could make. My story postponed all that.

The evening moved on with no more mention of Scrooby or New York. Katelyn set up the sofa as my bed. They invited me to join them Saturday afternoon at their health club a few blocks away. I declined. They each had chores before and after their workouts. I hadn't been in

Manhattan in a long time. I would take my exercise walking the city, maybe go to one of the museums along Central Park. I awoke early, grateful the evening's wine was not punishing my head. I showered and dressed quickly and bought a large coffee, banana, corn muffin, and the *Times* at the corner store. I returned to eat my breakfast before Katelyn or Gareth had risen. After twenty minutes, with my paper tucked under my arm, I walked to Queens Boulevard and took the R-train to Manhattan's Fifty-Seventh Street and Seventh Avenue where I got off and crossed to Central Park. Last night I said walking through Boston Common that March morning was like being in a black-and-white movie, which wasn't quite the truth. It was just cold and gray. Manhattan better fit the description.

The colorless surroundings here were more like a charcoal dream world, an immersion into old movies made on locations throughout the city. They were gritty, fast-living places where cops and hoodlums in long wool coats and wide-brimmed hats found jaded women and druggie jazzmen, and where sleazy guys and power brokers wrought their deals in ritzy clubs and grimy bars. Everyone lived and died to bluesy clarinets and muted trumpets. New York City had become a maker of celluloid illusions, and for me that was enough. I wanted nothing else from New York but its celebrity. I could take or leave it as the occasional tourist. I didn't live here. And I never would.

I didn't put it quite that way at the restaurant Saturday night. Again Katelyn praised Gareth's accomplishment and listed the multiple troves her hopes expected. Right after the waiter left the menus, she asked about my day in the city. I said it was a good day for a walk—partly sunny, almost sixty degrees. She pressed me for details, and I listed all the different kinds of people. A sidewalk vendor sold me my lunch—a hot dog slathered and piled with everything the man had, together with coffee and an enormous pretzel—something I always wanted to try during a visit to Central Park.

"I went down to St. Thomas Fifth Avenue but missed the lunchtime service, so I hung out for a while before strolling back to Fifty-Seventh and Seventh for the return train."

Our dinners came, and we said nothing else about my day. The Mets won, so had the Red Sox. The Yankees lost. Even during spring training, Gareth and I concluded this meant goodness had prevailed throughout the cosmos. Over dessert Katelyn asked what I would like to do Sunday.

"Well, I had a very nice nap late this afternoon while you two were out. I think I'll head back tonight."

Katelyn's voice rose with each sentence she spoke. "But why, Daddy? You always stay the weekend and go back early Monday mornings. Please, you'll get home way after midnight." Gareth put his hand on her forearm.

"I'm sorry, Katelyn. I love you both, but I just want to get back home. I've had a great time. Easter is coming. The choir has to get in extra practices. It's a busy time at church. I'm sorry. I should have told you sooner."

"Can't that church—"

Katelyn stopped herself and looked at Gareth as though it were his turn to say something. He said nothing. He probably figured it out yesterday afternoon when I watched the Phillies pitcher walk from the mound to the dugout.

Katelyn looked at me. "It's a long drive. I'll worry all night."

"I'll be fine, Katelyn."

I paid the check. My daughter was silent during the brief walk back to their building and the elevator ride to the sixth floor. Before I reached for my things, Gareth hugged me. Katelyn put her hands on my shoulders and kissed my cheek. I grabbed the overnight bag and Gareth's manuscript.

Katelyn said, "Next time you'll stay longer. Okay? Call when you get home. I don't care how late."

"I'll make good time."

The Beetle's gas gauge showed a full tank. I had filled up after my return from Manhattan and found a parking space closer to the apartment. A turn around the block sent me back toward the Grand Central Parkway, the RFK Bridge, Route 95, New England, and Scrooby where Jerry held two tickets for Haydn's *Creation*.

I made good time.

CHAPTER 6

Wen spoke to Qiao-Yun at least once a week. I asked Wen to relay my concern for Qiao-Yun and her family. Every Sunday Wen gave me a report. The first said Qiao-Yun's father was dying. The second said he died. All the others were the same: "She have much to do for family."

The Sunday after I returned from New York, Wen had a new message for me. "Qiao-Yun be back two weeks from this coming Saturday."

I wouldn't have much time. The concert was at three, not after coffee hour as Jerry had said. I would ask her the Sunday after her return—if she came to church. I bought Jerry's tickets before choir practice, thinking I would ask her today or Palm Sunday or Easter. Instead, it would be the Sunday after Easter, the very day of the concert.

"She'll be in church the Sunday she come back," Wen said without my asking.

The timing would be close. Meanwhile, other things needed attention. Midweek I went to the Bay View Nursing home—a curious name since the ocean was not visible from there—and visited Anita Colefax, a woman I barely knew but who knew me from my senior warden column in the parish newsletter.

Anita sat in a wheel chair just inside her room, which she shared with another woman who sat asleep in a wheelchair by the room's rear window. The roommate looked much older than Anita, and Anita looked younger than ninety. She wore the kind of pastel pants suit older women wear, especially nursing home residents who have precious little closet space, but she also had a pearl necklace and earrings, which together with her silver, well-coifed hair, gave her a confident look compatible with her stocky frame and bright blue eyes. She gave an approving smile to my Communion kit and me. The chair closest to Anita stood by the door, piled with stuffed animals.

"I used to have cats," Anita said. "They won't let us have pets here, so my daughter brought me those. It's silly I know. You can put them on the bed."

I knew nursing homes. My mother spent the last twenty years of her life in one, passing time by not recovering from her stroke. At sixty-five she had an apartment about a half-hour drive from my house, a car, and a clerical job in Boston. One Friday she came home fearful she had made a data-entry error that her boss would need days to straighten out. This terror, plus a lifetime's habitual anxiety, triggered her stroke. How she discovered her mistake and why she didn't tell her boss before she left for the weekend I never found out. My mother seldom made much sense after the stroke. She took to her bed for two days and called me, saying with slurred speech she didn't feel well. I called Fran, and the instant we saw our mother I called an ambulance. The hospital report stated her chances for a full recovery disintegrated during the 48-hour delay between Charlotte Pentheny's stroke and her son's calling the ambulance.

The hospital hooked her to an array of monitors and tubes. They got her stabilized, which for my mother meant minimal capabilities. Rehabilitation training helped a little, at first. She was always cold, and her mouth drooped slightly. Within a month hopes for her walking again ended; she was forever wheelchair-bound, and her left arm's coldness turned into constant pain. The nursing home became her last residence. Fran and I visited her as often as we could. My Saturday afternoons belonged to mother. The visits varied little. She might ask an opening question but didn't listen to the answer. An hour-long monologue started, filled with her complaints about the nursing home and dire warnings issued from the fundamentalist stations she heard on the radio and watched on television. One of them reported that homosexuals met in a bar two blocks from the White House to plot their agenda. Another time she heard Latin American rebels overran villages and confiscated the dolls Christian missionaries had given little girls. The rebels gave them Communist dolls instead. Her stations warned that terrorist cells operated from every mosque in the country and liberals encouraged them. Such alarms distressed Charlotte Pentheny, and she heard them every day. I tried to bring reason at first and then counseled her not to listen to crackpots. She assumed I was under great strain, whether at home or school or both. Otherwise, she said, I wouldn't be in such denial about Satan's hold on the world.

Falsehoods work better than truth when dealing with a person imprisoned in delusions. Charlotte had few emotional triumphs in her decline, but even those she would spin into the heebie-jeebies. Once when I visited her, she was consumed with fear and guilt because she had committed a wicked sin: she told a lie. The day before she was reaching for something on the table near her bed and lost her balance. Only the tucked-in top sheet saved her from landing on the floor.

Though jackknifed with her upper body hanging over the bed's edge, she managed to pull herself back in, violating a strict rule. Residents were supposed to summon an aide when they fell. Instead of rejoicing over her newfound dexterity, Charlotte suspected "the authorities" would find her out, strap her into her bed forever, and God would approve. When the nurse who delivered her meds noticed Charlotte's knitted blanket on the floor and her spilled fruit drink, she asked if my mother had fallen. Charlotte said she dropped some things, nothing else. The next day she rattled to me the whole story and berated herself for showing any degree of independence and self-reliance. "Stupid arrogance," she called it. I suspect she found such behavior too close to the secular humanism her Bible-thumpers railed against. Whenever my mother needed soothing, I turned truth to the wall and relied on creativity.

"Well, Mum, you needn't worry. I bet you forgot the rule in Deuteronomy about little old ladies. They get to tell three lies every year. You have two more to go."

Few joys in life can prompt the jubilation and bliss on my mother's face when she heard my bogus scripture. Forever afterwards, Charlotte believed my reassurances—until she forgot them. She gleefully praised her son to Fran because he was reading the Bible again.

I was reading the Bible but not Deuteronomy. About this same time I started going to St. Joseph's, and Charlotte was transferred to the Alzheimer's wing, which the nursing home more accurately should have called the dementia wing or the end of the world because "Alzheimer's" was applied broadly. Any sustained confusion would do. Charlotte always had a roommate whom she seldom noticed. They changed through the years, but none went home again. They went away. Two died after ambulances rushed them off to the hospital. One died in her bed next to Charlotte's. Two others died sitting in their wheelchairs waiting for God knows what. In the Alzheimer's wing waiting made the present manageable, though nothing better ever came along. Our visits to mother always included greetings to her various roommates. When they went away, we were reminded that our mother's time was not far off.

Charlotte Pentheny was eighty-five when she died in the Alzheimer wing. After everything else had failed, her heart did too. Anita Colefax at ninety was a nursing home rookie, a robust elderly person who fell down one day. That fall decreed she couldn't live alone and would never walk again unassisted. Neither her daughter in Scrooby nor her daughter in South Carolina had room or abundant time for her. I understood. The Bay View Nursing Home followed.

I put Anita's stuffed animals on the bed and sat down, placing the Communion kit on the rollaway table, and noticed the family pictures on her bureau and wall. Her husband Frank died four years earlier.

"I got a call from Diane saying you were coming," she said and closed the *National Geographic* she was reading. "I haven't been in church for a year or so, but I remember you. I remember that article you wrote in the newsletter when you stepped down as senior warden when your wife got sick. How are you, Stephen?"

"I'm okay, Anita."

For most of St. Joseph's parishioners that year, Easter came too early with flat grey skies and a damp chill made worse with sharp winds. All the great words about Holy Week came and went with cut flowers. The wonderful took only momentary hold. My Lent ended the Sunday after Easter when I left the changing room and headed to the rear of the sanctuary where the choir lingered before lining up for the procession to start the service. Qiao-Yun was back. She sat in the same third pew seat alongside Wen. I still had to get her alone long enough to ask her to the O.C.F.C concert that afternoon. I decided to talk to her before the service began.

Only one person sat in the second pew, a woman who always complained to the junior and senior wardens whenever the sound system didn't work. It failed far less often than she thought. The woman seemed pleased when I said good morning. I kept smiling as I angled a step to face the next pew. Wen sat immediately in front of me. I wished her good morning.

"Good morning, Stephen," Wen said almost laughing and took my extended hand briefly before letting it go.

Qiao-Yun's hand reached towards mine. I took it and felt the touch. I looked at her face and felt her eyes' penetration.

"I'm glad you're back, Qiao-Yun. I'm very sorry about your father. How is your family doing?"

"Thank you. They good. I glad I'm back."

"I would like to talk to you. Will you have coffee with me later, upstairs?"

"Yes. I will like that. This time Wen have her own car."

We agreed to meet in the parish hall after the service. I walked toward the back of the church while at the same time Diane and the acolytes entered from the opposite side. Janice Patterson played a two-minute prelude, and I stood next to Jerry who thumbed his hymnal's pages in preparation for the procession and murmured in a voice just audible over the organ's music.

"You remember the last scene in *Dark Passage* when Bogart is sitting in that Peruvian bar, the one he went to every night for a year after fleeing the States for a murder he didn't commit, and he waited for Bacall because she promised she'd find it no matter what and they could always be together?"

"I presume you have a reason for asking me this right now."

"Just picture that last scene. Bogie's eyes lift from his glass to the doorway, and there stands Bacall looking back at him. And then the camera returns to Bogie's face. It's gorgeous. It's the greatest single frame of film in his career, maybe anyone's career."

"And your point?"

As usual Diane announced the opening hymn as a way to let everyone know the service was about to start even though its page number was listed in the printed bulletins the greeters handed out.

"It's gorgeous," Jerry said. "That's all."

Janice Patterson pounded out an introductory refrain on the organ, and the choir and congregation started singing. The lead acolyte who carried the cross started the processional march. The service had begun, and my full-throated resonance matched Jerry's booming bass.

I had no other duties this Sunday other than to worship and sing, but imaginings of how coffee with Qiao-Yun would go overwhelmed my attention. I barely followed the readings, caught none of Diane's sermon, and heard little of the Communion liturgy. As a child I was a notorious daydreamer who would have astonished my teachers had they known that after a three-year hitch in the Navy I got into a college, earned two Master's degrees, and become a teacher myself. Little from the service found a way into my head this first Sunday after Easter. Instead, I kept thinking about Qiao-Yun. How to ask the question? What if she said no? What if she said yes? Should I pick her up? Meet her there? What if she said yes and didn't like the concert? What if I didn't like the concert? When Diane read the Gospel passage, she stood in the center aisle among the congregants. The choir pivoted left to watch her. My focus went to the third pew. At the reading's end, the congregation responded, "Praise to you, Lord Christ." I mumbled the phrase, a word behind the others.

Standing with the choir after the recessional hymn, Diane spoke the final words from the same spot where she had announced the opening hymn.

"Great sermon," I said before working my way down the center aisle, my senior warden good cheer parading at an accelerated pace. Qiao-Yun passed through the left hallway entrance, and I darted around her to the choir room beyond where I quickly stashed my music folder and hymnal. I grabbed my sport jacket from a hanger and hastily draped the robe in its place with the cotta slung over it. I was through the door with only one sleeve in the jacket and charged up the stairs to the parish hall.

Qiao-Yun stood to the side of the coffee urns with a paper cup in one hand and paper plate in the other. She was talking to Olivia Finch and Josefa Garcia. Jo sat nearby with her twin five-year-old daughters who were licking frosting off their cupcakes. Qiao-Yun wore a short-sleeve cream sweater and a dark blue ankle-length knit dress that made her look statuesque. Her long silver earrings and necklace matched. I took two steps towards her. She made a head gesture indicating the counter with the pastries. The line had dwindled. I raised my index finger to say, yes, I'll grab some refreshment and then join you momentarily. Qiao-Yun's head and shoulders moved as she chuckled. With half a bagel and two chocolate chip cookies on my plate, I drew a cup of coffee and moved toward Qiao-Yun.

Olivia started to introduce us. I explained Qiao-Yun and I had already met, and something about the way I said that made Olivia's face take on an all-knowing look.

Olivia said she had to get going. Jo was busy helping her girls wipe their faces and put their jackets on. She seemed in a hurry to move the kids along. I asked them if they liked the cupcakes. The twins barely had a chance to answer before Jo said something about their brother's soccer game and quick-stepped to the door with a little girl at each hand, Olivia right behind them. Whatever reasons they had to skedaddle, leaving Qiao-Yun and me alone had to be one of them. Qiao-Yun looked amused.

I pointed to a corner table. "Shall we sit down?" A pre-teen girl and her younger sister drank fruit punch at one end. We sat at the other.

"Thank you for coming to coffee hour," I said.

"I'm glad you ask me."

"I've never been to Asia. It must be a very long flight." I was running out of rehearsed lines.

"From Boston to San Francisco six hours and then from San Francisco to Taipei about fourteen. My family lives in Taichung. It's a long bus ride, two hours. I do it once a year, two times in the last six months."

"You father was ill when you were last home?"

"Yes, and he sick the year before."

An all too familiar voice calling my name interrupted us.

Harriet Pringle, her hair in a new reddish tint and her hands filled with coffee cup and pastry plate, slid with clunky dodges between tables and chairs. Seated people pulled their chairs and stomachs into their tables or pushed their chairs away to make a path for her.

"Stephen," she said again as soon as she stood alongside me, "a bunch of us have decided to go to brunch at the Harbor Side. It's marvelous. You should come along."

My head tilted upwards. "Harriet, you remember Qiao-Yun Wang?"

"Oh, Yes." Harriet snapped Qiao-Yun a tight-lipped grin. "How are you?"

"I'm good," Qiao-Yun said.

Harriet refocused on me, her mouth now agape with toothy self-confidence. "It's all you can eat. You can't go wrong."

"I've made plans, Harriet, maybe some other time."

If Harriet had any brains at all, she would have sensed my rigid courtesy was telling her to get lost. I contemplated spilling my coffee in her lap if she sat down. Much to my relief she acted as though someone across the room beckoned her attention. She said something about my missing a lovely time. As Harriet barreled away, she tossed, "I'll just have to book a busy man like you earlier," over her shoulder.

"Is she your friend?" Qiao-Yun asked.

My answer had an unintentional robotic meter. "We go to the same church."

The sound of Qiao-Yun's laughter made me laugh too.

"I'm sure she very nice person," Qiao-Yun said, "but I don't think you like her very much."

"Harriet's okay. She just gets ideas some times."

"I see that."

I looked behind me to make sure Harriet was out of earshot before saying I really did have plans for the afternoon. "Have you ever heard of the Old Colony Festival Chorus?"

"Huh?"

I explained it was a chorus like the church choir but much bigger and today they were singing music written by Joseph Haydn, an Austrian composer who lived over two hundred years ago. "Do you like this kind of music?"

"Yes."

"The concert starts at three o'clock at the Church of the Covenant. I have two tickets. Would you like to go with me?"

"Yes."

Forty-two years had passed since I last asked a young woman for a date.

"I can pick you up, or we could meet there."

"That better," she said. "I teach Chinese private lesson near center of town. Where concert exactly?"

I explained the location, and Qiao-Yun said she knew the church; she just didn't know its name. She would meet me at two forty-five.

At two-thirty I stood outside the classic, white-steeple church despite the cold front that entered after noon. Earlier I had gone home and pondered whether to swap my mock turtleneck for a shirt and tie. I decided to keep the jersey and my tweed jacket and chino ensemble. Lunch was a quick peanut butter and jelly sandwich to ward off stomach growls during the concert. I brushed my teeth and shaved again, my face burning, and toiled with my hair far longer than usual before driving to the downtown parking lot closest to the Church of the Covenant. Drizzle started, and I drew my raincoat together and tied the belt. The entrance's overhang kept my head and glasses dry. Concertgoers walked past while I shifted my vision from both lengths of the street to the corner before me. My watch and the clock on the stone Unitarian-Universalist Church across from me said two forty-five had come and gone. Six minutes later I saw Qiao-Yun briskly walking toward me. She wore glasses. When she stopped at the curb, I waved, and she waved back. She crossed the street and apologized for being late. I said she was right on time.

A rush of other ticket holders entered behind us. An usher handed everyone program booklets. Two sweeping wooden staircases led to the sanctuary. Polished woodwork and white paint defined the interior and pews, giving the room a simple elegance typical of Congregational churches. Muted light poured through the tall, clear windows. I spotted a pew midway down from the risers arrayed in front of the magnificent pulpit. A middle-aged woman sat there alone, and I guided Qiao-Yun into the pew after asking the woman if the remaining seats were taken. She said no and invited us to sit with her. I looked around and saw a pew filled with familiar faces, angels from St. Joseph's who smiled back as I nodded and waved in their direction. All along I hoped my attraction to Qiao-Yun wouldn't draw any notice. Two pews ahead a man and woman about my age called out Qiao-Yun's name, and she answered back. When she stood, I did too, and Qiao-Yun introduced everyone. The couple had been Tai Chi students.

"This my friend, Stephen."

An appropriate label, I thought. She could have said, "He goes to my church," or, "He asked me to this concert," which could be construed as, "He's this lonely old guy I know." "My friend" sounded so much better, a welcomed affirmation. The wife turned back again, and I was certain she was checking me out. Her wry look caused me to watch Qiao-Yun whose expression seemed to answer she agreed, which was very reassuring because I dared to perceive this silent communication between two women as glad approval even though I knew nothing about one of the women and very little about the other. We sat down. I determined to avoid dead-air pauses in our conversation.

"How long have you been in the United States?"

"I first come to graduate school at Springfield College. Then nine years ago I move here with my son. He now junior at Massachusetts Maritime Academy."

If she became a mother after college, the son was probably twenty, which meant she had to be in her early forties at least. I came very close to jerking a triumphant fist and shouting, "Yes!" A twenty-year difference could work. Of course, it could. Thirty years…well, I didn't have to think about that now, nor did I have to think about what "could work" meant. This news carried me through my next apprehension: whether the concert would be any good or Qiao-Yun would find it stuffy. Whatever she thought, Qiao-Yun might think the same about the guy who asked her to it.

"You must be very proud of him." I opened my program. "Let's see what this music is all about." As I turned my pages, Qiao-Yun flipped through hers. She had removed her glasses.

I skimmed the biographical blurbs about the soloists: the sopranos as Eve and Gabriel, the baritone as Adam, the tenor as Uriel, and the bass as Raphael. Reading on I discovered the libretto took elements from Genesis and Psalms and Milton's *Paradise Lost*. I knew these texts and noticed Qiao-Yun was reading a paragraph about the O.C.F.C. We looked up from our programs when the string quartet and percussionist entered and took their places followed by the chorus members. Jerry stood among the men, looking very much a bass with his broad shoulders and barrel chest. The five soloists entered. The organist came next. Once everyone was settled, the director entered. After acknowledging the applause, he tapped his baton, and the concert began.

I could barely discern a word anyone was singing, though the voices excelled. The program's notes included the libretto, and I started to read along. There was a lot to sing about. When I glanced at Qiao-Yun, she stared straight ahead. By the time God's Creation entered the fourth day, my churning stomach declared the peanut butter and jelly lunch was no longer sufficient. The thought of wandering off after the concert to eat alone while Qiao-Yun went her separate way felt so ridiculous it generated boldness. The printed program showed an intermission would divide the performance. Whether Qiao-Yun enjoyed the music was more important to me than the status of her son's father, a subject that concerned me very much, but neither unknown could match the immediate question. The chorus's intensity spiraled ever upwards proclaiming, "The Lord is great." Cheering applause flooded the Church of the Covenant. When it subsided and people shuffled to stretch their legs and tell each other how wonderful the first half was, I spoke to Qiao-Yun.

"I bet this will be over about five o'clock. Would you like to join me for dinner?"

Qiao-Yun showed no surprise at my question. "I hungry too. Where we go eat?"

We came in two cars. I pictured the restaurants a walking distance away. The beer and burger dens weren't appropriate. I considered the Indian and Thai places and didn't know whether they were too Asian or not Asian enough. I didn't want to suggest her ethnicity imposed a limited palate. It was one thing to be twenty years her senior; it was another to be a patronizing white guy.

"Do you like Mexican food?"

"I like very much," she said.

Ever since my invitation to coffee hour, Qiao-Yun had answered my questions perfectly, and now our afternoon would continue into dinner. We really were having a date.

"All right then. Fernando's Hacienda is a short walk away."

This was very good, quite wonderful actually, but I had to hide my self-satisfaction or look ridiculous.

My eyes fell on the program in my hand. "Isn't it good the words are printed for us? Otherwise, I couldn't keep track of who's singing what."

"What you mean?"

I showed Qiao-Yun the libretto with its listings of who sang what parts. "Here, from page four to seven you can see."

Qiao-Yun scanned the pages. "I'm so stupid. Everyone singing so good, but I have no idea what they say."

The chorus started filing back to the risers. I reassured Qiao-Yun, explaining that if I had a hard time following the story anyone whose first language was not English would probably find it impossible. I quickly retold the first half's narrative. Qiao-Yun said she understood. At the same time the choral director raised his baton, and for the next half hour Adam and Eve in successive solos joined with the choir in extolling God's goodness. Uriel declared them a happy pair. The chorus proclaimed Jehovah's praise shall evermore endure, with rousing concurrence from all the soloists in reverberating tones soaring to the final crescendo.

Some other composer and singers would have to explain the fall from Eden. Joseph Haydn and the Old Colony Festival Chorus were done. The audience gave them a standing ovation. While the musicians and singers left by side exits, Qiao-Yun and I worked our way through the crowd, down the grand stairs, and found Jerry surrounded by the St. Joseph's angels who hugged him and said how handsome he looked in his tuxedo and how proud he must be to have sung in such a glorious performance. Jerry introduced them to four nearby guys also in tuxedos. He said the five of them were headed to Linnehan's Irish Pub.

"If we drink enough dark ale, maybe Linnehan will fire up the karaoke machine. Would you care to join us?"

The angels tittered but said they had to get home. Jerry saw Qiao-Yun and me approaching, and his jokester demeanor changed. Other singers and audience members intermingled around them. Qiao-Yun hugged Jerry.

"You do so many things," she said, "fix my roof, be junior warden, sing in church choir, sing with concert today. You are awesome good!"

I congratulated the other singers and patted Jerry's back. "Thank you for a great afternoon. We're off to dinner."

Jerry asked where they were going, and Qiao-Yun told him. He said we made an excellent choice.

The drizzle stopped. Daylight Saving's murky sky gave sufficient light to the brick sidewalk, and Qiao-Yun put her arm though mine.

"Jerry your best friend. I can tell."

"You're right." The restaurant was in view across the street. "Jerry is my best friend."

Other concertgoers entered Fernando's before us. We waited a half-minute before the hostess showed us a table for two. Booths and tables surrounded us. The waitress brought menus and asked whether we wanted drinks. I asked Qiao-Yun what she would like. She said she would have what I had plus a glass of water with lemon and no ice. I ordered two glasses of the house Cabernet Sauvignon and two glasses of water with lemon and no ice. We opened our menus.

"I have idea," Qiao-Yun said. "We order different things and then we share. That way we get more flavors and learn about different food here. I been before, but this time I don't order what I had then. What you think?"

"I like that very much."

"Good. Let see what we want, and I pay half. The man shouldn't have to paying for everythings."

I would have gone along with whatever she proposed. We decided one of us would order the barbecue pork quesadilla and the other the beef enchiladas, each with its own spicy mix of vegetables and sauces. When the waitress brought the wine, I gave our order. When she left, I raised my glass.

"To the Old Colony Festival Chorus."

Qiao-Yun repeated this toast at twice my volume and tapped her glass against mine. We took deep drinks. Two couples seated at a booth duplicated Qiao-Yun's salute.

"Good job!" Qiao-Yun shouted.

The couples laughed, and toasts and cheers for the O.C.F.C. rolled through Fernando's tables and booths like the wave at a baseball park.

I wanted to tell Qiao-Yun everything. "I don't go out like this very often. What I mean is it's been a while since I've been out with a woman."

"Your wife die last summer. Do I say correct?"

I told her she was correct. "You're my first date since then."

"I think maybe this is so. I don't know why except everyone at church know you, so I hear things. Let me tell you my story. My husband, my son his father, he die too. I was teaching at my college in Taiwan. The father, he had very good education. He architect and contractor, start his own company. They build all over Asia. He die at construction in Taipei. Building collapse, kill five peoples. My son, eight years old, was with him and saw accident, but he not hurt."

"I'm so sorry."

"It was eleven years ago, a long time. Life go on. He had much life insurance. I move here with my son because I want American education for him. I buy my house."

"What's your son's name?"

"His American friends call him Ken. His Chinese name is Keung." I tried to imitate her pronunciation. "*Keeyung.*"

"Very good. Now I have question. Do you miss your wife?"

I hesitated. "Yes. But as you say, life goes on. For example, I think today is a very good day."

Qiao-Yun leaned toward me until her face was halfway across the table.

"I do too." She leaned back against her chair as the waitress arrived with our dinners. Qiao-Yun cut a section of her enchilada and put it on my plate and then cut a slice from my quesadilla and placed it on hers.

"If you like, I give you more of mine, and you give me more of yours. Okay?"

"Okay."

I cut a piece of the serving she gave me and tasted it, and she sampled my quesadilla. We looked at each other with full mouths and savored our food.

We freely took from both plates, and the more we talked, the less I heard her accent. From the time we arrived at Fernando's until we reached for our wallets, two hours passed. We spoke about our teaching careers, our comfort at St. Joseph's, and trust in Diane. When she asked what word best described Luke and Katelyn, I pondered a moment and said, "Honorable," and she said she could see it in me.

She told me about Keung's coming to the United States knowing no English and her joy with the ESL program in Scrooby schools and the scholarship Mass. Maritime had given him. Keung majored in international maritime business. I asked where she learned English.

She said a little in Taiwan and praised the adult literacy program at the Scrooby Public Library, and then she apologized for her English. I said it was very good and far superior to my Chinese. She also knew Taiwanese and a little Japanese. I said my high school and college French had pretty much deteriorated. She told me about Tai Chi and some Chinese philosophy about a cosmic energy I couldn't quite believe but didn't disbelieve either. I told her a little about George Herbert. She said she could imagine him from my explanation even though she seldom read literature, English or Chinese.

From her early teens onward, she had been an athlete always in training. She became Taiwan's martial arts champion and later received an athletic scholarship to college where she was invited to join the faculty after graduation, eventually becoming an associate professor of physical education. I was better suited for acting in school plays. During my teaching career I directed high school productions. I told her about Fran and Dom. Qiao-Yun had an older sister, a younger sister, and a younger brother. Her father, who treated her as his older son, came to Taiwan in 1949 with the Nationalist forces after the Communists overran the mainland. Her mother is Taiwanese. Her favorite aunt encouraged Qiao-Yun's interest in athletics and helped her get into a college-prep boarding school. My favorite aunt, my father's younger sister, was the only adult from my childhood who made me feel important.

We interrupted our dialogue only to eat and laugh some more and, at her suggestion, enter each other's number in our cell phones. Qiao-Yun had parked her eight year-old Honda two blocks from Fernando's. I walked her to it, and again she slipped her arm through mine and kept it there until we reached the car. She took her keys from her purse and unlocked the car door.

Qiao-Yun turned and hugged me, her head pressed against my chest. She said, "Goodnight, Stephen."

I spoke softly. "Good night, Qiao-Yun."

She opened the door and got behind the wheel. After putting her glasses on, she started the engine; her headlights tuned bright. Qiao-Yun waved just before she pulled onto the street and swung towards South Scrooby.

I waved back and didn't lower my hand until her car was out of view.

CHAPTER 7

I had work to do. Stubborn leaves squatted all over my back yard and gathered as defiant gangs in places where the wind had banked them against the house and within shrubs. How they got under rocks I'll never know. The leaves didn't move easily, often expelled only with ferocious stokes or diligent picking. For most of the year, leaves adorned my world, from their first appearances as infant buds to their lush green fullness through summer and bright reds and yellows in the fall, but come late autumn they turned to lifeless brown rubbish. Leaves fell according to a predisposed schedule. Every year was the same. Some dropped early, still sporting tint; some fell later when autumn winds drove them to the ground and then across properties until they littered everywhere and lodged against or into something. In October I raked the early fallen leaves while noticing that others clung to their home branches until winter's violence dislodged the most resilient.

This April morning I scraped and pulled the stubborn leaves and gathered them into mounds. Then I wheelbarrowed the loads to the edge of the woods behind the closed-up swimming pool. I started whistling to fill the air, put the wheelbarrow down, and light footed across the lawn. The opening notes to *Singin' in the Rain* bounced my steps as they did Gene Kelly's in my favorite movie sequence. I grabbed the rake and held it with the flared end up. I started to sing. My legs took long side glides and twinkle-toe steps. I was dancing with a rake.

Lunchtime I called Qiao-Yun.

"I just wanted to tell you again what a great time I had yesterday. Maybe we could see each other tonight."

Qiao-Yun said she enjoyed the day too. She told me her Tai Chi students were preparing for a competition. She was giving extra instructions but could meet me near the center of town at eight o'clock. We could go for a walk before she went home.

"There's the parking lot by the grist mill," I said. "If it's not too cold, we could stroll through Founders' Gardens. If the weather's bad, we can make other plans."

"Sound good. I see you eight o'clock. I eat early. You too."

After lunch I collected my tools, pleased with my initiative and excited about the evening ahead. Revitalizing the lawn had to wait.

The air was changing, and with it I switched tasks. The morning's scattered clouds found each other and layered into a chilly overcast made colder by increased winds. I looked like a ragged, unbathed drudge but put off my shower until later to be at my most fresh before leaving for the Olde Grist Mill. I went to my study where my yellow pad held the first draft about George Herbert's "Providence," a long, complicated poem about whether God's hand guided every event in the universe. Some religious people think they have God all figured out. Herbert isn't like them. For him God is unknowable but not imperceptible. Trying to understand "Providence" cluttered my afternoon, though this stanza stood out:

> The sea, which seems to stop the traveller,
> Is by a ship the speedier passage made.
> The windes, who think they rule the mariner,
> Are rul'd by him, and taught to serve his trade.

Thoughts about the day before caused me to take my pen and free write. An hour passed before I stopped. My path to clarity still meandered through ambiguities. I edited the notes about "Providence," typed them into the computer, and edited again. It remained garbled prose. I needed a break. Besides, I was hungry and had to cook a dinner and then ready myself for meeting Qiao-Yun. George Herbert and I would rendezvous later. I started whistling *Singin' in the Rain*.

Gareth once told me there are two kinds of history, big and small. What we learn in school is the big stuff—kings, presidents, battles, and such—history's headlines. Small history is what ordinary people do. Gareth thought small history the more fascinating. For example, everyone knows Scrooby's first English settlers arrived in 1620, but few know they loved to eat eels. They became quite skilled at trapping them. At low tide they picked lobsters, crabs, and clams from the beach and could have become the founders of the New England clambake. Unfortunately the Book of Leviticus forbids the eating of shellfish, and the Puritans took Leviticus so seriously they collected ocean crustaceans only to use them as bait while whetting their appetites for eels. They also decided not to name a local river for their king but for their favorite delicacy, which they caught in wicker traps lowered into the running water. The Eel River and other sources of fresh water made Scrooby habitable—a point the local Indians, the Wampanoags, had experienced for centuries and the English discovered when they realized they weren't at the mouth of the Hudson, their intended destination, and had to make do where they were.

The stream closest to their village they named Town Brook. The Indians taught the English how to catch herring in Town Brook and then use the fish to fertilize their cornfields. This and other examples of the Indians' neighborliness saved the settlers from extinction. The newcomers responded by giving the place an English name, and before the century was over they obliterated the Wampanoags and all the other tribes in Massachusetts, Rhode Island, and Connecticut. On a nearby hill stands a statue of Massasoit, the Wampanoag chief. He doesn't face Founders' Garden. He faces the sea. Scrooby is a place where small history and big history collide.

Later English generations, less interested in Leviticus and more in industry, built a gristmill on the banks of Town Brook about a quarter mile from where the water empties into the Atlantic. The original mill and its successors rose and fell with time, but by the mid-twentieth century a re-creation stood, a tourist attraction, its paddle wheel driving two mighty granite circles against each other within a little museum and gift shop on a boardwalk shared with a restaurant, The Olde Mill Stream. Main Street arched over Town Brook. Not far from this bridge, the state owned a wide lawn bordering the stone-buttressed waterfront. Along the shoreline ran Water Street, with the state park on one side and at its end Founders' Gardens on the other. Through the two parks and under Water Street, Town Brook twisted to the ocean. Scrooby took much pride in Founders' Gardens.

The grass already was thick green, and tulip and daffodil sprouts protruded from carefully mulched flowerbeds. A few monuments to Scrooby's first families stood among the pruned shrubs and park benches. Twenty years ago a monument to all of Scrooby's immigrants joined them. Over the last century hardly any arrivals from foreign lands had English names. I had been reading Gareth's *The Ellis Island Principle*, its focus being the ways diverse immigrants found mutuality in their common struggles. "Mutuality" is a word no one hears anymore, except in January when speakers at memorial services and breakfasts quote Dr. King. The immigrants' monument reminded me of Gareth's book.

Upstream near the gristmill, parking spaces bordered a small pond. I easily found a spot for my VW. Monday night was the slowest at The Olde Mill Stream, and an unyielding wind chilled the moist air. On summer nights romance roamed from Mill Pond to the sea. Strolling couples owned the evenings. Ice cream shops on Water Street did very well. On summer weekends wedding parties posed for pictures, but this April night with a winter's attitude drew only me who had hoped the weather would allow a prelude to those soft summer nights when amour wafted through Founders' Gardens.

A thick, winter coat would have been a smart choice. Instead, I decided to look good rather than practical, wearing my best-fitting jeans—the ones that flattened my belly without my sucking it in— a black sweater, and the brown leather jacket Cara let me buy on sale fifteen years earlier. The jacket's age gave it and me character, as though I were a pilot who had flown over jungles and deserts in single-engine crates—an adventurer who could do anything he wanted.

Qiao-Yun's Honda drew up alongside my Beetle. I stepped from my car and walked to her door. She again wore glasses for driving, and a wool brimmed hat ran across her forehead. It looked perfect. Her eyes and smile widened when she saw me. Qiao-Yun put her glasses in a compartment above the windshield.

"I know your car. I think everyone at church know your car," she said as she rose from her seat, grabbed her purse, and closed the door. "You wait long for me?"

"No, I just got here myself. We're both right on time."

"That's good. You want to walk a little bit?"

She pronounced *That's* as *Das* and *little bit* as *leetle beet*.

"Yes, I would. I haven't been here in a long time. Years ago I brought my kids. We bought bags of crushed corn at the Mill Store and fed the geese and ducks on the pond. Birds all over the place heard about the treats here."

"One my students tell me same story. She say town won't let people do that anymore because the place smell like bird shit."

Qiao-Yun suddenly looked embarrassed. "Oh, I use bad word. Sorry."

"That's okay," I said. "It's a perfectly good word, one of the oldest in the English language."

Qiao-Yun peered beyond to where the mill's security lights revealed two ducks on the pond. "And the birds, they still here."

"And they still shit."

Qiao-Yun had the sweetest laugh.

From the parking lot we sauntered past The Olde Mill Stream to the walkway along Town Brook. I asked her about the class she had just finished.

"Every year martial arts competition, all kinds. My students enter

Tai Chi. Judges score how well they doing form. In other martial arts people fight. Tai Chi different. Two my students do weapons form. One do sword. One do fan. Three do hand set, Tai Chi with no weapon. Most my classes this kind. Form must be exactly right. Everyone want more practice. Judges watch very close."

"So Tai Chi people do exhibitions sort of like figure skating?"

Qiao-Yun slipped her hand through my arm. "Something like that."

The walkway ran along the granite embankments above the flowing brook. A guardrail hugged the embankment's edge for another two hundred yards until Town Brook reached Founders' Gardens where it narrowed and rose almost to the level of the grass. The walkway turned dark as it passed under Main Street. When two shadowy male figures appeared at the opposite end, I wondered whether I had made a terrible mistake. One man turned to face us as though he would bar our path, and I felt Qiao-Yun's hand pull away.

"Hello Stephanos!" the shadow yelled. "Stephanos! Bous Stephanos!

"What he say?" Qiao-Yun asked.

"It's okay. I know these guys," I said. We approached the two men, and I greeted them by name: the tall one, Justin; the other, Paul.

"Good evening, Stephanos," Justin said. He was my height and wore a soiled parka with a Miami Dolphins logo. A red-brown beard covered his lower face and extended well below his zipped collar.

Paul's long dark hair curled from under his knit cap. He too had a full-growth beard. He was bundled in layers of clothes topped with a hooded sweatshirt that hung to his thighs.

"Out for a stroll?" Justin asked.

"Yes," Qiao-Yun said. "We go Founders' Gardens."

I asked the two men how they were doing.

"About the same," Justin said.

Paul nodded. "Will we see you in the fall?"

I hoped they wouldn't and knew they would. "I'll be there."

The two men wished us a good night. We answered in kind before leaving the underpass for Founders' Gardens, which was dimly lit from a few light poles within and the street lights beyond.

Qiao-Yun put her hand through my arm again. "How you know those men?"

I told her about an organization in town called the Task Force for the Homeless. From November through March five churches take turns giving homeless men a place to stay in their parish halls. Volunteers prepare a supper for them, and two chaperones stay the night. Everyone sleeps on rubber mattresses on the floor with sheets and blankets provided. Most chaperones bring a sleeping bag and pillow. Quite a few people at St. Joseph's help out. I was a chaperone. It wasn't much, just one night every five weeks through the winter. That's how I knew Justin and Paul. Qiao-Yun asked why men were homeless.

"Most of them are alcoholics or addicts."

Qiao-Yun halted. We stood next to a wooden footbridge that crossed Town Brook.

"Why that guy call your name that way, Stephanoodoo or somethings?"

"There's a novel written a hundred years ago about a young man named Stephen. It takes place in Ireland. One of Stephen's school friends calls him 'Stephanos,' just kidding the way friends do. Justin knows I've read the book. In fact, I use to teach it."

"I don't understand."

"Well, sometimes I get into conversations with these guys, get to know them a little, and they get to know something about me. Justin knows I'm a retired teacher and have been through some changes lately and I'm trying to write."

"About the George, the poet?"

"Yes, and, well, this Stephen character, who's a lot like the author of the book, is going through some changes too. He wants to be a writer."

"So that man not making fun of you?"

"He's just clowning a bit and in his own way, I guess, telling me to keep up with my writing."

"Is he your friend?"

The Task Force had a halfway house for the guys in recovery. Justin and Paul had yet to qualify. Some guys who used the winter overnights at the churches later disappeared, moving on to better or worse lives. A few of these homeless men we saw again every year. Justin was one of those.

"Not really."

Qiao-Yun looked back towards the tunnel and saw Justin and Paul still leaning against the entrance. "We have this in my country too."

I glanced toward the tunnel and turned back, facing Qiao-Yun. "I don't know Paul very well. He was new this year. Justin was an English major like me. I suppose we're alike in some ways."

Qiao-Yun gripped my forearms and raised her face as close to mine as she could push it. Her intensity grew as she spoke. "If he so smart, why he can't be more like you? He nothing like you. You good father and good husband. You own house. You teacher and do many things for peoples. He not like you, and he know it. That why he play smart person with you."

Justin and Paul probably had been drinking all day and would drink some more before the night ended.

"Thank you," I said.

"You are welcome. I don't mean to yell at you."

The last rays of sunset dissipated, and the windblown mist grew thicker, chilling us both.

"You didn't yell at me. But I don't think either of us can get any pleasure from this cold. Shall we go someplace else?"

Qiao-Yun slid her hand through my arm again. "Good idea. Where?"

Adjacent to Founder's Garden was Holland Street. It led back to the center of town. I didn't want to re-walk the path we had taken.

"Well, if we walk up this hill, we'll be close to The Coffee Plus. Is that okay?"

"Perfect," Qiao-Yun said. "Let's go."

Holland Street slanted up from Water Street back to Main Street. Above the incline from where the two streets crossed stood the First Parish Church with Burial Hill, Scrooby's oldest cemetery, behind it. To the right of First Parish stood the Church of the Covenant. We began the climb from Water Street. When First Parish's steeple came in view, I started a lesson in small history.

"For as long as Europeans have been on this continent, there have been squabbles over religion."

"What is squabble?" Qiao-Yun asked.

"An argument, or in this case a fight—many fights."

"Yes, I know that about America. In Taiwan seventy-percent of peoples Buddhist. They don't bother Christians. Christians don't bother them."

"That's good. We Americans are getting better at how we treat people we think are different, though some Americans still have a ways to go. This has been an important subject with me since I was a teenager. Right now we're walking one of the oldest streets in America. I think the oldest."

I explained why the original English settlers built a fort where First Parish sits at the top of the hill. They also used it as a meetinghouse and place for Sunday worship. Holland Street was just a dirt path back then with thatched-roof houses and small gardens plus fields of corn and wheat beyond them. The first church was rebuilt in stone in the nineteenth century. The original worshippers had very definite ideas about God, so definite they thought everyone else's were wrong. That's why they left England for Holland and then here. The Dutch thought everyone rated religious freedom. The Puritans believed only they deserved such liberty. Two hundred years later when the stone church went up, most of their descendants had developed other ideas.

"The new thinkers believed God is one thing or person not Father, Son, and Holy Spirit, and they thought the old thinkers were too narrow minded. The members who still believed the traditional way got angry and sad over that, so they moved across the street and built the Church of the Covenant. This was going on all over New England."

I paused when we reached the corner with Main Street and both churches were visible in the midtown lights.

"There's a lot of history here in Scrooby. All kinds of churches are in town now. There's a synagogue down the street. Muslim families live in Scrooby too. Maybe someday we'll have a mosque. And of course there are many people who don't go to any church."

Two cars came up Holland Street. I moved to block Qiao-Yun from the biting wind while we waited for them to pass through the intersection. We could see The Coffee Plus a few doors down.

"You say you always interest in Americans' difference," Qiao-Yun said. "I know it more than religion. I study American history for becoming citizen. Squabbles really bad. Many people very mean. Some still are. Do I say correct?"

"You say correct."

"Why you tell me this churches story?"

"I'm not sure. My son-in-law teaches history. He's written a book. I like stories. They're always about changes. Holland Street got me thinking."

"I think you good teacher."

"Thank you. I think you're a good teacher too."

The Coffee Plus was nearly empty. A tired teenage girl and a woman in her fifties stood behind the counter. Three round metal tables and two booths took up most of the floor space. Racks for donuts and muffins behind the counter held scarce samplings. Qiao-Yun and I were relieved to be out of the stinging cold.

I never drink coffee in the nighttime. Qiao-Yun recommended hot chocolate. I ordered two. The girl filled two small cups and placed them on the counter.

I looked at Qiao-Yun. "Would you like a donut or something?"

"The muffins are the freshest," said the older woman and rattled off the two available kinds.

Qiao-Yun asked me to share a banana nut with her. I said that sounded very good. The girl placed the order on a tray, and I paid. Qiao-Yun took extra napkins from a dispenser and a plastic knife. We sat at a table nearest the window. The wet glass distorted the outdoor lights into yellow glares that fell and spread along the wet pavement. I took a cautious sip from my steaming chocolate, and Qiao-Yun sliced the muffin in half with gentle strokes. She took a bite and pushed the paper plate towards me.

"Very good. Have some."

I usually avoided eating this late at night, but Qiao-Yun's offer replayed the sharing of our meal at Fernando's. I lifted the muffin to my mouth and found the fruity sweetness absolutely delicious.

"In Taiwan we have places like this but not the same. Tea very good. Coffee and chocolate not good."

"I suppose Scrooby, the United States, is very different from Taiwan. But you're a citizen here."

"I in ceremony in Boston last June, almost one year now. I also citizen of Taiwan."

"It seems you're at home in both countries."

"At Springfield College where I got Master's not bad because other Asian peoples there. When I first live in Scrooby, not so good, but then I meet Chinese women who live nearby. We see each other all the time. Wen bring me to St. Joseph's. I play mahjong every Wednesday with my Chinese lady friends. All my students are Americans. So I have Chinese and American friends."

I pictured Wen and Qiao-Yun sitting across from Jerry at the Epiphany dinner. "Your Chinese friends must be very important to you. I'm very glad Wen brought you to St. Joseph's."

Qiao-Yun wrapped her hands around her cup. She raised her eyes to me. "I'm glad she do that too."

I wanted to place a hand on hers. Instead, I took another bite of my muffin half.

"So what you do tomorrow?" Qiao-Yun asked. "You write? Do work for church?"

"I'll work in my yard some more. I did a little of that today. I'll write some more too. There's also a woman in a nursing home. Her name is Anita. I started visiting her last week. I'll definitely visit her tomorrow or Wednesday."

"In my country we don't have nursing home, not like here. Family take care of old ones."

"Some nursing homes are better than others. You'd like Anita. She'll be ninety-one in September. She's very bright and funny too."

Qiao-Yun grinned. "Oh, so we have a next date? You take me to nursing home?"

"Well, I was about to ask you about tomorrow night. If you're free, maybe we could have dinner again or see a movie or something."

"I cannot. Tomorrow I have three Tai Chi classes and then my Mandarin student come to my house. We do class together there every other Tuesday night. But Wednesday you come to my house. I cooking you dinner. Okay?"

"I would like that very much."

Qiao-Yun took her business card from her purse and wrote her home address on it. I knew the street.

"Come six o'clock," she said. "You don't need to bringing anythings—oh, maybe drink if you like."

For leisurely tourists on a warm night, the walk from The Coffee Plus to the gristmill's parking lot took fifteen minutes. We made it in a third the time. I was eager to get through the damp cold quickly and was loaded with—there was no getting around it—first-kiss anxieties. I sensed Qiao-Yun was feeling something similar and would think me a timid fool or worse if I didn't try. If I contemplated this any more, I would, as Jerry put it, get all weird.

When we got to her Honda, my move towards her caused the arm she had at my side to fold around me as my arms embraced her. We held each other with both hands on the other's back. Our bodies drew together. I bent my knees and lowered my head. Her face lifted to receive my mouth which pressed against hers, first gently, and then with a soft moving pressure. She deepened the intensity. I held her tighter, feeling her breasts against my chest. We squeezed closer, our kiss still lingering, until she very, very slowly pulled back.

I had to catch my breath. "Thank you for meeting me tonight."

"You are welcome."

Driving home, I listened to the jazz program on the public radio station and recognized Art Tatum's *Moonglow*. I pulled the VW into the garage and entered the house through the side door. I had left my cell phone on the bureau and noticed the message light on the land phone was blinking. I pushed the voice mail button and heard Katelyn saying she had good news. No matter what time I got in, I was to call her. After two rings, I heard Gareth's voice and asked what the good news was.

"I better let Katelyn tell you. I'll get her."

If Gareth had found a publisher, he would have said so. I heard the rustle of the phone going from one person to the other and Gareth's voice saying, "It's your dad." And then I heard Katelyn.

"Daddy? Are you ready? You're going to be a grandfather!"

Katelyn was ecstatic and said she was feeling fine and her doctor was great. "We hadn't planned to get pregnant, she said, "but we're very happy." If only Cara had lived long enough, I thought. Katelyn must have felt that way too. We didn't say these things now. The moment had to be cherished. It made us both happy, and we hadn't had a great happiness together in a very long time. She said the doctor's office and the hospital were in lower Manhattan, a few subway stops from her job. I wondered whether she suspected this when I was in New York a few weeks ago. She said she got the news today.

"I'm due in November."

I said nothing is wilder than an expectant grandfather turned loose in a shopping mall. She should give some instructions, at least whether I was buying for a granddaughter or a grandson—not that it mattered. I'd go equally insane with pink or blue. The more I talked the more I painted cartoons of my going out of control, running through the neighborhood like a horseless Paul Revere waking people and yelling, "The baby is coming! The baby is coming!" And I would stop strangers to tell them the news and hire a skywriter to spread "Katelyn is with child. Rejoice all you people!" Katelyn laughed wildly and said she expected as much from me, and I worked at making her laugh some more, which she did until she told me to stop.

I promised to visit in a week or two. Katelyn said she looked forward to that very much. She sounded so young.

"And what's new with you, Dad?" she asked. "Where were you tonight? Some church meeting, I bet."

"Well, not quite, something different."

I paused and switched the phone from one hand to the other. Katelyn broke the silence.

"Like what?"

"Choir," I said. "I mean dinner with the choir. We all went out to dinner. It was nice."

CHAPTER 8

Wednesday morning I sat on my weight lifting bench pushing through a third set of overhead presses with two ten-pound disks on either side of the barbell—a skinny guy's notion of pumping iron. It was the final exercise of an hour-long workout that included forty minutes on an elliptical stepping machine and one hundred stomach crunches.

During breaks I recalled Tuesday's telephone conversation with Qiao-Yun. I told her about putting my house on the market. Much had to be done to get it ready for a showing. I would hire Jerry to replace some rotted trim and make a few cosmetic fixes. Qiao-Yun asked why I wanted to sell the house. My answer complained about the upkeep. This was a lot easier than saying too many memories lived here. She talked about her class at White Pines, the upscale golf club and condo complex in South Scrooby not far from her house. The pricey condo fees included an all-purpose function room where Qiao-Yun taught Tai Chi classes twice a week.

"In winter many White Pines students go to Florida," she said. "Then I work only at my school and have extra time. I like that. In Taiwan I teaching classes and running competitions with thousand athletes and hundred staff."

I liked having just enough work to do to keep me occupied without all the teacher deadlines and stresses. Qiao-Yun understood. She didn't want to work as hard as she did in Taiwan. "Peoples should enjoy life."

I said nothing about Katelyn's pregnancy.

My final set of barbell presses, the heaviest, usually ended at the sixth repetition. Today I pushed up two more. My self-congratulations ended with a phone call from Diane who listen to me explain why I was out of breath.

"I'm delighted you're paying so much attention to physical fitness," she said. "But we have a nine o'clock meeting. It's seven past."

Fifteen minutes later I stood unshaven in Diane's office, still dressed in wrinkled nylon pants and frayed sweatshirt. Her roomy office was arranged into two spaces. One side held her desk, bookcases, file cabinets, and computer. The other side was for small meetings and consultations. It had a coffee table in the middle with a sofa on one side and two overstuffed chairs on the other, with a rocker and assorted chairs on the edges. A box of tissues was always on the coffee table.

I sat on the sofa because Diane had her favorite big chair. Qiao-Yun probably sat on this same sofa when she first met with Diane. I pictured Qiao-Yun, the way she laughed at Fernando's and her beautiful face under a street light just before our lips touched and her stern look when she said Justin was nothing like me. Suddenly I realized the vestry meeting was tonight. In fact, Diane said so when she called, but it didn't register. Vestry meetings are always the third Wednesday of the month. I knew that. I wrote it on my calendar months ago, but it was printed nowhere in my mind when I accepted Qiao-Yun's dinner invitation. Diane walked from her desk with a folder and notebook and sat down after dismissing my apologies. Her ten o'clock had cancelled, so we had plenty of time. We usually said a prayer before our meetings.

"Your turn," Diane said.

I said my usual gratitude for unspecified blessings and then asked for guidance to do God's will. I ended with "We ask this in Jesus name. Amen."

"Amen." Diane said. She opened her folder and scanned a document she knew very well. "Before we start, I have to tell you what a great job you did with that committee. I'm going to steal your methods."

She held up a piece of paper titled "The Essential Qualities of an Excellent Music Program."

Those methods weren't exactly mine. Half way through my teaching career, I moved away from always giving lectures as though the instructor were the only smart person in the room and instead used cooperative learning techniques any teacher could master by reading a few professional publications and experimenting a little.

"This sheet defines an excellent music program," Diane said, and she read the four key points, each with three or four sub-criteria. She stopped about six times to say how much she liked a particular item. Her voice kept on going through the whole page, and I barely heard any of this because how could I leave a dinner date before seven o'clock or tell Qiao-Yun we should start eating sometime after nine-thirty? Qiao-Yun would think me a muddle-headed jerk. I was about to tell Diane I had to make an important phone call when she put her folder on the table between us.

"You know Janice won't go for any of this. She might say she does, but she won't, which means this is nothing more than fantasy as long as she's the music director."

Diane was talking about Janice Patterson, but my head was all consumed with Qiao-Yun until Diane's rap on Janice switched me to memories of my old superintendent, Bob Norris, who had nothing to do with either problem facing me now. This ended when Diane stated what she wanted.

"We have to replace Janice with a music director committed to the 'Essential Qualities of an Excellent Music Program.'"

All along I didn't want Janice to be the issue. Standards, outcomes—the stuff curriculum coordinators think about—became the focus I imposed on the Music Committee, but the challenge had been about a personality all along. Janice had to be fired for the same reason I was fired as English Department Coordinator. She didn't fit the prevailing mold. I got the Music Committee to specify necessary changes. Janice could have joined in or thrown herself against it. She chose to do nothing and hoped nothing would happen. Three years ago I couldn't bring myself to do what Bob wanted, which was to go along with the boss and shut up. I just couldn't. So I was dumped. The same would happen to Janice Patterson, even though her resistance was passive and mine was anything but. As for Qiao-Yun, only God knows why I screwed up the dinner date. Sooner or later the vestry would have to address the Janice problem—I recognized that from the start—and maybe my not-so-scattered brain wanted me someplace else Wednesday night.

"Do you think I'm right?" Diane asked.

We were meeting about serious church business, and I let myself get distracted worrying about the dinner date with Qiao-Yun. This gave way to my old grudge with Bob. Diane needed me on her side. She couldn't grow St. Joseph's membership if every service offered boring music. That's why she created the committee and put me in charge. Excellent music could do people a lot of good, and what we had wasn't coming close. The rector and senior warden had to fix that. Of course, Diane was right. She wanted the vestry to approve "The Essential Qualities." Whatever loyalty Janice might have gained from past vestries had withered. Later we would ask the Music Committee to rewrite the director's job description to fit the new standards. The vestry would approve it next month, and the redefined position would be posted.

"What happens to Janice?" I asked.

"She could apply, with the understanding she would have to meet the job description. Who knows, maybe nobody else will want the position at the salary we can afford."

We were launching a big risk. If no one decent applied, Janice would be more entrenched than ever. If we found someone dynamic who would commit to "The Essential Qualities," Janice's departure could be disruptive. Unimaginative leaders always have staunch followers. Bob Norris taught me that.

I still had a faint hope for Janice. "Maybe she can present a case why she's the person to make 'The Essential Qualities' happen."

"You're in the choir. Do you really believe that?"

I got a vision of Jerry vaulting over the piano during choir rehearsal and grabbing Janice's throat between his massive hands—his face radiant with manic smile, hers contorted with bulging eyes and protruding tongue. Then I imagined Olivia Finch cheerfully slipping arsenic in Janice's cup some Sunday during coffee hour.

"It would be nice, but, no, I don't really believe that."

With this settled, at least for the moment, we went over other agenda items. The cash flow meant the treasurer would again need to take funds from investments to pay bills. We needed replacements for two Sunday school teachers stepping down in June, but this could wait. Larger stuff loomed. The Episcopal Bishop of Massachusetts gave priests permission to bless gay and lesbian marriages, which were legal in this state, at the time the only one with such wisdom. We had two couples, one of each, whom Diane didn't name. They hoped she would bless their unions. Diane was ready, and I agreed. The vestry would agree too, we figured, although some parishioners wouldn't. But the rector didn't need anyone's consent. In other business the vestry had to spend money to replace our broken-down photocopier. Jerry had three bids. We would delay reports from two subcommittees who never had anything new to say. Our conversation meandered to other topics until Diane asked how I was doing.

My concert date with Qiao-Yun had no doubt become common knowledge. A few people might know we ate at Fernando's. Of course no one knew about the Monday night kiss, but almost any rumor could be afoot by now. Months ago Fran learned about my attraction to Qiao-Yun. Jerry witnessed a lot more. But aside from getting information out of Wen, I hadn't talked about this to anyone except those three.

"Last Sunday I went on a date. I took Qiao-Yun Wang to the Old

Colony Festival Chorus concert."

Diane tried to suppress her smile. It didn't work. "How was it?"

I made no effort to suppress mine. "Quite nice, actually."

"Tell me more."

Diane heard all about my getting Jerry's tickets and asking Qiao-Yun out during coffee hour and the concert itself and my working up the nerve to ask her to dinner and her acceptance. "And she's not too young for me."

"No. She isn't."

"Yesterday morning I was raking leaves in the backyard and started whistling *Singin' in the Rain*. I danced with my rake the way Gene Kelly danced with his umbrella."

"I can see you doing something like that."

"Because you know I'm crazy."

"It's a good crazy. Isn't the song about being ready for love?"

As so often happened, Diane and I were going in the same direction, but her thoughts ran about a dozen steps ahead of mine. Her face had permission written all over it, and I got scared.

"I'm not sure. Let's just say the flesh is willing, but the spirit is weak."

"Stephen, many widows and widowers have gone through this. When the lucky ones get an impulse to dance, as you did yesterday, they do."

"Maybe I've been too impulsive." I explained my screw-up about tonight. "I have to call her right away."

"She'll be fine. You'll be fine. Trust me."

"There's something else. Katelyn is pregnant. She's due in November."

Saying those words for the first time, especially to Diane, choked me up.

"That's wonderful, Stephen."

Sitting in my VW outside St. Joseph's, I took out my cell phone. Qiao-Yun almost shouted over a cacophony of women's voices in the background.

"I play mahjong on Wednesdays," she said. In the background came more prattle. Someone said something with "Stephen" in it. Lots of laughter followed it.

"I'm sorry," Qiao-Yun yelled. "They make fun of me, say I should get back to game."

"I'm the one who should be sorry. There's a vestry meeting tonight. I forgot. I can't come to dinner. I'm very sorry."

Earlier she must have told her friends about me, and here I was breaking a date, her dinner of all things, at the last moment with her Chinese lady friends all around her. They would want to know everything, and soon she would tell them that this American guy who had seemed so nice was really an idiot.

The mahjong players quieted down, and Qiao-Yun's volume lowered. "What time your meeting?"

"Seven."

"I home at five. Dinner ready five-thirty. Okay?"

I said yes immediately. "I'm very sorry. You're very understanding."

"You make mistake. That's all. We both needs to eating. Dinner simple easy. I make all the time. Hope you like." She told me again to be there at five-thirty. "I go back to game now. Goodbye, Stephen."

This was very interesting. A guy calls a woman he's dated only twice—if you want to call Monday night a date—and has kissed once to say he's backing out of dinner at her house, and she says not to worry, they both have to eat anyway, and he can come over for a quick bite. Was this typical? I didn't think so. Sure, I could do that with Jerry (Hey, Jerry, I can't meet you at Linnehan's tonight because I forgot something), and he'd call me a moron and say okay, no problem, or I would say the same if he called to stand me up. It was like Diane's being so casual when I forgot our meeting to discuss the prospect of firing someone. Jerry's my best friend, and forgiveness is Diane's stock-in-trade. Qiao-Yun was my—well, she wasn't really my anything—but she rated a lot more consideration.

No label could fit her: an Episcopal martial arts champion who is young and beautiful and could attract legions of guys but goes to a concert of archaic music with a sixty-two-year-old doofus who half the time can't keep track of where the hell he's supposed to be, a guy she later kisses with such ardor he becomes transfixed, a process beginning the first time her hand touched his, reconfiguring him from the dour, self-obsessed fool he had been into someone he can't quite figure out but certain this emerging, new self is a definite improvement, and then forgiving him when he tramples her invitation for more.

Then again maybe I wasn't so transfixed. After all, I didn't tell my motherless daughter her father went out on a date or tell Qiao-Yun I was going to be a grandfather.

Well at least I was decent enough to visit Anita Colefax. I went home, cleaned up, and made lunch. When I arrived at the Bay View Nursing Home, Anita's roommate sat in a wheel chair and looked out the window. She didn't hear me enter, and I didn't want to disturb her. Anita wasn't there. An aide spotted me and said Anita was in the dining hall. I left the Communion kit on her table and walked from her wing to the center of the building. With lunch over and the tables cleared, the dining hall became the social activities room. Anita sat with five other women. Few men lived in Bay View. I had noticed the same at my mother's nursing home. The dining room's sound system played Glen Miller's *Chattanooga Choo Choo*, and Anita saw me standing at the entrance. She beckoned me and introduced her pals.

"This is Helen, Wanda, Vicky, Lulu, and Gilda. And this is Stephen, the nice man from my church I was telling you about."

My mother would never have remembered all five names.

An aide offered to get me a chair, but Anita said we were going back to her room. I thought this a good idea, especially after the music changed to Patti Paige's *How Much Is That Doggy in the Window?*

Her roommate hadn't moved from her window and took no notice when we returned. Anita called out to her. "Esther, it's Stephen. Say hello to Stephen."

Esther sat motionless while Anita waited for a response. "I don't know what she sees out there."

Our service took about ten minutes. The mini liturgy fit on one sheet of paper. The kit contained a few wafers and a small vial of wine that Diane had blessed and a second vial with water. It also held a candle, which I lit, and a small silver-coated cup and plate. Like all routines, Communions can slip into drone and habit. The Eucharistic minister is supposed to generate a conversation to avoid that. For the Gospel reading I brought a copy of what was read at St. Joseph's the previous Sunday.

We did the service together, alternating prayers. I read the passage from John's Gospel where Thomas doubts the risen Jesus standing before him is the real thing. I asked Anita what she thought.

"Thomas is like most people," she said. "He wanted proof."

"Is that bad?"

"Jesus didn't think so. He could have told Thomas to stop being so bullheaded. Instead, he showed him his wounds and let him touch them."

"Why do you think he did that?"

"Why not? Thomas wasn't a bad person. They had been together from the start." Anita removed the TV remote from the table to give me more room to set up Communion. "Why do you think Jesus did that?"

Anita waited for my answer. "For the same reasons," I said.

We read the Nicene Creed together and a prayer for people in need, adding names of specific persons. Anita mentioned Esther. I said, "Katelyn, Luke, and Gareth." Anita included her two daughters, several other names, and me.

After our service I began repacking the Communion kit. "How's everything at St. Joseph's?" Anita asked, as she glanced across the room at Esther.

I said everything was okay and the vestry would meet that night to discuss routine business.

"And you?" she asked. "Anything new going on?"

When I saw Anita the previous week, another four days would pass before I could ask Qiao-Yun to the O.C.F.C. concert. It made no sense to get into all that since I wasn't sure where this story was going and didn't want to set up a cliffhanger that ended badly. "Why burden Anita with a dead-end fairy tale?" I told myself, which was a crock. My only concern was how pathetic I'd look the following visit if Qiao-Yun had turned me down or, worse, she said yes but somewhere down the line it all fell apart, the fault being all mine. For now I had a fairy tale that got off to a good start, but telling this to my priest was one thing; telling someone else was much different. So I told her about Katelyn.

"I spoke with my daughter the other night. She's pregnant, due in November."

Anita's eyes went to the photos on her bureau and wall before she congratulated me. I spotted her late husband Frank in a group photo. In another taken about ten years ago he and Anita sat together. She had one grandson, three granddaughters, and one great-grandson. She talked about a portrait of two little girls seated on either side of a younger boy. The girls wore pink dresses, and their brother wore a white shirt and bow tie. Thirty years ago Anita bought these outfits and took the kids to the photographer. She had two prints made. One became a surprise anniversary gift for the kids' parents. She kept the other.

I repeated almost word-for-word all my silliness with Katelyn about the crazy grandfather I'd be. Anita said I would make an excellent grandfather and spoke about watching generations grow up.

The more she talked the more she slipped into vague generalities I couldn't piece together. This went on until Anita pointed towards the portrait of the two sisters and their brother.

"They're all grown up now. The boy lives in Middleboro, drives a truck all over the country. The oldest girl lives in Vermont. She's divorced. The other girl lives here in Scrooby. She visited me two months ago."

I lifted from her bureau a framed wallet-sized photo of a newborn wrapped in a blue blanket. "And this guy is your great-grandson. Isn't he?"

"That's Ronnie, my granddaughter Amy's boy. He'll be four in August. They're in South Carolina. I haven't seen him yet."

Ronnie and Amy were among the names Anita spoke earlier during Communion.

The Pastoral Care Ministry visited hospitalized parishioners, nursing home residents, and shut-ins as often as they could. We needed more volunteers. Anita saw few visitors from St. Joseph's. Anita's nearest daughter, the mother of the three kids in the portrait, worked full time and cared for her invalid husband. The daughter came when she could. I put Ronnie's picture back on the bureau and took a leap of faith.

"I mentioned you to another parishioner. She might tag along with me sometime."

"That would be nice. Is she someone I know?"

"No, she isn't, but you'll like her."

"What's her name?"

"Qiao-Yun Wang."

I sat down on the edge of the bed and told Anita everything. As she listened to my tale, her face showed all she heard, from the Epiphany dinner to the mahjong phone call. She threw her hands in the air and gleamed when I said we kissed each other goodnight.

Anita said she would love to meet Qiao-Yun. "And I'll put in a good word for you."

"That's why I want you two to meet."

Anita's broad smile expanded, then gradually withdrew, and her eyes tightened. "Have you told your children?"

If I shut my eyes, I could still see Anita's photos, her bed with its pillows and the pale orange afghan a St. Joseph's angel had brought, her single bureau, the closet she and Esther shared, the room's open doorway precluding privacy, the white walls and tiled floor beyond, the hospital curtain rail between the two beds, and the now dozing Esther in her wheelchair by the window, her chin almost touching her collarbone.

"I'm not sure what they can handle right now," I said.

A nurse and an aid entered. They pulled the curtain around Esther's bed, blocking my view of her by the window, and disappeared behind. A kind voice spoke Esther's name and said it was time for her medication. More was spoken, but I couldn't make out the words. Meanwhile, Anita's face said she had more to tell me and wished we were alone again. I almost said it was time for me to go when shuffling sounds joined the muffled voices. They stopped, and the nurse's arm jutted from the curtain and pulled it back. Esther lay in bed with the blanket to her neck, and the two women left. The table between Anita and me stood about four feet high, a rectangular metal stand on wheels typical in hospitals and nursing homes. Anita nudged it to one side and pedal-stepped her wheelchair towards me.

Her hand reached out and touched my knee. "Let me give you some advice. The question isn't what your kids can handle."

"I don't follow."

"Whatever it is you want, don't wait for proof."

For a second I figured Anita's intrusive nature was what made Esther clam up. I knew better, though. Someone had set a year as the rule. No one knows who. I lasted nine months, the time between Cara's death and the present. Or was it four months, the time between Cara's death and my first seeing Qiao-Yun after the eight o'clock service with Jerry and Wen? Two months later I pursued her. Whatever the count, it wasn't a year.

"I have friends who say I worry too much."

"Now you have another one."

"Qiao-Yun invited me to dinner before my vestry meeting tonight."

"If she's a good cook, your kids should hear about it, don't you think?"

Anita was right, of course, but I couldn't bring myself to say so. Instead I picked up the Communion kit. "Ask me again next week."

I kissed her forehead and left.

CHAPTER 9

Easy to find, Qiao-Yun's street came just before South Scrooby High School. The drive from my house near the northwest town line took thirty minutes in rush hour traffic. Her house was set about seventy-five yards back on a crushed stone driveway that sloped through a grove of scrub pines and looped by the side door. More weeds than grass populated what little lawn she had, and the house, a two-floor design popular in the early nineties, looked its age but not shabby. Maybe two years could pass before the trim needed fresh paint. I parked my car alongside her Honda. Qiao-Yun stepped from the house's side door wearing jeans and a black sweater. As always he looked great.

"Welcome. You coming right on time."

I had stopped at a florist and bought the biggest ready-made multicolored bouquet the woman had. She wrapped it in pink paper with a white ribbon and bow. Qiao-Yun's face lit up.

"For me?"

"I hope you like them." I held the flowers toward her.

As her left hand covered my right, the other reached behind my neck and drew my face to hers. I kept my hold on the flowers as her hand dropped and slipped up my back. We kissed deeply, and our embrace tightened. She brought me into the house.

The way she kicked off her shoes and lined them with others near the door announced this was the custom. I followed her example, and she led me to the dining table beyond the kitchen counter. I saw parts of her living room. Framed Chinese watercolors and calligraphy hung on the walls. A sofa and love seat near the fireplace looked as old as the house. The dining room table looked newer. She had two places already set, one at the head of the table and one to its side where she gestured for me to sit, and the aroma from the stove suggested meat and vegetables mixed with other, unfamiliar flavors, all pleasant.

Qiao-Yun filled a vase with water and unwrapped the bouquet. "You want drink? I made tea."

"Tea would be very nice."

She brought a small, white porcelain pot to the table decorated with blue dragons, the same design on the Chinese teacups. "You pour yourself. I start scallion pancakes."

I watched her scoot behind the counter. "What's a scallion

pancake?"

She faced the stove. "Very fast, you see. Very good. I get from Asian supermarket in Quincy. Let me see. I read box. It made with 'enriched flour, malted barley flour, scallion, onion, soybean oil, sesame oil,' ah, many things, like pancake."

The air filled with the loud sizzle of oil in a pan, and I imagined something like a tortilla, a dish I seldom had. In fact, before last Sunday I couldn't remember my last time in Fernando's. The teasing aroma suggested delights neither Mexican nor typical of American Chinese restaurants. I poured some tea into my cup and drank a little. Qiao-Yun talked while the stove's hisses and crackles settled down.

"These cook very fast, one minute each sides, and I bring other things to put in. You like tea?"

It certainly wasn't teabag Oolong. "Very much. What kind is it?"

"High mountain tea from my country, I'm glad you like."

Qiao-Yun had three burners going. Over one she flipped a scallion pancake while in a second frying pan she stirred what I guessed was the meat and vegetable filling. On the third she had a pot going. I noticed the place settings with chopsticks and small porcelain spoons. Mine also had a fork. Each had a plate and a bowl. She scurried to the table bringing two wooden squares, each about seven inches to a side, which I presumed would protect the tablecloth from hot dishes. I was right because she returned with a huge skillet loaded with beef chunks, onions, broccoli, and assorted peppers in one hand and in the other a pot with some kind of soup with noodles.

"Can I help you?" I asked.

She turned and dashed back to the kitchen. "Yes, ladle soup. I get pancakes. Oh, before you do that, here, take flowers. Put on table." When she handed me the vase, her eyes peeked from behind the tall spread of stems and colors. "They very beautiful."

I could tell the soup's broth and meat came from a chicken. The noodles were the length of spaghetti strands. I filled our bowls, and she returned with a platter of scallion pancakes and a bowl of spinach leaves. She sat down and said we should dig in. "Be careful. Very hot."

She lowered her face close to the table and spooned some soup into her mouth with a loud slurping noise. In my childhood home I never made sounds when eating, certainly not a slurp. Conversation was allowed as long as mouths were foodless or, like my parents, the diners had mastered the art of speaking clearly with their mouths quarter-full and closed. My grandmother—my mother's mother who lived with us—had a special privilege. She slobbered every liquid and lip-smacked every morsel she consumed. Though Fran and I had been indoctrinated that only animals made sounds when eating, we still had to put up with Gammy's noise at every family meal. Our confusion festered into nervous intolerance. Gammy's teeth, my mother once explained, meaning her dentures, weren't right. Why Gammy couldn't get proper ones we never learned. Much later we realized she and misfortune had been companions for a very long time. My mother insisted her two kids eat quietly. In everything having to do with manners, my father's view was "Do what your mother says." Lessons like this stick. Katelyn and Luke heard my admonitions since they were old enough to hold a spoon. Mouth sounds were impolite. Besides, they reminded me of Gammy, a memory less than splendid.

Qiao-Yun placed a scallion pancake on her plate. "I show you."

Tongs rested on the side of the skillet with the beef and vegetables. She loaded this filling on the pancake, added the spinach, and rolled it like a taco. She passed the plate to me. "Give me yours," she said and repeated the maneuver. From her roll-up she bit off one end. Some of the filling spilled onto her plate. She chewed her mouthful and then used her chopsticks to pick up what had dropped. I quietly took a bite.

"You like?" she asked.

"It's delicious." I wasn't lying.

"I'm glad you like. Try your soup."

I dipped my spoon into the broth and sampled a chicken noodle soup unlike anything from a can. "This is excellent too. What's in it?"

Qiao-Yun said she often ate chicken and always saved the broth. The noodles came from the Asian grocery store she mentioned earlier. To the bubbling soup she had added two raw scrambled eggs and peas and corn and "spices but not super spicy." All this was interesting, but as she twirled noodles around her chopsticks, I stopped caring about what we ate and instead worried about how she ate.

Qiao-Yun inserted the chopsticks into her mouth and inhaled the great white coil with heavy, wet sucking. I hadn't seen her eat this way in public. In her home she returned to habits that were probably acceptable to most of the world's population but were a dead sure appetite killer for me. Back in 1989 when the United States invaded Panama, the Army played loud rock music through huge speakers outside President Manuel Noriega's palace believing the racket would crumble his resolve. It was a dumb idea. But if anyone ever wanted a quick surrender from me, just blast some open-mouth chewing sounds and I'd fold in twenty seconds. Now this fascinating, beautiful woman was close to turning my stomach. I needed divine intervention. What came was Paul Muni.

In 1937 MGM made a movie of Peal Buck's *The Good Earth*, a novel about China. White actors played the leads and just about every other role. I saw it twice on TV about twenty years apart. Paul Muni played a Chinese peasant who grew wealthy, and Luise Rainer played his wife. That's all I remembered except for three scenes. One showed a throng of locusts swirling down on a wheat field. The two others held close-ups of Muni. The first came early. He's eating rice from a bowl. He's using chopsticks, no easy trick, but Muni looks like he knows what he's doing. When he gets to the final grains, Muni tips the bowl to his mouth, and pressing the chopsticks together he uses them to scrape the remaining rice into his slurpy, inhaling mouth. He isn't eating like a bumpkin. That's the point. He's eating like an Asian. I remembered sensing this. For all its insincere attempts at multiculturalism, Hollywood had this right. Utensils dictate table manners. What you can do with knives and forks, you can't do with chopsticks, nor should anyone try. The mission is to get food into your gut. I don't know what Chinese people think of *The Good Earth*. For me, Muni and Rainer avoided cliché portrayals. Their characters were human beings first, with a civilization older than Europe's, and I don't think most American audiences in 1937 knew that about Asians. Muni ate like an authentic person. The second close-up of him I remembered came in the movie's last shot. He says his wife, the Rainer character, is "the good earth." This is how my chaotic mind works. As long as Qiao-Yun's slurps brought me to Gammy and my parents' edicts, we were in trouble. Once Paul Muni walked in, I went from being an irritated head case to someone who could take the unpleasant and stick it behind a lovely screen. After all, Qiao-Yun looked perfect, and her dinner was delicious. We would talk just as we had before.

"Tell me about your mahjong friends."

"They all Chinese ladies. Three from Taiwan, one from China."

"I sensed the ladies enjoyed themselves when we spoke on the phone."

I explained how Diane reminded me about vestry tonight and how my friendship with Anita keeps growing. Qiao-Yun remembered my mentioning her before and said she would like to meet Anita. What I needed to tell her was Katelyn's news, and I was embarrassed because I didn't tell her Tuesday.

"Monday night after I got home my daughter called." I bit off more pancake. My measured chewing gave me a few seconds. "She's going to have a baby."

Qiao-Yun put down her chopsticks. "So you going to be grandfather." Her smile and eyes filled her face. "Congratulation!"

"I meant to tell you yesterday but..." I realized I should never have started this sentence because there was no way to end it without sounding like a ninny.

"But what?" Qiao-Yun rolled noodles on her chopsticks.

Paul Muni couldn't get me out of this one. Neither could Clark Gable, Cary Grant, or Gary Cooper who late in their careers made movies with actresses half their ages or younger—and no one bought it. Well, okay, Cary Grant could get away with anything, but Gable, at sixty-one, died from a heart attack after making *The Misfits* with Marilyn Monroe.

"Look, you ought to know how old I am. I'm sixty-two." And then I asked the question I had determined wasn't a problem. But I asked it anyway. "Is that too old for you?"

Qiao-Yun's mouth was full. "We'll see." She finished chewing and swallowed. "I'm forty-five. You already tell me you have two grown children, one married, so of course you be grandfather soon. I'm old enough to be grandmother. So let me ask you question. Am I too old for you?"

Over the past two minutes I had manufactured a reason why she wasn't good enough for me and another why I wasn't good enough for her. Both were crazy.

"We'll see," I said.

"Good answer."

Qiao-Yun twirled more noodles on her chopsticks, and I did a fair imitation. After we consumed our soup, her chopsticks squeezed a piece of beef. I tried with a piece from my plate. She tried not to laugh. "Let me show you."

She put her chopsticks down and then picked each one up with her left hand and set it in her right between fingers and thumb. "Don't move the bottom one. Make the upper one do the work to grabbing against the bottom."

She picked up a sliced pepper. "You try."

I targeted a chunk of beef and almost clamped it, but the upper stick wouldn't do what I wanted, and the lower wouldn't stay in place.

The next try went better. I clutched my prey and got it four inches off the plate before the grip slipped. A third try was worse than the first. We laughed.

I put down my chopsticks. "If I didn't have that damn meeting at seven, I'd keep at this. So I'm shifting to my fork, but only for the sake of time, you understand, and a warm meal."

"Of course, senior warden duty first. Chopstick practice later."

After I finished what was on my plate, Qiao-Yun rolled me another pancake. "Tell me about your daughter."

With this question I realized there will come a time when these two women would meet.

"She and her husband, Gareth, are very happy, though I don't think they planned to have a baby now. She's due in November."

"You happy too?"

"Yes, I am, though Gareth's position at the college doesn't pay well and they'll miss Katelyn's income."

"I had baby and worked same time. It not easy, but womens do it."

Cara didn't return to work until Katelyn and Luke started school. I remember some teacher colleagues who took maternity leaves and were back in school right away. Others resigned and returned years later or never. I knew nothing about daycare, especially in Queens. I decided not to fill that hole with worries.

"You'll have to tell me how you did that." I looked at my watch. "My meeting starts soon. We have a lot on the agenda. This has been a wonderful meal. Let me take you out Friday. I'd say tomorrow, but I have choir practice."

"That sound very nice. Where we eat?"

I told her wherever she wanted. She asked whether I wanted Chinese food again. "But not American Chinese food like round here. We could go to restaurant in Quincy where Asian people go."

Exotic flavors still danced in my mouth. I couldn't refuse. We agreed I should pick her up at five o'clock Friday afternoon. She walked me to the door, and with one hand against the wall, I slipped my shoes back on and bent to tie them. When I stood up, she put her arms around me. We kissed. Her tight embrace said she wanted me to stay.

I almost changed my mind. "I'll see you Friday and call you tomorrow. Meanwhile, I'll practice using chopsticks."

"Hold on." Qiao-Yun dashed to the kitchen and returned with a wooden pair and said what sounded like *kwhy-zuh*. "You try. But don't worry. They have forks in Quincy restaurant too."

I tried to imitate her word for chopsticks. "*Kwhy-zuh.*"

"Very good!" she said. I had spoken Chinese.

CHAPTER 10

St. Joseph's by-laws say the rector chairs the vestry meetings or can delegate this role to another. Diane gave the job to me. She and I were the first to arrive. We dispersed the agendas around the two tables that were pushed together in a cramped room used for committee meetings. The treasurer, Charlie Prendergast, soon joined us. He distributed monthly tally sheets as he maneuvered his squat body from place to place. The others gradually entered, took their seats, and perused their handouts.

First came the oldest, Fred Divol. Next came Dwayne Parsons, whose boyish face disguised his forty-two years. Josefa Garcia followed Dwayne. Jo was the Scrooby police and fire dispatcher. With a notebook in hand, the parish clerk, Irene Covey, took her seat. She taught third grade in my old school system and would retire in June, seven years after her eligibility for full pension. She exuded the image of a no-nonsense disciplinarian who didn't smile until November, but every June her kids began their summer vacations crying because Mrs. Covey wouldn't be their teacher again. Dr. Nick Bellini, a chiropractor built like a gymnast, entered and headed for the seat alongside Dwayne. At thirty-six Nick was the youngest member of the vestry, a stark contrast to the portly Paul Bellamy, the second oldest member, who sat to my left. I knew Nick professionally. He treated my back pain a year ago and predicted my high-impact running would do more damage than he could fix. I changed my exercise routine. After Olivia and Jerry entered, in came Rachel Arnold, an alto in the choir. She lived with her husband, Edgar, and her mother-in-law. Neither Edgar nor his mother came to church. I knew the vestry members fairly well, but Dwayne Parsons least of all. He had attended the eight o'clock ever since he joined the church two years ago. Diane thought he would be a very positive presence on the vestry. He volunteered at the food pantry twice a week, and he helped the Men's Group sell hotdogs during the Fourth of July parade that passed by St. Joseph's. Other than that, I knew little about him. To his credit, he never missed a meeting, never wasted time with off-hand prattle, and always voted for the budget.

Vestry meetings follow a pre-set format. First there's a meditation before we get on with business. Each month we rotate which member brings copies of something inspirational. The member reads it aloud while the others follow the copies he or she brings. We discuss it for about ten minutes, and the meditation closes with someone else reading it again. It's usually a good warm-up exercise before we get on with parish business. It's supposed to remind us we're a vestry and not a corporation board of directors. Some vestry members liked to get material from the Internet. Others relied on the Bible or the Book of Common Prayer. Jerry once brought his guitar and verses from a hymn none of us had heard before. He got us singing.

Fred Divol had served on various vestries since his twenties. He had been a lay Eucharistic minister for fifty years and was a past treasurer, junior warden, and senior warden. He brought this month's meditation, The Parable of the Prodigal Son. Fred went to the Saturday five o'clock services. I heard he was a Korean War veteran. Fred never talked about it. After the war he returned home and went to work at the Scrooby Savings Bank, eventually becoming a loan officer, a job he held until his retirement over a decade ago. Thin and lantern jawed with round eyeglasses atop his long pointed nose, Fred looked like a flinty old Yankee banker, but his reputation said he was the go-to guy for anyone needing a break.

Fred passed his photocopies around the table. "It's the King James Version. I hope that's okay."

Everyone said this was fine, and two said it's good to hear the old language again. Fred started to read when Harriet Pringle burst in, all smiles and apologies as she thumped her way towards the empty seat half way around. Fred started again, and we followed the familiar story about the man with two sons. The younger asks for his inheritance early, gets it, and leaves the farm. The older son stays with the father, loyally working hard to keep the place prosperous. The prodigal son quickly squanders his birthright. With no money or friends left, he hires out to a pig farmer. It was a terrible job. Ashamed and hungry, he decides to return home. He confesses all to his father and asks for a job as the old man's lowest of servants. Instead, the father embraces him and orders a celebration. The older son resents such attention for his wayward brother and complains that he, not the younger son, rates recognition and praise. The father tells him to be happy because the son who died has come back to life.

I asked the group, as was the usual procedure, what they saw in this story that is especially meaningful for us, the vestry. Silence hovered longer than I would have expected given how well known this story is. Sitting opposite my end of the table, Diane kept her eyes on the photocopy. She rarely spoke during the meditations. I asked again, and meager commentaries sputtered forth: "...forgiveness... God is a nice father too... kids will be kids...first read this in Sunday school...fine story...great parable." Jerry and Olivia looked at each other as though they both had very definite ideas. They waited for Fred to speak. He leaned forward with both elbows on the table.

"There's just three people in this story. When I was a kid, twelve or so, I thought the younger brother got a good deal, and I was glad his father forgave him. I didn't think much more about it until many years later. I was married, holding down two jobs, helping out around the church too, always one project or another. That's when I thought the prodigal son's deal was too good. The way the older son tells it, you'd think the father never gave him so much as a thank you in all the years he toiled on that farm. By the time my four kids were grown, I saw things the way the father sees them. He loves his two sons the same. The thing is I identify with all three characters, not just separately over the years. I mean right now, all three, have for a long time."

Harriet Pringle issued her toothy endorsement. "Well, I just think this is a wonderful story, Fred."

Jerry closed his eyes. Four members nodded their agreement. Fred perused the faces around him and placed his hands palm down on the table. Diane glanced up at me.

"Who'd like to give this passage a second reading?" I asked.

Dwayne volunteered. He read beautifully.

The minutes from last month's meeting were accepted. I called on Charlie Prendergast for his report. He spoke through his closely cropped white goatee. His double chin bulged underneath. Charlie had six pages detailing how the cash flow compared with the budget. As usual Charlie said he borrowed from the "rainy day fund," meaning he transferred money from the parish's endowments, much of it left to the parish by people who died long ago. Although most members dutifully followed his recitation of numbers and occasionally asked for clarifications referencing budget line items with spending variations from one month to the next, the treasurer's report always bored the hell out of me. I yearned to wander outside and look up in perfect silence at the stars. Charlie finished. I asked for a motion to accept the treasurer's report.

"So moved," said Jo Garcia. Olivia seconded. The vote was unanimous. I called for the junior warden's report. Jerry said the contracted work to sand and re-stain the main doors and rewire a backdoor security light was done. The bills matched the estimates approved at the January meeting.

"That's my report, but I need your approval for a big expenditure."

He held copies of three bids, each designating a particular photocopier and service contract. He divided the stack in half and passed a handful to the two members sitting next to him. I noticed we were five minutes behind schedule.

"While these bids are making the rounds, can I have a motion to accept the junior warden's report?" I said.

Dwayne made the motion, and the second came from Nick. Jerry took over right after the motion unanimously passed. "The papers you hold in your hand I had copied at Olde Towne Printing because the machine in our office has all the life and reliability of a beached whale. And if you asked Alice she'd tell you the two smell about the same. We need a new photocopier."

Alice was Alice Flynn, the parish secretary and Diane's most vital and trusted aide, much more so than the two wardens. Alice's most vital aides were her computer and photocopier. Jerry brought three bids detailing different machines' functions, warranties, service contracts, and prices. This was a standard practice that Charlie insisted the vestry adopt last year for any purchase over a thousand dollars. Jerry also brought scattered throughout these bids a catalog of numbers without meaning unless they were preceded by dollar signs or followed by "months" or "copies." Few did. The rest gave specifications about pixels, platforms, graphics, guides, and kits and dual things and universal things and things that would "full bleed."

Jerry understood this data no better than I did. The only factor worth noting was that St. Joseph's needed a machine that could do routine copying and turn out worship service leaflets, black and white for weekend services and color for Christmas and Easter and a few other occasions. Durability and cost counted next. Jerry gave us the required three bids.

The first cost too much even with a five-year warranty and guaranteed service because the copier had tons more versatility than we needed. Its gargantuan size, Jerry explained, meant he would have to partition off a Sunday school classroom to house it, another expense, which would locate the beast away from the office. The second option, though tiny and very cheap, was slow and fragile. For technical assistance the manufacturer offered a website. The third bid cost seven thousand dollars less than the first and two thousand more than the second. It could do all the necessary jobs. Its two-year warranty and service contract were renewable for a moderate fee. It would easily slip into the current copier's space.

Jerry summarized the third's most attractive virtue. "Alice likes it."

Ordinarily, Charlie would argue for the lowest bid, but he knew a treasurer might endure a rector's scorn but not the parish secretary's. Jerry made his recommendation. Jo moved it, and Paul seconded. The motion carried unanimously. Diane thanked the Vestry. I moved on.

"The next item on the agenda is the senior warden. I bring you a report from the Music Committee."

Rachel Arnold, who sat directly across from Olivia, joined the choir shortly after Janice Patterson arrived at St. Joseph's. I remembered her throwing back a lot of thickly spiked eggnog at the choir's Christmas party and then started pressing me about the Music Committee. After only one meeting I had little to say. Rachel accused me of being coy. "Well, whatever you people do," she said, "you should remember what our parish owes Janice." Her speech slurred with ire. From behind me Jerry whispered, "Yes, do remember that."

Now Rachel eyed Diane who was passing around copies of "The Essential Qualities of an Excellent Music Program" while I reviewed how the vestry, at Diane's request, had asked the rector to form a committee to determine what could be done to support the music program at St. Joseph's and how the committee's members, each endorsed by the vestry, had decided they would make no budget recommendations until they had established the program's overall goals.

"The paper before you is the result of that effort," I said. "Please give it a careful reading."

It took a while.

The first reaction came from Irene. "I don't think any church, even a cathedral, can be this excellent."

Whenever Paul Bellamy spoke at vestry meetings, a sonorous breath announced he had something to say. He started talking about a business trip to Atlanta. One night having nothing else to do he wandered by a church with a huge banner announcing a choir festival. He went inside.

"About a dozen choirs—some all white, some all black, some both—performed, not a bad one in the bunch," he said, "but the choirs I remember blew the roof off the place. These 'Essential Qualities,' remind me what I got that night. And all kinds of denominations were there. It can be done."

"If Paul says this can happen," Jo said. "I believe him."

Irene didn't doubt Paul. "But," she added, "with all due respect to the Music Committee, raising a bar is one thing; reaching it is something else again."

Rachel, who had been scribbling notes and underlining, took this as her cue. "I'm all for high goals—as long as they're not too high."

I wanted to jump in, but Olivia beat me to it. "I don't understand, Rachel. Please explain."

"Well, let's try this one: 'Challenges the program's leaders.' That's a pretty loaded statement."

Olivia's voice matched her placid face. "Loaded? How so?"

Rachel's jaw tightened. "Well, Olivia, it's been what, two years, since you've been in the choir? Maybe you've forgotten how hard Janice works. She challenges herself all the time."

Unmoved, Olivia answered back. "That being the case, Rachel, the standard you cite isn't too high."

At this point I sensed two main groups in the room—those who suppressed their laughter, with uneven degrees of success, and those who feared a fistfight would erupt.

Diane stepped in, speaking like a good shepherd. "Rachel, you'll recall we put the Music Committee together with Olivia representing the vestry and Stephen acting as chair. The vestry had directed Stephen to invite Janice. She declined. How many times, Stephen?"

"Three, twice before we met and later after the holidays."

"Did she say why?" Nick asked.

"She said she was very busy and thought the committee would work best without her."

Diane continued. "And although I believe the committee did an outstanding job, I can see how someone might view these standards as some kind of criticism of Janice because they were written without her input and they might seem to suggest that not a single one of these goals is currently evident here at St. Joseph's. That would be a shame."

I imagined the look on Jerry's face but didn't look his way.

Rachel wasn't done. "Thank you, Diane, but I have some other concerns with this sheet."

"Let's get a motion and a second," I said, "and then we can get into a discussion."

Jo said, "I move we accept the Music Committee's document 'The Essential Qualities of an Excellent Music Program.'"

Irene began writing on her notepad and stopped. "What are we accepting these as?"

Jo looked at me. Jerry said, "How about as guiding principles for St. Joseph's Parish?"

"So moved," Jo said. Paul Bellamy seconded. I asked for discussion.

Rachel's eyes darted to and from her marked-up paper. "Let's look at some more of these. There are some serious problems. I mean, do we really want to have dance and theater in our church? Someone please explain to me what alternative music is. Everything but traditional music is alternative. It could be anything and will tell the adult members, especially the older ones, this isn't their kind of church anymore. And what about 'Recognizes and respects multiple cultures and identities'? Where is that in the Book of Common Prayer? And here's some grandness for you: 'bolsters worshippers' commitments to the Baptismal Covenant.' Where did the Music Committee get that one?"

"I suspect from the Book of Common Prayer," Dwayne said, "page three-hundred four."

Irene's sardonic look told me which way she would vote.

The sides were lining up against Rachel. Even she could see it. She slowed down and adjusted her delivery.

"You're right, Dwayne. Let me rephrase that last one because it's really my central point. I think the Baptismal Covenant is very important. Of course, it is. The same is true for getting people 'to serve God in the world' or 'the congregation's spiritual understandings' or a lot of other ideals listed here. But this is something between an individual and God or the priest. It's not the choir's responsibility. You can't lay it on them. And let's get honest. You can't lay it on Janice. That's not fair, not fair at all."

"I'd like to say something." Charlie Prendergast had only to twist his neck slightly to fix his eyes on Diane or me. He started with Diane. "I know what it's like to be on a committee and get caught up in good intentions. That's the problem I have with this document, even though it has its good points. Janice knows St. Joseph's has been spending more than it takes in for years. That's why she hasn't raised her budget request, except for a slight increase in her salary. As treasurer I know some people think we should spend more on music, like hire trumpet players and violinists for Christmas Eve or replace the sound system."

Charlie shifted his focus to me. "You make this paper official parish policy, and there's no stopping the extravagances that will follow."

"Charlie's right," Harriet Pringle said. "And Rachel's point about grandness really hit it on the head. We are a traditional church. I think the people who make pledges every year want to keep it that way. Making changes because we want to get trendy would be an awful mistake."

Paul took another deep breath and let it out slowly. "In my old job I spent a lot of time looking at proposals. If I read them looking only for flaws and loopholes, that's all I'd see. That's not what my boss paid me to do."

"I agree with Paul," Nick said. "If you took out all the items Rachel mentioned, you might as well as take out anything that hints at religion. You might as well trash the whole thing. I like this paper fine the way it is."

The discussion went on. Nearly everyone voiced an opinion. I counted votes. Jerry, Olivia, Paul, Nick, Jo, Irene and Dwayne were firm on one side. Rachel and Charlie stood on the other. Harriet would vote with Rachel. I knew that from the start, though I wasn't sure about Fred Divol, who had said nothing.

Diane asked Irene to read the motion again. She flipped a page in her notebook. "To accept the Music Committee's document, 'The Essential Qualities of an Excellent Music Program,' as guiding principles for St. Joseph's Parish."

Diane thanked Irene. "In my view there's nothing in that motion or the 'Essential Qualities of an Excellent Music Program' that threatens our traditions. Ultimately, how we worship at St. Joseph's is determined foremost by the Canons of the Episcopal Church, and our parish by-laws, which say the rector and elected lay leadership and Annual Meeting govern how we get things done here, and this includes approving a budget. Before you now are some proposed guiding principles. They don't outweigh our most long-established authorities."

We were twenty minutes over schedule. I studied Fred while Diane spoke. He would vote to accept. I was certain of it now. Maybe Charlie would too, even though he fretted about church finances.

Rachel could count as well as I could. "It's getting late," she said. "We might as well vote."

"Let's vote," Harriet said.

"Okay, if there is no further discussion or objection," I said and waited an appropriate interval. "I think you all know the motion. All those in favor, please say 'Aye.'"

All but three vestry members responded.

"All those opposed say 'No.'"

Harriet's voice was strident. Rachel's less so. Charlie's almost mute.

"The motion carries. Next on the agenda is the rector's report."

Diane had already passed out the one-page summary of her activities over the last month, a summary that fell way short of detailing what happened over four seventy-hour workweeks. My watch said seven minutes after nine. Everyone looked at the wall clock behind me.

"Just let me add two points of information you should know," Diane said.

I figured Jerry and Olivia suspected "The Essential Qualities" needed follow-up action. That would be Diane's first point of information. No single piece of paper would affect how Janice ran the music program. I bet Rachel saw it coming too. But Diane's second point meant a huge policy change.

It was a bigger surprise too. The Massachusetts Supreme Court had stated gay marriages in this state were legal. Since churches didn't have to comply, most denominations kept silent about the ruling, except the most conservative, who denounced it, and the most liberal, who cheered. The Book of Common Prayer has a service in which a priest blesses a previous civil marriage. The Episcopal Church of the United States made this blessing available to Massachusetts gay couples, and our diocesan bishop encouraged this. The next likely step was allowing priests to perform the actual wedding. Right wing commentators and TV evangelists cranked up their railings against what they called activist judges in league with degenerates. They weren't alone. Even some Episcopalians agreed, and I wondered how many reactionaries went to St. Joseph's. At least one was on the vestry.

Diane opened with her first and less controversial point. "We have job descriptions for all three of our staff members. They're quite good. I think you, Fred, were the senior warden when these were developed back in the eighties."

"Yes, I was. A vestry subcommittee and the rector prepared the drafts."

"They're so good, in fact, two of the three still work very well, the ones for the parish secretary and the sextant. But with the approval of 'The Essential Qualities of an Excellent Music Program,' the music director's specifications need revisiting."

Fred said this was an excellent idea and he would be pleased to make the motion.

"We might not need that," Diane said. "In a month or two the Music Committee could have a draft description ready for the vestry."

Whether they were glad to escape a chore or to see a firm step follow their vote, every face but three beamed endorsement. I promised that when the draft was ready it would be on the next meeting's agenda. Charlie still looked worried. Rachel stayed quiet, a smart move because now her only shot was fighting the job description's changes once they were presented. Harriet's hard stare slid from Olivia to Jerry to Diane before landing on me.

Diane went to her second point, the one she hadn't discussed with me until this morning. "Recently I received two requests from couples who were married in civil ceremonies who want to have their marriages blessed. In each case this will be a ceremony for a same-sex couple— one for two women and one for two men—and these will be the first such blessings here. I wanted the vestry to be aware. I scheduled these services for June and July."

"That's not very far off," Nick said.

I wasn't sure what Nick meant, neither was Olivia. "Is that a problem?" she asked.

"No, it's not," Nick answered. "In fact, I bet we'll be one of the first in the diocese to have blessings of gay marriages. Is that right, Diane?"

Diane's answer showed much was going on. "At the clergy meeting last week, the bishop said a lot of rectors were getting similar requests. He urged we do the same pre-marriage counseling sessions we do with straight couples and then go ahead."

"Will they?" Harriet asked. "I mean will all the other rectors do these services?"

"I'm not sure about all."

Harriet all but crooned the next question. "And why's that do you suppose?"

"I don't have an answer," Diane said. "But I have no problem doing this. In fact, I'm happy to do it. I've met with both couples."

Harriet wasn't finished. "Why do you want to make holy matrimony available to people who—"

Charlie Prendergast interrupted: "—want to get married. In fact, they already are. All they're asking is to get blessed."

Harriet snapped. "If some parishes will bless these marriages and others won't, they'll flock to the ones that do. It's like I said before. The people who come to St. Joseph's come because they like it the way it is."

Dwayne glared at Harriet. "What bothers you more, two private ceremonies involving people you don't know or the likelihood these people might join our parish and maybe bring their friends?"

"Let me ask you a question, Dwayne. Which would you rather us be, St. Joseph's Episcopal Church or the Homosexual Church of Scrooby? Because, that's the choice!"

I wanted to speak, but Fred Divol beat me to it. "Harriet, you'll have to forgive me. If you have a problem with the rector going ahead and blessing these marriages, and it's obvious you do, what's the next step?"

Harriet had to come up with something or shut her mouth. "Okay, I have a motion. Here it is. The rector can't bless any homosexual marriages until the vestry determines the will of the parish on this issue."

Irene put down her pen. "Would you like to explain how the vestry will discern the will of the parish?"

"It doesn't matter," Fred said. "I have a point of order, Stephen."

I wasn't the least bit surprised and asked Fred to continue.

"Harriet, you can't make a motion that's not in conformity with the Episcopal Church. Canon law says the bishop and priest are within their rights to conduct any service in the prayer book for anyone they deem duly sincere and prepared for that service. I'm paraphrasing, but that's the gist of it."

Harriet seethed, but she didn't say anything. All that remained was for me to rule Fred's point of order valid. Business was done. Now all we needed was a motion to adjourn, which came from Paul. Nick seconded it. It was nine-thirty, a half-hour over time. I called the vote. No one voted no. Harriet didn't vote at all.

Rachel left first. Harriet waited until members seated between her and the door moved out. Fred walked with her. I couldn't hear what he said amid the various echoes of goodnight. Whatever it was it wouldn't work, not with Harriet and not, I feared, with other parishioners too.

Jerry and Olivia were the last to leave except for Diane and me. Jerry gently patted my back. Olivia squeezed my arm.

"Do you have some time tomorrow night?" Diane asked. "I'd like to debrief with you a little."

"I have choir at seven but can skip it."

She said we could meet at six.

Diane headed toward her office, her gait slow. I too felt very tired. In the parking lot the newly repaired security light illuminated my car. The distant foghorn in Scrooby Bay lowed a long, solitary note. I beeped the VW's electronic key. As I climbed in and tugged the shoulder harness, my cell phone rang. With one hand tangled in the strap, the other fumbled in my pocket. The phone rang twice more before I could answer. It was Qiao-Yun.

"Your meeting, it over? You must be home now."

"It just ended. We ran longer than usual. I'm leaving the church now."

"I wanted to say goodnight."

"That's very sweet."

"Your meeting go okay?"

"It went okay." The light in Diane's office was still on. "I'll call you tomorrow."

"That be very nice. Good night, Stephen."

"Good night, Qiao-Yun."

I freed my hand from the shoulder harness and started the engine. In the passenger seat were Qiao-Yun's chopsticks. I remembered the word. *Kwy-zuh.*

CHAPTER 11

I thought Diane the smartest person I had ever known and couldn't remember her ever being anything but confident. It was more than her collar and all the authority that came with it. She was three decades younger, yet I would throw myself in front of a train for her if she said it were a good idea.

Now she looked anxious. "Fred tripped up Harriet with a legalism, a clever tactic, and I'm glad no one else spoke against the blessings. But there will be an Act Two and an Act Three."

In an hour I would be in choir. Rachel must have blabbed to Janice everything about last night. This wouldn't be some breach of vestry security, but it could be a prelude to their working the choir with horror stories of how the vestry crucified Janice the Innocent. This didn't worry Diane. Instead, she wanted to talk about gay marriage, fearing—and this is what got me, her being afraid—that this issue threatened a worse mess.

Okay, I thought, let's take this in order. "What's Act Two?"

Diane explained that the vestry's stand against Harriet probably didn't mirror how the greater parish would react to gays and lesbians getting their marriages blessed at St. Joseph's. She and I had recruited most of the vestry and officers over the last two years. Harriet and Rachel were elected before that. Even with Harriet, who had to be involved in everything, and Rachel, who needed excuses to get out of her gloomy house, we had a reliable vestry.

I said the members typified the parish. "The worst any homophobic grumblers can do is make gay and lesbian worshippers feel unwelcome here. There are too many open-minded parishioners who will do just the reverse."

"You don't know Act Three."

But I did. Or to put it more accurately, it was something I had suspected for over a year, and it wove through my thinking all day.

That morning I exercised and phoned Qiao-Yun. I would pick her up at five o'clock Friday afternoon for the drive to Quincy and dinner at a restaurant serving authentic Chinese food. She told me to practice using my *kwhy-zuh*. I thanked her again for the gift. She told me the Mandarin word for "thank you" is *shyeh-shyeh*. I repeated the word, and she said, "*Bookuhchee*," which she said means, "you're welcome." So I repeated that word too and then *shyeh-shyeh* and *kwhy-zuh* again, and Qiao-Yun said, "*Dwayluh.*" She sang it, with a dotted half note for the first syllable. It means "correct," and I repeated *dwayluh*, singing it the way she did.

For lunch I slapped together a ham and cheese sandwich followed by a chocolate chip cookie that I broke into seven pieces and tried to eat with my new chopsticks. I nabbed only three and picked up the others with my fingers. I marked this a victory and practiced a second time with an apple I cut into eight pieces. Their juiciness made the slices slippery and my efforts truly fruitless until I used one chopstick to skewer them one-by-one. I tallied these into my score and felt quite proud. Still, I decided to use a fork at the restaurant Friday unless later practices between now and then brought a breakthrough; otherwise, Qiao-Yun would have to endure my spastic attempts at *kwhy-zuh* self-feeding until closing time—not very romantic.

After lunch I turned to George Herbert who filled up my afternoon and blended with my thoughts about last night's meeting and Diane.

Since I couldn't unravel "Providence" any more, I decided nobody understands the Infinite because everyone is finite. No wonder Herbert often got frustrated. He couldn't see what he wanted to see, though he could perceive vistas I struggled to comprehend. This faith held him together and brought a context for all the fragmented experiences he otherwise couldn't shape into a whole. For example, he wrote a three-poem sequence about Love, the big divine version. It's so big he couldn't pour it all into one cup. He instead filled up "Love I," "Love II," and "Love III."

Educators who know their craft would call what Herbert and I do "constructivist learning" lessons. People construct meanings for the new from the new and from everything else they've already learned, provided, first, they're open to new experiences. Without these two dynamics old beliefs go unchallenged. Poetry assaults old beliefs, which is why most people avoid it. Diane encouraged my reading George Herbert's poetry. She knew it would do me good. It has, and it has helped me better understand her.

At the outset "Love I" establishes two categories of love. There's "Immortal Love" which "Sprung from that beauty which can never fade," and there's "mortal love" to which humanity often gives the glory that Immortal Love should receive. The most notable manifestation of the original is Christ, the Incarnation, the Redeemer sent to suffer for all humankind. That's the backstory. But it's not the only story relevant to Immortal Love. I'll return to this. Contrasted with the Real Thing is the puny stuff we humans have "parceled out" as our "invention." We often forget Immortal Love is what made us. George says we start inventing the lesser loves from our mortal resources, "heart and brain," because that's all we appreciate with our nearsighted vision. But where did we get heart and brain? George says they're the "workmanship" of Immortal Love, the Real Thing. Enter irony. These lesser loves can't be entirely worthless if Immortal Love created the hearts and brains that made them.

An English major who doesn't enjoy irony shouldn't be trusted. Christians who can't appreciate irony are fundamentalists, no matter their denominations. They believe everything in the Bible because they think God dictated it to holy stenographers. They don't do constructivist learning. They wouldn't be caught dead doing it. Here's the irony in "Love I": all true loves come from the same Source.

George's metaphor in "Love II" is "Immortal Heat" which he contrasts with "a scarf or a glove." For me the Jesus story helps us understand why God's true being is Love. But we still don't really comprehend that Love. We do, however, comprehend scarves and gloves, which we know aren't hot but they do ward off cold. Coming anywhere close to understanding Love requires humility. Our cherished sense of independence is really "Dust blown by wit." It makes people blind. If we could only tear and blink our way through the vanity of self-entitlement, we might see the proper Illumination "And praise him who did make and mend our eyes." How we can do this takes up "Love III."

To frame his "Love I" and "Love II" ironies, George uses the four quatrains and couplet of the English sonnet. With its sturdy, reliable meter and rhyme scheme the sonnet is indeed a formal form, but "Love III" employs a new pattern. Its meter and rhyme present a dialogue. The Lord God confronts a lost soul (George says "I") who fears he just wandered into a banquet prepared for someone far better than he.

Immortal Love welcomes him, yet the wanderer, feeling "Guilty of dust and sin," wants out. All he can say is: "I cannot look on thee." Love being Love takes the fellow's hand, smiles, and says: "Who made the eyes but I?" It's as though Love in a voice as sweet as Olivia Finch's says: *Don't tell me what you can or cannot do. You can see me. Just lift your stupid head.* The wanderer confesses he has misused this gift of sight. He pleads to take himself and his shame off to some dingy place where they deserve each other. "And know not, says Love, who bore the blame?" In Christian talk we call this the "Atonement." George was a priest. Like Diane he took Holy Communion's symbolism deeply to heart. Love is both the feast and the server. "You must sit down, says Love, and taste my meat." The wanderer obeys, and George writes "Finis," which is more irony. Nothing is complete. The transformation, the healing, has only started. George quotes a Gospel passage to end "Love III." It's from Luke's second chapter, the Christmas story, when an angel appears to shepherds and says:

Glory be to God on high
And on earth peace
Good will towards men.

Peace and good will. That's the point. Their source is Immortal Love, and because we originated from that same Heat we can generate this warmth, both inwardly and outwardly in spiritual and mortal forms. No attempt to rank all our lesser loves makes any sense unless it helps us discern when we're perpetuating peace and good will and when we're behaving like self-absorbed nitwits. More irony: George wasn't telling me something I didn't already know. We have the same essential knowledge, and we keep forgetting it. We also have the good sense to adopt routines that help us remember again. George is much better at this than I am. It's the difference between a poet and a guy who writes about poetry.

"So what's Act Three?" I asked.

"I'm a lesbian."

Diane sat in her usual chair. I sat across on the sofa. She wore a sky blue blouse with her cleric color, together with beige slacks and a charcoal jacket. Between her breasts hung the light chain necklace with cross she often wore on the job. On her left lapel was pinned a pewter dove.

"It doesn't make a damn bit of difference."

"I knew you would say that."

"I'm not alone."

"There's a story."

"You don't have to tell it."

"Yes, I do."

Diane grew up all over the world. Her father was a career Air Force officer who sometimes flew U-2s among other assignments, including stints at the Pentagon and NATO in Brussels. Like her younger brother and sister, she was a straight-*A* student who made friends easily when her father's transfers moved the family about. At age ten Diane knew she wanted to be an Episcopal priest shortly after her family joined a parish in Arlington, Virginia. I imagined a child celebrating fanciful communions and baptisms with her little friends. She majored in Religious Studies at William and Mary while attending a church in Williamsburg that later sponsored her for the priesthood. This led to her enrollment at Virginia Theological Seminary. All her steps from there through ordination and an assistant rector's gig in Richmond I learned about when she applied to St. Joseph's. She said during her interview she wanted to come to Scrooby because she had visited the town on her way to a Cape Cod vacation.

Diane summarized all this for me again. "It really wasn't Scrooby, you know. When my father retired from the Air Force, he became a lobbyist, the quintessential military-industrial complex guy. Everybody in Washington knew him. He wrote checks. My parents still live there. I did everything high school and college kids do—the maniacally proper ones, I mean—and was sure I was following the vocation God wanted for me and I wanted too. Within a year after ordination, I looked for a job in the Diocese of Massachusetts. I wasn't exactly sure why. 'A new environment,' I told myself."

"Was it?"

"Yes. But not entirely new. I had an experience in Richmond, an encounter with another woman. She was older. What followed happened because I needed something to happen, and I had had feelings like this before—unfocused usually, fragmented, and unconsummated. This woman understood because she had come out years before. She was very kind too. She was protective."

"She sounds very important to you."

"She is. One night we had dinner at her condo. A lot of conversation. And then…" As Diane spoke, she glimpsed out the window to my left. When she looked back, a faint smile came and went. "And that was it. I knew."

I thought of Qiao-Yun.

"As I said, she was protective. She's very sweet. I told her about my growing up, those rites of passage years. The sports, parties, summer camps, school clubs, dates, proms—everything I did and kept external while living with confusion on the inside. She understood. I moved here, not exactly looking for adventure, just wanting to do

God's work, which had to include a deeper, more honest, understanding of myself."

"Was that difficult?"

"I don't think it's a gimme for anyone. Wouldn't you agree?"

I remembered all the times I had sat here doing most of the talking the way Diane was now. "It's easier when the right person helps."

"Being a single priest has its challenges. I don't make close friendships with parishioners, as you know. I think professional boundaries are important."

"You said as much during the interviews."

"There's a priest in Cambridge who's my spiritual advisor, a wonderful man. I've confided in him. I have clergy friends, and through them I'm part of a larger social circle in the Boston area, mostly college faculty and artists. Two months ago I met a woman. It lasted a few weeks and ended. Everything about it is over, except my approval of who I am."

"This is quite an Act Three."

"It does have its moments."

Soon choir practice would start. Diane explained her plan. She wanted a one-on-one with each vestry member. Her message would be brief: she's a lesbian; she discovered this about herself in recent years; she's not in a committed relationship; the bishop knows all about it and supports her. She will continue to serve St. Joseph's Parish. She will write a letter going to every member. She might give a sermon on the subject. What came next she didn't know.

Most parishioners, we figured, could deal with this. Some wouldn't. If a vestry member had a good idea about how to proceed, she would consider it. If Harriet or Rachel freaked, Diane was ready. She didn't anticipate any other vestry member getting sour. If any did, she knew her stance. Most of all, she wanted to get the word out. It was time.

I told her we should meet again soon. "You need a local person you can count on, and I need to feel I'm helping you."

"You are helping me, Stephen. I'm very grateful. We have to meet soon about Janice. She and I spoke an hour ago. She knew all about the music director vote last night."

"Rachel."

"Of course. Janice wants to see us both. Can you come Tuesday morning, ten o'clock?"

I said that was fine with me. Diane said she wasn't sure what Janice wanted. "Probably assurances. We need to set up a meeting with her anyway. I told her that."

I remembered when Bob Norris fired me. He made sure the assistant superintendent and high school principal were there too. They said nothing. This was different, and I had to stop remembering.

"We should pray," I said. "Then I have to get going. I can't be late for choir."

"Whose turn?"

"Yours."

"Let's say the Lord's Prayer."

We prayed the words together, slowly.

When she stood up, I did too. The top of her head slid under my chin. We hugged. We hadn't done that since Cara died.

"We'll talk again soon," she said.

I followed the corridor from the rector's office to the sanctuary door nearest the altar, which was open to allow choir members to pass through. At the altar I stopped and bowed and paused. The next door brought me to the choir room. Two sopranos entered behind me, and we took our folders and hymnals from the rows of cabinet slots Jerry had built for the choir two years ago. Janice had piled copies of Sunday's worship bulletin and next week's anthem atop the upright piano. She sat behind it penciling notes on her copy. I don't think she saw me. The choir's pre-practice hubbub seemed no different from any other night. When I greeted folks, they all answered as friendly as ever, even Rachel.

I worked my way to the bass's row and Jerry, who was bent forward and explaining to the one tenor how to patch his lawn. I sat down as he advised plenty of water, twice a day for the first two weeks.

"Don't be like Stephen. He'd save himself a lot of backache and money putting in new seed every year if he just watered properly."

"Pay no attention to Jerry," I said. "He just likes talking behind my aching back."

Janice placed her score on the music rack. Jerry tilted his head toward me. "Diane wants to meet after the ten o'clock Sunday. I bet she wants to see us about last night's meeting."

"She and I have already met. This is just you and Diane."

Janice said, "Okay. Let's get started. Let's do some warm-ups."

Everyone stood, and Janice struck a chord. The choir sang a roller-coaster sequence of *oh-wee-oh-wee-oh-wee-oh-wee-oh*. It wasn't the same

Wizard of Oz tune sung by the guards in the wicked witch's castle, but it always made me think of that scene. Janice upped the chord, and we sang the sounds again: a continuous, climbing sequence ending three repetitions after the notes became too high for the basses. We did it again, this time alternating *oohs* and *ahs*. Next we looked at the hymns listed in the bulletin. Janice wanted us to sing just one verse of each tonight since they were all familiar to us.

Jerry leaned toward me again as I turned my hymnal's pages to the processional. "What did you two talk about?"

I answered in his murmured tone. "The same thing she'll discuss with you."

Jerry put his folder aside and picked up his hymnal. "Are you going to tell me what's going on?"

"Certainly."

"When?"

"Right now. Turn to page three-hundred eighty-four."

Janice played a brief intro. We started singing: "Fairest Lord Jesus ruler of all nature..."

Jerry didn't pester me with more questions until we were in the parking lot two hours later. Choir practice followed its familiar routine. After we sang the first verse of the processional, we practiced the sequence hymn that comes before the Gospel reading and the recessional. We then worked on the anthems for the next two Sundays.

I had good reason to suspect Rachel and Janice of fermenting ill will, but nothing happened this night. Jerry believed they were plotting something. The news that Diane wanted to meet with him alone and my clamming up about its purpose had set him off more than I realized. He followed me to my car and looked around to make sure no one could hear him, all his wise-guy posturing gone.

"Is Diane pissed at me?"

Jerry could mess with me in a lot of ways, but surprise was rarely one of them. "What are you talking about?"

Choir members ambled to their cars, saying good night. Cars pulled from the lot.

"Didn't it strike you funny that Janice and Rachel acted as though there had been no vote about the music director last night?"

I told Jerry about Janice's upcoming meeting with Diane and me Tuesday morning. "I'll find out what Janice wants. Diane and I will tell her what we know, which is the same you and the vestry know."

"Janice asked for this meeting?"

"Yes."

"And the day before this meeting Diane wants to meet with me. What's this all about?"

"Look, all I can tell you is your meeting with Diane has nothing to do with the music director business."

"What are you not telling me?"

Jerry and I met thirteen years ago. We started going to St. Joseph's within a month of each other. He became my best friend. Cara liked him too, even though she thought he drank too much. She trusted his workmanship. He built our two-car garage almost single-handedly. Over the years we met some of his girlfriends, none lasted a year, most only a few weeks. Jerry never talked about St. Joseph's in front of Cara. He sensed anytime we talked about something that didn't involve or interest her she would feel excluded. He saw this well before I did. Instead, he would fascinate her with details about carpentry and landscaping. She even took notes.

His finances were always boom or bust. A full wallet meant he had abundant work. March through November provided the most. Winters sapped his savings. He lived in a two-room apartment next to the boatyard. With no mortgage, he had no debts. He didn't have a credit card. "I can't be trusted with such a thing."

Despite his roles in parish leadership, Jerry avoided filling out an annual pledge card. Instead, he gave St. Joseph's countless evenings and off days and did projects. I knew hardly anything about his family or his life before St. Joseph's. He was an only child whose parents were dead. He was baptized and confirmed an Episcopalian, stopped going to church while an undergraduate, and started again twenty-years later. He never explained why he didn't finish his Ph.D. dissertation or why he gave up classical scholarship to work with his hands. He said he learned his crafts "here and there." Jerry claimed he didn't care what anyone said about him. I knew better.

"You're as close to Diane as I am," I said.

The parking lot emptied except for my VW and Jerry's pickup. He looked around again to make sure we were alone.

"I had a few pops before last night's meeting. I usually do."

I said it wasn't noticeable to me. He said that's because I seldom saw him when he didn't have a few under his belt. "Diane can always tell. She's nice about it, but last month she told me to knock it off before vestry meetings."

"That's not why she wants to see you."

He didn't believe me. "Everyone knows I think Janice is a shitty choir director. If Janice can make me look like a drunken sot, that makes her look good. You think I don't know how this game is played?"

"Think whatever you want about Janice and Rachel. But if you think Diane and I are playing games you're crazy." Jerry was wrong. But he wasn't crazy. I had to tell him something. "Diane wants to talk to you about herself, not about you. Don't ask me anymore. I've said too much already."

That got to him. "She's okay, isn't she?"

"She's okay."

Jerry looked as though he wanted to crawl under his truck and stay there. "I'm sorry, Stephen. I was worried and—"

"I understand."

Jerry's right hand slid into his pocket. He fumbled for his keys. "Would you like to go to Linnehan's?"

I wanted to go home. "It's getting late. Some other time. Okay?"

"I guess you're right. Sure, some other time."

I waited until Jerry started his engine before leaving the parking lot. We both descended the hill to Court Street. I turned right. In my rearview mirror I saw Jerry turn left toward downtown Scrooby. I shifted from first to second, uncertain whether he would go straight home. Maybe I should have gone to Linnehan's with him. My speed rose slightly. At third gear his taillights were out of view. I could have slowed and turned around at the strip mall thirty yards ahead. The VW surged forward. I shifted into fourth then fifth.

CHAPTER 12

The next day I called Fran. "You ought to know I have a date tonight."

"Could it be with Qiao-Yun Wang, that amazing Taiwanese-Scrooby woman you met at church?"

"As a matter of fact, this will be our fourth date—fourth, that is, if you count a banana nut muffin and scallion pancakes."

We had been talking to each other like this for as far back as I could remember. Fran answered as though my last sentence made sense.

"Oh, do tell me more."

Fran got a summary, enough to say she needn't worry. The conversation ended with my big sister's encouragement. A few minutes later, I drove to Qiao-Yun's house.

The young, shoeless Asian man at the side door stood taller than my six feet. He wore jeans, and his maroon jersey wrapped a lean torso honed in a gym. He had close-cropped black hair. He looked like a nice guy and spoke with a faint accent.

"You must be Stephen. I'm Ken."

I shook his hand and followed him to the living room, mindful to remove my shoes and place them alongside the array by the door. His shoes, about two sizes bigger than mine, looked enormous next to his mother's.

Keung gestured towards the living room's sofa and chairs arranged in front of the bay window. To the left were the front door and stairs leading to the second floor.

"She'll be right down."

I sat on the sofa. "Your mother tells me you go to Mass. Maritime." This was an old guy's idea of how to start a conversation with a college student, not very original.

"I have one more year after this one." Keung lowered his frame into the chair across from me. "My mother says you two met at church."

I ran through the Epiphany dinner and our first date after Qiao-Yun's trip to Taiwan—a quick synopsis that prompted me to remember something I should have said right off. "I'm sorry about your grandfather."

Keung said his grandfather was a good man. For a second he looked a little uneasy. He reverted to Mass. Maritime. "My major is international maritime business. I like it, even if I have to be at a college that makes us wear uniforms and follow a lot of regimentation."

"That must be an interesting mix. I was in the Navy for three years. College came later—big difference, two different worlds, especially back then."

Forty years ago liberal arts students and business majors didn't talk to each other. Haircuts and clothes labeled who was who. Back then I looked like a typical English major, which meant I looked like an anti-war protester. Most business majors dressed like interns in the Nixon White House.

Upstairs a door opened and closed. Keung asked, "You two had a good time at the concert last Sunday?"

"We got to know each other a little during dinner afterwards. Tonight we're going to a restaurant in Quincy."

"She told me, the China Sea. You'll like it."

Footsteps lightly thudded down the stairs as Qiao-Yun's voice sang, "I'm ready." She landed with her arms outstretched like a victorious gymnast spun from a horizontal bar. She put one foot forward and half-pivoted, angling her right arm above her head. High heel shoes dangled from her fingers. Her left hand rested on her hip. She wore a long dark blue dress slit above the knees. She had matching earrings and necklace set with aqua tinted stones.

"You like?"

I stood up. "Very much."

Keung stood too. "Looking good, Mama." He had his mother's smile.

Qiao-Yun asked about the weather. April's first warm day had turned chilly by late afternoon. I advised a light coat, and Qiao-Yun stepped towards the closet.

I turned to her son. "I'm glad we met, Keung."

I could tell he liked my calling him by his Chinese name. "I am too, Stephen."

Qiao-Yun lifted a thin, black coat and a gossamer silver scarf from the closet. I took them from her hand and held the coat open as she put it on. She looped her scarf over her collar. I wore an open-neck blue shirt, tan slacks, and brown sport coat. Next to her they looked like clearance rack markdowns. Qiao-Yun stepped into her high heels.

She put her hand in mine to steady herself. By the side door Keung wished us a pleasant night while I slipped into my loafers. Qiao-Yun kissed his cheek. Stepping into the driveway, she again held my hand until I opened the car door.

This was Qiao-Yun's first ride in the Beetle. A forty-five minute drive lay ahead, leading to a place she knew but I didn't, though I knew Quincy. Cara grew up there. We were married in a Catholic church a half-mile from her parents' house. For five years we rented a Quincy apartment back when the city had two Chinese restaurants, each offering the oily fried rice, spareribs, and chop suey Americans expected. Qiao-Yun said many Asians had since moved to Quincy, and with them came much better restaurants.

Qiao-Yun could dine anywhere the way she was dressed. She said I looked very nice.

I was happy for the compliment. "You're very beautiful."

"I like to dressing up. The restaurant not fancy. I don't care. We have good time. Okay?"

I headed north on Route 3, also called the Southeast Expressway, a title often undeserved, but tonight traffic moved with few slowdowns. Qiao-Yun had me take the first exit closest to Quincy, which meant a drive from Weymouth along a mostly commercial stretch that maintained an unrelenting drabness, and then we passed the old Fore River Shipyard, once a steady job site of constant welding sparks and clanging, now a refueling pier and parking lot. At different times in my life I had lived not far from here.

"Keung seems like a very nice young man."

Qiao-Yun's looked pleased. "Why you think this way?"

Ahead the traffic light by the shipyard changed to yellow. I slowed down and stopped as it turned red.

"Well, we had a brief but very pleasant chat. It's obvious he loves his mother. And he looks like you."

"All my friends say Keung look like me."

The light turned green. I moved the VW through the intersection and climbed a hill before Qiao-Yun spoke again. "He look like his father too."

I asked how often Keung came home.

"Almost every weekends. He hate college food. He want my cooking instead."

"I don't blame him. What will he eat tonight?"

"I already make his favorite, noodle soup and dumplings. But I tell him he must come straight home today after classes. I want him to meeting you."

"So let me get this straight. His ticket for soup and dumplings was to get home in time to meet me?"

"I make good plan, do you think?"

I said she made an excellent plan.

Before the age of suburban shopping malls, Quincy was the place to go. When Fran and I were kids, all our new clothes came from the stores along or near Hancock Street. They all closed in the sixties, out-priced by the big chains dominating the malls and replaced by transient businesses or emptiness. With them went the specialty shops and eateries serving the same customers. Quincy Center turned grim by the time Cara and I had our apartment. Much had changed since then.

I parked across from the China Sea, following Qiao-Yun's directions. New stores, restaurants, boutiques, and a health center crowded among office spaces, most of their signs in alphabets I couldn't read. Traffic crawled. Busy pedestrians filed by, entering one place, exiting another. Quincy billed itself the City of Presidents. Its most notable historic site was the big, old house where John Adams died, July 4, 1826, and where his son, John Quincy Adams, and their descendants had lived. Few people milling by the China Sea Restaurant looked anything like them.

The restaurant's décor confirmed Qiao-Yun's description. A dozen square small tables and two huge round tables spread from the street window. Almost every one was taken. The back wall held three rectangular water tanks: the first for a lone hand-sized tropical fish striped black and yellow, the second for six slumbering brownish creatures sad-faced and tubular. The third held a mound of spider-leg crabs. A soundless widescreen television near the front window showed three generations of Asians, Chinese I presumed, arguing in a living room. Asian subtitles ran beneath. Near the water tanks I saw a glassed-in kitchen with cooked chickens and ducks suspended behind the windows. Here and there green bamboo sprouted from flowerpots. A single hung painting showed a pagoda by a waterfall amidst mountains and trees leaved like broccoli. Opposite, a framed poster gave a harbor view of a modern seaport, possibly Hong Kong, aglow at night.

Qiao-Yun and the hostess greeted each other in Chinese. Two small tables were unoccupied. Qiao-Yun said something to the hostess. Behind us the door opened, and people jammed into the narrow foyer.

The hostess led us inward. Before handing out menus she set down a spoon next to each plate; on the other side she placed chopsticks.

"Chinese people come here all the time," Qiao-Yun said. "They have food like in my country."

Nearby four young women worked their chopsticks like hungry sandpipers on a low tide beach. They were the only non-Asians in the place besides me. I envied their *kwhy-zuh* dexterity.

"The food must be as good as your scallion pancakes," I said.

"You see." Qiao-Yun opened her menu. I opened mine. Everything was in Chinese with smaller English translations, and every offering had a number preceded by a letter categorizing the selections: the *A*-group for appetizers, *V* for vegetables, *R* for rice, *S* for seafood, *B* for beef, *P* for pork, etc.—nineteen groupings altogether, most with at least twenty specialties. I had no idea what to get.

"Would you like me to order for us both?" Qiao-Yun asked.

I said this was a wise suggestion. "But please don't order anything with jellyfish in it or the soup called 'fish maw with black mushrooms.'"

A waitress brought a pot of tea and two cups. She asked for drink orders. Qiao-Yun said she wanted water, no ice, and lemon. I ordered the same, even though the wine and beer prices beat Scrooby's. When the waitress returned with the water, Qiao-Yun rattled off her choices, sometimes pointing to an item number. The TV program looked like a soap opera. No one looked happy. The waitress left us, and I asked Qiao-Yun about the show. She said it was a favorite in China and Taiwan.

I mentioned the writing at the bottom of the screen. "I've never seen closed captions in Chinese characters before."

"They not close caption."

I looked again. The print wasn't white figures set within a black border. "You mean Chinese programs have Chinese subtitles?"

Qiao-Yun saw my bewilderment. "China has many dialects. For examples, some people speak Mandarin. Some speak Cantonese, like in Hong Kong. Shanghai people speak Shanghainese. My mother speak Taiwanese."

I remembered hearing something about this and almost responded with a Henry Higgins quip about English.

Qiao-Yun kept explaining. "Dialect like total difference language. People speak difference dialect don't understand the other. But all Chinese writing the same. Dialect doesn't matter. So actor on TV they speak Mandarin. Everyone understand, if they can read. In China, many, many dialect, but everyone read same writing."

I started to get it. Chinese characters aren't phonetic. They're pictures. Imagine a bus station with dozens people from all over China. No two speak the same dialect, but all read the same newspaper.

"That's amazing," I said. "Westerners can't do that."

The waitress brought a plate of chicken appetizers and spring rolls and two cups of soup that Qiao-Yun identified as seaweed with pork and shrimp. I enjoyed both.

Qiao-Yun picked up a chicken piece with her fingers. I spooned more soup. "Much here difference for you. Do I say correct?"

Her tone had changed. Something similar happened during the drive when she said Keung looked like his father.

"In some ways, yes." I drank some tea and lifted a spring roll with my fingers. "In other ways, not so much."

"America like that for me."

I was right about her mood shift, and there was something telling about her reference to Taiwan as "my country," which I had heard before. She had lived in the U.S. for a decade and became an American citizen a year ago.

"I know my English not good."

She had said this at Fernando's. I praised her for speaking multiple languages and reminded her I could speak only one. I asked whether Mandarin was the dialect she spoke most often.

"It official language in Taiwan and China. I told you about my auntie. She pay for my boarding school. We study Mandarin like American student study English. All that part of my story. You know a little bit. I want you to knowing more."

Qiao-Yun's English had irregular patterns. Sometimes she left verbs out of sentences or misused tenses; other times she didn't. Sometimes she confused pronoun genders. She often swapped plural with singular nouns and used odd constructions for possessives. I later learned Mandarin's third person singular pronoun, *ta*, covers both *he* and *she*, and nouns in Mandarin don't change with number. The verbs don't have tenses. In English no consistent rule determines how a noun can be changed to an adjective. Qiao-Yun got around these riddles using noun forms as modifiers. For a person native to an ancient, uncorrupted language like Mandarin, learning a multi-based, contradictory hybrid like English must be difficult—about as daunting as phonetic readers would find learning Chinese calligraphy.

"If I not go to boarding school when I little girl, I would not go to Taichung to my college. My auntie she think me special girl and want me have good education. Taichung a big city, over a million peoples. In high school and college I train all the time with other athletes. We compete in tournament, have no time for boy-girl things. My husband his family live in Taichung. I meet him there when I twenty-two. He my first boyfriend. He architect, very smart. When he graduate from college, he and friends start construction company. They do very well. So my husband is rich, powerful man when he in his twenties. But he not powerful in his house. My husband his mother run everythings there."

"I'm sorry," I said. "I didn't quite get that last part. The mother and son ran everything?"

"No, I say wrong. She, the mother, she runs everythings. In house he do what she say."

I had to listen very carefully because emotion more than accent formed and constricted her every word.

"In Asia a son must honor parents. My husband the only son. Tradition say my mother-in-law cannot live alone. We never have our own house. He say we must live with her. She treat me like servant. I get up four in morning to clean house before I go teaching my classes. She inspect, make me do again what she don't like. I come home and cook dinner for them. If she don't like, she throw away, say I'm useless. She say I give her my salary. Her son say I give her my salary. I do. She controls everythings. She never nice to me."

Qiao-Yun's voice cracked. A wet film formed over her eyes. Tears fell. She used her napkin to wipe her face. I took my handkerchief from my inside pocket and gave it to her. She blew her nose. She apologized. I said it was okay, and Qiao-Yun continued, digging ever deeper into what I realized was a cruel past.

"She say to him I am bad wife. He should beat me. He do, but he stop when I get pregnant. I take my baby to school with me, to the day care. For little while, all seem better. My son he getting older. He, what you say, toddler. I still do housework every day. I teach classes, coach martial art teams. I take my son everywhere. When I run tournament in Taiwan, Japan, Singapore, all over Asia, mother-in-law say to her son he should have girlfriend. He do. She have baby. I say mother-in-law can no more have my salary. She say I am bad woman. He beat me. This time I hit back. He don't hit me again, never. But I very sad, don't know what to do. I call my father. He come to house. He say, 'Get your son. You come with me.' Mother-in-law and husband they say, 'No.' My father he say, 'Yes.' They shut up. I pack one little bag, boy things, take Keung from bed, and go with my father. My father say in car, 'You cannot go back there.' I don't. I get divorce. Keung's father, he feel bad, very bad. He not a bad man. He give us money. Few years later I have chance to go United States for graduate school. My parents take care of Keung. I go to America, Massachusetts, Springfield College. I leave my son behind."

I had known guys like her husband, though not as extreme. I never knew anyone as evil as the mother-in-law. Still, I believed every word Qiao-Yun said. I had seen some awful parents in my time, obsessive and delusional, their arrogance rooted in fears that went back through generations of nutty parents. Qiao-Yun's story held a painful timelessness. Telling her story brought her back into it. People were watching us now. They couldn't hear her, but they saw her cry.

Qiao-Yun realized the attention. She had more to tell, and she wanted to get through it quickly before the waitress brought our dinner.

"When I come to Springfield, I afraid. My English much worse than now. Another teacher from my department he already there, in his last semester. He help me a lot. Other Asian students there, and Americans very good to me. I work hard. College have tutors help me write papers. With everyone helping me, I do good. I not afraid anymore, not of America. But I miss Taiwan. I miss my son. He stay with my parents in Taichung, but I afraid he will forget me. I get very sad. And the day after I get my Master's degree, my husband take Keung with him on trip to Taipei. That when he have accident at building. Keung see his father die."

Qiao-Yun stopped. She looked like a boxer who must back-pedal to shake off hurts and catch his breath before moving in for another exchange of blows against an opponent who could tear him apart. Her shoulders rose and lowered twice before she spoke again.

"I go back to Taiwan. I do everthings. Keung stay with my auntie in Taipei until I get there. I bring him back to Taichung. I bring husband's ashes back to Taichung, give them to mother-in-law. Mother-in-law, she say she have no more son. She want her grandson. No way. No way. She never get my son!"

Qiao-Yun's voice rose almost to a shout, and people turned their heads our way again. She took a drink from her water glass.

"I go back to teaching and coaching and work very hard. My

students like me very much. Years go by. My family not good. I have two sisters. Their marriage bad. Husbands leave them. My brother, he the youngest, he drink with his friends every night. They need me to solving all their problems. My parents don't know what to do. Since I little girl my father treat me like I'm the older son. My siblings say I the lucky one. Mother-in-law go to court to getting my son. I don't like Keung's school. They make him memory all the time. They don't let him thinking. I want go back to America. My college say okay. They pay my salary if I only stay United States one year. Professor from my college who go to Springfield with me say Massachusetts have good schools and Scrooby have good ESL. So I move to Scrooby. Keung go to Scrooby school. We buy house with Keung father life insurance."

Qiao Yun explained that over the next few years she split time between Taiwan and Scrooby, teaching college classes there and Tai Chi here. She needed her Taiwan salary, but Keung's school was in Scrooby. Luckily she met Wen who volunteered to care for Keung while Qiao-Yun taught one semester every year in Taiwan. Meanwhile the mother-in-law went to court to get custody of her grandson. Keung's grandmother lost, but it cost Qiao-Yun much of the money her husband bequeathed her, which she believed he left fearing something like this would happen.

Qiao-Yun got an unpaid leave and stayed in the United States.

"I like America. I get by with money I earn here. But Keung he miss Taiwan. Mother-in-law, she turn nice. I let her talk to him on phone. She say she want us back in Taiwan. Keung he think her good grandmother. I don't say bad things. My department chairman he know me since I student athlete. He say I should be in Taiwan. I don't know."

Qiao-Yun needed my handkerchief again.

"I divorce woman," she said. "Some peoples call me bad woman, bad mother. Some peoples say I have no gratitude. You should know this. I'm sorry."

Last November Qiao-Yun and Wen sat with Jerry at St. Joseph's, the first time I saw her. She looked unhappy, and now I knew why.

"You're not a bad woman," I said. "Don't ever think that."

Qiao-Yun's hand still held my handkerchief. I stretched my hand across the table and placed it on hers. "Bad mothers don't raise good sons. I'm sorry people have hurt you. They make me angry. And you're entitled to make choices about your own life."

"I don't want you angry."

"It's not you. It's them."

"I don't hate peoples. Life better now. Keung is good boy. I have house and friends and work. The grandmother not mean to me anymore."

My hand stayed on hers, and the tension left her face.

"You're really something," I said.

"What you mean?"

"You're a very good and brave person, Qiao-Yun."

Around us faces turned away relieved the great drama at our table seemed resolved. The waitress arrived with a heavy tray. She gave us each bowls of steamed rice before she spread our table with more heaping platters. I asked Qiao-Yun what she ordered.

She pointed to each dish, very happy to have something different to talk about. "This one beef, pork, and bean sprouts. This one stir-fried squid. This one all vegetables. We eat everythings. Okay? You try."

"Watch this," I said.

I picked up my chops sticks, using my left hand to maneuver them into the right, and found the balance. I brought the *kwhy-zuh* to a sliver of squid. My fingers squeezed and held on with a safecracker's finesse. I raised the *kwhy-zuh* and delivered their prize to my gaping mouth. I chewed slowly and swallowed. Qiao-Yun applauded.

"You like very much, huh? Do I say correct?"

I sang my answer the way I first heard her pronounce the word: "*Dwayluh.*" She was correct.

CHAPTER 13

During the drive back to Scrooby, we decided I should keep the doggy bag of leftovers. This was Qiao-Yun's idea. We also decided to stop at my house for a glass of wine. This was my idea. Between Quincy and my house, I developed other notions too, some about Qiao-Yun and some about me.

Any sensible view of Qiao-Yun's marriage would label her a victim of her mother-in-law's malevolence and husband's contorted sense of self. She became more than a victim, though, once she stood up to them. I learned the difference between victims and heroes a long time ago watching the Civil Rights Movement play out on television. Qiao-Yun answered betrayal and exploitation with patience and later with resistance. She answered her mother-in-law's madness with forgiveness. She also did her duty—to her family, her students, herself, and most of all her son.

Forgiving the mother-in-law got to me the most. Nobody screwed me over worse than Bob Norris. It was mild stuff compared to what Qiao-Yun went through. Still, as nonphysical muggings go, getting canned as English Department head messed me up terribly—the one irony I couldn't smile about. The good guy was labeled a menace while the bad guy strengthened his power and demonstrated how transgressors are crushed. The witnesses went along and stayed quiet. I forgave Bob Norris. A year before my retirement I sent him a handwritten note saying we had known each other too long for either of us to hold any rancor and the next time I saw him I would greet him as a friend. He replied with a one-sentence email saying he was "delighted." Between then and my last day in school I saw him two or three times, always in a crowd. I didn't approach him. Mark Twain had a joke about quitting smoking: "I've done it hundreds of times." My forgiveness of Bob worked the same way. I did it every morning.

Qiao-Yun's forgiveness of her mother-in-law probably needed occasional refueling too. Her tears said as much. Anyone could see Qiao-Yun's strength of character. I told her so and said she deserved honesty from me too. After we retraced our path back to Route 3, I started in.

"My marriage had troubles too, nothing as hard as what you went through—nothing like that at all—but my wife and I married when we were very young."

Qiao-Yun asked how old we were on our wedding day.

"I was twenty-two. She was twenty. I was still in college."

Qiao-Yun said men in Taiwan wait longer. "Why you marry so young?"

"We met when I was in the Navy, stationed not far from here at an air base that's since been closed. She was seventeen, had just graduated from high school. A friend introduced us. Veterans could get government money for education. I took advantage of that when my enlistment ended. After two years of dating, we couldn't wait. We were kids in love."

Much of what I could say held too much historical clutter. I'm one of those people who lived through the sixties but missed their ride on the sexual revolution. A year after modernity began on a November afternoon in Dallas, I was in the Navy, living a half-hour drive from my parents' home and unaware until college what little I knew. Cara and I entered our wedding night as two virgins. We came close to losing that status many times before, but Cara was a good Catholic girl. Our make-out sessions, despite my hopeful groping, couldn't change that. Cara's priestly confessor insisted we must save ourselves for marriage. Sustained lingerings at second base with halted advances to third defined our sex life. Inside my Chevy's steamed-up windows religious indoctrination prevailed. Outside the world fell apart. It was the sixties.

We married between my freshman and sophomore years of college. After the wedding I stuck to my studies and worked in a publisher's mailroom afternoons and all through the summers. Cara worked as a secretary. No Woodstock for us. From time to time I joined thousands of students in Boston Common and shouted "Tricky Dick, Stop the War!" College wasn't drudgery. I loved literature classes and learned to write. Cara typed my papers and applauded the *A's* that came back. Still, neither of us admitted how each semester college kept changing me. Wherever Cara was, it seemed my head was someplace else. I started teaching. By 1980 most of those who went to Woodstock had consumed all they ever got from it. They craved new opiates and voted for Reagan. Cara and I had Katelyn and Luke, and we didn't vote for Reagan. Whatever our differences, politics wasn't one of them.

"I was twenty-three when I marry Keung father," Qiao-Yun said. "He almost thirty."

I said when two young and different people marry they usually don't know how great their differences are until later. "Over the years we tried making compromises, especially after the kids were born."

"What is comapize?"

I pronounced the word again. "It has many meanings. One is to try to keep a relationship going. You give a little to get a little, hoping all will be well. When you gave your mother-in-law your salary, you made a compromise. Sometimes it's a good idea. Sometimes it isn't."

"Your marriage need a lot of this…how you say?"

"Compromise. Yes."

I wanted Qiao-Yun to appreciate the complexity of my thirty-nine years with Cara. Maybe someday she would understand it. Maybe someday I would understand it better.

"There were times in my marriage when my wife—her name was Cara—and I were very close. We started out that way, and we ended that way. In between we had two children. We were very close when my daughter and son were born. We drew apart at times, sometimes very far apart and for long periods without our admitting how much. And then we became close again. When her parents died. When my parents died. The three times she fought cancer. And Christmas and birthdays. She gave great gifts."

"I think many marriages like that," Qiao-Yun said.

"I do too. That's where the compromises come in."

"Because you have to accepting whole package."

"Yes."

"Did you accept your wife her whole package?"

"When it was easy, yes."

"I don't understand."

"Some things I tried to compromise or deny. As I said, there were times we drew apart. We both were unhappy. I think the unhappiness came before the drawing apart, and then the drawing apart made us more unhappy. It got very bad."

"What make you and Cara unhappy?"

"We grew in different directions." I had spoken the worst cliché about marital breakdowns. "That's too easy. It was my fault. I took my work too seriously. It occupied almost all my time. Being a good father came in second. Cara came in a distant third. My work and my children became my identity, mostly my work."

I found myself pouring out more than I intended. "Cara didn't like my not paying attention to her, and I didn't like her wanting more from me. We weren't so different after all. Some people, some families, don't trust happiness."

I had been speaking to the windshield. I glanced at Qiao-Yun. The dashboard lights revealed a face that said she knew what I meant. Of course she did.

Fran and I grew up in a house of fear. Cara did too. Her mother and all her aunts were nervous women. Her father never started a hug in his life. Somehow my big sister Fran discovered early in her life you have to choose between fear and happiness. She made the right choice. It came long before Cara and I even knew such a choice was possible.

The last person to hear this story was Diane when I was an emotional mess last July. Before that I never discussed it with anyone, except Cara and a counselor, not even to Fran.

"Why you not divorce?" Qiao-Yun asked.

"We almost did. I moved out and got an apartment. We hired lawyers and stayed separated for ten months. I couldn't go through with it. I wanted my family together again."

"How old your kids?" Qiao-Yun asked.

"Katelyn was in high school, Luke in middle school. It was hard on my daughter and son—hardest on my daughter, I think."

"Did you have girl friend? Did she have boyfriend?"

"She had no one. I'm sure of it. If some woman made a play for me, I would have gone along. That opportunity never happened, and I didn't seek it out. Instead I drank a lot."

"What happened?"

"I couldn't handle the separation and told Cara I didn't want a divorce. What she said was very wise and loving. We were crying to each other on the phone. We went to marriage counseling, and I moved back home."

"Then what happens?"

"Our marriage got better."

"Because you really love each other."

"We had to be in our late forties before we realized how much. But two years later Cara had breast cancer."

I gave the basic details. Cara had a mastectomy on one side. Five years after that she had cancer again. The surgery wasn't as bad, but she went through chemotherapy and radiation again.

"When I turned sixty she had a surprise birthday party for me. She had to call a lot of people she didn't know well, teachers at my school and friends from church. She was a very private and shy person, but she did it. It was a great party. And then a year ago last fall, a different cancer struck her. It spread quickly. She was very brave."

I felt Qiao-Yun's hand touch my right elbow. It slowly brushed up my arm and stopped at my shoulder. "Are you okay, Stephen?"

I lifted my left hand from the wheel and placed it on hers.

The first Scrooby exit was a quarter-mile ahead.

We entered my house through the side door. Qiao-Yun asked to use my bathroom. I pointed the way and then raced to the john upstairs. I was back in the kitchen with a winged corkscrew and the chilled bottle on the counter when she appeared. I seldom drank Riesling, and this bottle cost much more than the cheap wine my palate knew best. Selecting it and then cleaning the house took up most of my day. I opened the bottle and filled two crystal glasses half way.

I handed one to Qiao-Yun. "Would you like me to show you the place?"

"All right."

I took my glass and stepped into the living room-dining room space. The only family photos on display were Katelyn's and Luke's high school graduation portraits on the spinet piano. The cabinet holding the television and CD player stood at one end of the combined rooms, the dining table and chairs at the other. The fireplace connected to a central chimney. The sofa and dining table were against its opposite wall. A love seat met the sofa at a right angle.

"Do you play piano?" Qiao-Yun asked.

"No, but Luke and Katelyn do. Their mother did a little." I walked toward the piano and pointed to their pictures.

"They are very good looking." Qiao-Yun looked around the room as though she expected to see other photos.

Shortly after our reconciliation Cara took a six-week course in painting watercolors. Her two completed pieces, a seascape and a wooded scene, hung on the wall behind the sofa. I pointed them out. Qiao-Yun examined each carefully.

"She very good. I did watercolor painting too, Chinese style. I show you sometime."

I said that would interest me very much and led Qiao-Yun towards my study. She spotted the framed snapshot of the four of us taken fifteen years ago.

"Your wife, she very beautiful."

"That was taken shortly after Katelyn started college."

Qiao-Yun looked at my bookcases and notepad on my desk.

"This where you writing about the George."

"Mostly here. There's really not much more to see. Upstairs are two empty bedrooms and a bathroom."

Here we were sipping wine and wandering about the first floor with only my bedroom left unseen. If I skipped the bedroom, she might think I was hiding an unmade bed with dirty laundry and empty pizza boxes strewn about. If I showed her the bedroom, she might think I was inviting her to join me in a demonstration of how well the mattress could stand up to sustained activity. All I really wanted to do was show her where I lived. I backed into the corridor and opened the door to my left.

"And this is the bedroom."

Qiao-Yun looked in. The bed made, the bureaus clean and dusted, drawers closed with nothing protruding, the carpeted floor bare—everything in its place. I didn't mention that the queen-sized bed was really two metal-framed twins lashed together. We never had a proper master bedroom set, and for much of our marriage we had an old double bed Cara's aunt gave us. When we bought this house, we had the space for a queen size. Cara found the two twins on sale. Years later during the hospice weeks, Cara needed a hospital bed. I dismantled one of the twins, the one closest to the door, to make room for its big replacement. Cara had always slept on the side farthest from the door. For the final three weeks of her life, I slept on that side; she slept on what had been mine. After Cara died and the hospital bed was removed, I put the old assembly back the way it was and returned to sleeping closest to the door. Cara didn't die in this bed; she died in this room, a distinction important to me.

I gestured toward the living room.

CHAPTER 14

Before my first class with Qiao-Yun, the only people I ever saw doing Tai Chi wore swaying cuffless shirts hung over baggy pants in a massive hillside dance televised January 1, 2000—quite a contrast to what Americans usually saw of China: Nixon in 1972 and Tiananmen Square in 1989 along with assorted street sweepers, bicyclists, dams, the Great Wall, floods, earthquakes, the Forbidden City's plaza, and rows of rigid, stern-faced marching soldiers. Later U. S. presidents and their secretaries of state took turns posing with Chinese leaders who had traded their Mao jackets for suits and ties. Nearly all my other visions of China appeared in grainy black and white film. For Taiwan I pictured an almond-shaped spec in the far Pacific and Chiang Kai-Shek in tailored uniforms. Meanwhile Tai Chi remained that hillside throng and clothes sold nowhere near Scrooby.

During the drive back to her house, Qiao-Yun said she had a nine AM class tomorrow. "You should come."

With less than honest cheerfulness I agreed. "What should I wear?"

My question amused her. "You exercise all the time. What you wear?"

"The usual gym clothes depending on the time of year."

"All my students do same thing. Be comfortable. But no sneakers. Go barefoot. Later, you want I take you Chinatown to buying Tai Chi shoes." She meant Boston's Chinatown. I had eaten there once a long time ago.

Entering her driveway, I noticed the light in an upstairs window. "Keung's been waiting up for you."

"He on computer with friends in Taiwan."

I saw her pleasure with that upstairs light. We walked to her door and kissed for the last time this night.

"See you in class," she said.

Six o'clock Saturday morning my entire exercise wardrobe lay strewn across my bed. Near frantic with vanity and dismay, I stood in my skivvies inspecting the mess. Until summer gave color to my skinny legs, I wouldn't wear shorts to Tai Chi class. The fleece-lined winter running pants would probably cascade sweat to my bare feet. My old, cotton sweat pants had one side of the drawstring forever lost in the waistband. All my other pants looked like hell. I tore through the pile again and found a lightweight polyester pair slightly wrinkled. For no clear reason I determined the correct t-shirt shouldn't have lettering or images. Navy blue looked best. I had two. One didn't have a frayed neckline. I pulled it on and studied my reflection. Not bad.

Qiao-Yun's classroom took up half of a single-floor, flat-roofed building. It needed paint, and the surrounding asphalt buckled from wear and frost heaves. The building's other half held a beauty salon. At 8:50 cars took up all the front spaces. I parked the VW in the rear and walked around to the door lettered "Tai Chi with Qiao-Yun" and joined six women and two men gathered outside. They eyed me the way the new kid always gets looked over. I tried not to appear self-conscious. Everyone wore a black t-shirt featuring a white circle around a large white crane in flight. The backsides showed the yin-yang symbol. Not one of these people looked Asian.

One fellow stuck out his hand and said his name. I took it and said mine, and the others introduced themselves. The circled crane, I discovered, was Qiao-Yun's logo. One woman asked, "Have you studied Tai Chi before?"

A voice from behind drowned my one-word answer. "I thought you might end up here sooner or later."

Jo Garcia, wearing the uniform t-shirt, approached the group. It had never occurred to me that someone familiar, especially someone from St. Joseph's, took Qiao-Yun's Tai Chi class. Then again, I knew little about Jo other than she had three kids, worked as a 911 dispatcher, and voted right at vestry meetings.

Jo gave me a hug. "A lot of people saw you and Qiao-Yun at the O.C.F.C. concert."

Qiao-Yun arrived right behind Jo holding her key ring. She wore black tights and the logo t-shirt. She saw me but acted as though she didn't. "Let's go inside. Class start right away."

Qiao-Yun opened the door and flipped on the lights, revealing an open space with hard-wood floors. One wall held large mirrors. The women stashed their purses in a corner, and I joined the men who emptied their pockets and placed the contents on a shelf. Qiao-Yun stepped to a CD player and pressed a button. Music from Asian strings flowed into the room while her students removed their shoes. I followed their lead. Qiao-Yun stood at one-end of the rectangular room, mirrors behind her. Right away the students formed two lines across the room's width. I opted for the second.

"Stephen, you come to front line," Qiao-Yun said, sounding nothing like she did nine hours ago. "This is Stephen. He new student today."

The faces in the mirrors approved.

"Okay," Qiao-Yun said. "Let's do warm-up."

She stood straight with her feet shoulder-width apart and lowered her head slowly, tucking her chin, and then raised it until her eyes could see the ceiling. She slowly repeated this up-down action, and I followed along until she said, "Side." She turned her heard horizontally from one shoulder gradually back to the other. She repeated the action several times. "Rotate," Qiao-Yun said, and her head motion changed to three vertical turns. She said, "Reverse," and the motion went in the opposite direction. She breathed slowly, as did the students around me. I wondered whether they could hear my neck's grinding sound. Qiao-Yun moved her warm-up exercises to the shoulders, arms, wrists, hips, and ankles. With each sequence she had us rotating joints and stretching, not anything I was accustomed to doing. All the other students knew the drill. With just a word or two, Qiao-Yun transitioned from one movement to the next.

The warm-up came in two phases, first an easy head-to-toes progression followed by another downward sequence devoted to muscles and tendons. These were a little more familiar to me, especially the legwork, but a lot more difficult. When Qiao-Yun had us bend over and touch the floor, my stiffness rioted, after which came squats and floor work that shoved and hauled my leg and back muscles to positions unvisited since childhood. Qiao-Yun's elasticity defied human anatomy. I saw myself in the mirror and tried not to show pain. I failed. Jo Garcia was probably the only student under fifty. At least one man and a woman looked over seventy. My creakiness produced the lone moaner in the room. The last exercise, called "shaky-shaky," had us shimmy and wiggle like flags in a hurricane.

All that remained before Tai Chi started was "dusting." Qiao-Yun slapped and brushed herself all over, as did the others. The purpose, Qiao-Yun explained after she ordered me to pound my flesh harder, was to rid the body of "old *Qi.*" I had no idea what that meant other than a recollection of something she said at Fernando's. In fact, I didn't know the word was spelled *Q-i.* In Pinyin a *ch* sound is spelled with a *q,* just like with Qiao-Yun's name.

Qiao-Yun said something about "Parts One, Two, and Three." Students could decide among themselves which part they wished to practice. She designated Jo and me a fourth group.

"Show him Introductory Breathing and Qi Ball Hands," Qiao-Yun said before she moved off to work with the other groups.

We had a corner of the room to ourselves. Jo asked, "What do you know about Tai Chi?"

I hunched my shoulders. "Nothing."

"Okay," Jo said. "First you need to face me with your feet shoulder-width apart. Relax. As you listen to me, breathe slowly. If you can do that, you'll own the two basic principles of Tai Chi. Start with a stable foundation and breathe steady. Keep it slow."

If I ever have to call an emergency number, I hope Jo answers the phone. Her voice purred calmness and assurance. Breathing to her explanation was like breathing to the *Moonlight Sonata*. Jo knew a lot about Tai Chi. It's represented by the yin-yang symbol. Everyone has seen it: a circle bisected by a wavy line; one side is black, and the other is white with a smaller black circle inside the white and a white circle inside the black. Tai Chi goes back three thousand years and has many forms. In that time billions of people practiced the art. The form Qiao-Yun taught has thirty-seven steps. Jo said Qiao-Yun studied long to become a master, a *sifu*, learning her discipline from an apostolic succession of masters going back many centuries. That's how sacred Jo made it seem.

"So what's Qi?" I asked.

"I'm coming to that. Just listen. Focus on your breathing."

I took about five more slow, deep breaths.

"Qi," Jo said, "is all around us and within us. It falls to the earth from the sky. We absorb it from both directions. It's good for us. It's energy. With the right kind of physical movements and breathing, we can send this energy throughout our bodies. We have channels for doing this, but no Western medical book mentions them. Qi can go to joints and muscles and internal organs."

The *chi* in Tai Chi has a different meaning, something really huge. To explain it, Jo said, would take more time than we had.

"Let's get you started. Watch."

Facing me, Jo started shifting her weight from side to side as though her feet straddled a seesaw. Her feet didn't move. "Now you."

I followed her action, matching her pace and direction and feeling a little stress in my knees and thighs. I studied Jo's shifting and got into her rhythm. After a while, though, monotony set in, and my focus dimmed. Our face-to-face weight shifting reminded me of the scene in the Marx brothers' *Duck Soup* when Harpo and Groucho, both in nightshirts and sleeping caps, faced each other in a doorway. Harpo copied every move Groucho made, trying to make Groucho believe he saw himself in a full-length mirror.

Jo said, "Keep your back straight and stop grinning."

I obeyed, and we continued until she changed her position, this time with one foot planted about three feet in front of the other, again shoulder-width apart. Now we stood alongside each other and shifted fore and aft rather than port and starboard.

Jo said, "Every step in Tai Chi begins with the lower body moving first, usually a weight shift like the ones we've been doing. It works on the same principle as walking or dancing or climbing stairs. You can't move one foot unless the other bears your weight. If you always keep your weight equally distributed, you go nowhere, just like in life. If you want to go somewhere, you have to shift first. In Tai Chi the legs flex, but the spine remains straight."

If Jo ever played high school sports, I could see her in field hockey or softball. She looked like a catcher. She had legs like Qiao-Yun's, muscular but very feminine. Her body was compact without being stout. She had long, curly chestnut hair.

"Look at my feet," she said. "They're pointing straight ahead, what we call 'twelve o'clock.' Now watch."

She shifted her weight to her left side and pivoted the right foot. "This is called 'open the door.' My right foot is at three o'clock."

Jo told me to open and close first my right foot and then my left, achievements I pulled off without her having to tell me when to shift my weight.

She looked pleased. "Now I'm going to model Introductory Breathing."

Jo slowly—every move in Tai Chi is slow—started with her feet together and then drew them apart keeping her hands by her side and palms facing downward. Then she raised her arms about shoulder high. They seemed to float into position. She pushed her hands straight out, drew them back and returned them to her side.

She repeated her movements. "See how I'm standing at attention. Notice how my heels are together and my toes are apart. My back is straight. I take a breath and my palms face the floor, absorbing Qi from the earth, and my knees bend. I draw my left foot away from the right and set it shoulder-width apart. I shift my weight slightly to set both feet pointed forward. I breathe out. I breathe in, and my arms rise while my elbows stay at my side. I extend the arms outward but not all the way. I breathe out. I bring my hands back as I breathe in. I return my hands to the sides of the legs legs while I breathe out."

Jo told me to follow along as she repeated and narrated the action. My mind didn't wander. I imitated her deep inhales and exhales, sensing a flow in my actions similar to hers. My arms floated up and out and returned. My wrists stayed loose, my shoulders relaxed; my lungs filled and emptied like a dozing cat's.

"Again," Jo said, and we did it all two more times.

Introductory Breathing is just that, an introduction. It sets the tempo. The first step comes next. Jo said every step has a name.

"Some are named for animals, like Monkey Walking Backwards and Crane's Stance. Some have names that explain what you do, like Separate Leg and Maintain Space. Some refer back to martial arts, like Shoulder Attack and Low Punch. Some have poetic names, like Cloudy Hands and Seven Stars."

Jo showed me how the first step ends. She stood erect the way we did after Introductory Breathing and placed her left foot forward in the fore-and-aft shifting position we practiced earlier. She kept her weight forward and back straight. Her upper left arm extended out and the forearm angled across her chest, the palm facing inward. Her right hand dropped down, her hand above the knee with her palm facing the floor.

"This is Qi Ball Hands. How we get here from Introductory Breathing takes some foot and torso work."

Jo showed me a stance called "hold the ball," an occasional transition between steps. The imaginary sphere is no bigger than a soccer ball. It's held below shoulder level, the upper hand determined by which side of the body the ball starts. To get me from the end of Introductory Breathing through Hold the Ball to Qi Ball Hands took a while. Jo modeled and narrated twice, and after that I had to duplicate her movements.

Standing with feet apart, I shifted my weight to the left side. "Now you can open the door on the right," Jo said, which I did, and then shifted my weight to the right. "Hold the ball" meant my right hand went on top, the left under the invisible sphere. I got this much down by the third run-through. The rest was harder. With weight still on my right foot, I was supposed to push my left foot forward. "But not directly forward or you'll end up in a narrow stance. Go a little bit to the left." I tried this and got better whenever I remembered to keep my knees slightly bent through the whole form. My weight now had to shift to the forward foot, and two events should follow. One, my torso, which had been aimed right when I grabbed that ball, had to turn forward. Two, my ball-holding hands had to change position. The right came down to protect the right knee, and the left came up to protect the chest, creating the position Jo modeled earlier. "Your weight is still mostly forward. That's good because you need to close the back door halfway." I kept forgetting to close that damn door. "Now balance your weight evenly."

There I was posed with my back straight, the forward knee bent and the other straight and my weight anchored in flat-footed sturdiness, resembling a clay gladiator whose shield and sword had rotted away but he stood a fierce dude nonetheless. Qiao-Yun walked by.

"Good job," she said.

I didn't know whether Qiao-Yun meant this for Jo or me, but I took it as the cue to relax my stance, which I did and wondered what the other thirty-six steps were like and how anyone could remember them. This was stuff so complicated I couldn't imagine synchronizing all this precision without someone like Jo calling every move. She read my mind.

"No one gets this right off. With practice you won't have to think so much. Muscle memory takes over."

At that moment my leg muscles remembered I hadn't been very nice to them, and they were letting me know about it. Qiao-Yun called the four groups back to the original two lines. "We do whole form now."

I figured this was a lovely time for me to sit down and observe people who knew what they're doing. Qiao-Yun had different ideas.

"Stephen, you stand here, middle of class. Watch me. Don't worry. Do best you can. When we turn different direction, you watch other student. Okay?"

"Sure," I said, uncertain of everything except my imminent, clumsy display amid everyone else's blissful oneness with the universe. Qiao-Yun reminded us to follow our breathing and try to stay together. She turned her back and stood at attention the same as Jo had done when she modeled the first stance.

"Begin," Qiao-Yun said, and her knees flexed and her palms faced the floor. Everyone else did the same, and for a mindless moment my apprehensions faded. Already I could do what the others did. My confidence lasted through Introductory Breathing and Qi Ball Hands. Then it imploded.

I felt oafish, though the others didn't seem to care about my stumbling all over the place.

Meanwhile Qiao-Yun narrated the whole form with instructions like "weight back," "hold the ball," "close the door," "step right," "step left," "push hands, " and all those names Jo listed plus more. I followed, always a full clumsy step behind the others, often on the wrong foot like a half-drunk city dweller at his first country line dance. It was awful.

The final step returned us to the beginning—heels together, toes apart, back straight, and hands at our sides. Qiao-Yun turned around and faced us. Her weight transferred to her right foot with her left slightly forward.

"Courtesy," she said.

Her left arm rose and bent to the right at an upward angle, creating a straight line to her fingertips like the pitch of a roof. Her right hand made a similar move toward the left, but this hand became a fist gently pressed against the left's palm. In the mirror the other students repeated her gesture. I tried to copy them. Qiao-Yun dropped her hands and walked toward me.

"Keep weight back," she said, "put left toe forward." She grabbed both my hands to widen the angle where they met. "Better. Good job." All the while the other students held their positions.

Qiao-Yun turned her upper body from one side to the other, her eyes focusing along the two lines of students. "*Shyeh-shyeh,*" she said. I remembered this means thank you.

The students said, "*Shyeh-shyeh,*" and turned their upper bodies toward each other. I copied them. When Qiao-Yun released her courtesy stance, the others did too.

One of the women said, "Breakfast," and the group divided into those who said they had to get going and those eager to eat. With a neighbor watching her kids at home, Jo needed to take off. She sat next to me as I put on my shoes. I complimented her patience with me.

"At work I sometimes deal with morons who call nine-one-one when their toilet backs up. You're easy, Stephen. I saw you *fee da frew.*"

"I what?"

"*Fee da frew*. It's Qiao-Yunlish. It means 'feel the flow.'" I could see it when we kept repeating Introductory Breathing."

"I'll have to remember that, *fee da frew*."

Jo finished tying her laces. "Are you going to breakfast? They usually go to that little place across the street."

The others encouraged me to join them, Qiao-Yun among them. She sounded sweet again. "Come, Stephen. You will like."

Six of us crossed the street, and the waitress let us push two tables together. The three women and one other man maneuvered their chairs and left Qiao-Yun and me facing each other. The conversation turned into testimonials for Tai Chi. I could only nod. The students praised their sifu. When our meals came, Qiao-Yun and I reestablished our weekend schedules. We would see each other tomorrow at church and at my house for dinner. I didn't mention my other weekend plans. I had to call Katelyn and Luke. If Jerry didn't call me Sunday afternoon, I would phone him. His meeting with Diane followed the ten o'clock service. Qiao-Yun and I had our separate grocery shopping to do. For me it was buying the meat and veggies for our Sunday dinner. I also wanted the really good wine Fran and Dom served. Meanwhile, Qiao-Yun and Keung were off to the Asian supermarket in Quincy. They had their Saturday night planned. I had mine, a movie.

When I was a boy, the Cameo Theater in South Weymouth geared its Saturday matinees for kids. We filled every seat. For twenty-five cents we saw two feature films, usually reissued westerns and war epics, about half directed by John Ford. A zillion cartoons always came first. Sometimes we got first-run monster movies. If giant bugs or dinosaurs defrosted by nuclear bomb tests weren't attacking major cities, flying saucers bent on world conquest showed up. The genres barely changed until one remarkable Saturday when the marquee blazoned "MARLON BRANDO in 'JULIUS CAESAR.'"

I knew about Brando because Fran thought he was "intense," the adjective she used when our mother was in the room. I think the Cameo's management thought *Julius Caesar* was another sword and sandal movie. A young, bare-chested Brando dominated the poster, and since he was hot box office, somebody figured preteens would love to watch him thrust and slash his way through the ancient world. Shakespeare's name meant nothing to kids bordering puberty. We came bringing our usual action-filled expectations, which dissipated ten minutes into the first reel. Not one sword flashed. More to the kids' dismay, the characters wouldn't shut up. Vexed and bewildered, kids squirmed in their seats. They got up to pee or get more popcorn, and within a half-hour their endurance expired. They trooped up the sloping aisles and past the exit signs to familiar daylight. The bloody Ides of March rewarded the more patient, but soon they too joined the evacuation, leaving just the heavy-eyed and passive behind. I stayed, transfixed. Every gesture, every word, including the many I didn't understand, rooted my English-major destiny. I still loved that movie, and it was on a commercial-free station tonight.

After shopping and putting the groceries away and doing household chores, I grew anxious. Four more hours needed to pass before *Julius Caesar.* Sitting down with George Herbert didn't attract me. Too much occupied my mind, and rather than rehearse my Qiao-Yun revelations to Katelyn and Luke, which I started doing in the supermarket, I picked up the phone.

Luke came first. He had news of his own. His band broke up, but he met another guitarist whose tastes ran like his. Luke appreciated this guy's versatility as much as this other guitarist admired Luke's playing. It turned out Luke's new friend had many musician buddies, all of them more serious than the ones in Luke's old band. They liked his songs. Among them Luke found a drummer, keyboardist, and bass player. They knew someone who rented studio time at an affordable rate and another guy who booked bands for local clubs.

"We're still in the rehearsal stage, but this is the most fun I've had playing with a group."

He asked what was new.

"I took a Tai Chi class today taught by a woman who goes to my church."

I spoke Qiao-Yun's name and described the O.C.F.C concert and a little bit about the dinner at Fernando's. I said she was from Taiwan and she was very nice. "I thought it would be fun to take her class. It was. I guess you could say we're friends."

The best way to describe Luke's response is to say it differed from Katelyn's. I called her next. She also had good news. An agent liked Gareth's manuscript, and Katelyn's doctor thought she was doing very well.

"I'm starting to show. Gareth says I'm getting sexier."

Katelyn chatted on about her two babies—the one she was carrying and the one Gareth wrote. Finally she asked how I was doing.

"I started a Tai Chi class today."

I don't know whether it's because Katelyn is the older child or because she's the daughter, but she always comes on as though she has her father all figured out. I told Katelyn everything her brother heard about Qiao-Yun. He didn't ask her age. Katelyn did.

"Mid-forties," I said and held my silent phone while she processed.

"Are you two dating?"

"Well, as I said, we had dinner, and I'm sure we will again."

"I see," she said, her voice stagnant.

"It's been ten months, Katelyn."

She tried to sound agreeable. "I know, Daddy." I wished she tried harder.

Luke was easier. When I said Qiao-Yun had been Taiwan's martial arts champion, he joked I better behave myself. I didn't try to reassure Katelyn further except to say that we would talk again.

A few hours later Brando's Marc Antony stood over James Mason's fallen Brutus. All through the movie my mind kept rerunning the conversations with Katelyn and Luke. At ten the next morning, far from Rome and Philippi, Jerry and I marched side-by-side singing the processional hymn. In the third row Qiao-Yun sang alongside Wen. After the service I went upstairs to coffee hour. When I sat with Qiao-Yun and Wen, they stopped speaking Mandarin. Qiao-Yun asked about my evening. I told her I watched a favorite old movie. She said she wanted to see any movie that's a favorite of mine. I asked about her night, and she listed everything she and Keung had for dinner. They had a good time, she said, and they planned an afternoon walk along the Cape Cod Canal, not far from Mass. Maritime.

Qiao-Yun had to drive Wen home. "I see you at six tonight."

"I hope you like roast pork."

She does," Wen said. "But will she like your cooking?"

Qiao-Yun laughed. "We'll see."

I drove home confident in my dinner plans. I had written out all the numbers before leaving for church—oven temperature and time per pound, with extra minutes for the baked potatoes. I had an Internet recipe for mixed carrots, broccoli, and zucchini simmered in Italian salad dressing. Fran, Dom, and Jerry raved when I served it at Christmas. I stopped at a bakery and bought fresh roles.

I put out the best tablecloth, plates, and silverware—things sparking memories I quickly edged aside. With candle and matches at the ready, half my work was done. I snapped on the TV in time to hear the National Anthem playing at Fenway. After five innings the Sox had a four-zip lead over the Rays. Jerry called. He had met with Diane right after this morning's service. They skipped coffee hour. Jerry sounded ready for action.

"Diane and I talked for over an hour. She told me everything. She's tough as nails, Stephen."

Like me, Jerry had no strategies for moving ahead other than to support Diane in whatever ways she wanted. Jerry also expected everything would work out well. "But it's a huge issue," he added.

I agreed. Jerry said he and I should get together sometime soon. "Let's have dinner at Linnehan's. We haven't done that in ages."

It had been a while. After tonight I had no idea about Qiao-Yun's schedule. For me every night this coming week was hers, though the loose ends at St. Joseph's could change things fast. I'd know better after I met with Diane and Janice Tuesday morning. No telling how events might develop, plus I wanted all the time with Qiao-Yun I could get. Even so, I hadn't had any fun with Jerry in a long while. We were due.

"How about tomorrow night?" I asked.

"Why not tonight?"

I told him why and summarized much of the past week. Jerry sounded almost as goofy as I did when Katelyn called to say she was pregnant. He liked hearing about that too. Then he asked what I was serving and how long the pork roast had been in the oven. Jerry sounded like the big brother even though I was twenty years older. We threw obscenities back and forth until I told him to shut up because my roast needed checking, the veggies were unprepared, and Qiao-Yun would be here any minute. He made me promise a full rundown tomorrow night.

I grimaced through a second shave and changed clothes. The Sox made a rout of it, winning nine to one. At four minutes to five the doorbell rang.

I had the oven open. The roast looked brown and juicy. I lowered the heat and shoved the pan back in. I wiped my hands and opened the kitchen door. Qiao-Yun slipped her glasses into her purse, its strap slung over a shoulder. She raised her eyes. The outdoor light caught her face in the shadows. She picked something up and stepped inside.

"Thank you for inviting me," she said. The purse slid to her wrist. Her right hand held a small overnight bag.

CHAPTER 15

Jerry got to Linnehan's first, grabbing the last high top, two-seat table. He looked terrible. It was good I called Qiao-Yun before leaving the house to make plans for tomorrow night. These hours with Jerry probably wouldn't leave me in great shape to do anything later. We ordered burgers for dinner and had just started our twenty-ounce dark ales, my first and his second, maybe his third, which meant there was no telling what he might say, but I didn't expect this.

"Do you ever wonder why I didn't finish that Ph.D.?"

I tried not to sound serious. "Wondering about you takes up too much of my time."

"Stephen, something happened this morning, something I need to explain to you."

Jerry's workdays started early. He liked to get to his job site by eight. This morning was different. He had a lumber delivery that wouldn't arrive until noon at one house. At another he had scheduled an estimate for a front porch. The owner couldn't meet him until ten-thirty. Given this extra time, he decided to treat himself to a jumbo breakfast at the Corner Cafe across the street from Linnehan's. The unusually warm morning prompted the owner to set up four outdoor tables on the red brick sidewalk.

"I never made it inside. I turned around and walked away. Harriet was sitting at one of those tables."

I couldn't imagine why Harriet Pringle's presence at a restaurant would chase Jerry off.

"The person sitting next to her was someone I knew twenty years ago when I was in grad school and teaching introductory Latin classes. This woman with Harriet had been one of my students. I tried to make like I didn't see them, but they both saw me."

"You never told me you had a teaching fellowship."

"For a while I was good at it."

In all the years I had known him he never seemed so disturbed, except last Thursday after choir practice.

"Her name is Cheryl," Jerry said. "I recognized her right off. If Harriet were younger and slimmer, they would look a lot alike, but I never made the connection, maybe because I never thought anyone with a Master's degree could come from the same gene pool as Harriet. Cheryl could be her younger sister, cousin, or something. I know

Harriet has only one kid, a son who had moved away. California wasn't it?"

"If this Cheryl had a Master's, what was she doing in your Intro to Latin class?"

"She wasn't in the Classics department. Her degree was in English, and she had just been accepted into the doctoral program. She needed a reading knowledge of a classical language. Taking two undergrad semesters was an option for meeting this requirement. She took my class."

Before Katelyn and Luke entered their teens, I got my M.A. in English. I pored through grad school catalogs dreaming of getting a Ph.D. It never happened.

"The university ran two accelerated semesters in the summer. Cheryl wanted to get the language requirement done right away. I was writing my dissertation, living like a threadbare, malnourished scholar. The summer gig suited me fine. All the other students were kids. Cheryl was no kid, and she wasn't much of a Latin student. But she looked sensational."

"And it was summer."

"It was summer."

I had to look away from Jerry's face. Almost every night locals and tourists filled these booths and tables as though determined to prove a theory he had repeated for years: "Sooner or later everyone comes to Linnehan's." I saw a young man sitting at the bar who looked familiar. I couldn't recall his name and made a point not to try right now, but he probably was in one of my Senior English classes. He was sitting with a dark-haired, dark-eyed beauty. She enjoyed his company.

"Not that summer was any excuse." Jerry spotted the waitress, her hands balancing two plates, heading our way. She gave us our dinners and took his order for two more tall ales.

"It was the first summer since tenth grade I didn't work construction or landscaping, and the only work I've done since then is construction and landscaping."

The guy at the bar saw me. I told Jerry our dinner would get cold fast. Like an obedient child, he forked a French fry. He didn't notice when my former student and I gave each other acknowledging nods.

"We all knew the boundary rules, faculty and T.A.'s alike, even though nothing specific had been written down. It's the kind of topic academia never defines unless forced to. I noticed Cheryl the first day of class. In college I studied hard and reveled in bacchanalia—summa cum laude day and night. Why stop with a B.A.? I applied to grad schools and got in, which brought great scholarly pursuits but my sex life was monastic."

"Because of the boundaries."

"Not really."

Jerry explained there were always rumors about some prof poking somebody or getting poked. No one got hurt, so the stories went, so nothing more was said. What really got to him was the teaching. It wasn't just a job to defray tuition. He lived five miles off campus in a tiny attic room, drove an oil-burning Chevy pickup, seldom had two dimes to rub together, and loved his job.

His voice faded into a coarse whisper. "It was almost enough."

As Jerry told me more, I realized that Cheryl was the kind of person who believes success comes only to those who know how to trade. Jerry had no idea whether he had been set up from the start, a late afternoon encounter outside the library, or Cheryl's guile kicked in once her traction skidded. Mostly, he blamed himself.

"For a while there, I thought I loved her. Imagine that."

Cheryl never studied. For her conjugation was no fun with verbs. Jerry offered extra help, which she avoided. Cheryl offered hers, which he took time and again. When he warned her she had to ace the final exam to get the credit she needed, Cheryl acted unconcerned as though another tug on his fly would get her through. It didn't. She flunked the exam. He flunked her. She ran to the dean and didn't tell Jerry.

"I get called to his office, too dumb to know what's going on, and the chairman of the department is there with him."

They had a paper, a statement, Cheryl's version of what happened. The dean read it aloud. The chairman sat with his hands folded on the table and stared at his thumbs. The dean finished reading and asked for Jerry's response. He told him it was a distortion but didn't deny the key facts. She was his student. They had a sexual relationship.

"And then there's the killer. The dean asks, 'Did you try to entice her into having an inappropriate affection for you?' It's like putting me in the same category as child molesters."

"What did you say to them?"

"I saw the obvious. They'd crush my nuts with vice grips and think themselves white knights. I despised them."

I asked whether something could have been done. It was a ridiculous question. Cheryl had something to trade, a scandal. From the administrators' perspective Jerry had nil. For the good of all concerned, the dean said, Jerry should reconsider Cheryl's grade.

"I told them to go fuck themselves."

"What about Cheryl?"

"I later heard she dropped out after the fall semester and moved to New York."

"Did you see her again?"

"Not until this morning."

I could picture Jerry telling off his two bosses and storming back to his one-room apartment and throwing everything he owned in the back of his pickup and burning rubber as he made his getaway. Thirteen years ago he ended up in Scrooby and St. Joseph's.

"I can guess what Harriet said to Cheryl," he said. "There goes that booze-soaked son of a bitch from my church. And Cheryl would smirk and say, Oh, Jerry Devereux, I know him."

Whatever Harriet knew about Jerry and Cheryl she didn't learn until this morning. She would have used it a long time ago. I said so to Jerry.

"Well, you can bet she knows now. She'll claim I'm a sex fiend in league with a lesbian priest to turn St. Joseph's over to a bunch of perverts and his buddy the senior warden is cheering all the way."

I couldn't put this past Harriet but confirming his fears wouldn't make Jerry feel any better. I went into a long monologue about the difference between the crazy, bigoted notions people get and the actions they actually take. Not every racist fire bombs a bus. Jerry saw through all of it.

"She hates you too, Stephen. A mind this wretched thinks you tossed her over for Qiao-Yun, but she won't tell it that way. She'll say you and Qiao-Yun had it going on before Cara died."

When mud gets thrown, pieces always stick. Bob Norris taught me that, yet I wanted to believe Jerry was overreacting.

"Whatever Harriet might win, she's got to know it would be nothing compared to what she would lose."

"Stephen, we're not talking about a rational person! And whatever she wins will cause a world of hurt. "

"But she needs a plan—when to strike and who to get on her side."

"Nothing is more contagious than stupidity."

I tried to reassure us both. "We have time. She doesn't know about Diane."

"But that will come this week. Diane's going to tell the vestry members individually. Remember?"

I reminded him about my ten o'clock meeting tomorrow morning with Diane and Janice. He ordered me to get there early before Janice showed up.

His voice softened. "Diane heard my story two years ago."

Our waitress brought the fresh ales, and we drained what was left in the ones we had.

Jerry slowly pushed his chair back from the table. "Harriet needs a few days to plan her next move, and she probably wants to give me time to squirm."

"How's that going?"

"Severely. But not because of her." He rose from his seat and back pedaled an unsteady step. "I gotta take a leak."

Jerry headed towards the men's room. His work boots thumped each concentrated step.

My former student and the young woman eased away from the bar into the light. I remembered his name, Sean, and placed his graduating year in the mid-nineties when I taught only seniors. According to Bob Norris, the administration had no choice. I was a tough act to follow. He explained it this way: "You're best suited for older kids."

Sean and the woman walked towards me. If she had been one of my students, I would have remembered. Sean's face had matured. The couple could be on the cover of a health club's brochure. I stood up.

"Mr. Pentheny," Sean said, "you probably don't remember me."

I spoke Sean's full name and stuck out my hand. He took it firmly and introduced his wife, Adiba. She gave my hand a firm squeeze. I repeated her name.

"I've heard so much about you, Mr. Pentheny."

"It's all true," Sean said.

"So you did play *Alice's Restaurant* in class the day before Thanksgiving?"

"I'm an advocate for cultural literacy."

"You did a lot more," Sean said. "I'll always remember what you called the 'dialectical relationship between thought and language.'"

"That line wasn't original with me."

I asked Sean about his life since high school. He said he met Adiba in Philadelphia when they were law students. They had lived in Philly ever since.

Adiba said they worked in the public defender's office.

Sean asked what was new with me. I said I was retired and did some volunteer work through my church. Sean said they were visiting his family. They had tickets for Fenway the next night. He asked if I were writing. My answer called it random essays about a favorite poet, George Herbert.

"Didn't he write a poem that looked like a pair of wings, something to do with Easter?"

"He did." It was in the senior's anthology.

We chatted for a few more minutes. Linnehan's patrons noticed our laughter. As Sean and Adiba were leaving, she embraced me.

Sitting alone, I leaned back in self-satisfaction, which soon triggered memories of people unlike Sean who thought me a fool. Bob Norris led the list. It didn't help when I cracked a joke about him in the faculty room. This happened during his first year as principal. He appeared on the classroom TVs the morning of Halloween wearing a Frankenstein mask. The junior girl who read the morning announcements said the principal had a special message, and the camera zoomed in on Bob. I don't remember what he said. Probably no one does, though right afterwards in the faculty room two habitually cranky guys had something new to gripe about. They asked what I thought of Bob's performance. My response was, "You mean Boris?" That's all they needed. "Boris Norris" took off and ran through the faculty's ranks. By second lunch it became the joke of the day.

Five years before, Bob had the gumption to become an assistant principal, a job he endured better than I would have. Our friendship eroded after he became principal. His authenticity proved too weak for the position's grinding tasks, and he resorted to sleights of hand, a skill he honed from then on. Nothing substantial about the school ever really got better, but he claimed great improvements anyway and gave kids awards, lots of awards, as though bestowing accolades brought him kickbacks.

One year he launched a contest before the Christmas break. Every homeroom would decorate its door. At the December faculty meeting Bob said festive corridors make a school happy. Every homeroom teacher had to comply. In a public school everyone knew religious implications cause trouble. "Just stress joy," Bob said. The freshman, sophomore, junior, and senior class presidents would be the judges, together with the principal, which meant if class loyalties held firm the homeroom with two of the five votes would win and the same plurality would decide second, third, and fourth places. Bob designed prizes for the champion homerooms, coupons good for credit against any one-night assignment the students chose to blow off. Many teachers thought this a dandy idea. The teachers who didn't have homerooms snickered. Those of us who believed our assignments weren't frivolous seethed. Bob ordered extra art supplies which the Student Council made available in the cafeteria. When Bob informed the kids during morning announcements, my homeroom students glared at me. With eyes rolling I asked for volunteers to stay after school and get this done. The students, all seniors, got the hint. Relieved because each had better things to do, none volunteered. "Don't worry," I said. That afternoon I taped sheets of white construction paper all over the door and with a black marker scrawled, "Stopping by Woods on a Snowy Evening."

Bob was pissed. He didn't speak to me for a week and then caught me late one afternoon as I was leaving school. We were alone. He stood three inches shorter and weighed about forty pounds more. His tie cost more than my shoes; his gelled dark hair defied age.

"Stephen, have you walked around this building lately? I do every morning, and let me tell you the door decorating contest has really brightened up the place, except your room."

"Gee, Bob," I said. "I didn't know the Christmas spirit is all about competition."

"Your door is a mockery."

"Yes, Bob, I know." I walked away.

He didn't like that. My sarcasm had gone too far, not because he was my boss but because he was my friend—or used to be. I needed to make peace. The day before Christmas vacation I went to his office bearing a gift, a book carefully wrapped in shiny green paper with silver stars and wide red ribbon in a bow. He was surprised and mystified. I stayed a few minutes. We talked about our holiday plans and reminisced a little about the days when we both taught English. Finally, he asked whether he could open the gift now. I said he should.

He undid the wrapping, read the book's title, and looked at me not sure what to make of it.

"Read the inscription." I said.

He did: "To Bob, with warm regards from your fellow teacher—Stephen."

We wished each other a merry Christmas. It was the last truly amiable meeting we ever had. The book was *The Poetry of Robert Frost*.

Two and a half years later Bob was the superintendent. He came with the most energetic educational master plan he could conceive. He called it "The Enlightenment." It merged all his notions about awards with a program advanced by a corporation that manufactured class rings and sports trophies. When our district joined, the company paid for the banners proclaiming "Welcome to the Enlightenment" hung throughout the five elementary schools, the two middle schools, and the high school. The company provided the software and thick textured stationery for printing certificates, and for good reason: the banners and awards featured the company's name and logo. "Enlightened" students, according to Bob, were those determined to win their teacher's favor as one of the two "best" or the one deemed "most improved." An elementary teacher had a single class from which to find these elites. Middle and high school teachers selected winners from each of their five classes. No changes in number allowed. Every teacher got nomination forms, except those who taught special needs kids. Awards also went to any student who had perfect attendance for the year. Even though honor rolls plus local scholarships for graduating seniors had been in public education for over a century, Bob's talent for ballyhoo projected the Enlightened students as the district's imperial guard.

"This rewards not just academic performance," Bob decreed. "Kids will know their full selves have been judged—character, leadership, appearance, and attitude." Its innovation was the "incentives," another name for the certificates passed out at the evening awards ceremonies scheduled in late spring. There was more. In late spring one school day featured two hours of outdoor games and ice cream only the Enlightened students could attend. All the other kids stayed in their classes. At these restricted field days the superintendent made a special guest appearance to pass out ribbons to all who competed in the games. The winners got gold; the others got blue.

No one complained. Many teachers and parents, but far fewer students, thought the Enlightenment wonderful. The teachers' union executive board saw the selection process as another example of the administration's coming up with additional tasks not specified in the contract, but they let it go. I hated the whole goddamn thing from the start and made an appointment to see the superintendent. His office was across town.

Bob offered a seat in front of his huge desk and closed the door.

"What's on your mind, Stephen?"

I waited until he had settled into his deep leather swivel chair. "It's about the Enlightenment Program, Bob. I need you to hear me out."

"You're jumping ranks, you know. This is district policy voted on by the school committee."

I suspected he might stiff me. "If you prefer, I'll leave now and write you a twenty-page memo and send it up the chain of command."

The idea of my leaving must have appealed to him, but Bob didn't want his administrative team reading anything unless it came from his office. "My door is always open, Stephen. You know that. I'm just stating protocol. Go ahead. I'm listening."

I began with my most gentle, carefully reasoned argument. I didn't question his goals. I argued pragmatism and cited research. Rewards systems in schools don't work. The emphasis gets shifted away from learning lessons to winning prizes. "For example," I said, "suppose you promise kids pizzas if they read a certain number of books. Over time, you might increase their appetite for pepperoni but not their desire for reading."

Bob was unmoved. He said I had ignored a pile of other research.

"What research is that, Bob?" I knew he had nothing except junk published fifty years ago or gobbledygook from the ring and trophy company.

"Trust me. It's there."

I didn't trust him. He could tell.

"The most convincing research is right here," Bob added. "You didn't go to any of those Enlightenment award ceremonies. You never saw those happy kids and parents."

I told him he'd get the same response if he walked through a shopping mall and randomly handed out five-dollar bills. A few people might get excited about a gimmick like this the first or second time it's tried. After that it's not enough. People will want a new gimmick when what they need is substance. The Enlightenment hadn't a shred of substance.

"I resent your terminology," Bob said.

"Look, you want to make things better. I understand. All over the country too often teachers, kids, and subject matter aren't coming together in meaningful ways. It's no secret. It's why we're stuck with state-mandated exams."

"You think I don't know that? You think we're not addressing that? You've been to the meetings. I expect department heads like you to get those scores up!"

"Then explain how the Enlightenment Program helps teachers do a better job?"

Our voices had been climbing over each other since I called his baby a gimmick. Bob paused. I waited. He picked up a pen from his desk and twirled it about ten times before he put it down. He leaned forward, his arms on his desk and fingers intertwined. He spoke slowly.

"Here's how it works, Stephen. You might not like it. But it works. We get a bunch of kids—say fifteen percent of the entire student population—and we treat them like royalty for a day or two. They're all good kids. No one questions that. They're exemplary because they do what we want them to do. Their numbers never go down. Every year we will have fifteen percent of the kids we can make a big deal about. Their parents love it because they feel validated. I know what you're thinking. What about all the other kids? Well, some might feel jealous, and that's okay. You know why?"

His tone made me uneasy. I remembered his Frankenstein mask.

"I'll tell you why," he said. "Because some of those jealous kids are going to make up their minds they too want to be royalty. Maybe only a few. I don't mind. They'll be better kids for trying."

"And all the others?"

Bob tilted back in his chair. "They'll still have to live up to state standards or they don't graduate. That's why I love education reform. And here's what the school committee loves, and the whole community loves, about a program like this—and this is true everywhere the Enlightenment goes. Even with the kids who don't give a shit about awards, we're planting seeds. Later on, maybe five or ten years later, they'll realize there are only two kinds of people in this world, winners and losers. And they'll remember the Enlightenment and realize they missed their chance. But here's what so great about America, they get second chances. Not all will take them. After all, there will always be losers."

I had to ask, even though I feared what he would say. "Second chances to do what?"

"To do what they're told. It's the biggest lesson taxpayers want schools to teach."

He was beyond reason. I could see that now, yet I couldn't leave. "Bob, do you believe learning has value for its own sake?"

"Sure."

"Could you explain what that value is?"

"I'll leave that to philosophers like you." Bob couldn't have been more serious. "I have a school district to run."

Before I left, Bob said he appreciated my dropping by and was glad we had cleared the air. I drove home to Cara and repeated the whole conversation. We sat on the couch, and I drank a double scotch. She pulled me to her shoulder and said she loved me. The next day she said, "Be careful. Whatever Bob says about you to others, they will believe it even if they know it isn't true."

He must have said something. Then again maybe he didn't need to. Six weeks earlier a woman in my department approached me. She held one of the Enlightenment nomination forms the central office sent to every teacher. We had known each for over a decade.

"What am I supposed to do with this stupid thing, Stephen?"

I put a hand on her shoulder. "Whatever you damn well please."

The next day she fingered through the one hundred and six names in her rank book and selected the ten "best" students and five "most improved." Every teacher but one, the English Department chairman, submitted forms. A year later she had the job.

"Because we've known each other for so long," Bob said when he summoned me to his office and announced the change, with the assistant superintendent and high school principal alongside him, "this is very difficult for me personally."

"You make it look easy," I said.

It was easy. I had started a rebellion without bothering to look over my shoulder. I made people uncomfortable. It didn't matter that professional journals published my articles about teaching composition and literature. In fact, that made matters worse.

I watched Sean open Linnehan's door for Adiba. He gave me a quick wave and followed her to the sidewalk. I could still see them through the big front window. Adiba slipped her arm around his. They crossed the street and disappeared into the darkness and the window's reflections.

My attention swung to Jerry. A minute later he sat across from me again. His face aglow, he raised his glass.

"To the Reverend Diane Fleming."

"The Reverend Diane Fleming." Our glasses clinked, and we swilled our brews like pirates.

A hamburger at Linnehan's requires two hands and much attention. Jerry handed me a napkin. "As I was leaving the can, I saw you with that couple who just left. They looked very glad to see you. Do I know them?"

I wiped my mouth and fingers. "Probably not. They went to college with Katelyn, haven't seen them since commencement."

CHAPTER 16

I shouldn't have had that third twenty-ouncer. The next morning a sore head and arid mouth scolded me. I am one acquainted with hangovers. This one pardoned my stomach and bowels enough to permit a half-hour on the elliptical stepper before a cold cereal breakfast and the necessaries for launching my day. Jerry had to be in much worse shape. By the time we got around to talking about Qiao-Yun, he and sobriety had parted ways, a condition he usually handled with experienced skill. While I nursed my last dark ale, he heard my story. I said very little about Qiao-Yun's terrible marriage or her staying at my house Sunday night. But he understood she and I had advanced way beyond passing notes in homeroom. I thanked him for the kicks in the ass. Hearing this pleased him very much. Jerry said I shouldn't worry about Katelyn. Consuming another two ales to my one, he sat enchanted, the earlier distress tucked far behind. We resolved to take on whatever campaign Harriet might wage. What remained was my finding the means to get him home safely.

"Not to worry," he said. "I will walk."

He had left his pickup at home across from the boatyard. I offered to drive him the short mile to his place. He said I should follow his example and go with him. I asked how many ales he had put away.

"Several."

"Which is several more than my three. I can drive all right. The question is: Can you walk across the street?"

Jerry called me an old fart and claimed a young buck like him could drink me under the table. The waitress brought the check. He studied it and couldn't do the math for the tip. Instead, he demanded to pay for the burgers and drinks and make the tip my contribution. I figured the total, and we paid fifty-fifty, despite his protests, and then we returned to the previous argument about who was going where and how. This ended outside Linnehan's where North Street meets Main Street. To shut me up, Jerry carefully itemized his walk home, how North Street sloped to Water Street where he would turn right and trace the coastline until he reached the boatyard and then cross to his door.

He stopped yammering about my ability to drive. Jerry knew my limit. Regardless of the trouble a breathalyzer might bring, I always managed the fifteen-minute drive between Linnehan's and my house.

He said I should give him credit for leaving his truck home in the first place. I called him a wise and prudent man. We hugged each other and went our different directions: he with both hands in his pockets down North Street and I fifty yards down Main to my VW. But before I moved, I watched him pass under two streetlights. He kept a slow but steady gait.

Tuesday morning the stars threw down their spears.

I arrived at St. Joseph's hoping Diane's schedule would give me thirty minutes before Janice showed up. The upper half of the parish office's Dutch doors were open, and Alice Flynn sat at her desk peering at her computer screen. Few church members could remember the previous parish secretary. Alice usually wore a prim, collared dress, this one a pastel yellow print. She looked like everyone's favorite aunt. I never entered her space without making sure she first noticed my presence.

Alice looked up, her greeting jubilant. "The new photocopier will be here Thursday, all installed and ready to run off the Sunday bulletins. I'm so excited."

I said this was very good news.

Alice knew all the details from the last vestry meeting. "Diane called Jerry's presentation a masterpiece."

I said it was and opened the bottom door. Alice made a slight nod over her shoulder. "There's no one with her."

I strolled by Alice's desk towards the alcove separating the two offices and knocked on Diane's open door. Her head poked out from the bookshelves partially hiding her.

"I'm glad you're early."

Even though Diane possessed a remarkable talent for handling the unexpected, she preferred well-planned meetings. We hadn't prepared for Janice beyond our getting the vestry's commitments to the Essential Qualities for an Excellent Music Program and the development of new job specs for the music director. Neither of us was certain why Janice wanted this meeting. I brought a more pressing problem.

"Before we get to Janice, I have to tell you something Jerry told me last night that we think you need to know."

She gestured for us to take our usual seats by the coffee table. "Okay."

I started in right away, telling her first how Jerry related to me the story she heard two years ago. Then I detailed Jerry's seeing Cheryl yesterday morning with Harriet, how disturbing this was for him because he feared Harriet now had a weapon she could twist into a denunciation of the rector.

Diane disagreed. "No one at St. Joseph's would try that."

"Harriet is neurotic enough to say anything."

"She's not malicious, and it's unfair to call her neurotic."

"What if you're wrong?"

"We'll muddle through."

Diane said Jerry was still upset about what happened a long time ago and seeing Cheryl, if indeed that's who he saw, triggered all that emotion again. "Don't add this to the already low opinion you two have of Harriet."

I came to tell her there was a problem, and she was calling Jerry and me the problem. It didn't sit well. "So what do you propose?"

Diane recommended prayerful thought about how to proceed. She had scheduled her meetings with the vestry members and already met with a few. Her letter to the parish was almost done. She'd show me the draft when ready. We would talk more about Harriet tomorrow. In a few minutes Janice will arrive.

"Can we talk about that now?" Diane paused—an obvious signal for me to refocus. I tried.

She outlined her plan. "The vestry voted to stick with the Music Committee, and that puts Janice in jeopardy. If she's anxious, let me do the talking. Let's be as gentle as possible. If she's feisty—"

"—Let me do the talking. I'll talk procedures. Their legitimacy speaks for itself."

Diane saw I was still stewing. She had accused Jerry and me of overreacting; and as much as I resented this, she might be right, at least partially. Harriet was a jerk, not a monster, but vicious acts don't require monsters. I wanted to push Diane further after we finished with Janice. And as for Janice, she would do everyone a huge favor if she walked in right now and thanked us for saving her from her own incompetence.

Something stole Diane's attention. Alice stood in the doorway, rigid, her gaping eyes fixed on Diane who rose from her chair. Alice looked at me and tried to speak. Her throat closed. She took one step forward. Her focus jumped back to Diane. Again she tried to speak.

"The State Police called." Alice's lips barely moved. "An accident. Last night. Jerry Devereaux. Jerry is dead."

Manners, proper etiquette, were essential at a time like this, more essential really than acknowledging the cause of Alice's turmoil. It was too absurd. The night before, under the streetlights, Jerry proved his invulnerability. I had watched him. Therefore, Jerry could not be dead, and there had been no accident. And Diane said, "How? Alice. How?" Alice's face contorted, and she started crying. I had never seen her cry before, and as Diane ran to her and embraced her, I thought this a most unusual sight, such unveiled emotion coming from a person, an adult, who was near wailing, and here was Diane showing such compassion. It was all so very touching. I didn't know whether to feel embarrassed or privileged. In fact, I sat there pondering which was the more appropriate response. I could have sat there forever weighing this question as though I were a monk safe in his cloister wondering what he would say come the one moment each year when his abbot suspended the brothers' vow of silence. And Alice kept on crying, which was the proper response because it gave me the time I needed, the necessary time, to decide whether I should feel embarrassed or privileged to be witnessing Alice's extraordinary sorrow. You just go ahead, Alice, and let it all out, and, yes, Diane, that's a good priest, give her what comfort you can, and, Alice, you don't have to answer Diane's questions, even though she means well, because there is no answer because Jerry isn't dead and there was no accident, and there's really no need for all these tears, but since you feel you must cry, I will abide with you, though I don't know whether to feel embarrassed or privileged.

The details, what few there were, gradually stumbled forth. The Massachusetts State Police had called. Someone driving Jerry's pickup swerved off Route 3 down an embankment and rolled over twice. Some other motorist called in the accident. A cruiser and ambulance arrived. The pickup's driver, unconscious, terribly banged up, and bleeding internally died in the ambulance dashing to take him to the nearest hospital, the South Coast Medical Center, four miles from the next exit. The cops had the truck's registration and the dead man's license. Manila folders and papers strewn throughout the truck's cab included construction contracts, an assortment of bills, and the minutes of seven past meetings of the Vestry, St. Joseph's Episcopal Church, Scrooby, Massachusetts—Jerry's name on them all. The state trooper who called never actually stated Jerry was dead. He said he was reporting a fatality involving a person who might be affiliated with St. Joseph's and asking whether anyone at the church knew a Gerard

Devereaux. Alice answered we did have a parishioner by that name. Still, Jerry wasn't really dead, not officially. The officer needed two persons to come to the South Coast Medical Center to make the identification. Alice said she would tell the rector. She took the officer's number and said someone would get back to him in a few minutes. We got Alice to sit down on the couch, and we sat with her until she regained enough composure to stop crying and breathe normally and tell us what the officer said. I got her a glass of water, and Diane went to her desk and made two calls.

I needed to know where the hell Jerry was. He couldn't be this dead guy. Jerry walked home last night. I watched him, and now I pictured him unconscious in the bushes outside his apartment house, having been mugged, no doubt, by some bastard who got his just deserts after grabbing Jerry's wallet and keys and stealing his truck. And Jerry needs his truck. His livelihood depends on it. We'll have to do something about that. I stood up and took my cell phone from my pocket and called Jerry's cell phone. The state trooper thinks his problem is a body needing identification when the real trouble is an altogether different person, a missing person, the victim of foul play, and this cop is too lazy and too stupid to consider the obvious when he should be pulling his head out of his ass and getting the Massachusetts State Police and the Scrooby Police and the Scrooby County Sheriff's Department out looking for Jerry. All this raged in my head through the ten rings before I heard Jerry's voice.

"This is Jerry Devereaux. I can't answer your call right now. Please leave me your name and number, and I'll get back to you as soon as I can. Thank you."

Jerry set his phone at ten rings before his voice mail kicked in because if he were on the job any number of things could keep him from answering, and if his table saw were running he might not hear the phone at all. That was probably it. He had that damn saw whining like a wounded banshee and he couldn't hear a jumbo jet a hundred feet over head. I called again.

Each ring was supposed to be the last before Jerry's voice, his real voice, filled the prolonged, intermittent emptiness. The count went to ten.

"This is Jerry Devereaux. I can't answer—"

I snapped my phone shut.

At the opposite end of the office, Diane held her receiver. She turned away. I could tell her first call had been to Janice. She said something about a pastoral emergency and promised to call again before nightfall. The second call went to the state cop who phoned earlier. Diane listened. She muttered something about "...myself and a church lay officer who knew Mr. Devereaux" before she hung up.

Diane turned her chair and spoke across the room. "It looks very bad, Stephen." She said we had to go to the South Coast Medical Center. "An official identification needs two persons, unless an immediate relative does it. A cruiser will be here soon. I told them you and I would be ready."

Forty years ago I had to go to the morgue at Boston City Hospital to identify my father. A heart attack killed him while he drove on Morrissey Boulevard in Dorchester. It was the classic movie scene in a morgue. One wall held stainless steel drawers. With a Boston Police sergeant by my side, the attendant pulled a drawer, and out came the sheeted body. The attendant drew back the sheet. My father's hair looked more white than gray, and I had never seen him without his teeth.

"We're the closest Jerry has to family," I said.

Alice broke down again. Diane went to her side, putting Alice between us, and Alice cried on Diane's shoulder. I put a hand on Alice's back. I didn't cry, not then, because everything the state cop reported still had a huge hole in it. Jerry had said nothing about going back out once he got home. He was too drunk to drive. His day was done. We parted around nine. If the cops said he never made it home—he fell into the ocean and drowned or staggered onto Water Street and got run over—that I might believe, and his death would be my fault. I should have protected him, walked with him, made sure he got home safely. But I didn't screw up. He never got so drunk he couldn't navigate a familiar half-mile walk, and I had seen him drunker than he was last night. So what the hell was he doing four towns away on Route 3? It made no sense.

Alice stopped crying. Diane told her to go home. Alice refused. She would feel no better at home, she said. Better it would be if she stayed at her desk and finished typing Sunday's worship booklet. With Diane out of the building, someone should answer the phone, especially if news about the accident got out. People would call. Alice could explain until everything was sure. She would be useful. Alice took two tissues from the box on the coffee table. She blotted her face and blew her nose.

"Let me be of some help," Alice said and didn't wait for an answer. She walked back to the outer office.

Diane followed her to the door and closed it. She walked back to her chair across from the couch and sat down.

"The police say the driver's blood-alcohol content was point-one-two-oh."

"Is that a high number?"

"Way too high to drive. The truck might have been going as fast as ninety. I have to ask you this, Stephen. Where were you guys last night?"

"I told you. We met at Linnehan's for dinner. I got there around seven. We ate and had a few ales—that is, I had three and he had more. We talked about different things, mostly this business with Harriet and Cheryl, and went our separate ways a little after nine."

Before Diane could ask the difficult question about letting him drive, I explained that Jerry had left his truck at his place and walked home. "And that's what I don't understand, Diane. Jerry knew when he left his apartment for Linnehan's that two hours later he would be in no shape to drive home. He planned it that way, and then to walk home, get in his truck, and head north on Route 3 doesn't add up."

Diane started to say something when her phone rang. She went to it, listened, and said, "Please tell him we'll be right out."

I rose from the couch. Diane said, "The state trooper is here to take us to South Coast Medical."

I started towards the door. Diane put a hand up as if to stop me.

"Whatever we say in the car, let's not talk about last night. There's a lot we don't know, and I don't want us speculating in front of the police."

Diane took a cloth bag from behind her desk and went to her bookcase. She took down two copies of the Book of Common Prayer. She pulled open her file cabinet and thumbed through folders until she found the one she wanted. She put the books in the bag and handed it to me.

"Now we can go."

CHAPTER 17

Diane and I rode in the cruiser and said nothing. The trees were budding as they did every spring, a few precocious oaks a tad greener than the others. The scenery was very familiar to me. The highway's construction had started in the late fifties when I was a boy. Route 3 runs to the Cape Cod Canal. From there to Provincetown it's Route 6. From Quincy northward through Boston and into New Hampshire and beyond, it becomes Interstate Route 93—the same stretch with three different names. My father worked in Boston all his life. My homeland had been the towns along Route 3 where anyone who needed to travel more than a few miles north or south found this state highway the quickest course, which meant it often became the slowest. When traffic is lighter, as is usually the case at night, hardly anyone obeys the speed limit. Jerry never did. The highway expands from two lanes to three not far from the exit closest to the South Coast Medical Center. According to the state cop, Jerry's truck never made it to the wider road. The wreck was gone before we passed the site, revealing no telltale rubble or tire tracks or mangled grass or lacerated tree.

At the hospital's main entrance we met another state trooper, a sergeant, with a clipboard and forms. He asked our names and checked his papers. The sergeant asked our addresses and wrote them down, careful to get the spelling right. He took us down a floor and through a zigzag grid of corridors to a barren twelve-by-twelve room well away from the hospital's usual traffic. All it had were metal cabinets along two walls. We waited. An attendant entered to check that we were there, and then he wheeled in a gurney. A white blanket covered the long, broad-shouldered, still figure underneath. The sergeant asked if we were ready to make the identification. Diane said yes, and the attendant pulled the blanket to the body's collarbone. We saw the lifeless, expressionless face, his eyes closed.

"That's Gerard Devereaux," Diane said.

The sergeant waited a moment. "And you, sir?"

I said, "That's Gerard Devereaux."

Diane asked the sergeant if we could have some time to say prayers. He motioned to the attendant, and they went outside. We took the two prayer books from the cloth bag. Diane spoke the page numbers. The words were familiar to me. Last July I called Diane the morning Cara died. I made a sequence of phone calls then, all prearranged. The first went to the hospice nurse. She had the legal authority to certify a death. The second went to the Douglas Funeral Home. The third went to Diane. She came right away with Olivia Finch and Jerry. The fourth went to Fran and Dom. These four joined Diane and me to read "The Ministration at the Time of Death," standing around the bed before the hospice nurse and the professionally somber-faced team from Douglas's arrived. Katelyn and Luke, who had been staying at the house the past week, chose not to participate. Gareth stayed with Katelyn. The nurse came and checked Cara's signs. She disconnected the morphine I-V.

Ten months later Diane and I were reading the words again. Less than three pages, the prayers and responses confront death with assertions of faith. One is the presence of the Trinity, and the other is the departed's transformation into something other than nothingness. In three prayers Diane asked God, "That it may please you…" Three times I followed with: "We beseech you to hear us, good Lord." The stations of Creator and created define the protocol. It's old, one-sided, contrived, humbling—and the only way to go when someone dies because it defies futility. Diane and I read the last prayer together. It said Jerry was God's servant, he was a lamb, and he was a sinner: "Receive him into the arms of your mercy, into the blessed rest of your everlasting peace, and into the glorious company of the saints in light. Amen."

We speak these ancient words for ourselves mostly. They lift us from time and space and take us to the edge of eternity. It's the loneliest place to be unless you bring awe and wonder, and then it becomes the only place with context, the mystery that fills a vacuum, if only part way.

Diane opened the door and told the sergeant we were done. As the attendant put his hands on the gurney, my eyes fell on the sergeant's chevrons, and his sleeve turned from gray to dark blue, the uniform of the Boston Police sergeant who had been with me forty years before when I identified my dead father, the first of the three unadorned corpses I've seen in my life. I pictured each one again, and my mouth turned bitter with the acidic aftertaste of last night's ale and fried dinner and the undigested milk and cereal of this morning's breakfast.

I asked the attendant where the men's room was. He pointed and said, "Three doors down." I ran.

Diane stood alone when I reentered the corridor. "Are you okay?" she asked.

I told her I was okay.

Are you sure?" She handed me a bottle of water. "Here, have some of this."

My throat burned from the retching, and the cool water soothed. Diane took a striped mint from her purse. "This too," she said.

I pealed the wrapper from the mint. "Do you always travel so well prepared?"

"With mints, yes. I bought the water from a machine down the hall." She put her hand on my shoulder. "Are you sure you're okay?"

"I'm okay. Thank you." I put the mint in my mouth.

The state trooper is waiting to take us back. Can we talk for a minute before we go outside?"

I muttered, "Sure."

We found our way back to the entrance and stopped at a row of chairs. We sat down. Diane spoke barely above a whisper. "Did you know Jerry appointed the rector of St. Joseph's the executor of his estate?"

I remembered his saying this a few years ago when the columbarium was installed. He bought one of the niches. "He has no living relatives," I said. "It's not much of an estate."

"His will leaves everything to the church. He had a life insurance policy. St. Joseph's is the beneficiary. I'm going to call Fred Divol for advice. He's been an executor. I need your help too."

Making a few bucks for St. Joseph's was the last thing on Diane's mind. "Whatever you need," I said.

"Do you know Jerry's landlord?"

"He lives on the first floor." I gave Diane his name.

I'm going to call him and explain what happened. This is where I need your help. Someone has to get into Jerry's apartment."

"You want this done soon?"

"Yes. I want to know where Jerry was going last night."

"You think the answer is in his apartment?"

"Maybe, if that's where his cell phone is."

Diane explained. While I was in the men's room, she asked the sergeant whether Jerry had listed her or me as emergency contacts on his phone. The folder she brought contained a copy of Jerry's will naming her as executor. She wanted his cell phone, and she planned to use this document and her collar to get it from the state

171

police. She didn't tell the sergeant Jerry's cell was his only phone or her reason for wanting it. What if someone called him? And whatever that someone had to say, it was enough to make Jerry head north on Route 3. The phone's list of recent calls would identify the number if not the caller. The sergeant checked his clipboard and said they didn't find a cell phone.

Riding back to Scrooby, Diane reviewed the legal business she settled with the police and hospital. I must have been out of action quite a while. She got a lot done, including a call to the Douglas Funeral Home.

"Their visiting times are booked for the next few days, but they will do everything else. We could do a viewing at our sanctuary and have the funeral the next day. What do you think?"

I didn't want to see the inside of Douglas's again, especially if Jerry's wake were in the same parlor where Cara's had been.

"He would prefer our sanctuary."

I said the choir will want to sing at the funeral. Diane said I should give the eulogy. The police cruiser slowed down. The state trooper took the second Scrooby exit. Soon we arrived at St. Joseph's. Alice greeted us and asked if we were hungry. Diane looked at me. Alice offered to call the deli down the street. I said I'd have whatever Diane ordered.

I took out my keys. "Excuse me for a minute."

I walked down the corridor to the sanctuary's side door. It opened alongside the organ. The altar was to my left, and ahead were the choir stalls. Multicolored light slanted through the huge stained glass windows making the nave's pews visible. The chancel and altar remained in darkness with barely enough light spilling through the open door to reveal the place where Jerry sat every Sunday. In the choir stalls the men took up the last pew, and Jerry always sat the farthest to the right. I groped through the darkness and took his seat. I removed my glasses and placed them on the pew and reached for my handkerchief. Hideous, violent sobs erupted and wouldn't stop until they ran their awful, immeasurable course. I lifted my heavy head. The handkerchief went to my runny nose and wet face. I put my glasses back on. Across the chancel a woman's silhouette stood framed within the open side door. I heard Qiao-Yun's voice.

"Stephen, I'm so sorry."

I tried to stand, but my knees wouldn't move. I tried a second time and willed myself upright and clunked along the pew. Qiao-Yun rushed past the altar and met me in the purblind darkness. My desperate arms pressed her to me.

Qiao-Yun trembled and held me tight. "Diane, she call me from hospital."

We walked towards the hallway beyond. I closed the sanctuary door and locked it. We entered the room where the vestry meets and brought two folding chairs together.

"Diane tell me about Jerry. She say you need me, say you be at church in little while."

I couldn't stop talking about Jerry and babbled a string of tributes. Qiao-Yun said Jerry invited Wen and her to sit with him at the Epiphany dinner.

"I think he know you be there."

"He did."

For the next twenty minutes I revealed what Jerry told me at Linnehan's and included what Diane had confided to us. Qiao-Yun listened. She didn't trust Harriet and said women like Cheryl were nothing new. She called Jerry an honorable man. The thought of anyone hurting Diane angered her. When I explained the little we knew about his accident, she said Diane was right to find out all we could.

We heard soft footsteps coming from the office. Alice peered around the doorway. Her face begged forgiveness for interrupting. Lunch had arrived.

Sandwiches and a green salad spread across Diane's coffee table. Qiao-Yun and I sat on the couch while Diane spoke into her desk phone. "Thank you, Mr. Swenson." Hank Swenson was Jerry's landlord. Diane crossed to the coffee table and took her usual seat. She prayed a one-sentence grace before she praised the deli's wraps and salads while opening three bottles of iced tea and pouring them into cups. "Dig in. There's plenty."

Qiao-Yun had chicken salad. I had ham. We swapped halves. Diane noticed.

"Qiao-Yun," I said, "knows all about my conversation with Jerry last night, all of it. I realize that runs ahead of your schedule."

It's okay," Diane said. "Yesterday afternoon I met separately with Fred Divol and Jo Garcia. I saw Olivia last night. They were very supportive. And Alice knows everything."

I asked what we needed to do. Diane's single concern was Jerry. She had just finished sending an email announcement to the parish. To us she recommended a viewing Thursday at St. Joseph's. The cremation could be scheduled for Friday and the funeral Saturday morning at ten.

Qiao-Yun said she wanted to help. "I will cancel Saturday morning class. What you need now?"

Diane said there was something Qiao-Yun and I could do together this afternoon. She looked at me. "That is, if you're up for it."

"You were talking to Hank Swenson."

"I don't want you to go alone."

Qiao-Yun said she didn't have a class until five.

"There's something else," Diane said. "While you're there, for the viewing…"

She didn't have to finish her sentence. Jerry didn't own a suit. At least I never saw him in one, except the tuxedo he bought at a fire sale for the O.C.F.C. concerts.

"He has a blue blazer," I said.

"Perfect. The other items, I have a list from Douglas's."

I didn't need the list.

From the church to Jerry's apartment I drove along Water Street. Three years ago Jerry completely gutted and remodeled the old house where he lived. He made a deal with Hank Swenson when he converted the rundown Victorian into three apartments. Jerry swapped his labor for two years of free rent in the second floor apartment he created. With Hank as Jerry's helper, it was a good deal for them both. Not long ago I asked Jerry what would happen next year when the agreement expired. He said he could never afford the rent. The house was too nice, especially with its views of the town and ocean from the wrap-around deck he built. He said he had been encouraging Hank to take up sailing. Jerry had sketched plans for a twenty-foot boat, a new job for a new lease.

Jerry's carpentry created the house's interior and exterior renovations. Hank's apartment took up half of the first and second floors. Jerry installed a second, prefab spiral stairway. Hank's parents had the other first-floor apartment. I rang Hank's doorbell. He expected me. I introduced him to Qiao-Yun. His wife had gone to Boston with his parents for the day. His two kids were in school. He dreaded telling them.

Hank invited us into the main hallway and took us up the original staircase. Jerry preferred the deck's outdoor steps to access his apartment. I had never used the central staircase before. Hank gave me the key and said there was no hurry to return it. He walked downstairs.

Jerry's apartment took up half the second floor. Aside from the bedroom, the closet, and the bathroom, it was an open space. Wood paneling covered the walls. When I first saw the place, I asked Jerry what kind of wood it was. He knew I couldn't tell oak from pine.

"Norwegian," he said.

An L-shaped bookcase ran the full height of wall opposite the bedroom and the rear wall, stopping at the door to the deck and outside stairs. Jerry stacked his books in categories. The Greek and Latin classics took up a quarter of the shelves. The rest included tomes about theology, linguistics, art history, and architecture. He had jazz and classical music commentaries, the Weavers songbook, and rafts of rock and blues anthologies. Other volumes covered carpentry, gardening and landscape design, followed by what looked like the complete works of Walter Mosley and various other novels. Some assorted cookbooks took space nearest the kitchen. His computer and printer stood atop a card table next to a badly worn swivel chair. Two wooden crates held a circular saw and extra tools. The only other pieces of furniture were a reupholstered sofa that faced the entertainment cabinet he built and a rocking chair he had refinished. In front of the couch there was a coffee table. A picnic table and benches that he made crowded the kitchen. The entertainment cabinet held his bulky old television, cable box, and assorted players including a phonograph, speakers, and stacks of CDs and LPs. A tall, leafy potted plant was on one side of the sofa, an end table with lamp on the other. His two guitars, one in a gig bag, leaned against it.

Aside from my first visit when I helped him move in, I had been here only a few times, little more than quick pickups or drop-offs. Qiao-Yun's eyes panned the room once and returned to the bookcases. With the door closed I could see the refrigerator, sink, and counter space that extended towards the back exit.

"Do you think his cell phone in bedroom?" Qiao-Yun asked.

I had never seen Jerry's bedroom except for a quick glance that first time. Its closet and bureau drawers held the clothes for the viewing. Qiao-Yun said she would check to see whether the phone was there. If I called his phone and it were in the apartment, we would hear the ringing. I started to reach into my pocket, an action that made me twist slightly. I spotted something behind a bowl at the end of the kitchen counter.

"There it is," I said. Qiao-Yun followed my gaze.

I picked up the phone. It was the old kind that flipped open like the communicators in the original *Star Trek* series. I fumbled with the menu and pressed through it twice before I found the recent calls. After my calls this morning, the next two listings showed the same number and different times—9:51 last night and 12:06 this morning.

"Someone did call him."

"Who?"

I kept the number highlighted and pressed the call button. The unanswered rings came as a relief. I had no idea what to say to this person. The ringing stopped, and one of those impersonal recordings came on. When the tone sounded, I said nothing and flipped Jerry's phone shut.

"I got a voicemail."

"Whose?"

"Someone named Cheryl Sinclair."

CHAPTER 18

Everybody was worried about me.

Before leaving Jerry's apartment, I took both the phone and the charger and added Cheryl's number to my phone's contact list. I drove Qiao-Yun back to St. Joseph's. We kissed in the church parking lot. She invited me to dinner and insisted I stay the night. After Diane's call this morning, Qiao-Yun cancelled her Tuesday night Mandarin class. I promised to be at her house by seven. We kissed again and held it long.

As Qiao-Yun's car grated over the dirt lot, I walked to St. Joseph's side entrance and used my key to get in. Alice had left. Diane stood in the parish office amidst pale shadows. I held up Jerry's cell phone and told her about the Cheryl call.

Diane said she had suspected something like this. "My guess is Cheryl told him where she was staying, and he wanted to see her."

The fatigue in my legs returned. I leaned against a file cabinet.

Diane asked, "Do you think she was trying to manipulate him?"

"I doubt she'd get very far."

"Do you think he wanted to manipulate her?"

"The only person Jerry could manipulate was me, and he knew it. Do you still believe Harriet isn't a threat?"

"I figured she'd be contentious but not hateful."

"Do you believe that now?"

"Jerry didn't. Do you think he would speed off looking for Cheryl if his focus weren't Harriet?"

"I don't think he could ever get that drunk."

"Neither do I." Diane looked exhausted. I probably looked the same way to her. "Promise me you won't call Cheryl again."

"I can't make that promise."

"You have more important things to do than call her."

She asked about Katelyn and Luke. I will call them, I said, my sister too. Diane said Olivia had scanned Jerry's photo from the parish directory. She wanted to enlarge it and buy a frame. It would stand on a table with the urn during the funeral. Olivia had just left.

"And there's something else," Diane said. "I don't want you to be alone tonight."

"I'll be with Qiao-Yun."

"That's good, Stephen." Diane peered out at the parking lot. "I like the way you two say goodbye to each other."

One stop interrupted my drive home. I went across the street to Douglas's. A stocky young man in a dark suit with a black and grey striped tie stood inside the foyer. He called me Mr. Pentheny. Last July he handled all my dealings with the funeral home. I remembered his first name, John. Diane had told him to expect me.

In one hand I held a wooden coat hanger with a pair of grey dress slacks and a white shirt under a blue blazer. A pale blue tie draped the jacket's lapels. In the other hand I had a plastic bag with underwear and a pair of black socks. "These are for Jerry Devereaux."

John said he was sorry for my loss. He meant it. I glimpsed the hallway outside the parlor used for Cara's wake. Last July Fran collected Cara's things and delivered them. Five years earlier she did the same when our mother died. Forty years ago I brought my father's clothes to the funeral home near his welding shop in Dorchester, a short distance from the neighborhood where he grew up. Gathering Jerry's clothes took little time. His closet wasn't cluttered. He usually wore jeans, even to church. Alongside the blazer hung his two pairs of dress pants: one grey, the other tan. He had two ties and seven shirts on hangers, including three flannels. His concert tuxedo hung inside a garment bag. I found the rest in his bureau's top two drawers. Come Friday morning the clothes I brought, Jerry, and the mortician's artistry would go up in flames. Saturday, the urn would be present at the funeral, followed by the committal at the columbarium, the final page in Jerry's ashes-to-ashes narrative.

Two miles from home my cell phone rang. It was Olivia. I could barely hear her. She was the first vestry member Diane called. She went straight to St. Joseph's.

"I didn't want to be alone."

I welled up. "Diane said you took care of Jerry's picture."

"I have the software." A tight throat constricted her speech. "Diane asked me to serve the chalice at the funeral. She said you're doing the eulogy."

"I need to do it right."

"You will."

I explained getting Jerry's clothes but didn't mention the cell phone. "Qiao-Yun was with me. I'll be with her tonight."

"I feel better knowing that."

I feared she was going to ask details about the accident. She didn't. We planned to see each other the next afternoon to prepare the funeral.

As soon as I entered the house, I grabbed a glass and the quart of scotch Dom gave me for Christmas. I poured three fingers neat and plopped on the couch. I savored the taste and let the single malt's smoothness linger. Before long a mild numbness began, but not enough, not unless the next hour went entirely to alcohol. I called Fran first. It was supposed to be brief. In the background I could hear Dom ask what was wrong. She repeated my words exactly: "Jerry wrecked his truck last night. He's dead." Dom said something about me, and Fran answered, "I don't know. Let me talk to him."

And so we talked. I did most of it, recounting Alice's horrified announcement and my reaction, the ride to the barren room, Jerry's body and the visions that followed, the vomiting and tears, Jerry's clothes, and the delivery to Douglas's. Fran asked about the wake and funeral, and she relayed my answer to Dom.

She asked the tough question. "Had he been drinking?"

The only way I could answer was to tell her everything. I couldn't shut up. I told her about Diane, Harriet, Linnehan's, Jerry's accounts of what happened twenty years ago and yesterday morning, and my last view of him alive. I told her about the cell phone and Cheryl Sinclair.

Fran asked a few questions to make sure she was hearing me right. She said I was carrying too big a load. She sounded like Diane, saying I shouldn't be alone. "Come here. Stay the night."

"That's very sweet, but I won't be alone. I'm staying with Qiao-Yun."

I explained how Jerry brought us together. Fran said Jerry knew what he was doing. I promised to call her again tomorrow.

Luke would take Jerry's death hard. In all my life the happiest kid I ever saw was my son on his twelfth birthday when we gave him his first guitar. He started lessons right away and progressed faster than his fingertips could build up calluses.

Whenever Jerry brought his guitar to the house, he and Luke descended to the basement where they improvised melodies and exchanges. Out of view, Cara and I sat on the stairs and listened. It was beautiful. As the years went on, these improvisations became more complex. Jerry said Luke made him a better player. Luke said Jerry made him better.

Of the four Penthenys, Luke was the most intuitive. He went to college to satisfy his parents. He majored in Philosophy because he distrusted most things utilitarian unless they served the making of music—like his hoard of instruments and his stockpile of electronic equipment and arcane parts. Cara's idea of a shopping spree was a Saturday morning at yard sales. Luke often tagged along in search of recordings. The older the format the more he treasured the find. Vinyls, including 45s, outnumbered his CDs—another trait he shared with Jerry.

A week after Luke's college graduation, he drove to the Pacific Northwest by way of the Mississippi Delta through a route he made up as he went along. Before Luke left, I told Jerry about his hazy plan. Jerry wasn't surprised. In fact, he already knew. "No one grows up," he said, "without first going on a journey." It was the sort of aphorism he'd make up or had read in some ancient myth. Luke's trek ended when the hand-me-down clunker he drove coughed twice and passed out one rainy morning at the opposite end of the continent from Scrooby and couldn't revive without an overhaul worth more than the car. The precious Seattle sun came out, and Luke liked the city it unveiled. Then he called us. He transferred his savings into an apartment's first, last, and deposit, and a bicycle. Within a week he announced his job at a food co-op and praised the two clubs where he performed at open mics. He came back to Scrooby for his sister's wedding and his mother's dying. In between Cara and I visited him once and stayed three days. Her illnesses prevented other trips.

My glass held a puddle of scotch. I emptied it and called my son. I avoided lame euphemisms and condensed the secondary details into "no one else was hurt" and immediately realized how ridiculous that sounded. I didn't say anything about Linnehan's and said little about identifying the body except that Diane was with me. I listed the wake and funeral times and explained why the police called the church office. Like Fran, Luke must have wondered whether Jerry had been drinking. That's not what he asked.

"Dad, are you okay?"

"That's what I should be asking you."

Luke repeated his question.

"I have friends here," I said.

"Qiao-Yun must know how close you guys were."

It was the first time he said her name, and it sounded good. I described how Jerry finagled the Epiphany dinner meeting and how he needled me to take her to the O.C.F.C. concert.

Luke choked up. "He was always looking out for you, wasn't he?"

I pictured Jerry walking under a lamppost on North Street.

"I'm coming home," Luke said. "I can catch a flight today."

At Cara's funeral Luke and Jerry sang a song Pete Seeger recorded about growing a garden inch-by-inch and row-by-row. At the third chorus, they beckoned the congregation to join them. I tried, so did Katelyn and Gareth. We broke down. Luke and Jerry barely finished. Luke sounded that way now.

"It's good you're coming," I said.

Luke dismissed my offer to pay his airfare. His income tax refund had come the day before. Anticipating my questions, he said his band was ready for the first gig and could get by without him for a few days. He had unused vacation time too.

"None of that matters anyway," he said.

Luke asked about Katelyn and Gareth. I told him they were my next call. He would phone them too. For now he wanted to go online and buy his plane ticket.

"It means a lot to know you're not alone," he said.

One more call remained before I left for Qiao-Yun's house. Gareth answered, which was a relief. Katelyn was at a routine prenatal consultation. I gave Gareth the same details Luke heard. He said they were coming to the wake and funeral. What struck me was his terrible sadness. Gareth had met Jerry only twice. I assumed Katelyn viewed him as her father's church and drinking buddy, one activity pretty much like the other, but then she also witnessed how beautifully he made music with Luke and the comic relief he gave her mother.

"Katelyn and I were talking about Jerry Saturday night," Gareth said. "It was shortly after your call."

I asked him to explain, but first he wanted to pronounce the Tai Chi instructor's name correctly. Katelyn wasn't sure she had it right. He asked me to say it, and he repeated my sounds.

"Jerry set me up with her," I said.

"We thought so, and we talked about you and Jerry for much of the weekend. Katelyn asked if my father had a friend like him. I said few men do."

Gareth paused a few seconds. "The more we talked the more Katelyn understood how much Jerry cared about you."

His voice got stronger, and he asked about Qiao-Yun. I described the Epiphany dinner and the O.C.F.C. concert and all the spontaneity at Fernando's, none of which would have happened without Jerry's two tickets and his commandment I couldn't take my sister.

"I'm staying with her tonight."

Gareth said that was good. "Katelyn will think so too." I wasn't so sure. He asked about Luke. I said the news hit him hard and they could expect his call. Gareth said Katelyn planned to call me tonight.

"She said so this morning." Again I heard his sadness. "You can count on it now."

We ended with his assurance they will arrive Thursday and stay until Sunday.

Four phone calls. Only Fran asked the tough question. Maybe the others didn't want me to be the one to tell them. I started crying again. The scotch was wearing off, and a second glass wasn't going to change anything. My clothes felt heavy and dingy as though I had spent a week camping in them. I stripped everything off and soaked under a long, steamy shower, then dressed and packed an overnight bag.

The drive to Qiao-Yun's house slowed in relentless traffic that bulged off Route 3 onto Scrooby's streets. My left hand found two CD's in the door's pocket. Without looking, I pulled out a Thelonious Monk and slipped it into the dashboard's slot. My tired brain wanted Monk's quirky rhythms to carry me some place where a piano mattered more than anything—a distraction that lasted until a distant red light made me and the three cars in front crawl to a stop. My attention fell to the passenger seat and Jerry's phone.

The voicemail. I hadn't checked his voicemail.

I flipped the phone open. My thumb clumsily pounded through irrelevant menus. I found the right button. Jerry hadn't set up a password. The usual ringing came, followed by a feminine sing-song announcing a message. Then another woman spoke, her silky voice wrapped in unease:

"It's been two hours, Jerry, and you haven't come. I hope you're okay. My plane leaves at six-forty this morning. I'll say goodnight now."

The light changed to green. The guy behind me leaned on his horn.

CHAPTER 19

The orange sun had begun its decent behind the tall pines surrounding Qiao-Yun's house. I knocked on the back door and peered through its windows. Qiao-Yun approached wearing tight jeans and a white collared blouse tucked behind a wide belt and buckle. Pale rhinestones in a paisley loop dotted one thigh of her jeans. The blouse's open neck revealed a hint of cleavage. I walked through the open doorway. She stepped in close. Her magic hands touched my back as mine moved behind hers.

I half wanted to push her backwards down the hall. We would kiss and stumble and grab each other until we reached the couch and fell into unstoppable, breathy groping and fumbling with belts, buttons, and zippers; and with her empty jeans and panties flung on the rug and my khaki slacks and boxer shorts knotted at my feet we would shove and grind into moaning, shuddering tremors that left us drooping over each other, having exorcised every tension that had bound us since noon when she saw me bawling my brains out in the choir stalls.

The other half of me just wanted to sit down.

Sunday night we finally turned bold and saucy. Monday morning spontaneity ruled a second time, and we nestled lazy and satiated. She asked me to call her later in the day. I did. She wanted to hear my voice. We spoke only for a minute or two, and I never stopped thinking about her until my rendezvous with Jerry at Linnehan's, a date with my buddy that brought no objections from Qiao-Yun. In fact, she encouraged it, saying she had to make some calls to Taiwan. The thirty-six hour difference between our time zone and theirs made her evenings coincide with mid-to-late mornings there. Tonight, Tuesday, was to be our second night.

As soon as Qiao-Yun's arms opened to me, I dropped my bag. Our mouths and tongues gently pressed into each other, she standing on slippered toes while I bent my knees and lowered my head. Qiao-Yun took a half step back and looked at me tenderly as though my eyes revealed more than I could ever know about myself.

"Would you like a drink?" she asked. "I have plum wine from Taiwan my friend give me."

I could still taste Dom's scotch. "A glass of water would be fine."

My toes pressed the heel of each shoe and shunted them to the side. I followed Qiao-Yun to the kitchen. Before she drew a pitcher of chilled water from the fridge, she sliced a wedge of lemon on her cutting board and placed it in the glass. She turned on three of the stove's gas burners. The fourth already pulsed fire under a two-handled pot. She adjusted the flames with twists of her wrist. Juicy chicken sections, fish fillets in an herbal sauce, and a green vegetable I later learned was bok choi soon simmered in separate pans, while the pot held a soup invisible through the steamed glass cover. I asked about a squat cylindrical gizmo plugged into the counter's electric outlet. Qiao-Yun said it was a rice cooker. She went to work. My job was to drink my water and stay out of the way.

While she tied on an apron, I started summarizing my afternoon calls, beginning with Luke's decision to come east for the funeral. I mentioned tomorrow's meeting with Olivia and Diane and said my talk with Fran lasted the longest because we both had much to say. Qiao-Yun had difficulty remembering English names. I had to remind her who Olivia was. The Chinese custom is to call people by a title. Siblings and children, for example, could be Older Brother or Older Sister, Younger Brother or Younger Sister. Qiao Yun followed my narrative better when I spoke about Sister, Son, Brother-in-Law, Daughter, and Daughter's Husband. As I rattled on, Qiao-Yun's attention focused mainly on the tasks before her. She moved like an octopus working a fast-paced assembly line. The exhibition ended when the pans' sizzles and crackles subsided after she turned off the burners. With a glance over her shoulder, she reached back and popped the top of the rice cooker. A vapor puff shot upward, and she handed me a spatula.

"Put rice on plates," she said, taking charge. "Bring plates to table. I bring other food."

While I followed orders and scooped two servings of rice onto the plates, she placed the soup pot on the counter and had the fish, chicken, and bok choi on separate platters. She made two sorties from the stove to the table in the time it took me to complete my one-way assignment. I put the plates in spaces between chopsticks on one side and bowls with comma-shaped porcelain spoons on the other. Qiao-Yun pulled off her apron as she returned to the kitchen a third time. She brought back a teapot. She brought back her smile too.

"Good job," she said and kissed my cheek. "Let's eat."

We sat in the same places we took last week. While Qiao-Yun ladled soup into our bowls, I continued my phone call summaries.

"Daughter's Husband was very sad to hear about Jerry, and he said Daughter will be sad too. They will come to the wake and funeral."

Qiao-Yun responded in monotone. "Your whole family, they come. That's good."

"You will like them, and they will like you."

Sunday night Qiao-Yun had asked about my kids. I praised Gareth's compassion and his book, and I praised Luke's sensitivity and his talent. I said Katelyn was very beautiful. Qiao-Yun saw through that. She wanted more. I told her about the last trip to New York. Qiao-Yun must have wondered how Katelyn would react if they met. It worried me too.

I could see that question again on Qiao-Yun's face as she loaded our plates with food. She needed to hear what passed between Gareth and me. It took a while because context is everything. There were the backstories. My explaining all this to Qiao-Yun sputtered and meandered. She listened very carefully, and then she said something that surprised me.

"Your daughter, she is like you."

Years ago Cara said this whenever Katelyn personified the adolescent tag team of petulance and self-doubt. I hoped Qiao-Yun meant something else.

"What makes you say that?"

"Many things."

"Like what?"

"I tell you one." Qiao-Yun poured tea into my cup. "She thinks."

"Is that good?"

"The way you do it, yes—most the time."

Seven hours had passed since our lunch with Diane. We dove in. I studied Qiao-Yun's *kwhy-zuh* technique and tried to imitate it, which meant I pinched chunks of food and bit off chewable segments. Separating the fish from its skeleton required more deftness. Spooning the soup, a savory liquid with two Chinese dumplings and shallot bits and other things, was the easiest. Qiao-Yun watched my performance. I put on a show. She liked it. Meanwhile my palate unwrapped layers of flavors. Qiao-Yun spoke to me in Mandarin. It sounded like "*How chir mah?*"

She saw my bewilderment. "I ask if your dinner taste good. '*Mah*' at end of sentence make a question."

"It's delicious," I said.

"Thank you. But if I say *how chir mah?*, what do you say?

I had to think about this a little. Qiao-Yun's voice went up when she said *mah*. "Ask me again," I said.

185

"How chir mah?"

Like a kid in a breakfast cereal commercial, I sat up straight and proclaimed, "*How chir!*"

Qiao-Yun glowed. "*Dwayluh!* Excellent, Stephen. *How* mean good. *Chir* mean to eat. *Shyeh-shyeh.*"

My brain cells did a nanosecond word search. I hoisted my teacup and said, "*Bookuhchee.*"

Qiao-Yun applauded. "You remember!"

Before I could answer with a bow, her disposition suddenly changed. She lowered her head; her eyes closed. She brought her napkin to her mouth, stealing time to bring herself back. She lifted her face and returned the napkin to her lap.

Qiao-Yun said, "You remember" again, very softly.

We spoke little more for the rest of our meal. I started the cleanup, scraping from her plate onto mine and collecting the cups. With polite directions, she told me where things went and said nothing else. Clearing off a table and loading a dishwasher were nothing new to me. When we were done, her silence still loomed between us. Somebody had to say something. I pulled Jerry's cell phone from my pocket.

"Cheryl left Jerry a voicemail."

We sat at the dining table. I played the message. Qiao-Yun listened with a code breaker's concentration. She asked me to play it a second time and then a third.

"What do you think?" I asked.

"Has Diane heard this?"

I explained that Jerry's voicemail hadn't occurred to me until just before my arrival at the house. "But I did tell Diane about the first call, the one Jerry answered, when I was at the church this afternoon."

"It was her idea you take Jerry's cell phone when we at his apartment today. Do I say correct?"

"Yes."

"So what you two think about that call?"

"We think Cheryl saw him at the Corner Cafe and probably wanted to warn him about Harriet. He went to meet her, hoping Cheryl could settle Harriet down."

Qiao-Yun suspected Cheryl found Jerry's number through an on-line directory. "I don't think Harriet know about the Cheryl call," she said.

"My guess is she was calling from a place within twenty miles of Boston. I bet she was in the city."

"Yes, and she alone. Maybe she on business."

"Which means coming down to Scrooby was a side trip."

"Even if she stay in Boston, she need to get up early, like four-thirty to make her flight. Her first call almost ten o'clock. She waiting long time before call again. She not get many sleep that night."

"Does she sound worried about him?"

"She say she hope he okay. She worry. She say 'Goodnight.'"

I wondered whether Qiao-Yun accepted the theories Diane and I invented and hoped were true. Maybe St. Joseph's church had nothing to do with why Jerry wanted to see Cheryl and why Cheryl waited long into the night to see him.

"Stephen, we should call Cheryl. She might not know Jerry die."

"Diane doesn't want me to call Cheryl."

"So what you do?"

I didn't have an answer or a chance to think of one. My cell phone rang. The caller ID showed Katelyn.

"It's my daughter."

Qiao-Yun said, "I make more tea."

She walked behind the kitchen counter. I talked to Katelyn who sounded awful and said Gareth told her everything. My phone felt like it weighed ten pounds. Katelyn talked about Jerry's love for our family, and I said he touched many people. Qiao-Yun headed down the hallway. I heard the bathroom door close. I asked Katelyn about her doctor's appointment. She said all went well. She said Luke called. His flight arrives in Boston tomorrow night. He emailed me the details. She and Gareth will drive up Thursday for the wake and stay until Sunday or longer. They plan to arrive after lunch. Katelyn asked about me, was I with Qiao-Yun. I said she cooked me a delicious dinner. Could she speak to Qiao-Yun, Katelyn asked. A week ago I couldn't admit Qiao-Yun existed. I heard the bathroom door open and Qiao-Yun's returning steps. I beckoned her towards me and pantomimed Katelyn's request. Qiao-Yun nodded. I said Qiao-Yun was right here and handed her the phone. Qiao-Yun said, "Hello," and I watched her face while Katelyn spoke.

Despite everything Gareth told me, I could imagine Katelyn telling Qiao-Yun to stay the hell away from her father; he didn't need some scheming foreigner screwing up his fragile mind any more than it already was. Qiao-Yun didn't look wary when she took the phone. Her expression remained fixed while Katelyn spoke. Qiao-Yun said, "Yes."

Katelyn said something. Qiao-Yun said, "Thank you." Katelyn spoke again. Qiao-Yun said, "You're welcome."

Qiao-Yun looked at me. "Family very important to your father."

Qiao-Yun listened some more. She said, "His name Keung." She listened again. She said "Yes" twice and "Thank you" once again. Katelyn said something. Qiao-Yun answered "Yes" a third time and handed the phone back to me.

The first thing Katelyn said was she thought it good Qiao-Yun was with me. "Aunt Fran called. We made plans, and we want Qiao-Yun to be part of them."

According to Katelyn and Fran by seven o'clock Thursday night the wake would be over and everyone would be hungry. Gareth and Katelyn wanted to take the family to one of Scrooby's best restaurants. Qiao-Yun will come. Fran and Katelyn foresaw some of the church women preparing a lunch after the funeral. Fran will call the church tomorrow. Katelyn and Fran will help. Qiao-Yun said she will too. Saturday night Dom is cooking for everybody. Qiao-Yun is bringing Keung.

"So, Daddy, don't worry about food." My daughter could barely finish her sentence.

Katelyn coughed and reminded me to check my email for Luke's arrival time. She would see me Thursday afternoon and call tomorrow. I should call her if I needed anything. I closed my phone and set it on the table.

"Katelyn," Qiao-Yun said, "she sound very nice."

"She is."

Qiao-Yun's two hands reached for mine. "Come," she said. "You look tired."

Fatigue had been my general condition since morning. Aches and numbness compounded as I plodded up the creaking stairs. Qiao-Yun turned on the overhead light. Its dim wattage outlined a layout like my second floor: a short corridor with a room on both sides with a bathroom between them. I glimpsed two large paintings veiled in shade. One looked like a watercolor of a rooster. The other featured all kinds of birds flocking toward a much bigger, pheasant-like creature. Exhaustion blurred the other details. We turned right.

The hall light faintly spread into the dark bedroom. Qiao-Yun undressed. I watched. Naked, she undid the buttons on my shirt and stroked my chest. Her hands pushed the sleeves down my arms. The shirt dropped to the floor. She undid my belt and the button of my pants, and she pulled the zipper. The pants descended. Her fingers slipped inside my boxers. She stretched the elastic waist. The boxers fell. I lifted each foot from the clothes gathered at my ankles and moved my hands to her back. As her arms enfolded me, I drew her tight against me. We kissed. Qiao-Yun walked to the hall light switch and shut it off. She returned to the bed. She peeled back the covers and lowered herself between the sheets. I crawled in next to her.

CHAPTER 20

For breakfast Qiao-Yun prepared a plate of six steamed buns she called *baozhih*, each about the size of an orange. Her coffee was excellent. We listed our plans for the day. I wanted to see Anita in the morning and meet Olivia and Diane in the afternoon. Diane, I assumed, would have Janice Patterson join us to complete the funeral's music preparations. Qiao-Yun volunteered to help after her two morning classes. It was the closest we came to talking about Jerry.

I broke open my first *baozhih* and smelled its sweet aroma. Qiao-Yun cautioned that the filling needed to cool a little, and then she asked a question no one ever asked me before.

"Stephen, what you think about most the time?"

My lifelong habit was to answer odd questions with a joke. Years ago a history teacher whose comprehension of social justice came from Ayn Rand declared I was "a closed-minded, collectivist." He challenged me to name a prominent conservative I respected. "Sure," I said, "Clint Eastwood. *Million Dollar Baby* is wonderful."

"I understand family and friends," Qiao-Yun said. "You think about them a lot, I know. But what other thing?"

I had no joke. "Probably my career as a teacher."

Qiao-Yun asked what I remembered the most.

"Being fired as the English Department coordinator."

Qiao-Yun wasn't sure whether a coordinator and department chairman were the same. I explained they were.

"How you lose your job? Why they do this to you?"

"It's a long story."

Qiao-Yun glanced at the kitchen clock. "In forty-five minute I leave for my class."

If I had ever put this story behind me, memories might have withered, but of course this wasn't the case.

"There was this guy who taught English a few doors down from me. His name was Bob."

By the story's end, I had emptied my large coffee mug and finished two more *baozhihs*. Qiao-Yun understood everything. Not every teacher would. She had been an athlete, a fierce competitor, a coach, and a classroom teacher. She could fill my garage with her medals and trophies, yet she saw the Enlightenment for the sham it was.

I told her about my forgiving Bob but having to do it again every day. She knew what that was like. I waited for her explanation about why she had launched this conversation in the first place. It didn't come.

We both saw the clock. If she wanted to get to class on time, she would have to leave right away. I had a full day ahead but no clear sense of why she brought up this subject. I remembered her saying Friday night she wasn't sure whether she would stay in the United States. The possibility of her leaving sounded remote then. After all, coming to America, getting Keung through public school and into college, and the two of them becoming U.S. citizens was a great story. Put that together with the wicked Taiwanese mother-in-law, and Qiao-Yun had plenty of reasons for remaining in Scrooby. But there was more on the other side: she was an associate professor and an internationally recognized champion and coach. Of course her old department head wanted her back. If I had his job, I'd want her back too.

While I brushed my teeth in the first-floor bathroom and she used the one upstairs, I told myself not to worry. Last night was special. In fact, every moment we had spent together was special. I spat out my toothpaste. *Special!* What a candy ass word. I wiped my mouth and jolted to the second floor. Too much had happened in my life without my being able to do anything about it. Not this time. Qiao-Yun met me in the hallway. She must have thought something horrible happened. I caught my breath.

"I have something to tell you."

I took both her hands in mine and looked into those eyes.

"I love you, Qiao-Yun." I pulled her close. Her cheek pressed against my chest.

Time stopped.

She spoke without moving. "I love you too, Stephen."

Qiao-Yun lifted her face. She was crying.

Whenever I brought Communion to Anita, it took a while to find a parking space at the Bay View Nursing Home. Most visitors arrived late morning or after lunch. The doctors got the few reserved spots. The incoming day staff hustled to get the residents up and dressed. I learned the routine when my mother was in a nursing home. Getting to the Bay View a little after nine pushed things a bit. I had good reason. This visit with Anita might take more time than the others, and I had household chores to finish before lunch. But if I got there too early she might not be dressed or the cleanup crew would be shuffling in and out of her room while I stood around on a wet floor. I had two hopes: one was the nursing home had an efficient staff, and the other was Anita didn't need much assistance. Plenty of parking spaces rewarded my early arrival, and my hopes rang true. Ready for her day, Anita sat in her wheelchair, her back to me, her silver hair perfectly brushed in place. The curtain was drawn around Esther's bed.

Anita had a visitor. One look at Charlie Prendergast told me he and Anita were talking about Jerry.

"Stephen, I'm so sorry," he said.

Anita spun her chair around, her face pale and drawn. I placed the Communion kit on the bed and put my hands on her shoulders. "This is a terrible loss," she said. She praised Jerry's kind heart, even though she barely knew him.

Charlie explained that he and Anita had been neighbors long ago. Diane had asked him to visit Anita when she called with the news about Jerry, thinking it would be easier for me if Anita knew before I visited her. If Diane's schedule weren't so full, she'd do it herself. Whatever Charlie told Anita, it was more than I would have expected. I kissed her cheek and turned to Charlie. We hugged. We had never done that before.

I opened the Communion kit and invited Charlie to stay. He had to go. Diane wanted to meet with him at nine-thirty. He looked at his watch.

"It's funny," he said. "On Sunday Diane asked me to meet with her this morning. I have no idea what it's about. She didn't explain, except to say that it's important."

I broke eye contact. Charlie noticed. "Do you know what's going on?"

"It's best Diane told you."

He started toward the door and stopped. He turned back. "Stephen, if I can—I mean, the funeral or anything else. Please let me know."

I was grateful for his offer and told him so. Charlie left. I pulled a chair alongside Anita and opened the Communion kit. She said, "You looked a little surprised to find Charlie here."

"How often does he come?"

"Every now and then. Twenty years ago we lived in the same neighborhood. His family grew. His job got better. They moved to their current house. It's much bigger than the two-bedroom ranches where we lived."

I came less prepared than usual. In the past I brought the service leaflet for the previous Sunday. Today I used my backup photocopy of three brief Gospel choices in the Book of Common Prayer. After I set out the two wafers, I opened the vials of water and wine and poured a little of each into the miniature chalice. With little thought, I chose a verse from John. We read it together.

Jesus said, "Abide in me, as I in you. As the branch cannot bear fruit by itself, unless it abides in the vine, neither can you, unless you abide in me. I am the vine, you are the branches... "

I didn't ask Anita what she thought of this verse, and she offered nothing. We just kept going as though we had agreed to let the sacrament stand by itself because any talk of the words' relevance to the immediate here-and-now would lead to only one place.

So neither of us mentioned Jerry. Instead, when we finished our service, Anita asked about Charlie. "Are you two friends?"

"We both care about St. Joseph's."

Anita leaned forward in her chair. "I know what you're saying. It takes a while to know Charlie."

According to Anita her husband Frank never got their neighbor to say more than a few words. One spring Charlie bought a snow blower on sale. The following winter five northeasters battered the Massachusetts coast. When it came to snow removal, Frank was like I used to be. The first storm left eighteen inches. When it stopped, Frank grabbed his shovel. After twenty hard minutes, he cleared only his front steps. Next door, Charlie—barely visible behind a massive white plume—uncovered his entire driveway. Frank, exhausted, sat in his kitchen taking a break and heard the blaring machine draw closer. He went to the window, and there was Charlie and his snow blower doing what would have taken Frank all day to do, even with Anita's help. Frank dashed outside to thank him. Charlie hollered over the engine's racket that he was just having fun with his new toy. The subsequent storms that year also brought Charlie and his snow blower. Six months later Charlie put his house on the market. He said his new home had a half-acre of lawn and an eighty-foot driveway. He bought a lawn tractor with a snow blower attachment. Charlie said Frank could have his old snow blower for fifty dollars. Though used, it was worth about eight times more.

An aide stuck her head through Anita's doorway and asked if she would be going to the dayroom for breakfast. Anita rarely ate from a tray in her room. She said she'd be along shortly.

"Now tell me about that romance of yours."

"I took your advice about telling my family. They're happy for me."

Anita said she had been praying for just that. On my way out I wheeled her to breakfast. We had two corridors to travel filled with caregivers and cleaning staff and other residents in wheelchairs. We didn't try to talk over the commotion except for Anita's saying hello to everyone by name as we passed through.

At the dayroom's entrance I stopped the chair and stepped in front of Anita to say goodbye with a promise to see her next week.

"There's something else you should know about Charlie," she said. I maneuvered the chair to the side so the others could get by. "Across the street from us lived a woman named Harriet McCutcheon. She sometimes went to St. Joseph's. After her divorce, she moved closer to downtown."

I knew only one Harriet at St. Joseph's. Anita made no attempt to connect the two. When Harriet McCutcheon divorced her husband, he got custody of their twelve-year old son. Anita said the boy was a "very sweet but lonely little guy; a lot of kids made fun of him." Harriet agreed to the settlement because that's what the boy wanted. She got the rest, the house and just about everything in it. The husband, Ernie, had a brother who owned a citrus farm in Florida. The brother wanted Ernie to work for him. Ernie jumped at the offer. The brother sent Ernie money to help him make the move. Ernie needed more. Charlie lent it to him.

Driving home, I pictured Charlie sitting across from Diane and reassuring her. At the last vestry meeting he supported same-sex marriages. Then I thought about Qiao-Yun and the two Chinese art works hanging in her upstairs hallway.

This morning I had showered and dressed first. The pictures caught my attention while Qiao-Yun showered. One was a watercolor. The other was finely stitched embroidery. Each took up a lot of space. Broad, sparse strokes defined the watercolor. They made a rooster and hen, both white and gray with a touch of red. A bunch of black blotches shaped like chicks gathered by their feet among strands of green grass. The embroidery's shapes came in multi-hued threads. These were birds too: sparrows, thrushes, herons, finches, ducks, and swallows. A radiant pheasant-like creature perched on a low branch, and roses bloomed around it. Chinese writing was stitched near the top. Next to the Chinese characters there was a square mark in red ink. While I studied the embroidery, Qiao-Yun entered the hall. She was wrapped in a towel.

"My father give me that one," she said.

"It's beautiful."

Qiao-Yun pointed to the center bird. "This is the phoenix. All other birds show courtesy to her." The writing stated this, she explained. She said Hunan is famous for its tapestries. Her father came from Hunan. A few years before his death, he returned home to get a tapestry for Qiao-Yun. "In Chinese culture," she said, "the dragon is good thing. The dragon is male. The phoenix is female. She dragon's mate. Both very spiritual."

"Tell me about the painting," I said.

It came from Taiwan. The inscription meant peaceful family. It too had square red stamps. She said Chinese artists don't sign their works. They use an inked chop, a small engraved block of wood. "Not just artists. Many peoples have their own chop. I have."

I asked her about the artist.

"He my painting teacher."

I was astonished she ever found time to take up watercolors.

Qiao-Yun's moist hair glistened, and she smelled like orchids. "It was after my surgery."

The operation was a hysterectomy. Twelve years ago she had uterine cancer.

Between the Bay View and my house I stopped at a supermarket and loaded a shopping cart with groceries and household items. Baskets of hanging flowers caught my eye on the way to the checkout counter. I bought two. My house needed color. The flowers' tags identified them as petunias and pansies. The house needed a good cleaning too, especially the upstairs bedrooms and bathroom. Guests were coming. As soon as I got home, I booted up the computer and read Luke's email. His plane landed at seven-thirty. With the outdoor plants watered and suspended from hooks outside the kitchen, I laid on fresh bedding upstairs and stocked the second bathroom with amenities and clean towels. I scrubbed up the place. Downstairs took less time. Beforehand, I ran the washing machine and midway through the chores tossed the clean laundry into the dryer. A plate of leftovers from Sunday's dinner became my microwaved lunch. When the dryer stopped, I folded and put away everything that didn't require pressing. I set up the ironing board and went through shirts and pants while eating lunch and watching the afternoon local news. With family traveling my way, I needed to know the weather forecast. No rain in sight. I hadn't finished cleaning up the yard. Out came the wheelbarrow and rake. Another half-hour made the front yard presentable.

My clothes needed changing. With that done I jumped into the VW and headed towards St. Joseph's where Olivia and Diane would join me in planning Jerry's funeral. I almost didn't make it because, like texting, there ought to be a law against mentally composing a eulogy while driving. I ran a stop sign and almost crashed into a moving van.

I didn't see Olivia's car in St. Joseph's parking lot. She'd be along soon enough, and I had a little time before our meeting began. Diane's office door was open. Her soft, telephone voice faintly carried into the outer office. Alice sat at her computer typing Sunday's order of worship. Diane appeared in the doorframe.

"I just got off the phone with Janice. She won't be joining our meeting this afternoon. In fact, she won't be playing organ at Jerry's funeral."

Everyone knew Janice and Jerry resented each other, and I knew she was every inch as self-absorbed as Jerry said she was. Still, it surprised me she couldn't suspend all that for a parishioner's funeral.

"Did she give a reason?"

"Yeah, a load of nonsense sprinkled with words like 'inappropriate.' She won't be at choir rehearsal or Sunday's services or any other services. She quit."

Alice gasped. Diane drew a wry smile. "Perhaps I should have been more tactful after she blew off Jerry's funeral."

An essential quality of an excellent priest is balls. Janice didn't phone just to boycott Jerry's funeral, not directly anyway. She wanted a deal or at least the promise of one. She thought she had something to trade. If she could be trusted to rehearse the choir and play the organ for the funeral of a man—"with all due respect for the departed," Diane quoted—who disdained her music choices and had caused her great personal stress, she should be trusted to carry on her duties as music director without the Music Committee's intrigues and humiliating insinuations. Janice figured that we couldn't get a decent substitute in time; meanwhile, if necessary, she and her allies could always project her departure as the product of the senior warden and rector's skullduggery. In other words, Janice was stupid. No one pushes the Reverend Diane Fleming around.

But getting a substitute right away wouldn't be easy. We had a parishioner, Willard Willoughby, who fancied himself an organist. He wasn't a professional musician. Jerry had a code name for him, "Willard Solid B," because Willard always hit the right notes of any composition eighty-five percent of the time. He drove people nuts. Four years had passed since Willard last filled in for Janice, whose infrequent, scheduled absences allowed Diane ample time to put together a replacement ensemble of musicians whom Jerry often led with his guitar.

Diane said she would make some calls and turned towards her office.

I saw Olivia's car pull into the parking lot and felt confident that somehow we could cobble together enough singers and musicians for the service. Olivia or Diane would think of something. The assumption that Janice would prepare that part of the funeral service was brainless anyway. Her exit was addition through subtraction, the phrase Olivia spoke when I filled her in. We decided to forget the music question and focus on the words: who would say what and when?

I told Alice we would be in the conference room. There was a white board there. We would start pouring over the Book of Common Prayer and post ideas. Alice reached into her desk drawer and pulled out two yellow legal pads, two pens, and an unopened box of markers. She had put them aside just for us. In the conference room there were Bibles and prayer books, hymnals too. She said Diane would join us shortly. Alice told us to get a move on as though we'd be late for our school bus. I picked up the writing supplies.

"One more thing before we start," I said, "a question maybe one of you could answer for me. It's about Harriet Pringle."

Curiosity lit up both faces.

"When she first came here, did she have a different name."

Olivia spoke first. "She did. It was—"

Alice finished her sentence. "McCutcheon."

CHAPTER 21

During our short walk from the parish office to the conference room, I related the Charlie Prendergast stories Anita told me. As Olivia put it, "He'll be on the right side."

We were sitting at the table. I predicted we would know soon enough because Diane and Charlie met this morning. I barely finished when Diane walked in. She pulled out a chair and sat across from us.

"If you're keeping score, here's how it stands with the vestry. So far I've spoken to you two, Jo Garcia, Charlie, Fred Divol, Dwayne Parsons, and Jerry." Her saying Jerry's name made it sound like he was still in the mix. "Everyone was supportive. Late this afternoon I meet with Irene Covey and tonight with Paul Bellamy, then Harriet. Rachel comes tomorrow morning. I'm on pace to get to all members before the wake."

"Any predictions?" Olivia asked.

"We're okay" is all Diane said.

I asked whether Rachel and Harriet knew about her coming out. She didn't think so. The music program and same sex marriages were enough to set them off—with a bunch of tangential issues, real and imaginary, tossed in. Olivia thought so too but offered a broader explanation, citing a problem Diane and I had discussed many times before.

"People hate change, and for a lot of parishioners, St. Joseph's is their spiritual home. They want it predictable."

Diane called it "shelter from the storm."

I quoted Shakespeare's Caesar: "...as constant as the northern star."

We had other work. I reached for a prayer book and opened to the service called "The Burial of the Dead." Diane and Olivia opened to the same place. When it comes to baptizing a child or ordaining a priest, the Book of Common Prayer provides a single format and language. Communions and funerals are different. Our first decision was whether to use Rite I, which was written in a seventeenth-century English, or Rite II, which was written in contemporary language. Diane suggested Rite I for the funeral, which surprised me more than a little. Jerry would want a Communion included, but we put off choosing from the Rite I and four Rite II offerings. Next came selections of listed prayers and scriptural suggestions, and that created the toughest options, a process complicated by the freedom to insert any other verses. Diane said she had another meeting scheduled and asked Olivia and me to whittle down the possibilities. She recommended we delay any discussion of music.

We still had a lot to figure out. Diane offered one reassurance. "About the Committal, everything will be set for the columbarium on Saturday." She meant Jerry's ashes would be ready and his niche would be open.

"And there's something else, something the vestry needs to address pretty soon," Diane added. "The church needs a junior warden."

There was no sense in Diane being anything but blunt. Saturday an urn containing Jerry's ashes would get locked away while his parish workload persisted untended. We couldn't fulfill one responsibility and ignore the other. The parish by-laws gave the vestry the power to appoint his replacement until the next annual meeting.

"Bill Forsythe will be here shortly. We talked last night, and I asked him to become junior warden. I'll get his answer today. If he says yes, the vestry will have a brief special meeting after Sunday's service."

"That's only four days away," Olivia said. "I doubt anyone on the vestry knows him."

I first met Bill and his wife Jen at the Epiphany dinner in January. Later during Qiao-Yun's trip to Taiwan, we chatted once over Sunday coffee. He spoke mostly about his daughter Becky and her talent for drawing and painting. He seemed like a nice guy. Apparently Diane thought he was capable. St. Joseph's buildings and grounds would make any homeowner tremble. Maintenance problems lurked all over the place. Only a fool would want to be junior warden. Fortunately, savvy priests like Diane cultivate fools. From personal experience, Olivia understood that much. The problem was choosing someone who had only been a member less than half a year.

Diane had her reasons. Bill and Jen had been taking Confirmation classes with her. They were very serious. They liked St. Joseph's and the Episcopal Church. Bill was an architect. He knew how to construct buildings and what makes them fall apart. If he took the job and someone complained, that person could run against him next February—that is, if Bill chose to run, and he need not commit to that.

"As for a vote Sunday, why wait? Bill would be a good fit."

Since Bill took Diane's Confirmation class, she knew his soul as well as she knew ours. St. Joseph's had mentors who prepared teenagers for Confirmation in weekly meetings over several months. The rector met with the mentors and confirmands at the outset and near the end. Confirmation concluded with a special service. A bishop came and with a laying on of hands formally did the deed. When adults sought Confirmation—which, by the way, is a process leading to a deeper sense of faith—Diane took them on. Her goal wasn't about the individual's attaining worthiness for a sacred ritual; rather, the issue was whether the individual could confirm the church's worthiness—and which version of the church.

"When I asked Bill to take on this job, I explained the sexuality issues. He knows everything."

We needed no further definition of what "good fit" meant.

"One more thing," Diane said.

I noticed she had her key ring with her. She picked from its collection what I recognized as St. Joseph's master key, the same as mine. She handed us hymnals and took one for herself.

"I want you to hear something."

Diane beckoned us to follow her out into the corridor and the sanctuary's side door. She unlocked it. We entered the vaulted gray darkness. Diane bowed to the altar and spun around. She wanted lights and disappeared down the chancel's steps toward the panel box in the side foyer. I heard two loud clicks. The chancel's overheads snapped on. Wedged between the pulpit and the electric keyboard, the sound system's console came alive in rows of red and green lights. Diane darted up the steps. She squatted in front of the console and pressed three buttons. The electric keyboard stretched atop an x-shaped stand. Diane slid into the metal chair behind it.

"I'm not very good at this," she said.

I didn't know she could play at all. Her hands pressed three quick chords. She looked up. "I told you to put off any thoughts about Jerry's music until we know about an organist. But even if I have to play the tune myself, the congregation has to sing *Teach Me, My God and King*. Listen.

It was a simple tune, just eight bars, and familiar the way hymns often are. Diane played without missing a note and in perfect time, her eyes never leaving her fingers until she finished.

She placed her hands in her lap and lifted her head.

"A few months ago Jerry and I were talking about church music. He mentioned *Teach Me, My God and King*. The lyricist, an English poet, was someone he had been reading."

200

Diane told us to find page five hundred ninety-two. Olivia and I flipped through the numbers. Composers' names are listed under each hymn. That's where I looked first.

Words: George Herbert (1593-1633)

The title would have tipped off a better scholar. It's the opening words of a George Herbert poem, "The Elixir":

Teach me, my God and King
In all things thee to see,
And what I do in anything,
I do for thee.

"It's been one of my favorites since I was a teenager," Diane said. "Let's sing it."

While Diane focused on her playing, Olivia and I sang feebly. By the second verse Olivia got stronger. I barely made a sound. When we finished, Olivia said we should definitely include *Teach Me, My God and King.*

If I didn't get out of the sanctuary right away, I risked falling apart worse than yesterday's meltdown. Olivia saw it coming. She said we should get back to the conference room. Diane told us she would shut off everything and lock up. I headed towards the doorway. Olivia stayed behind.

My rubbery legs got me back to the conference room. I dropped into the nearest chair and turned to the hymnal's index of authors. Four other hymns featured George's poetry. I should have known that. I bet Jerry did. Minutes passed. I heard the jangle of Diane's turning keys. She hurried towards the office without stopping to apologize for setting me up, not that I expected it.

Olivia delayed her return. The two women probably made a quick pact. One would give me solitude while the other met with Bill Forsythe. Maybe Diane had a chance to tell Olivia about my trying to write a George Herbert book. Maybe I had told her months ago. I couldn't remember. Some people knew. Only Diane, I thought, was familiar with George's work or cared that I used to teach some of it. My writing the book was her idea. Seventeenth-century English poetry wasn't something Jerry studied. But he read George Herbert. I should have known. Olivia came in and sat next to me. She spoke softly: "Shall we get back to work?"

"In a few minutes."

I asked whether this morning's paper had anything about Jerry. Olivia had read a two-paragraph story. It listed only the who, what, where, when, and how—no why, mercifully no blood-alcohol report. The death notice said less. She asked what I knew.

I said a woman Jerry met a long time ago phoned him. This woman knew Harriet and what she was planning. "Jerry went to see her. Before he left, he called me. On the way he had the accident."

If I had been hooked up to a polygraph, the damn thing would have exploded.

"He sounded good, Liv, sober. It was shit luck, a freak thing."

"What else, Stephen?"

"That's all I know. He said he was in a hurry."

"How did she know Jerry?"

"All he said was they met a long time ago."

If Diane had her way, I'd realize Cheryl would never give me all the facts and the truth had little to do with them anyway. That was the theme of her *Teach Me, My God and King* exercise.

"When you find out more, Stephen, you will tell me." Olivia wasn't making a request.

"I promise, Liv."

We needed a change in topic.

"Do you know anything about Chinese art?" I asked.

Olivia rolled her eyes. "No, but I suspect you do."

"Qiao-Yun has Chinese art all over her house."

Olivia listened carefully as I described the watercolor and the tapestry. "They sound beautiful," she said.

"She brought them here from Taiwan. That's a long way. They must be very important to her."

I told Olivia about our dates and dinners and our natural ease with each other. From Jo Garcia she had learned about Qiao-Yun's Tai Chi classes and her martial arts reputation. She also heard Qiao-Yun's son was a college student. I said nothing else about the paintings, their sources—a Taiwanese artist who taught her while she fought the scariest of diseases and her father whose iconic tapestry came from China—and their themes of family and loyalty. I left out my suspicion that the college teaching job still had a hold on her. Instead, I labeled everything as a love story in full bloom and summarized last night's phone call from Katelyn.

Three hours later I was driving through the Ted Williams Tunnel under Boston Harbor. Ahead came Logan Airport and my son Luke. The airport exit brought a series of signs itemizing which airlines used which terminals. Some people glean data rapidly. I've never been one of them, a fact Luke figured out the first time I helped him with this homework and he realized his old man, unlike his mother and sister, read the same way he did. Yesterday's email listed Luke's airline, flight number, landing time, and, for my special benefit, identified the terminal. With "Terminal C" in my memory's front row, I exited the tunnel with my concentration set on bypassing "A" and "B" and remembering the difference between "Arrivals" and "Departures"— the first task suspenseful but not complicated, the second tangled in too much thinking until common sense took over.

Prior to that my mind danced to earlier matters settled back at St. Joseph's. We had solved the music problem. Or to be more exact, Bill Forsythe did. He knew a guy, his wife's brother, Nate, who had just finished a Master's program at the New England Conservatory. Nate loved conducting choral music, and a church choir would do just fine. He held two part-time jobs teaching piano and voice in local music schools. For extra cash he played in a jazz combo, getting occasional gigs in clubs ranging from southern New Hampshire to Rhode Island. Nate could play any keyboard instrument, including big old church organs. He was coming to St. Joseph's ready to rehearse and lead the choir for Jerry's funeral. He would sing with his band.

The Nate acquisition came in two stages constructed in Diane's office while two doors down Olivia and I worked on the funeral. First, after Bill agreed to become junior warden, Diane explained the blow-up with Janice and the need for an interim music director, and Bill recommended his brother-in-law. Bill had helped Nate write his résumé. He ran to his car and came back with a laptop containing the file. With that and very little discussion, Diane asked Bill to call Nate immediately, which he did. Once Bill explained the situation, he handed the phone to Diane. This conversation became the second stage, and Nate, a twenty-four year-old choral director needing no persuasion, jumped to lead the music for the funeral and the scheduled weekend services.

Meanwhile back in the conference room, Olivia and I carried on. We chose Rite I for the funeral. The custom in Episcopal services calls for two readings from the Old Testament, one a psalm, and two selections from the New Testament. The Burial of the Dead service lists suggestions. Reading and choosing these passages took up the most time. We liked Psalm 121, a passage from Isaiah, one from Revelation, and another from John. Olivia offered to do the Isaiah reading. The priest always reads the Gospel. We needed two more volunteers, someone to lead a responsive reading of the psalm and another to read from Revelation. We didn't know who. To make sure the service didn't drag, we chose the most succinct Rite II Eucharist. All the prayer options for the Committal we left to Diane. The eulogy belonged to me. Diane would give a homily. For music at this point, all we had was *Teach Me, My Lord and King* and probably a song Luke would perform.

After their meeting, Bill and Diane came to the conference room. That was when Olivia and I heard about Nate. Diane said Fred Divol had phoned. He was a trustee for the Old Colony Festival Chorus. He offered to call O.C.F.C. members. Nate needed rehearsal time Friday. Fred promised singers. Alice joined us and started taking notes. Qiao-Yun came in right behind her. Alice offered to read the passage from Revelation. I asked Qiao-Yun to lead the responsive reading of Psalm 121. She feared her accent disqualified her. I handed her a prayer book. We practiced a run-through together. Everyone said she did fine.

At Logan Airport the best place to meet a passenger is the luggage carousels. After parking the car and traversing to Terminal C and taking the elevator four stops down, I found the main floor with its check-in lines, stores and eateries, and the TV screens detailing flights. Luke's plane was on time. I hurried down the stairs and found Carousel 2. When its jolt to action signaled the plane had emptied, I hunched over the belt and watched the open shoot about to disgorge tumbling suitcases. Behind me footsteps and shuffles announced the disembarked travelers. I shifted my attention to the tops of heads and the figures beyond. A tall, disheveled young man stood with one hand attached to a guitar case and the other pressed against his ear. My cell phone rang. The carousel chugged on. I edged and squeezed my way back through the advancing crowd. Luke set his guitar case on the floor and opened his arms.

I found my way out of the airport, never an easy task, and drove under the sea and city to reunite with Route 3. Familiar with my multi-tasking limitations, Luke said little until we cleared Logan. His flight was uneventful. He slept through most of it and landed hungry. Everything Katelyn resolved last night he already knew. He looked forward to the family dinners later this week and to meeting Qiao-Yun and Keung. He asked me to run through the schedule.

"The wake will be tomorrow from four to seven at St. Joseph's. Friday the body will be cremated. The funeral is Saturday morning at eleven."

Luke adjusted his seat. After six hours in economy class, his long legs needed a stretch. I told him about the afternoon's planning session, saving Nate's story for the end. Luke thought having a jazz combo a great idea. I asked him if he knew the old gospel tune *Just a Closer Walk with Thee*. He asked me to hum it. He recognized it right away.

I said it's one of those tunes you might hear at a New Orleans funeral procession. They start off really mournful and then the band rips loose, swinging into something joyous. Luke said he could imagine how *Just a Closer Walk* could work that way. Diane suggested it.

Luke asked me about the rehearsal Friday. I said Nate would work with the choir Friday morning. His band will show up after lunch. The number of musicians varied with each gig. Sometimes it was a sestet, sometimes a smaller group. Sometimes Nate played and sang alone. It all depended on who was available. This time the band would have Nate on piano and vocals, a drummer, bassist, and guys on trombone, trumpet, and clarinet. Diane told Nate she knew an excellent guitarist. Whether he played with the band or did his own thing or both could be decided Friday. Nate said he and his buddies will jam with anyone, though they prefer excellence.

"I'd like to go to that rehearsal," Luke said. "He sounds like my kind of musician.

"You can have the car. I just need it in the morning, a Tai Chi class."

Bill Forsythe had written Nate's number down for me. I handed the paper to Luke. Boston's skyline diminished behind us

"Where would you like to eat?" I asked. "There's a good place not far from here."

"I'm up for anything," Luke said.

The next exit went to Quincy. I put on my blinker and headed for the China Sea.

CHAPTER 22

Thursday started with my drive to Tai Chi class. Sometime after noon, Katelyn and Gareth would arrive. During last night's dinner Luke asked why the wake was at St. Joseph's. According to Diane, Scrooby's funeral homes were booked. Luke asked about the casket. Would it be open? I didn't know. Diane had made all the arrangements with Douglas's. Sometime today I had to call her anyway. I had to call Fran too. I didn't want anyone with Jerry's full story accidentally launching gossip. Conversations during the wake might lead to just that. I also decided to keep Katelyn, Gareth, and Luke in the dark a while longer. Luke asked about Qiao-Yun. He hoped to meet her before the wake. She was a step ahead of him. Before I left St. Joseph's for the airport, Qiao-Yun said she would arrive at my house Thursday afternoon and serve tea.

Before I went to bed, I called her. She told me she was bringing everything—pots and cups and Chinese cakes too. She liked hearing that Luke was looking forward to meeting her. She encouraged me to come to her class today and tomorrow.

I parked in the same place behind Qiao-Yun's school. As I entered, two women came right behind me. One I recognized from Saturday's class. We didn't have any time for gabby hellos and introductions because Qiao-Yun started her CD of Asian music. I yanked off my jacket and footwear and lined up with the others ready to follow the warm-up exercises. Altogether, nine of us faced our sifu. Six attended my previous class. Jo Garcia wasn't among them. Her rotating schedule kept her at the dispatcher's desk. Despite some erratic sleep, I felt more relaxed and found the warm-ups easier than the last time. Buying a circled crane t-shirt at the end of Saturday's class made me feel less conspicuous.

Once the joint-loosening and muscle-stretching exercises ended, Qiao-Yun had us do something she called Bear Spine. She stood with her feet shoulder-width apart and her knees slightly bent. With her shoulders slightly hunched forward and her arms bowed as though she were about to lift a barrel, she slowly turned her torso first to one side and then the other—or so it looked to me.

"Shift!" she commanded.

I stuck out my rear end.

"Stand up straight."

I tucked in my butt and stood at attention with my arms angled out like tent lines.

"Shift!" Qiao-Yun commanded again. Her voice sweetened. "Relax. Breath in...Turn."

I glimpsed the seasoned students. They really shifted their weight. The leg bearing the heaviest load showed a pronounced bend, while the other crooked slightly. They kept their knees slightly flexed, the first point Jo taught me. I made the correction. The breathing in came as the weight shifted. I followed along. With our lungs full we slowly exhaled in synch with turn.

"Stephen, shift more."

I thought my shifts were pretty good, but apparently Qiao-Yun thought them little more than dainty hip checks. "Use your legs more. Make your hands separate and in front."

Qiao-Yun stopped singling me out and said nothing for another five turns. If I were hopeless, she didn't say so.

We weren't done. Qiao-Yun said, "Bear Spine with Cloudy Hands," and her body transformed to a much more complicated version of what we were doing. The lower body's motion stayed the same.

The handwork was something else, a bedazzlement. She never missed a beat in the transition, and from what I could see the others in the class kept up just fine. To me everyone looked like haunted house explorers making their way through endless cobwebs. Class members extended their hands to one side, easy enough, but what came next wasn't. That's when the cobweb action got going, hands floating off in front of the face in sweeping curlicues that somehow ended with the hands on the body's opposite side ready for more. Meantime, the weight shifting continued in its unchanged rhythm. As inept as I felt copying the others, this motion wasn't entirely foreign to me. Jo Garcia had mentioned Cloudy Hands when she said every Tai Chi step has a name, and Qiao-Yun called out all the names when the class practiced the full form on Saturday. I had done this move in my klutzy imitations last time. It had footwork then; but this Cloudy Hands didn't, and that made it friendlier, even though I was getting none of it right, mainly because my hands weren't placed correctly from the outset. This I discovered when Qiao-Yun walked up to me and began making adjustments. She grabbed my wrists.

After twice calling "shift-breathe-in-Cloudy-Hands-breathe-out" in soft cadence, her grip guided my hands. She whispered, "Hold the ball," and that made all the sense in the world because it was one of the basics Jo taught me Saturday. To hold the imaginary ball to one side means the lower arm must stretch across the midsection and the ball rests on that hand. The hand on the same side as the ball controls the top. Reverse the hands' position, as I had been doing, and nothing good will follow. Get them right, and all else comes into play nicely, not at first—Qiao-Yun had to manipulate my gestures as she told me what to do—but the hands did find fluidity and merge it with the lower body's ever shifting balance. Qiao-Yun returned to her place, and I fell into my classmates' rhythm. From my ball-holding position the arms made a scissors action as the weight shifted and the lungs filled. My body turned, and my hands rolled the wrists so that when the turn ended the hands again held the ball on the opposite side while my breath slowly released. My hands ended up where they should be, each properly holding the invisible sphere, ready to flow again with a new weight shift back to the previous pose, and thus it went, back and forth: shift...breathe in...Cloudy Hands...breathe out...shift...breathe in...Cloudy Hands...breathe out...

Qiao-Yun said, "Ending." Her body faced center, her weight even on each foot. Her arms gracefully swung outward and then closed in front. She crossed her wrists. "Crossing Hands," she called it. Her weight shifted so she could slide one foot against the other; her heels came together with toes apart. I recognized this move. It was how she ended the Thirty-Seven Steps. Her hands folded inward and then down the sides of each leg. We all followed her lead. The warm-ups were done.

Qiao-Yun divided the class into three groups, each having a third of the whole form to practice. Students made their choices, and the nine became two doing Part One, three doing Part Two, and three doing Part Three. I didn't get a choice.

"Stephen, you with me," Qiao-Yun said.

We took a corner away from the others and the mirror, and Qiao-Yun assumed the first stance. She stood at attention with her heels together and toes apart. "Good," she said when I faced her and held the same position. She wanted to review Introductory Breathing and Qi Ball Hands. Even though five days had passed since Jo drilled me on these opening moves, I did okay and breathed correctly during the arm movements in Introductory Breathing. I kept my knees bent.

Now I was ready for the next step, Four Actions. Qiao-Yun told me to stand still while she demonstrated. She held the Qi Ball Hands position and then brought her weight forward. Her hands moved to hold the imaginary ball in front of her. With her weight on her left foot, she swung her right leg and maneuvered into a second Qi Ball Hands at a ninety-degree angle from the first, except this time she didn't stop. The feet stayed in place while the upper body, especially the arms and hands, pushed back and forth like someone doing vertical push-ups against thin air. At least that's how it appeared to me. Like all Tai Chi moves, Four Actions is loaded with subtleties. She demonstrated it again, this time narrating every move. I saw a little more. Her second Qi Ball Hands swept into the next phase without a pause. Her weight shifted to the forward foot. Her right hand extended forward with her arm angled to the right. She placed her left hand under the right elbow. She turned her torso leftward and the hands went with it. The left hand swung away from the right elbow and returned to find the right palm. She squared her posture towards the front. The left palm pushed the right forward. She separated them, pulled them back, and then she did the two-hand pumping move. I still missed more than I saw.

Practice followed observation. Bit by bit, Qiao-Yun put me through the whole thing—over and over. I went from doing none of it right to advancing through approximations of correctness, sometimes getting close to the real thing. It was all in the legs. What looked like elbow flexing wasn't. When the hands pushed forward, the legs took over and drove the back-and-forth motions. It isn't abstract choreography, a point I didn't quite get from Jo despite all her erudition about Qi and history. Qiao-Yun explained every movement as offensive or defensive thrusts and dodges. Her allusions to fighting, like the rhyme and meter in the epic poems European troubadours recited, framed the content. It's a mnemonic devise. I was becoming a constructivist learner of Tai Chi, which didn't happen until Qiao-Yun introduced imagination to my passionless copying. Four Actions means, first, you face whoever's coming at you and hold your ground; second, you grab the threat, take control, and pull him past you; third, push the next menace backward; and, fourth, re-coil, and push again, shoving some other villain out of the away. Qiao-Yun didn't explain it in those words, but what she did say gave me a better sense of how to move. It clicked for another reason too. Winning fights, even imaginary ones, had a very definite appeal.

Qiao-Yun had to check on her other students. I was to practice everything from Introductory Breathing through Four Actions for ten minutes. If I looked good when she returned, she'd teach me the next step, Single Whip. I went to work and immediately forgot the most essential point. I moved quickly and breathed fast. The martial arts analogy took over. It was macho pantomime, not Tai Chi. Qiao-Yun was talking to the group practicing Part One and didn't see my mistake. It was worse than a mistake. It was a stupid screw-up. I stopped and returned to basics. I slowed down. Introductory Breathing sets the metronome for the whole form. This time I completed a smooth Qi Ball Hands in one long breath. Four Actions had four breaths. I did it all again and again and again. Each repetition nestled me deeper into the pattern.

Qiao-Yun returned to our corner. She liked what I was doing. It was time for Single Whip. Qiao-Yun demonstrated. She said Single Whip comes up four times in the Thirty-Seven Steps, and it always follows a Four Actions. It had two obvious features. There was a straight-arm thrust while the fingers and thumb folded into a bird's beak, and the move ended with my facing the opposite direction from where Four Actions finished. It also had two weight shifts, a pivot, a pointed toe hold, and a long step while the other hand made a grand sweeping gesture that stopped with the palm faced out.

Qiao-Yun focused mostly on my balance and footwork. She left me alone to practice while she worked with the veterans. She wanted me to practice Single Whip and then put everything I knew into a continuous mini-form blending the progress made from Introductory Breathing through Four Actions with the newly learned mechanics of Single Whip. All I had to do was stay focused and practice.

I did two isolated Single Whips before returning to the beginning and splicing everything together. First I gave attention to the mechanics, but after the third repetition I focused on breathing, gradually reestablishing the continuity that grew with the additional move. A quasi muscle memory led the way. I was like an actor who frees himself from word recollection and conscious mannerisms. He lives within the dramatic moment. I was doing Stanislavsky Tai Chi. I liked it but still wasn't in the zone Jo predicted. I tried to imagine what the zone was like and couldn't come any closer than pretentious drivel rhapsodizing over Qi: a benevolent, immeasurable energy circulates throughout the body while slow breathing and precise graceful movements interweave and place cognition inside a cocoon of physicality from which the spirit emerges tranquil and supreme. I didn't achieve anything like this. I wanted it too much. Everything fell apart.

I started again. Get the mechanics right. Shift your weight. Keep your knees flexed. Be mindful of the wide stance. Move with intention. Don't approximate and don't improvise.

I didn't notice Qiao-Yun's return. "You do good, Stephen." I felt more than reassured.

If combinations of Qi Ball Hands, Four Actions, and Single Whip emerge four times in the form, I had learned twelve of the Thirty-Seven Steps. Linear thinking marked that a thirty-two percent advancement—a ridiculous notion, really. I hadn't mastered anything. When Qiao-Yun complimented my progress, she meant I was good enough for now. Any improvement required more time than the few minutes remaining.

Qiao-Yun led the class through the entire Thirty-Seven Steps. The form's first twenty seconds kindly granted me similarity with everyone else. Nothing like it followed. Even when my practiced steps reappeared, clumsiness shoved me into more blunders. Self-consciousness compounded the errors. Afterwards, as we put our shoes back on, the classmates who saw me Saturday claimed I showed much improvement. Apparently, a Tai Chi class was a good place to meet very nice, generous people.

Qiao-Yun had to drive across town for her class at Scrooby's senior center. We spoke briefly. She said my best work came when I blocked out distractions. She had to run. So did everyone else, but she seemed the most eager to move on. The place emptied.

My car pulled out after Qiao Yun's. We both headed north, and I followed for several miles. Her hasty exit bothered me. I wondered too about the Chinese tea ceremony she wanted to do with my family. Why do it, especially the first time she met them? The easiest answer was that she was Chinese, but this answer really wasn't so easy. My stop came first, the same florist I used last July. I told the woman behind the counter the time and place of Jerry's wake. She showed me what she had in the glass case and a book of sample layouts. I ordered the biggest and signed the card "The Pentheny Family."

On the way home, I called Diane and Fran. They agreed with me. Given Jerry's reputation, we could never shut down all talk he died a drunk driver, but we hoped the topic would go nowhere since his truck didn't hit another vehicle. I asked Diane about the casket during the wake. She said it would be open. I went along.

Last night Luke went to bed sometime after me. He was still on Pacific Time. Making my early breakfast, I brewed twice the usual coffee. When I returned, the pot was empty. It had been cleaned too. A familiar melody wafted from his room. Luke had plugged his guitar into the first amplifier we had given him, a little thing with less power than my stereo. Over and over he picked through *Just a Closer Walk with Thee*. With each repetition the tune got edgier. Then it writhed. Luke stretched and scraped it through contorted riffs. It screamed. He stopped in mid-phrase.

He paused and played again. Soft notes wanted to swing but couldn't.

I went upstairs.

The door was open. He stood in the room's shadows, his guitar suspended from the leather strap around his neck.

"I called Nate. He asked me to mess around with *A Closer Walk* and bring what I had to rehearsal tomorrow. How was Tai Chi?"

"It was okay. I heard you playing."

Luke lifted the strap over his head. He sat on the bed. His anguished face tilted up at me.

CHAPTER 23

Luke and I talked about what lay ahead—Katelyn and Gareth's arrival, tea with Qiao-Yun, the wake, and the funeral—mostly stuff we had discussed the night before. He wanted a schedule. Death's aftermath calls forth assignments. One was rehearsing with Nate.

Katelyn called from Route 95 in Connecticut. She and Gareth were stopping for lunch in Mystic. With luck they should arrive in Scrooby in two hours. Luke needed new strings and asked to borrow the VW. I handed him the keys and said he didn't have to hurry back.

I headed towards the basement and the elliptical stepper, but my mind turned to Diane and her way of seldom explaining herself completely to me. The Cheryl question hung in the air. Diane wanted me to forget the whole thing. We had been through this before. She predicted if Cheryl told me anything it would be a lie, at least in part. Diane had another reason too, the unstated one, and it had to do with Harriet. How could I ever forgive anyone connected to Jerry's crash, no matter how remote? It would be harder than forgiving myself, and I still hadn't done that. So what did I want? To build a case against Harriet so damning that Diane could badger a confession from her? And then, only then, after Harriet's public scorn, Diane would offer her the penitential rites of the Episcopal Church, which the hideous old bitch would refuse. She'd slither out of Scrooby, move in with Cheryl, and spend the rest of her miserable life driving her slutty relative crazy. As vengeful fantasies go, this seemed about right.

I turned on the TV in the basement and started a forty-minute regimen on the stepper. Commercials made me switch to the classic movie station. It showed a 1933 Tugboat Annie picture. I watched for about two minutes and switched to the news, hoping for a weather report. After the two anchors yakked happy gab, on came a typically curvaceous female meteorologist. She promised continued bright skies and mild temperatures through the weekend. I returned to Marie Dressler and Wallace Berry while the rest of my workout burned crap energy.

Luke hadn't returned. I imagined him getting a bite to eat or cruising around in his old man's car or strolling along the waterfront. The best time for me to clean up was now. I got all that done and checked my clothes for tonight. To fill up the time I reached for Gareth's manuscript. Before stretching out on the couch, I opened the living room windows for the first time this spring. I started reading a new chapter.

The poor and huddled immigrants traipsing down the gangplank at Ellis Island still had a long way to go. The American examiners who lined up to greet them saw strangers. They didn't like strangers. Strict criteria determined acceptance or rejection. Protocols superseded everything else. The newcomers needed documents showing someone here would take them in, and they needed to be sturdy enough to work and not be a public health risk. Using a buttonhook, a medical examiner, not always a doctor, lifted an immigrant's eyelids to check for trachoma and continued with the same instrument all day long. On Ellis Island common-sense hygiene remained an undeserved privilege. If a newcomer had trachoma or any other eye infection, there was a good chance the people next in line, maybe scores or hundreds, would catch it from the examiner's buttonhook. Records listed only the rejected. No one knows how many people Ellis Island infected.

I looked at my watch. Gareth and Katelyn would arrive soon. I made a bologna sandwich. Half way through it, I put my feet up on the couch again and returned to Gareth's pages. I often fell asleep with a book in my hands, regardless of whether the subject matter interested me, and this one did very much. Afternoon naps like this one began with semiconscious dreams, fleeting images with little relevance to what was read or to anything else, or so it seemed; and when I awoke they faded into memory's vapor. I stirred to sounds outside the house. A car pulled in—two cars, in fact. My family was home.

I was on my feet and in the driveway just as Katelyn opened the passenger door. Before this day ended, people would do a lot of hugging, much of it tearful. It started now. Luke spotted the Mini at a traffic light three miles from the house and followed it home. We four said little because we had too much to say and too few words. Gareth suggested we go into the house. He got the luggage. I led. Luke and Katelyn followed, each with an arm around the other's waist. When Katelyn walked in, she reenacted Luke's entrance from the night before. She stopped and turned her head to the right and then to the left and slowly spun a three-sixty, absorbing what is and remembering what was—few changes since her teenage years and nothing different from last July. Her longest gaze passed to the terraced garden where purple petals atop green stems had breached the soft earth.

Gareth clumped in carrying two suitcases. He put them down and started back out. Luke said he'd give him a hand. Gareth said he could get the rest, but Luke followed him out anyway.

Katelyn and I hadn't been alone since last September.

"In about a half-hour Qiao-Yun will be here," I said. "I hope you don't mind. She wanted to meet the family before the wake. I thought it a good idea."

Katelyn smiled. "It is a good idea."

"She's bringing tea, some cakes too or something."

Katelyn looked down at her tummy. "That's good. We're getting hungry."

Gareth reappeared carrying a black dress inside a clear plastic cover. Luke held a long garment bag. He closed the screen door behind him, leaving the other door open.

"I bet Gareth's suit is in better shape than mine," he said.

Luke's charcoal grey suit, having never left Scrooby, probably hung cockeyed in his old closet. Katelyn gave her brother the same frown Fran sometimes gave me. "Help Gareth get this upstairs, and I'll inspect your suit."

The two guys did as commanded. Katelyn turned towards me. "If he doesn't have a clean white shirt and a decent tie, he'll need to borrow them."

Katelyn crossed to the kitchen closet and grabbed the iron. "You get the ironing board," she said and walked towards the stairs. Like the two younger men, I did as told. We hadn't noticed that in Luke's shuffling to and from the Mini, he had brought in a shopping bag from the Beetle. As I set up the ironing board in his room, Luke sat on the bed pulling pins from a newly purchased dress shirt. Next to it was a necktie with a subdued dark print, the price tag not yet removed, and a new set of guitar strings. Katelyn plugged in the iron. I went downstairs while my guests changed clothes and spruced up. Overhead, busy footsteps and bathroom faucets evoked the last time such activity reverberated in this house. I shut my mind to it. Qiao-Yun would be here soon. I changed clothes.

I heard Qiao-Yun's car roll into the driveway at the same time Katelyn's light feet descended the stairs. I looked in the mirror and centered my tie. From the kitchen's screen door Qiao-Yun's voice sent an inquisitive "Hello." Katelyn greeted her. They talked. Most words I couldn't make out. Luke and Gareth bounded down the stairs. Qiao-Yun's voice rose as she carefully pronounced their names. Each ended with a difficult consonant sound. She got them right. The three Americans pronounced *Cheow-yune* perfectly. I heard Katelyn say "October." Soft chatter followed. I pulled on my jacket and delayed my entrance a few more seconds.

Everyone wore somber hues, the women in similar dresses: Qiao-Yun in dark grey, Katelyn in black. Luke's suit looked like mine. Gareth's had faint pinstripes.

Qiao-Yun had never seen me in a suit before. "You look nice, Stephen."

I stepped closer and gently pressed my lips against hers.

"So do you." I resisted turning around to see my daughter's face.

Qiao-Yun mentioned Katelyn's call Tuesday night. That got everyone talking about the upcoming dinners. Qiao-Yun said she looked forward to meeting Fran and Dom. Katelyn said she wanted to meet Keung.

Qiao-Yun asked Luke to give her a hand bringing in all the tea fixings she had loaded in her car. He followed her through the doorway with Gareth at his heels offering to help. Katelyn watched them go out.

"I like her," she said.

"What did you two talk about while I was in the bedroom?"

"Babies."

Luke returned carrying a cardboard box. Gareth carried a loaded tote bag. Qiao-Yun held the screen door for them. They set their parcels on the kitchen table, and we watched Qiao-Yun unpack. As soon as she brought a few cups to the dining table, Katelyn picked up the others and carried those over too. Together they transferred all of Qiao-Yun's tea ware except the food and the kettle. Qiao-Yun handed the kettle to me with a request to boil water. Gareth asked about the candles already on the table. Qiao-Yun said they should stay and asked Gareth to light them. Luke opened a counter drawer and handed Gareth a book of matches. We stepped away from the table and let Qiao-Yun take over.

Moving from the kitchen to the dining table, she set up the tea ceremony, using an assortment of cups and teapots, together with a porcelain bowl and a covered serving plate and a bunch of other things I couldn't identify. She transferred little cakes from a red tin decorated with gold dragons, and she sliced Asian pears. She had ten cups for five persons. None of the cups had handles. Five of them looked like elegant versions of typical cups in Chinese restaurants. The other five matched the first in finery, but they were slightly taller and narrower.

216

Qiao-Yun set out place mats of woven bamboo. She took the kettle from the stove and filled the first of her pots.

She handed Luke a CD and asked him to play it. We heard gentle strings and ethereal woodwinds. She played similar music during Tai Chi class. Qiao-Yun said she had forgotten something in her car. Watching her scurry out the door, I couldn't imagine what it could be, especially with all the paraphernalia she had already placed on the table. Katelyn, Gareth, and Luke's amused expressions turned quizzical because Qiao-Yun took longer than expected. When she re-entered, Katelyn's eyes widened, Gareth's too. Luke all but gulped. Qiao-Yun wore a knee-length Chinese robe over her dress. It radiated color. From ten feet away I could tell it was embroidered silk. The collar covered her neck. The stitched decorations reminded me of the tapestry her father had given her. Birds and plants in red, gold, and black threads embossed the bright green background. Five buttons made from intricately knotted fabric ends passed through tight loops. She asked us to sit down. Everyone's place had a carefully folded cloth napkin.

Qiao-Yun's implements and dress announced a formal event was unfolding. She would serve. We would receive. She poured hot water from the kettle to a pot and said, "*Wuhmen her chah.* It means 'We drink tea.'"

Katelyn and Gareth correctly repeated Qiao-Yun's Mandarin. Luke and I needed two tries. Using a long handled ladle Qiao-Yun scooped tealeaves into a second, smaller pot used for brewing. Into that pot she poured the hot water. She replaced the brewing pot's cover. Over a third pot used for serving, she placed a strainer before pouring the weak brew into it. Though I never expected microwaved mugs with tea bags, I hadn't anticipated a kettle and three pots before any tea made it to a cup.

"This tea from my country," Qiao-Yun said. "I could use other kind, but the tea must have fragrance."

She lined up the ten cups in two rows, one type behind the other. She removed the strainer from the serving pot and poured tea into each of the taller cups.

"Tea ceremony go back many years in China since Tang Dynasty, more than thousand years ago."

When she finished pouring the fifth cup, she put down the pot, and her hands returned to the front of the row. She inverted each stubby cup over its taller mate. Now with a row of cups atop cups, she placed her hands along the sides of one tall vessel with her thumbs pressing on the other. With a quick turn of her wrists, she flipped the two upside down, causing the liquid from one to flow into the other.

She repeated this action with the next three cups. As her hands surrounded the fifth, she said, "Tea ceremony have four principles. They are purity, reverence, harmony, and tranquility."

As Qiao-Yun continued, the others, like me, must have realized a Chinese tea ceremony had little to do with quenching thirst. It had become obvious when Qiao-Yun emptied each newly filled cup into a bowl and put it aside.

Gareth understood. "Qiao-Yun, I think I know why you poured the tea before it had much chance to brew."

Qiao-Yun lined up the ten cups again. She reached for the serving pot. "Tell me," she said.

"You were washing the cups in weak tea."

Qiao-Yun refilled the tall cups. Katelyn said, "It's about fragrance, isn't it?"

"Yes," Qiao-Yun said. She repeated all the steps except emptying the cups. This time she handed them to us. "Before you drink, smell your tea."

I rarely drank tea. When I did, it usually had an English name. What my nose sampled now was very different. But its appeal came laced with a vague foreboding I couldn't shake.

Qiao-Yun encouraged us to drink, and she passed around plates of "moon cakes" and fruit. She poured more tea, and we drank.

"Let me ask you," Qiao-Yun said as we finished and reached for our napkins, "do you like?"

Luke recalled a Seattle teahouse he visited with his bass player. "This is better," he said.

"Did you go to a formal tea ceremony?" Katelyn asked.

"No. We went in and sat by ourselves. We ordered tea and little cakes pictured on the menu."

"Did you first smell the tea?" Gareth asked.

"I don't even know what kind it was." Everyone but me laughed.

"In Taiwan," Qiao-Yun said. "We have many kind."

Luke asked, "Qiao-Yun, how often do you have tea ceremonies?"

"Not often," she said.

So when the mahjong gang got together every week, they might have tea and sweets, but not like this.

Gareth said, "This was lovely, Qiao-Yun."

We had just enough time to do the cleanup. Everyone helped clear off the table. I loaded the dishwasher. It was 3:30, time to leave because we were Jerry's family. The five of us went in two cars: Gareth, Katelyn, and Luke in the Mini, I with Qiao-Yun in her Honda. We arrived at quarter-to-four and entered St. Joseph's through the side door. Bill Forsythe met us. His wore a dark suit. With two simultaneous wakes across the street, he became the stand-in for Douglas's ushers.

"Everything has been set up in the sanctuary," Bill said. "We'll open the main doors in a few minutes."

I had given little thought about the wake's preparation, assuming John Douglas and Diane would get everything ready. Bill's presence made me realize volunteers from St. Joseph's must have helped too.

We had little room inside the tiny foyer. "If you would like to go in," Bill said, "you'll have some time to yourselves. Diane's there."

The door behind me opened. Fran and Dom entered. The seven of us crammed together.

As Bill back stepped into the corridor to make room, I felt the return of my long-standing ambivalence about wakes. When my grandmother died, I was twelve. Gammy's wake was my first, and the long-jawed, grease-painted old lady in the casket looked nothing like her—a vision still remembered. My father had an explanation: the woman in the casket wasn't really Gammy because she was in heaven. Silently I screamed, "Then what the hell are we doing here?" I carried this boyhood reaction ever since. Through the years morticians grew more adept, and my more experienced self understood wakes are about respect and farewells. Cara thought so too but hated the idea of death and cosmetics making her a spectacle.

I hadn't seen Fran and Dom since dinner at their house three weeks ago. Dom edged his hand towards Qiao-Yun and introduced himself. Fran and I embraced as though each wanted to absorb the other.

Qiao-Yun took Dom's hand and said her name. "Stephen say good things about you and your wife, his sister."

"He says good things about you."

Fran pulled her head back to see my face. "Are you okay?"

"It's good to have everyone here."

We changed partners. "Qiao-Yun," my sister said with faultless pronunciation, "I'm Fran."

Dom wrapped his arms around my shoulders. In the corridor Bill waited, his head lowered.

"We should go in," I said.

CHAPTER 24

Time pressed against Friday morning from both sides. Ahead lay another class with Qiao-Yun. I prayed it wouldn't be my only chance to see her today. Behind loomed yesterday's tea ceremony and the wake and the restaurant gathering that followed.

When we entered the sanctuary, Bill stayed by the side door. I saw the casket and bier placed before the chancel steps. Diane stood by. She greeted us individually. At the opposite end of the center aisle, Olivia waited for Bill's signal to open the big main doors. She foreshadowed our crumbled resolve not to cry. Only Diane had seen Jerry the way I had. All the others saw the body in the casket—an artifact brushed and polished like a knight's effigy in blue blazer and tie. Luke broke first. I think we all cried more for his pain than our own, Qiao-Yun included. Diane said a prayer. It offered gratitude for a good man's life and a plea for peace. Everyone said Amen. Diane left promising she would come to the house Friday. Bill nodded to Olivia.

We lined up to receive the visitors and gave no thought to our placement other than my position closest to the casket. At first Qiao-Yun stood next to me. After ten minutes she gave her spot to Luke, saying not a word, and went to the end alongside Gareth. An hour after people filed by and said their condolences, Qiao-Yun said she needed to sit down. She walked past seven pews of scattered mourners and sat with Wen. Qiao-Yun looked like she carried more troubles than I could count. It scared me. Tuesday night the word *remember* stole her away, and I couldn't forget her saying "my country" when she praised the tea in Taiwan, a place about as far as you could get from my America. She had used the expression before, but it didn't resonate the way it did now. As the passing visitors ebbed to an infrequent few, Gareth left Katelyn's side and angled himself between Luke and me. Maybe my face begged him closer. He said the tea ceremony was very beautiful. I said it beat the hell out of eye exams on Ellis Island. Wen left. Katelyn said her legs needed a rest. She walked half the length of the church and sat next to Qiao-Yun. Fran and Dom were two pews up from them.

Meanwhile Fred Divol, Irene Covey, and Paul Bellamy approached a second time. We stepped away from the casket. They worried about Diane. Paul asked if we could count on Bill. I said Diane knew what she was doing when she recruited him. Most vestry members came early. Jo Garcia had swapped shifts with another dispatcher. They stuck around greeting visitors who included all the angels who helped me in July. Alice Flynn stayed almost as long. Neither Harriet nor Rachel showed up. Irene said if those two didn't come they were in battle mode and that meant they were spreading the word about Diane, vestry confidentiality be damned.

Paul sounded more confident. "At worst a few people will be confused, and they'll be angry. If they leave St. Joseph's, let them go."

I said, "It's a sad day when the junior warden dies and two members of the vestry blow-off his wake."

Irene said, "Church fights get nasty."

Fred hoped we might not have a fight at all. He asked me to meet him for lunch tomorrow. He turned to the casket. "Tonight we have more important business."

I couldn't argue with that. My three vestry mates moved on. Qiao-Yun rose from her pew and came back to my side, Katelyn right behind her. I hoped Qiao-Yun's hand would reach for mine. It didn't.

Charlie Prendergast came at six o'clock right from work. I saw three of Jerry's old girl friends and about a dozen singers from the O.C.F.C who said they would rehearse with Nate tomorrow. Jerry's landlord, Hank Swenson, came along with his wife, parents, and two teenage boys. I met many of Jerry's past customers. I couldn't help watching for a younger, slimmer version of Harriet. The thought that Harriet would boycott Jerry's wake but Cheryl would come seemed too good to be true, and it was. By the end of the third hour, Harriet and Rachel still hadn't shown. Battle mode it was.

Olivia wanted one more look before the crew from Douglas's came. She moved toward the casket with her husband Ralph beside her. The vestry members stayed until the end. Dwayne Parsons and Nick Bellini walked to the main doors. Nick exited first, Dwayne a few steps behind him. Their leaving showed the few lingering mourners the three-hour wake had ended. A guy I had seen a few times in church came after the second hour. He left with Dwayne. Before the vestry members left, each spoke again to me. Bill said he would stay until all was done.

Katelyn had made dinner reservations for seven-thirty. She chose the Blue Cove, a quiet restaurant near Scrooby Beach. Qiao-Yun rode with me. As we continued through the center of town, she asked when my family last saw Diane. I said Cara's funeral.

"Do you think they thinking about that tonight?"

"Probably."

The number of people who came to Jerry's wake touched her. "Your sister and her husband, they very nice." Her words came slowly.

We passed Linnehan's.

The Mini arrived at the Blue Cove first. The three occupants gathered by the sea wall bordering the restaurant. Qiao-Yun parked next to them. We got out of the car. My sister and brother-in-law hadn't arrived yet. The calm sea rolled over beach pebbles below. The tide was full.

A car turned into the parking lot, its headlights catching us as it drew closer. It was Fran and Dom. Everyone was hungry. The hostess led us to two tables pushed together at the rear of the dining room. The waiter came. Dom and I ordered scotches; Luke, a local craft beer. Qiao-Yun and Katelyn asked for water with lemon and no ice. Gareth and Fran wanted white wine. We studied the menu. The Blue Cove had a reputation for good seafood, and that's what everyone ordered—our conversation limited to what menu items seemed best. No one ordered lobster.

Afterwards Fran wanted to know everything about Katelyn, Gareth, and Luke, and they went on about Gareth's publication details and Luke's new band. Luke said he was lucky to meet such great musicians. He was writing his best music for them, and they liked his work. There was a lot of talk about Katelyn's pregnancy. Fran updated news of her son Jim in Florida. He had a girlfriend. Qiao-Yun didn't speak until Fran asked her about Keung. Qiao-Yun said he went to Mass. Maritime. Luke praised the tea ceremony. Gareth and Katelyn jumped in as he described it to his aunt and uncle. Qiao-Yun gave short answers to Fran's and Dom's questions.

Fran asked about the weather. I said clear skies were predicted for the next three days. All through dinner we avoided talk about the previous three hours or the upcoming funeral. Luke raved about the bakery he passed today and the pies he would bring for tomorrow night's dessert. Katelyn volunteered a salad. Gareth promised more wine, and I offered an appetizer and had no idea what to bring. Katelyn said she'd help me. Dom said he and Fran had the main dish and veggies all planned. Qiao-Yun didn't speak until Fran asked her for another hors d'oeuvre. Qiao-Yun suggested Chinese dumplings. Fran said that sounded wonderful.

When I said goodnight to Qiao-Yun outside the Blue Cove, I asked her to meet me tomorrow night. She said Keung was coming home. They needed time together. She apologized for not telling me earlier. I asked about Friday morning's Tai Chi class. She said its focus was weapons, but I could still come and practice my form.

I went home in the Mini with Tai Chi least on my mind. Qiao-Yun's appointments loaded her Friday, and Keung owned the evening. Saturday had no space. Sunday morning my family would leave Scrooby. After the ten o'clock service the vestry would meet, and Harriet and Rachel would bring their mayhem. I had to find out what was going on with Qiao-Yun face-to-face, not a phone call. Tomorrow morning was the nearest window. Whatever Katelyn learned when she sat with Qiao-Yun she kept to herself. They said little to each other. Sooner or later, I supposed, Qiao-Yun would explain everything. Maybe my grief mistook her mood for something it wasn't.

Friday morning I drove to class. Along the way Fred called. He said Bill Forsythe was joining us for lunch. Two hours separated the end of class and noon. Qiao-Yun's schedule closed off all but a small piece of time for us to be alone. How much we needed I didn't know. Class started at eight-forty-five. I got there at eight-thirty, worried some other student would steal her attention, leaving me no chance to insist we had to talk after class.

Waiting in the parking lot, scornful of any car but hers that came down the street, I saw Qiao-Yun's Honda and sprang from the VW. An SUV drove in behind her. I recognized the driver from yesterday's class. My one chance was to intercept Qiao-Yun before she got to the door. Two more cars parked while Qiao-Yun exited hers. I pretended to be as cheerful as the sun-washed sky and made a beeline for the Honda. Qiao-Yun saw me coming.

We were about twenty feet apart. "Good morning," she said with a smile as showy as mine. "Today you see what weapons class is like." She wanted the others to hear us.

I matched her volume. "Well, I love to learn."

As we closed the distance between us, students opened their trunks and grabbed long carrying cases, and three more cars swerved into parking spots.

I had only seconds. "Do you have any time after class?" I whispered.

"Yes, but I teach at Senior Center at ten-thirty. It ten-minute drive."

If slowpokes and gabbers didn't drag out their leaving at ten, we'd barely have quarter of an hour to ourselves.

"I was hoping for more time."

"After that class I go two nursing homes and afternoon Mandarin class and reflexology session before cooking dinner for Keung."

Qiao-Yun looked over her shoulder. She turned back to me. "Stephen, I know I been strange."

"Help me understand why."

She didn't have a chance to answer. Eight students, each with an arm through a sling connected to a bag long enough for an Enfield rifle, surrounded us. They spouted greetings and asked whether I was taking the weapons class.

Qiao-Yun put on a big happy face. "Stephen wanting practice his Thirty-Seven Steps."

"Well, about four of them anyway," I said. Two of the students I hadn't met before. While we went through introductions, Qiao-Yun unlocked the door.

Pulling off my shoes, I watched the other students prepare for class. They zipped open their bags and unloaded steel swords. Each blade measured about a yard long and an inch wide with a sharp point. Long tassels hung from hilts. A closer look showed some swords had greater heft and thickness than others and all had dull edges, but every one could kill a man. The unpacking wasn't done. The students took out fans over a foot long. A gray-haired woman snapped hers open with what sounded like a dragon's chomp. The fan burst into a red semicircle with yellow ribs—a gruesome tool for anyone who likes to poke people's eyes out.

Qiao-Yun popped in a CD. I recognized the melody we heard during the tea ceremony. Distinctive *pings* and *poings* with lonely *coos* like a mourning dove's floated across the room. We spread into two lines with Qiao-Yun in front.

"Take a deep breath," she said, "and breathe out slowly."

Warm-ups started as usual, beginning with the head-to-toe sequence to loosen joints. They felt good and eased me into the muscle stretches that followed, which progressed with barely any discomfort. For coordination she put us through a sequence of Bear Spine and Cloudy Hands. Getting through those went much better than the last time. Qiao-Yun started a third set of exercises apparently geared for this class. She had us slowly sink into a deep squat. She called on one of the guys to count to five. In two-second intervals he said, "*Ee-er-san-szer-wu.*" Qiao-Yun stood erect. We followed. She sent us down again and called on the gray-haired woman to give the count. She did. Up we came. Qiao-Yun called for another squat.

"Stephen, you count."

I imitated the others. "*Ee-er-san-szer-wu.*"

Twice in the Thirty-Seven Steps comes a move Qiao-Yun called Descending. They follow a Single Whip, which ends with one foot placed ahead of the other and weight shifted forward. In this posture the back leg is free to move. In Descending the back foot makes a heel pivot to the rear followed by a ball pivot and another heel pivot, resulting in a wide spread between the two feet. Next the weight is shifted from front to back and forward again moving to an upright stance weighted on the left foot. There's hand work with this that I had yet to do right in my two previous classes, but the biggest challenge is to shift the weight so far backward the forward leg stays straight while the back leg bends sharply like the prow of a speed boat. No student descended lower than Qiao-Yun. Her butt nearly touched the floor. The strain on our hamstrings and front knees from such a deep dip was more than any student could control for long. I guessed weapon forms required similar splits.

To strengthen our legs Qiao-Yun had us stand with feet as far apart as we could push them and still haul ourselves upright with knees flexed. We had to shift from one side to the other. Jo Garcia put me through an easy version of this my first class. She wasn't interested in endurance or flexibility so much as making me experience attentive weight shifting. Jo had my feet shoulder-width apart. Qiao-Yun wanted at least twice that spread. We stretched far to the right, held, and then stretched far to the left. Qiao-Yun said, "Switch," each time. After one knee pushed towards a center position, the other knee pulled into the deep stretch. Back and forth we slowly went. I was relieved when the six shifts ended. It hurt, but I didn't groan.

With the warm-ups done, Qiao-Yun had us take another slow, deep breath and gradually let it out. "Okay," she said. "Let's do swords."

The students headed towards their stash of weapons. I didn't know what to do. Qiao-Yun walked to the storage closet. "I have something for you, Stephen. Come."

She opened the door and withdrew a wooden sword. "Beginners use this kind. You should try."

Qiao-Yun yanked a steel sword from its scabbard. "I review basics with class," she said. "Follow best you can."

I took the woody. It was a little shorter than the others and very light. The veterans lined up as before, swords in hand, their wrists rotating in tight figure eights. I copied their action.

Qiao-Yun repositioned her sword behind her bare left arm the way an assassin would hide a stiletto up his sleeve. She stood at attention. She wanted to drill the form's opening steps, which included the sword's transfer from the left hand to right. The form began with the same Introductory Breathing I learned earlier. It opened the stance. After that came a deep shift to the right. With the hilt grabbed in an upside-down grip, we had to swing the left arm across the body while the sword ran under the forearm. The tassels flew open like a racehorse's tail. Qiao-Yun called out the names of the next two steps, Rock and Roll and the one-legged Rooster's Stance. I had imitated similar moves in the previous classes. This time, wielding my squire's toy, I had to shift and sway and maintain a more challenging balance. The steps ended with the sword's exchange from one hand to the other. The grip changed in the process. The sword became an extension of the right arm, the point forward, and I suddenly got the idea that all this weapons stuff had little to do with violence. It was Tai Chi with props to make the synthesis of precise, slow movements and slow breathing more challenging, and perhaps with this challenge came a deeper experience of "the zone" Jo talked about, a more enhanced *fee da frew*. I was nowhere near getting there, of course, but my theory made better sense than assuming Qiao-Yun and her students pirouetted to homicidal fantasies.

When I directed high school plays, there always came a time deep in the rehearsal schedule when the first scenes needed review. Theater production is a recursive process, a rolling forward and then a rolling back to tighten blocking and timing. It also made actors reconnect with their characters' situations at the start, and this helped them interpret the later scenes better. Learning a Tai Chi form follows the same procedure. Bad habits can sink in. The leader has to undo marred memory and reinstall the good. That's what Qiao-Yun was doing with this drill; and because it was so repetitive and precise, a neophyte could follow along. I got these opening sword moves down faster than I got Qi Ball Hands and Four Actions with Jo. That wasn't Jo's fault. After all, Qiao-Yun was the Master, but there was something else.

With the drill complete, Qiao-Yun asked the students to run the entire sword form on their own. She also wanted to run through my few Tai Chi steps. I followed her back to the storage closet.

"I wasn't expecting an invitation to do sword," I said.

"Early in class you looking like you can handle it."

"Why's that?"

"You can count to five in Mandarin."

It was the kind of answer Jerry or Diane would have given. Behind Qiao-Yun the sword form carried on.

"Show me Introductory Breathing through Single Whip," Qiao-Yun said.

I did as told. Qiao-Yun liked what she saw, even though my every step and posture needed adjustment. I utilized leg muscles well, but the shifts should have gone deeper. My arms moved in the right directions, but they needed more extension. My hands lacked definition. My eyes appeared unaware of my body's motions. She complimented my wide stance and straight back. It meant I maintained Tai Chi's essential substructure. We worked on the flaws. She modeled. I copied. When I didn't get something right, she pulled or pushed wayward limbs into line. I caught on.

She wanted me to jump sequence as I did the last class and add the form's last two steps, Crossing Hands and Ending. "You do good, Stephen, but everythings must flow start to finish. Watch me."

Qiao-Yun began and ended in the same position. My challenge was to replicate her start and finish and everything in between.

"Concentrate and relax," Qiao-Yun said. She returned to the sword people, leaving me to draw all the parts into a journey that ended where it began.

In retrospect I see how Tai Chi, like a poem, doesn't give any news worth chasing; instead, it offers a different pursuit, one of balance, and in balance we find grace, and these are loaded terms. I breathed slowly and made calm, unconventional motions which poured from one into the other as a continuous, gentle wave.

My circular mini-forms filled the rest of the hour. The others finished with their swords and took up their fans. I didn't see their form as much as hear their fans' intermittent, raspy openings. After a while I didn't hear them at all. When Qiao-Yun said "Courtesy" to end the class, I was gliding into another Four Actions. She had to say, "Courtesy, Stephen," before I sprang into the stance—my right foot planted, the left foot on its toes, my right arm bent like the pitch of a roof, my right hand a fist pressed against the left palm.

We students said, "*Shyeh shyeh*."

"*Shyeh shyeh*," Qiao-Yun said.

The place cleared out fast. Everyone else, it seemed, had a Friday schedule as busy as Qiao-Yun's. By the time she shut off the music and stashed her fan in the storage closet, we were alone. Qiao-Yun sat on a bench and patted the space next to her. I sat down. She said I did very well today. I said it was my best class. She asked why.

"I guess I'm getting more used to Tai Chi."

"I see that."

"Before class I wasn't in the best frame of mind. During class I felt better."

"I see that too. "

She said she had a story to tell. She stood up and walked three steps away and lowered her head as though contemplating the right words. She turned around and faced me, her demeanor serious but absent the stress so evident last night.

"I tell you before about my college. I had scholarship. When I graduate, I had job there. When I go to Springfield College for Master's degree, government pay, give me salary too. When I move to America, I return Taiwan to teach every year. I spend summer months and month between semesters here. For past year I on leave. My college, the government, been very good to me. My department chairman want me back very much. Other professor, a woman, want me back more. I know her a long time. She recruit me to college. She help get me scholarship. She teach me many courses. She get me on faculty when I only have bachelor's degree. She my closest friend when I get divorce. She and chairman help me all the time. We talk on phone. She want me back too. On Saturday she say chairman will call Monday with final offer. If I don't go back, he must making other plans. He call when you with Jerry."

She told me the offer: a full professorship and a coaching schedule that wouldn't drive her into the ground. She'd have clout to reshape the outworn curriculum, something she had battled to do much as I had at my high school.

"My chairman and my professor, they know me since I seventeen. And there is more. Keung. When he graduate from college, he want go back to Asia."

"But you didn't say yes to the chairman."

"He give me one week to deciding."

Wednesday she got me to admit how much my old job influenced my sense of self. We both left our professions too soon. I sulked off wounded and sore. She left loaded with gratitude from individuals and a government that hated to see her go. No boss wanted me back. A nation wanted her. Qiao-Yun had three more days.

She sat next to me. "What you think?"

"I think all things must flow from a start to a finish. You wouldn't have begun teaching me the sword form, if you weren't staying to complete the job."

Qiao-Yun leaned her body into mine. She put her hands on my cheeks and drew my face to hers. She kissed me.

Qiao-Yun finished her story. She came close to turning down the job when her chairman called Monday night. Out of respect she agreed to take the week he gave her. Tuesday morning the mentor, the woman professor who had nurtured her career from its start, called Qiao-Yun and spooned out a fifty-gallon drum of motherly persuasion, everything from sugar to guilt. Over a month ago when her father died, Qiao-Yun pretty much determined her future belonged in America. She didn't say my entrance into her life pushed her closer. In fact, it might have complicated what was nearly settled. She didn't go into it, though she did say she liked my family very much and regretted last night she couldn't tell all to Katelyn. The tea ceremony was her way of explaining who she was. She told me about Keung. Despite all his academic success in America, he had never seen himself as anything other than Chinese. I thought it unusual that the parent assimilates into the new country better than the son. But I knew nothing about immigrants' struggles, especially Asians'. She wanted to level with him about the job offer and all the rest. Keung would get to have his say. Qiao-Yun didn't think he could change her mind.

"I know he be disappointed," she said.

He would have to argue something she hadn't already considered. Chances were he couldn't, yet the possibility remained open, however slightly. Sorting everything out with Keung wouldn't be easy, and Qiao-Yun's chairman and mentor still weighed on her. The chairman knew what he was doing when he wouldn't let her answer Monday night. He and the mentor were in cahoots. Letting their concoction marinate for a week had its effects; and though neither of us mentioned it, Qiao-Yun must have suspected her refusal would generate no blessings from either of them again. I felt bad for her. On the other hand, from my totally biased perspective she had made the right choice. Making a new life in America and leaving the old behind struck me as a very sensible course to follow, the very thing I had been doing in my own fumbling way since the Epiphany dinner when I held her hand and looked into those penetrating eyes.

When we parted last night at the Blue Cove, our kiss had about the same juice as the one Fran gave me. We more than made up for it now. Qiao-Yun promised to stop at my house tomorrow before going to the funeral. Keung was coming too.

Qiao-Yun had to hurry off. Luke called from St. Joseph's. Nate needed another bass for Sunday's service. Without the voices from the O.C.F.C., the Sunday choir would sound weaker than ever. I didn't want to sit with the choir during the funeral. I had enough to do and wanted to be with my family and Qiao-Yun. Sunday was different. Nate needed every choir member.

"Could you come to practice one-thirty this afternoon?" Luke asked.

"Tell Nate I'll be there."

CHAPTER 25

I steered the VW toward Scrooby's waterfront hoping for a parking space midpoint between Founders Garden and the Oceanside Cafe. A park department's green pick-up backed out, giving me an open space and abundant time before lunch with Fred and Bill. With a eulogy to write and a spiral notebook, I headed toward a marble bench alongside a flowering rhododendron and shut off my cell phone.

My sloppy handwriting worked away at lists and circles and arrows and more lists and sentence fragments and cross-outs and more words looking for lists to join or new ones to make. Every list got a title. All the while I kept big ideas cordoned off in a disciplined place. In my spiral laboratory observation and discovery came before confirmation. If Sean and Adiba were peering over my shoulder, he would explain this was how I taught my classes to compose. The little stuff piled into clumsy sentences that coagulated into hideous paragraphs, but they were much better than nothing because nothing comes from nothing— a basic principle ignored by teachers who think all life begins with topic sentences. Hideous paragraphs can be revised. My hour-long scribbles had meaning, and from them would come better prose pushing deeper thought and worthier language. That would come later, my work tonight.

At a table by a window, Fred and Bill sipped ice water as I entered the Oceanside Cafe. A third glass waited by the empty chair. They welcomed me to the table.

"We were talking about our kids," Fred said. "Bill's daughter is an artist, and my son is married to one, the smartest thing he ever did."

Fred, I noticed, had a knack for finding something in common with anyone. Bill said they arrived at the same time, a little early, hoping to get a good table before the lunch crowd streamed in. He asked how I was doing.

"Staying busy," I said, taking my seat. "I'm grateful for all the help."

"Diane called me," Fred said. "She's been trying to reach you. She heard we three were having lunch together."

Diane heard because Bill or Fred or both told her. Neither owned up. The waitress came and took our orders: tuna salads all around and ice tea.

Fred said, "Diane met with Harriet and then with Rachel. Neither session went well. No surprise there. They both called her this morning demanding the rector's sexuality be on the agenda for Sunday's meeting."

I could imagine Harriet making demands but not Rachel. Fred said Rachel came to her meeting knowing what Diane would say. Rachel's response was to mumble this is not acceptable. I asked Fred how Harriet reacted to Diane's revelation.

"'Like she drew three cards and got a straight flush.' That's how Diane put it."

"What's Diane's reaction?" I asked.

"She doesn't give a rat's ass—my words, not hers."

Fred explained he had known Harriet for a long time, remembered her husband and son slightly, but could never figure her out, except that she was the kind of person who feared that if she can't dominate other people they will dominate her. "There's a lot of folks like that. She's always in a conflict, whether she's laying on charm or assaulting someone."

"I've witnessed her attempts at charm. They don't work," I said.

Fred recalled the last vestry meeting. "And her combativeness doesn't work either."

"I've only been in her presence once," Bill said, "at the Epiphany dinner. I sized her up the same way."

People like Harriet generate judgments. They have to impress. They have to control. I remembered how she acted that night.

"I'm not afraid of anything she might try," Fred said. "She has no gift for winning—"

I interrupted. "But she doesn't have to win anything to cause a pile of hurt."

"You're right, Stephen, and that's the reason I wanted to talk to both of you."

Fred had a plan. It worked on two premises. First, Rachel was like a puppy in her loyalties and about as smart. She and Harriet would probably make calls asking certain parishioners, the ones easily shocked and most negative, to attend the vestry meeting after Sunday's ten o'clock service. Fred said he too will make calls and urge the other vestry members to make some too, reaching as many people as they can, including the ones Harriet would target. His second premise held that a sizable turnout would work in our favor because most people who went to St. Joseph's were sensible.

Fred's mouth slanted uncharacteristically. "Irene Covey is scheduled to bring the meditative reading for the next monthly meeting. She'll have one on Sunday. I don't know what. I hope that's okay with you, Stephen."

How could I object? All vestry meetings should proceed according to custom. The more Fred spoke the more interesting his plan became. He said Bill and I shouldn't make any calls. The senior warden, he explained, will chair the meeting as usual and can't appear to have a dog in this fight. The same reasoning applied to Bill because as the soon-to-be junior warden he shouldn't act like what he was, a political appointee. From a doctrinal perspective Harriet had no beef, the same situation she discovered when she tried to shut down same sex weddings. She could, however, percolate discord. How much depended partly on us.

Fred said Diane took an additional step. "She sent letters to every parishioner explaining what she told vestry members individually. People will get them in today's or tomorrow's mail."

Diane and I had discussed doing this after she showed a draft to me, which she didn't do.

"You look surprised, Stephen. You have to remember she wasn't writing about a church matter so much as a personal one. If she had reached you this morning, she would have told you."

"Does she know about your plans?" I asked.

"She knows the gist."

"Diane's under an awful strain," I said.

"Maybe not as much as you think."

Fred had all but taken charge because the senior warden's best friend's funeral came the day before the special vestry meeting. Fred was committed to protecting Diane and St. Joseph's. He needed room to do it his own way, hinting Diane should lay low and trust him. My job was to get through tomorrow and run a tight meeting on Sunday. I should appear impartial even though anyone with a brain knew I wasn't. Bill's job was to understand what he was getting into.

"You need another agenda item," Bill said. "It should come between the two you have."

Neither Fred nor I saw this coming, though we had seen enough of Bill to notice he wasn't one to sit quietly until someone gave him orders. "The church doesn't have a music director," he said, "and the vestry shouldn't wait three weeks before they do something."

He had a proposal. The agenda item needed only two words: "Music Director." The vestry should vote to accept Janice's resignation. The conventional next step called for the rector to hire substitute organists until the job was posted and filled. Bill offered an alternative solution, one long-term substitute, the guy who was leading the music at Jerry's funeral and the Sunday service.

"Think of them as an audition," Bill explained. "If you think he's qualified, let him have the long-term gig and apply for the permanent job."

I turned to Fred. "The young man Bill's talking about is his brother-in-law."

"So I've heard." Fred wasn't pleased. "Is this young man aware you're making this pitch?"

"He isn't even aware I'm up for junior warden."

"You haven't answered my question."

Bill's reply sounded like an elocution lesson. "He's asked nothing from me, and I've offered nothing."

I had to smooth this over.

Bill beat me too it. "I shouldn't have used the word 'audition.' I'm sorry, Stephen. You don't need that going through your head tomorrow."

Bill had more to say. He spoke like an architect. It was all about equilibrium. Janice's departure created an instability we shouldn't ignore.

"There will be no cry for Janice's return," I said.

Bill wasn't so sure. "For some people a terrible consistency has more appeal than uncertainty."

Fred wasn't happy. "Do either of you have any idea what Diane thinks of this?"

Bill did. "It's her recommendation. And there's something else. Nate is gay. He's engaged to the trumpet player. When you call the vestry members, Fred, you ought to tell them. Diane and I want them to know."

The waitress delivered our lunches. The usual back-and-forth with an attentive server followed. After she left, I waited for Fred to say something. He poured creamy dressing over his salad, spread it around, forked some lettuce, and chewed away in silence.

"I'll see Diane this afternoon," I said. "We'll put together an agenda based on both your suggestions. If there are any changes, I'll call you right away."

"I'd appreciate that," Fred said.

We spoke very little while we ate. Every table at the Oceanside was full. Outside our window tourists strolled through Founders Garden on their way to the restaurants and shops lining one side of Water Street. The harbor, speckled with moored boats, spread across the opposite side. Fred picked up the check. He insisted.

Everyone in the choir had spent the morning with Nate and his band, the O.C.F.C reinforcements, and Luke. When I showed up after lunch for choir practice, the core crew of five sopranos, six altos (Rachel, of course, not among them), a tenor, and two basses greeted me as their long-awaited prom date; and they practically fell on their knees rejoicing when Olivia walked in. Nobody mentioned Janice. Like me, Olivia had plenty to do during the funeral. She said she missed singing with the choir and wanted to join them for Sunday's service. Olivia was St. Joseph's best soprano, a fact Nate discovered right away. He reminded me of Luke, the same boyish innocence about him and the same slender build. He wasn't as tall as Luke, and his hair was cropped close. Nate had brought his own arrangement of the anthem, *Amazing Grace*. To make it work we had to sing from the balls of our feet, and we needed a soprano who could blast a descant. Olivia packed the voice and soul to do it. For the service's other hymns, Nate played the organ, and he got chords from St. Joseph's old pipes that made the sanctuary resonate like a mineshaft. For *Amazing Grace*, he played the electric keyboard and knocked out piano riffs we never sang to before. I fell behind a little at first, marveling at what was happening, but soon hit my notes dead-on and hard.

After choir practice, I sat in my car and worked on the eulogy again. This time I kept my cell phone on. Qiao-Yun called. She said she would miss me tonight. Keung agreed to help her practice Psalm 46. We talked for about twenty minutes, and my spirits, which had fallen during the eulogy writing, lifted. Afterwards I should have gone straight home. Instead, I returned to my spiral notebook. I still had more to do tonight.

By the time I got home, my priest was exiting through the kitchen door. In our driveway conversation I summarized the lunch time session with Bill and Fred, which unfolded exactly as she thought it would. Diane had just informed my family about all the drama at St. Joseph's.

"I wanted them to understand everything you're going through." Her tone said I mustn't worry about them. "How was choir practice? Luke says Nate could teach a sack of rocks to sing."

"He can." I asked her about the parish-wide letter she wrote.

"I brought you a copy. Katelyn put it on your desk. For Sunday's meeting I'm calling the final agenda item 'The Rector's Letter.'"

I predicted Nate was a shoo-in. As to the first item, I said she made a wise choice recruiting Bill. Diane said she'd write up the agenda and email it to the vestry, adding Irene Covey's turn with the opening meditation.

"How's the eulogy coming?" she asked.

"I worked on it before lunch and again after choir practice."

Diane said I should get some rest. "You will say all the right words, Stephen, and you will say them well."

As I entered the kitchen, Katelyn handed me a bottle of cold beer and asked how my day has been.

"I have come to rely on the kindness of strangers." My magnolia accent gave way to normal voice. "Diane says she filled you in about her and St. Joseph's.

"She did. She's wonderful."

Gareth and Luke were working on the backyard grill. It hadn't been fired up since the summer before last. They replaced the empty gas tank and high-fived when the ignition sparked flames.

Last night Katelyn sensed something was up between Qiao-Yun and me. She asked how this morning went. We sat together on the porch's old wicker sofa that Cara bought at a yard sale. I explained how Qiao-Yun's college department head wanted her back. I almost replayed her China Sea narrative but held off. I did say Keung saw his future in Asia. Qiao-Yun wanted to stay here. The two had much to talk about tonight. Katelyn predicted Keung, a guy she had yet to meet, would not oppose his mother's decision. I wasn't so sure. She knew nothing about Qiao-Yun's mother-in-law. According to Qiao-Yun, Keung talked to his grandmother once a week. Manipulators like her don't change.

Over a dinner of salads and grilled chicken, Gareth did most of the talking, all in response to my asking for his prediction about the vestry meeting Sunday. I read Diane's letter before we began eating. I showed it to Gareth. He read it aloud for Luke and Katelyn. It ran three paragraphs on one page. She used the words "lesbian" and "intimacy" and the phrases "after much prayerful reflection" and "joy in God's love." Diane had explained "her journey of self-discovery" to the bishop who was very supportive. She was "not now in a relationship." The letter explained that she had met individually with every vestry member, the wardens, treasurer, and parish clerk, saying two persons on the vestry had expressed disapproval and the others voiced their confidence in her and gave encouragement. I wondered when she made the three hundred copies to cover the parish's mailing list and stuffed the envelopes for everyone's mail today or tomorrow. Alice must have helped her, and they did it before she met with Harriet and Rachel. She closed her letter saying Sunday's sermon would explain her personal theology about same-sex issues.

Gareth passed the letter to Katelyn. "Diane's very smart and very tough," he said.

"She'll come through okay," I said.

Gareth vaguely nodded. "She shares your faith in the people of St. Joseph's." He shifted in his chair. "Have you read my next-to-last chapter, the one titled 'A Chinaman's Chance'? I mention it because it's relevant to what Diane is facing."

I hadn't read the chapter and wondered where Gareth was going with this. My tiny knowledge of the Chinese experience in America came mostly from a Grade Eight U. S. History text during my last two years teaching. The Chinese built the western end of the transcontinental railroad and faced immigration quotas. That was it.

I listened to Gareth's explanation. Anyone who cares about America's racial past knows the Indians barely survived systematic genocide and no one ever asked their views about illegal immigration. Black folks withstood centuries of slavery, Jim Crow, and trigger happy cops. Jews were told to go peddle their wares. Latinos keep paying for the Spanish Armada. Muslims, not financiers, lead watch lists. When it comes to the Chinese-Americans, few of us think beyond fortune cookies and laundries.

"You know what we did to Japanese-Americans during World War Two," Gareth began. "That kind of racism didn't start with Pearl Harbor. The dehumanizing of Asians began with the Chinese a century before. Diane will get better treatment from the people at your church, but antigay hysteria and hate crimes like the Defense of Marriage Act have deep roots in America's muck of intolerance. Until very recently gays and lesbians had a Chinaman's chance."

My father sometimes used the expression "a Chinaman's chance" whenever he meant no chance at all. I doubt he ever knew its origins, neither did I until Gareth told the story.

Most of the first Chinese, Gareth explained, nearly all men, came from Kwangtung. As soon as possible after their arrival in California, they sent money home, not only for their families but also for local projects like schools and hospitals. Mutuality was nothing new to these men. The Chinese who preceded the new arrivals provided food, shelter, and money for supplies. After the newcomers gained an income, they repaid their benefactors. Meanwhile, they confronted the blatant corruption and lawlessness of the Wild West. Most Americans they encountered were crude and loud. Violence asserted white supremacy. The Chinese got low-paying jobs or opened shops with little profit, despite their intelligence and tireless work ethic. When the Central Pacific started its eastward leg of the transcontinental railroad, the investors first thought the Chinese lacked the strength and stamina to do the work. Only a few were hired. They immediately proved their worth. In time over 10,000 were employed by the Central Pacific, which was the more difficult and hazardous of the two lines, the other being the Union Pacific, which also exploited immigrant labor, mostly Irish. After the completion of the railroad, anti-Chinese discrimination grew worse in California. Beatings and murders were commonplace. In 1868 the Fourteenth Amendment to the Constitution granted U.S. citizenship to all persons born in the U.S. Shortly afterwards the government denied naturalized citizenship to the Chinese, a policy that continued until 1943.

The first Chinese Exclusion Act came in 1882; it forbade Chinese immigration for ten years. It was modified to prohibit the coming of Chinese laborers to the U.S., allowing only bureaucrats, teachers, students, merchants, and travelers; but they rarely got a fair shake. Those who returned to visit families in China weren't allowed back into the U.S., even if they had property and families here. The west coast version of Ellis Island, Angel Island in San Francisco Bay, enforced the law. In 1892 more legislation stripped the Chinese of any protection in courts, and the Supreme Court of the United States said this was okay with them. A Chinaman's chance became synonymous with hopeless oppression. The Immigration Act of 1924 prohibited the immigration of all persons not eligible for citizenship. It included all Asians. This meant, among other injustices, that a married Chinese man already in the country could not bring his overseas wife and children here. Most of these men lived solitary, celibate lives.

"Which is precisely how most straight people want gays and lesbians to live." Gareth said. "That's what the good folks at St. Joseph's are up against."

He detailed one history of injustice to explain another. In his book he used the Chinese struggle as the template for summarizing institutional discrimination. To him America's story was a succession of choices between intolerance and wisdom. Too often the wrong side prevailed.

I got his point, but Gareth's template got me wondering about Keung. Nowadays where did a Chinese-American's best chances lie?

I was also curious about Diane's revelations. "Did Diane say anything about Jerry's cell phone?"

Katelyn, Gareth, and Luke shot the same blank expressions. I told them everything—from Linnehan's to finding Cheryl Sinclair's message. Katelyn asked questions, mostly about names. She wanted more information about Harriet. I told her what Anita told me.

"I noticed a cell phone on your desk. It wasn't yours," Katelyn said.

"It's Jerry's."

She asked to see it. After heading towards my study, she reappeared with Jerry's phone and went upstairs. Meanwhile Gareth scraped down the grill and I loaded the dishwasher. Luke dumped the garbage. I still had a eulogy to revise and went off to type my last handwritten draft into the computer. All that remained was getting through a public reading without falling apart. I printed the two-page text and picked up Gareth's manuscript and read his next-to-last chapter. The last he titled "Emma Lazarus." She wrote the poem engraved on the base of the Statue of Liberty. It's my favorite sonnet.

I left my study and clumped toward the TV sounds coming from the living room. Gareth and Luke were watching the Red Sox game in Oakland, a late starter here. Katelyn stayed upstairs. I plopped on the sofa. It was the fourth inning, no score. The A's were up, two outs. By the start of the fifth, I was asleep. Luke nudged me.

Morning hours never drag. From my closet I pulled the navy blue suit I wore at the wake and noticed someone had pressed sharp creases into the pants. I selected a white shirt with blue pinstripes and a tie dappled with multi-colored blossoms. I wore it every Easter. For the

Gospel reading Olivia and I chose John 14:1-6. In the New Revised Standard Version, Jesus says, "In my father's house there are many dwelling places." The King James gives the more elegant "many mansions." They both have the same follow-up sentence: "I go to prepare a place for you." We preferred the older language. It fits the central purpose of a Christian funeral. It means wear a dark suit but put on a colorful tie.

Gareth and Luke were already seated for the pancake breakfast Katelyn had prepared. My daughter looked me over. "Pretty tie." She poured my coffee.

We ate and cleaned up quickly. When we talked yesterday afternoon, Qiao-Yun said she and Keung should come to my house before going to St. Joseph's. Sending our kids through all the introductions at church minutes before a funeral didn't seem right to either of us. Though the funeral started at ten o'clock, everyone was ready by eight-thirty. Luke had to be first out the door. The band wanted his help for a sound check. I offered him my car. Katelyn and Gareth promised to meet Fran and Dom and a bunch of church angels to get lunch ready. Qiao-Yun would join them. When her car appeared at the top of the driveway, I opened the kitchen door.

Right away Keung became the center of attention. It was pleasantries all around, especially when Keung said he valued the friendship Jerry had given his mother. "My ma," he called her. I studied Qiao-Yun and read nothing happened last night to derail her decision.

It was time to go. I walked towards my study to get Luke the keys. Katelyn followed. She wanted to tell me something.

"I listened to Cheryl's message last night."

I spotted Jerry's phone back on my desk. "How many times?"

"A lot."

"What did you make of it?"

"You should take Diane's advice. Don't call Cheryl."

At the opposite end of the hallway, Luke stood holding his gig bag. I beckoned him forward. He took the keys from my hand. "See you in church."

"It's time Gareth and I were going too," Katelyn said.

Any further discussion about Cheryl would have to come later. Qiao-Yun suggested Keung and I stay longer. She wanted to leave with Gareth and Katelyn. Keung and I had no need to arrive at a funeral an hour before its start.

The two cars left. Keung and I sat at the kitchen counter. He said his mother practiced Psalm 46 with him the night before. She wanted to pronounce every syllable correctly.

"She wasn't sure about all the meaning, and I couldn't help her much."

I envisioned Diane or Olivia drawing Qiao-Yun away from the bustle in the parish hall and bringing her into the sanctuary so she could get accustomed to the light over the lectern and feel comfortable with the microphone.

"She'll get more coaching at the church."

I placed a mug in front of Keung and asked if he wanted coffee. He said no and looked around the kitchen before speaking again.

"Jerry finished the roof on our house in one day. He did a great job and charged far less than the two other estimates I got."

That job was typical of Jerry's work, I explained. Keung said my family seemed very nice. I said he made a good impression too.

He looked around the kitchen a second time. "You know my ma and I had a long talk last night."

"How did it go?"

"She's staying in America."

"What about you?"

"Probably not, but I want her to be happy."

"So do I, Keung."

"My ma said that about you."

"Do you think she's right?"

"She usually is." Keung reached for the empty mug. "Maybe I'll have some coffee after all."

St. Joseph's parking lot was full when we arrived. Keung found a space on the street. We entered through the main doors. People in choir robes, most of them from the O.C.F. C., crowded the rear of the church, their numbers spilling into the narthex. Acolytes, rarely seen at funerals—three girls and a boy in red robes and white cottas—fronted the procession. Dwayne Parsons and Olivia wore the white robes of Eucharistic ministers. Jo Garcia and Nick Bellini were greeters. Nick handed us service programs. At the edge of the chancel near the first step, the burnished chrome urn rested upon a small table. The air smelled of flowers. Arrangements surrounded the altar. Next to the urn Olivia's framed print of Jerry faced outward. Seven musicians squeezed in amongst the organ and electric keyboard—the drummer behind his kit, the clarinetist and trumpet player almost atop each other with the bass player and his stand-up instrument wedged against the wall. Nate sat behind the organ, the trombone player at his right shoulder. Luke sat in front of them. In the middle of the right front pew, Qiao-Yun, Katelyn, and Gareth left spaces for Keung and me. Diane in full vestments entered through the sanctuary's side door. Keung and I walked down the center aisle. Gareth and Katelyn slid to the right. Keung stepped across his mother and took the opened space. I went to Qiao-Yun's left, the aisle seat.

From the rear of the church Diane announced the page for the processional hymn. Nate struck the opening notes of *Teach Me, My God and King*. Everybody stood up.

CHAPTER 26

I remember Jerry's funeral in parts: disjointed remnants woven through the eulogy. Halfway into it I told a joke.

...That's a tough mix—a fierce sense of independence and a humble submission to the divine. It can cause psychological dissonance. Maybe that's why some of us thought Jerry was a little crazy...

Everybody laughed.

Olivia read Isaiah's promises about good news for the oppressed and comfort for those who mourn. Alice's passage from Revelation promised "death will be no more."

...Jerry did many things very well. He was a scholar of ancient Greek and Roman literature, but we here knew him as a skilled carpenter and horticulturist and as a musician and singer. He was also a mentor to our young people. Most of all he was an immensely lovable guy...

Qiao-Yun and the congregation alternated psalm verses proclaiming we will not fear and "a river makes glad the City of God." The choir sang, "...come Holy Spirit that sweetly flows in silent streams." Diane read, "Let not your heart be troubled."

...There's a talent scholars, craftsmen, and musicians share. They perceive how the parts make up the whole. Jerry had this intelligence, and he also had the very good sense to know his individual parts did not make a whole if all he had to patch them together was his determined self-reliance...

The band played solemnly. Nate sang, "I'll be satisfied as long as I walk close to Thee." Luke's guitar seared our hearts.

...We're supposed to love God and to love our neighbors as ourselves. That's no easy task. It isn't God's fault, though sometimes we think it is, and not all our neighbors are, well, neighborly. Jerry approached this problem the same way he would plant a garden—inch by inch, row by row...

Just before the Eucharist, Diane said all are welcomed to the Lord's table. It extends into infinity. Jerry has a seat. We joined the sacrament. The choir sang, "God be in my head and in my understanding."

...Jerry worked in our food pantry. He was our junior warden. He sang for us and played guitar and recorder for us. He sawed wood for us and hammered nails and drove screws for us. He planted flowers, shrubs, and grass for us. He taught our children and welcomed strangers and urged the risk-takers among us to follow their dreams. He did more acts of kindness than anyone knew. And he prayed for us and for himself...

Luke carried the urn to the columbarium, Diane behind him. I followed her with Qiao-Yun by my side, Katelyn and Gareth behind us. Everyone else stayed in the pews and leaned towards the side chapel and the open niche. Diane led the final prayers. From the chancel's top step Olivia watched and listened. She read the words we all read when we committed Jerry's ashes. Nate struck up the band. The closer walk soared into swing. I looked to Olivia. Her face wet with tears, she clapped her hands to the music's time. Her shoulders swayed. We followed her example.

Earlier in the week, Diane and I made a deal. I would pay for the musicians and flowers. St. Joseph's would pay for the cremation, Douglas's, and everything else with Jerry's life insurance. Diane thought Jerry's policy should cover all the expenses. I said no. She asked how much I wanted to throw in. I gave her a number. She proposed one much lower and wouldn't budge. Now with the funeral over, I hurried to pay my share as though Jerry's everlasting life stayed stuck in a waiting room until I did. In truth, my anxiety really wasn't all Jerry-based. I had a compulsion to pay bills.

With the service over I excused myself from the crowd around me and edged towards the band, reaching inside my jacket for the envelope and the check written early this morning. The drummer unscrewed cymbals. The bass player zipped wide the biggest gig bag. Horn players pulled at mouthpieces, and Nate slid music sheets into his briefcase. I entered this realm bringing thanks and praise, handshakes all around, and gave the envelope to Nate. From the sanctuary I dashed to the wall of mailboxes outside the office. As promised, Alice left me a note quoting the florist's bill. I put the note in one pocket and pulled a second envelope and a blank check from another. From a third I took a pen and wrote across the check's lines with concentrated legibility. The check went in the envelope. The envelope went in Alice's mailbox. Stepping into the corridor, I saw Qiao-Yun at the foot of the stairs leading to the parish hall. The others had gone ahead.

"You ready now?" she asked. "You must be hungry."

Qiao-Yun and I had almost the entire afternoon to ourselves. We headed to the waterfront. Holding hands, the old white dude and the gorgeous Chinese princess ambled past the sea and boats. Qiao-Yun confirmed what her eyes told me this morning. She was staying in Scrooby. Keung's future would play out in its own way. Qiao-Yun's future belonged to her. The lingering question from her department head had been answered. Only he remained unsure, and that would end Monday night. It was a beautiful day. We talked about the post-funeral lunch, having left Gareth, Katelyn, Luke, Olivia, and a few angels to finish the cleanup. Qiao-Yun said everyone thought the service was very nice. People went beyond speaking mere courtesies and instead showed they came away with what every church service should give: something to think about. An encounter with the mystical can illuminate a speck of truth. People talked about that. Shoulder to shoulder around the food table, they loaded plates with salads, wraps, and little pastries. They drank coffee and talked about Jerry, a more multifaceted fellow than most of them had realized, and they talked about the music because music goes to depths words seldom do. But they talked about the words too and the individuals who said them. "The best funeral I've ever been to," one woman said. I knew what she meant. I felt the same way. And soon they all talked about anything but the funeral, which was a necessary and proper change. They told funny stories. It was time. After a funeral people get free time—free, that is, from grief. We don't ask for it or make it, and it's anything but permanent. Free time just happens. I brought Olivia into an empty Sunday school classroom and confessed I hadn't told her everything about Jerry's accident. She said I always was a terrible liar and it was just a matter of time before I would level with her. She asked about Jerry's rush to Cheryl. I said Diane and Katelyn told me to forget it. Olivia wasn't so sure, but she didn't push, which was Qiao-Yun's response when I explained Olivia's reaction as we turned from the harbor up the inclined side street leading back to St. Joseph's

Keung took Qiao-Yun's car back to her house. He had studying to do, she said. My family went off in the Mini to improvise an afternoon of shopping and whatever else struck their fancy. I needed a nap. Qiao-Yun did too. Before Keung left he had taken an overnight bag and two hangers of clothes from his mother's car and put them in mine. Qiao-Yun checked to make sure her things were in the VW. Then she walked through the empty parish hall to the kitchen. From the refrigerator she withdrew two plastic bags containing the Chinese dumplings she promised to bring tonight. She had left them in the Honda and made sure before the service to stick them in the church's fridge. With Qiao-Yun next to me, I drove the Beetle back home. While she brought dumplings to the kitchen, I carried her bag and clothes to the bedroom. She joined me there, and we collapsed into an hour of bottomless sleep.

We awoke to the sound of the Mini's return. The three shoppers brought in groceries, some for tonight's dinner at Fran and Dom's house, including bottles of wine from vineyards unknown to my cheap tastes, plus bags of meats and veggies along with small packages and jars of essentials, as Katelyn called them, all from a gourmet market in the next town. My daughter decreed my refrigerator and cupboards needed proper stocking and I couldn't be trusted to do it right. Qiao-Yun laughed while Katelyn explained each item before handing it to Gareth who stored them away. Not to be outdone, Luke showed off the apple and blueberry pies bought at his now favorite bakery and claimed ownership of a paper bag holding the fixings for tonight's salad. He bragged about the salad-making skills he had developed working at his Seattle food co-op. Katelyn shooed everyone but her brother out of the kitchen so she could prepare stuffed quahogs. The original plans had Katelyn bring a salad and I would bring an appetizer. The brother and sister did it all. I didn't have to do anything. Whenever Dom cooked, Fran gladly stayed out of his way. For tonight he promised roast duck. The main course would be his doing. Fran would put out some kind of hors d'oeuvre. Together with Gareth's load of wine bottles, Qiao-Yun's dumplings, and Katelyn's clams, Fran's offerings would keep us satiated and occupied until Dom called us to dinner.

We were hungry too. And everyone needed a change of clothes and some sprucing up before we headed out. A half-hour later, with everyone generating the familiar sounds of running water and doors opening and closing with hurried footsteps on two floors, Katelyn and I nearly crashed into each other. Wrapped from collarbone to shins in my terrycloth bathrobe, she had bounded down the stairs to get her handbag, and I had sauntered into the living room while Qiao-Yun prepped before the bedroom's mirror. For a second Katelyn's wide-eyed stare made me think she wanted to tell me something. We did the comedic jig of two persons trying to get out of each other's way, twice going in the same direction until I did a matador's back step and she scurried by.

While Katelyn dressed, Qiao-Yun fried her dumplings and made a dip from bottles marked with Chinese characters. By the time we left the house, everyone had changed into casual clothes, the two women looking sexy and stylish in jeans, flowing blouses, and perfect makeup and jewelry. We guys looked like farmhands.

Keung arrived right on time. We all went in two cars. Luke rode with Keung. I wasn't sure whether Keung was happy about this dinner with a house full of people he barely knew. The drive took us to Route 3, Keung closely following in the Honda. We took the fourth exit north. Katelyn had insisted she and Qiao-Yun should ride in the back. It was my first time on Route 3 since Diane and I rode in the police cruiser. I gave that little thought, focused instead on the sight of Katelyn and Qiao-Yun squeezed together and blabbing away. Katelyn raved and hooted about Keung's good looks. Qiao-Yun loved it, especially when Katelyn turned bad girl. Like her mother, she could be a great clown. I peered behind my seat to watch. With leering eyes she purred and moaned about the hot Chinese boy toy.

Qiao-Yun was in stitches. "This what every mother want to hear about her son!" she screamed. Their laughter almost blew the Mini's roof off.

We were headed to a good place. The late afternoon sun gave golden tint to the tall marsh grass bordering the narrow, tidal river. As we left the shoreline, the Mini climbed a long gradual hill where shadowy pines studded one side and the sun-rich pines on the other basked their green in yellow light. Some of the most expensive homes in Massachusetts stand on oceanfront lots. Our destination was a roomy two-floor contemporary a mile inland about a fifth the size and a tenth the price of the seaside mansions. It was situated in the kind of town where at Christmas few homes displayed anything but white lights. Fran and Dom hung colored lights, a choice Cara applauded every year.

The protocols for a dinner party at my sister's house called for all beverages to be placed on a counter in the kitchen and opened as wanted. All appetizers after getting whatever treatments they needed in the kitchen were brought to the living room and arranged on a long glass-topped coffee table with a sofa and love seat taking two sides with overstuffed chairs opposite. After a period of drinking and chomping, custom sent hosts and guests to the dining room where they served themselves the sumptuous dinner arrayed on the perfectly set table. This routine and the house's elegant Mediterranean decor provided the basic routine. Everything else came as spontaneous overflows of good cheer.

Once inside the house and the greetings done, everyone with a responsibility went to work. Luke asked for a huge bowl and unpacked his salad ingredients. Dom, having already launched his specialties in pots and roasting pan, relinquished his work space to Katelyn and Qiao-Yun who made the final preparations to their quahogs and dumplings. Fran trotted to the living room with a plate of gourmet cheeses and wafers. She returned and popped off again with a handful of plates and forks. Meanwhile Gareth opened bottles of red and white wines and started pouring. Keung and I had it easy. We watched. Gareth handed me a glass of Pinot Grigio. Keung announced he didn't drink alcohol. Dom opened his refrigerator and rattled off the names of assorted fruit juices, a stock he loaded in preparation for Katelyn. She and Keung opted for cranberry.

Around the coffee table our conversation happily rambled. Most of it focused on the appetizers we all but shoveled down. Then Gareth asked Keung about life at a military academy, and Keung said he disliked the regimentation but confessed some of it was good for him. He asked Gareth about his book. Gareth looked at Katelyn whose face ordered him not to overcast the happy atmosphere she had been fanning since lunch.

Gareth tried answering Keung's question as simply as possible. He also sent a message to me. "It's about immigrants," he said. "Overall a very positive story, though I sounded like a grim, old pedagogue when talking about it last night."

"How could you sound grim about a positive subject?" Keung asked. Everyone looked at Gareth, no one harder than Katelyn.

"Well, let's just say over time America's tattered ideals have held up." Katelyn put a quahog on a plate and handed it to Keung. Luke passed him a fork and napkin. "I've had two of these already," he said. "You should try one."

Keung hesitated before speaking. "I look forward to reading your book." He tasted his stuffed clam and proclaimed it delicious. Gareth promised him an autographed copy.

My glass needed replenishing. I slipped off to the kitchen. From the oven Dom's duck wafted a tantalizing aroma. I spotted the wine Gareth served me and started filling my glass. Katelyn approached from behind.

She spoke gently. "I wasn't honest with you this morning. I mean about Jerry's phone."

"You said to forget about calling Cheryl. That sounded honest to me."

"Yes, that part was honest. You shouldn't call Cheryl."

"I don't understand

"I wanted to explain before we left the house but instead stepped around you. I called Cheryl Sinclair last night. She's an executive at a New York public relations firm. My company has worked with hers. She knows me."

Last night when Katelyn heard me say Cheryl's name, she got suspicious. Hearing the voicemail confirmed it. If two women who knew Jerry from opposite ends of a twenty-year span were to meet, New York City seemed as likely a place as any.

"Tiny world."

"After Harriet met with Diane on Thursday, she called Cheryl saying she had the ammunition to get rid of the priest and everyone else who was ruining St. Joseph's. That's how Harriet talked. In passing she said the junior warden died in a highway accident."

"Is Cheryl helping Harriet?"

"No. She had only come to Scrooby for a quick visit. Jerry was right in thinking Cheryl recognized him that morning outside the cafe, and Harriet saw him too. But he was wrong to fear Cheryl ever bought into Harriet's hatred."

"How did Cheryl know Harriet?"

"Exactly what Jerry guessed. Harriet is her mother's sister."

Cheryl's father died when she was little. Her mother died three months ago. Cheryl had organized a trade show in Boston last weekend. She stayed over to visit her aunt and soon regretted it."

"So she takes time to visit her dead mother's sister and finds herself having breakfast with a lunatic."

"That's what happened. Harriet ranted about St. Joseph's. It was all about Jerry and you and Diane and what she called the anything-goes-liberalism that was polluting her church with sodomites."

"That's pretty sophisticated vocabulary for Harriet, even if it is bullshit."

Gareth entered the kitchen. He took the bottle of Pinot Grigio still in my hand and filled his glass half way. "We live in a bullshit age, Stephen."

"Why did Cheryl call Jerry?"

"To warn him," Katelyn said. "You were right about that."

"Why should she care?"

"She never said. In Midtown Manhattan people keep their cares to a narrow few. The night she called him, she sat in the hotel bar and used her phone to scroll for carpenters in Scrooby. She told Jerry he shouldn't underestimate Harriet's bitterness and resolve."

"What did Jerry say?"

"He insisted on seeing her."

"Why?"

"I asked her that. Cheryl could barely talk. She said she had to go. That was it."

Katelyn took my wine glass and placed it on the counter. She wrapped her arms around my shoulders. She spoke into my ear, her voice a trace above a whisper. "You answered your question this morning at St. Joseph's."

Dom stepped through the kitchen archway. "If you folks will excuse me, I have to get dinner ready." He put on an apron and began tying the strings.

Very slowly Katelyn released her embrace. She offered to help Dom. He kindly waved her off, saying he had little left to do.

"Then let's get out of our chef's way," Gareth advised. He led us back to the living room.

When everyone sat down to Dom's dinner, Gareth served more wine. At Fran's suggestion Luke loaded his salad plate and passed the bowl to Keung, and on it went. Sharing the main course required many hands to start the rotations. The carved duck and vegetables got passed amid the clang and clatter of serving forks and spoons against plates. We ate as though gluttony were a celebrated virtue. Fran asked Qiao-Yun how often she returned to Taiwan, and that turned into a discussion about how best to get frequent flyer miles, which morphed into a list of everyone's favorite travel spots and that turned into a massive, tousled catalogue of other favorites including Peter Sellers movies, about which Qiao-Yun and Keung knew nothing, to contemporary pop songs and summer Olympic events, about which they knew a lot. At the end, with Luke's two pies left half uneaten, we formed a brigade clearing the table. That's all Fran and Dom would let us do.

During the front steps chorus of goodnights, the last word was Dom's, telling me to call him when I wanted to open the pool. I needed his help for other projects too, assorted fix-ups before putting my house on the market. These were projects Jerry would have done. And that reminded me about something Luke said at the China Sea about his journey that took him to a faraway place where he and musicians who understood him found each other. Now he could do the work he wanted most to do, and his journey had been Jerry's idea.

Qiao-Yun and I rode back to Scrooby with Katelyn and Gareth. I slid my key into the kitchen door. The driveway lit up as the Honda pulled in. Keung dropped off Luke. I held the door open for him and the others. We said our goodnights in the living room. Katelyn, Gareth, and Luke went upstairs. Qiao-Yun and I went to my room. I was done with thinking too much.

CHAPTER 27

"Great minds think alike."

The high school librarian, Mary O'Dell, said this to me my first year teaching while she pounded her date stamp on a black inkpad. She pressed it onto the card taped to the book that a long-haired girl in hip-hugger jeans wanted to check out. I had come to reserve time for my grade nine classes to receive their obligatory library orientations and waited my turn for Mrs. O'Dell's attention. Mary, I learned later, cursed any school assignment called a "report." She labeled the teachers who assigned them "flatlanders" and suspected they had no idea why civilizations would crumble without libraries. She encouraged the girl to read deeply and evaluate the information found in books. Reporting it wasn't enough.

"Isn't that right, Mr. Pentheny?" Mary added. It was the first time she asked my opinion about anything.

"Yes, indeed, Mrs. O'Dell." We remained co-subversives right up to her retirement four years later.

Before this Sunday morning ended, Mary's maxim about great minds occurred to me again.

According to Irene Covey's count, over half the ten o'clock congregation, about a hundred souls, trooped up the stairway to the parish hall, a massive number for coffee hour. A bevy of extra kitchen workers, the usual angels, joined the husband and wife who volunteered four months ago expecting far fewer patrons. The reinforcements plugged in an additional sixty-cup pot and covered the counter with platters of bagels, homemade muffins, and sliced fruit. At the same time Olivia and her husband Ralph helped Nick Bellini, Paul Bellamy, Dwayne Parsons, and the fellow I had seen before with Dwayne reconfigured the parish hall's eight-foot long tables into an angular theater in the round. Bill Forsythe helped as did Wen and Bill's wife Jen.

Fred Divol pulled me aside and flashed a sheaf of papers inside a manila folder. He wanted to give a copy to each vestry member. I read the brief paragraph and told him it might come in handy but to hold off.

In the chatter and noise of people getting refreshments and claiming their seats, I stood tiptoed trying to find Qiao-Yun. We became separated in the dense migration up the stairs. Fred's distraction ruined my sense of where Qiao-Yun had gone. The surrounding throng blocked my view. I wanted her to have a front row seat, and my head rotated like a periscope, my hunt ending at the glass doors by the back entrance and the handicap ramp. Charlie Prendergast pushed a wheel chair holding Anita Colfax.

During the service Diane carried the paten of wafers as she descended the chancel steps followed by the lay Eucharistic minister with a chalice of wine. I sat in Jerry's seat in the last row of the choir pews, a position that put Diane's destination out of view. I gave it little thought. Most Sundays one or two worshippers with limited mobility found Communion brought directly to them. Diane always knew where they were. Charlie must have escorted Anita to the ten o'clock. Now seeing Anita, I started towards the glass doors and felt a tug at my elbow. It came from Qiao-Yun. She had a cup of black coffee in one hand. The other held an unbuttered bagel on a plate.

"This for you."

"Where will you be sitting?"

Qiao-Yun pointed to an empty chair next to Wen who sat facing the three eight-footers pushed together for the vestry, forming a wide rectangle. Around it all the other tables had been lined in four sets of rows. Qiao-Yun squeezed my arm before heading to her seat. I put my refreshments in front of a chair that faced a lane keeping her in sight.

The crowd parted for Charlie and Anita as they headed to Qiao-Yun's table. Charlie pulled aside the folding chair and wheeled Anita in its space. I watched him introduce her to Qiao-Yun. At the same time the gathered assembly readied for drama. People jostled into position carrying their paper cups and plates. The vestry members took their places while the parishioners clamored through tight rows to claim the first open seats they found. Other parishioners stood like a stockade all along the hall's perimeter No one wanted the action delayed. I pulled rank on everyone's impatience and traipsed around the seated vestry to Anita. She saw me coming and puckered up. I stretched across her table and gave her a big kiss.

"Good of you to come."

"Thank Charlie."

Behind me Diane and Irene took their seats at one end of the vestry's rectangle. Jo Garcia and Fred Divol sat at the opposite end with my empty chair between them. From Jo's left sat Dwayne, Harriet, Rachel, and Charlie. The chairs opposite them held Olivia closest to Fred, and then Paul. A chair saved for Bill waited between Olivia and

Paul. Nick finished the line. Diane reached behind and gave copies of the agenda to Wen who took one and passed the stack on. Diane had already given copies to the vestry.

Having Qiao-Yun in view topped my stage-setting priorities. Now I had Anita too. Diane, who sat in front of them, didn't block my sight line as I took my place between Jo and Fred. From my vantage point it appeared Harriet could never look directly at Diane without noticing Anita. I wondered what she would make of that. On a conventional stage with a proscenium arch, actors speak through an invisible fourth wall between their world of illusion and the audience's supposed reality, yet nothing exciting happens during a performance unless the two worlds converge. It's a delicate irony. In a small, intimate house like the parish hall with the spectators surrounding the players, the fourth wall disappeared.

At eight this morning my family left for Queens. Luke's return flight departed from La Guardia. If traffic were good, they'd soon be crossing from Connecticut into New York. I had no intention of letting this meeting drag on all afternoon. I had to call Luke before he boarded, and with luck I could report to all three at the same time.

I called the meeting to order and welcomed the onlookers. Since this was a special meeting, I announced we would forgo the reading of the minutes until next time.

"It's the vestry's custom," I said, "to begin every meeting with a spiritual meditation." Across the long rectangle Irene's notebook lay open while she sent sheets of paper to her right and left.

As members passed copies along, I noticed Dwayne had a separate stack in his hand. "Stephen, is it okay if I distribute Irene's meditation to our guests?"

My curiosity doubled. "Good idea."

Dwayne gave half his papers to his friend. As the two men passed the papers throughout the gathering, I read my copy, three brief passages from the Bible, and saw exactly where Irene was going.

I explained the vestry's tradition of calling for a different member each month to bring us a few printed words for our contemplation before we start the business meeting. "This time Harriet has selected quotations from the Bible. The person who brings the meditation reads it aloud. Then we have a brief discussion, after which we ask for a second member to read it again."

Irene stood up, her rigid posture making her look taller than she really was. Although she spoke with a volume no one in the parish hall could miss, her focus fixed on the vestry members seated around the three tables.

"Before I start," she said as people's eyes went to the handout, "I'd like to give a little introduction about these passages. The first one is from Leviticus. The next one is from Romans. I discovered there's some controversy as to whether Paul wrote that letter. The last is from Galatians, and it's pretty certain Paul did write that."

To my left Harriet and Dwayne sat next to each other. Harriet, stone-faced, kept her attention on the paper. Dwayne focused on Harriet.

"One more thing," Irene added. "Of these three quotations you can believe each is the word of God, or you can believe none is. Or you can believe anything in between."

Every so often Episcopalians need to be reminded this is how we make sense of the Bible. Irene read her three passages aloud. Silence followed.

My thoughts returned to the morning drive to St. Joseph's. Qiao-Yun talked about Tai Chi. She said nothing could keep me from being a great practitioner except my tendency to have "monkey brain." By that she meant my letting memories of the past or concerns about the future mess with my concentration. I promised to get better. Right now, though, my monkey brain was swinging from Irene's three passages to Diane's sermon about grace.

We know hardly anything about the Bible's multiple authors, certainly a lot less than what's known about the composer of *Amazing Grace*. As a young man John Newton worked the cross-Atlantic slave trade until his conscience couldn't bear it any longer. Afterwards he became an Anglican priest. There's a movie about him with the same title. Newton's hymn was published in the late seventeen hundreds. It's partly a confession of what a moral lowlife he had been but mostly a song of joy. Everyone recognizes the tune. Even people who scoff at hymns can recite bits from the first verse.

In her sermon Diane summarized all this, but not before she said the lyrics can be interpreted in complementing ways. "God's love is not single-faceted," she said. "And for people like me, these words have a particular beauty."

A group of parishioners rose as one. They thumped and sidestepped from their pews and marched toward the rear doors. I counted them, only eight. Their walkout held everyone's attention until they cleared the sanctuary. The remaining congregants, with faces worried or annoyed, returned their attention to the pulpit.

Unruffled, Diane continued. She itemized her letter's essential points: that she was a lesbian; that everyone in the vestry had been told personally, all but two of them very supportive; and that the bishop stood by her. Then she went back to John Newton, who was ashamed of the "wretch" he once was. Diane explained that many people, especially the social outcasts with whom Jesus bonded so easily, also considered themselves wretches often because they believed the labels of unworthiness other people had pasted on them.

"Grace cannot be amazing," Diane said, "if it means only forgiveness of sins. Of course, it means that, but grace also means liberation from the frightful loneliness generated by cruel social and institutional traditions. Because too few people question these traditions, let me state some facts about people like me. First, we are okay. Second, God made gays, lesbians, bisexuals, and transgender people the way they are. Third, we like it. And, fourth, we're not leaving."

If someone had asked me to deliver a lecture about *Amazing Grace*, I would have gone on for at least an hour, trudging through every verse and word and trumpeting all sorts of righteous stuff about the peace that passes understanding and the human capacity to grow and learn and the power of God. I'd throw in some lines from George Herbert's "Love" poems too. It would have been pretty good, but Diane's sermon went much deeper and finished in a quarter the time. She included an observation I thought only an English teacher could spot, the shift in the lyrics' point of view. In verses one through four, the speaker is singular, a continuous use of *I* and *me*. Verse five is different.

Diane announced what the worshippers could see printed in their service bulletins. The offertory anthem was *Amazing Grace*. She asked the people to read along with the choir during the collection. She pointed out the hymnal page. But when the choir got to the last verse Diane wanted everyone to sing. She explained why.

"In verse five the only pronoun is *we*. The hymn is no longer an individual's affirmation. In the previous verses the voice is each one of us, a distinct person who like John Newton has his or her own unique history. In the last verse *we*"—Diane all but shouted the word— "transform our identities. We proclaim our Oneness with each other and with the Holy Trinity. United, people like you and people like me and all faithful people become the promise of the ages."

Monkey Brain looked to the left side of the vestry's abutting tables. Harriet, motionless between Rachel and Dwayne, appeared as inert as she did all through Diane's sermon.

When the disgruntled eight parishioners made their exit, Harriet didn't blink. After the sermon the congregation read in unison from the prayer book. The words enveloped a Christian creed from the fourth century, supplications for universal blessings, and our confession of sins. We lifted our eyes to Diane.

The priest recited the next paragraph. She beseeched the triune God to forgive our sins, strengthen our goodness, and keep us in eternal life.

Then she said: "The peace of the Lord be always with you."

The people said: "And also with you."

The worshippers rose and turned toward their neighbors, and the senior warden left Jerry's choir seat. He started with his choir mates and nearly bumped into Nate who had left the organ and crossed the chancel, reaching out to every hand he could touch.

I worked my way to the third pew. "Peace, Qiao-Yun."

"Peace, Stephen."

The word reverberated throughout the sanctuary, a sweet cacophony compared to the soundless parish hall after Irene read her three passages.

Every face in the parish hall shifted to me.

"Thank you, Irene." I asked the vestry for comments about the meditation.

Paul Bellamy made a faint guttural sound before speaking. "Well, in response to Irene's suggestion, I think the first two passages don't sound at all God-like. The third does."

No one else volunteered an opinion. They either agreed with Paul or they didn't. The argument could last another two thousand years. I waited about ten seconds.

"Before we move onto our next agenda item, which is to appoint an interim junior warden, would anyone like to read aloud Irene's meditation one more time?"

"I will," Jo said. She stayed seated and read each passage with an unhurried pace, her intonation treating the three exactly the same.

Leviticus, Chapter Twenty, Verse Thirteen. If a man lies with a man as with a woman, both of them have committed an abomination; they shall be put to death.

Romans Chapter One, Verses Twenty-Six through Twenty-Seven and Verse Thirty-Two. Their women exchanged natural intercourse for unnatural, and in the same way also the men, giving up natural intercourse with women, were consumed with passion for one another. They know God's decree, that those who practice such things deserve to die.

Galatians Chapter Three, Verses Twenty-Seven through Twenty-Eight. There is neither Jew nor Gentile, neither slave nor free, nor is there male and female, for you are all one in Christ Jesus.

Anyone interested in what Jesus had to say about same-sex relations could pore through the four gospels forever and find not a word. Jesus thought other issues much more important, like what was Stephen Pentheny going to do about Harriet Pringle.

During the service Monkey Brain behaved himself. Qiao-Yun released my hand. Diagonally across the aisle, I saw Harriet. The kids from Sunday school streamed in. I looked around for Rachel and couldn't find her. Two little girls took the open space between Harriet and their parents. That family and maybe the people in the pew in front and the pew behind might have been the only persons who initiated the peace with Harriet. I eased myself back from Qiao-Yun and stood in the center aisle.

It was just a matter of putting one foot in front of the other four or five times and sticking my hand out.

"Peace, Harriet."

She responded with a gripless hand and a muffled word, her eyes someplace else.

After Jo finished the second reading, I asked Diane to introduce Bill Forsythe. He sat next to Jen. Diane asked him to stand up. She explained that Bill and Jen and their daughter Becky were new members of St. Joseph's parish. She said she encouraged him to seek this ministry because he was an experienced architect who understood the maintenance problems of a building the size and age of St. Joseph's. Diane asked Bill to say a few words.

"I thank the vestry for their consideration," Bill said. "If I am appointed, you will get my best efforts. But as you know, I'll have very big shoes to fill."

I asked for a motion and spied on Harriet one last time. Her frame remained stock-still, her face lowered. I took a bite from the bagel Qiao-Yun gave me.

Nick Bellini's chair squeaked as he leaned forward. "I move we appoint Bill Forsythe to fill the remainder of the junior warden's term."

I waited while Irene jotted Nick's motion in her notebook before I asked for a second. A chorus of voices answered. Irene looked up from her notebook.

"Sounded like Fred said it first," I said.

Irene whispered as she wrote, "Seconded by Fred Divol."

I asked for discussion. There was none. I called the vote. Another chorus answered "Aye." No one voted in the negative. No one abstained. Harriet and Rachel didn't vote.

Applause broke out for the second time today.

Diane heard the first after her sermon. It came in gradual but escalating sputters, the kind of applause that grows once the reticent realize they can't do a one-handed clap. It got louder and continued, the volume swelling and piling into a clamorous ovation. The choir stood up, Olivia the first to rise. I looked to the congregation. Perhaps some people stayed seated, and maybe a few regretted they didn't bolt for the door with the others when Diane started her sermon. I couldn't tell. Too many of St. Joseph's faithful were on their feet.

I invited Bill to the vestry table.

"Our next agenda item regards the music director. I'm sure everyone noticed we had a different organist this morning. His name is Nathan Empson. He was here yesterday for Jerry's funeral. Nate joined us because of developments this week."

Ten minutes before the service, when I invited Diane to lunch with Qiao-Yun and me, we were huddled in the sacristy while two Altar Guild women scurried in and out collecting everything needed to set up Communion.

"How do you want to handle Bill's and Nate's appointments?" Diane asked.

"I'll set 'em up, you do the rest."

We ad libbed through Bill's because it was easy. The vestry was appointing someone to a job no one else wanted. This next one boded difficulties. Janice had been music director for a long time. My "developments this week" sounded better than saying Janice ran out on us and the new junior warden slipped his brother-in-law in her place.

"The rector will explain the details," I said.

Diane began slowly. "I doubt everyone here has heard of Janice's sudden decision to resign as music director effective immediately."

I expected gasps. There were none.

Diane continued. "I have only Janice's telephone call to me but presume there will be a letter coming soon."

A voice I hadn't heard since Wednesday's vestry meeting stepped on Diane's last syllable. "It was mailed yesterday."

Diane's face turned to the speaker. "Thank you, Rachel. That's very reassuring."

The rector didn't explain why Janice quit, and no one asked. She stuck to the essentials: Janice is gone and needs to be replaced. "At their next meeting the vestry will see Janice's letter and will vote to formally accept her decision with deep regret, I'm sure."

Rachel descended back into the semi-catatonic state she shared with Harriet. I looked over at Olivia who, like me, stayed deadpan.

Diane stated we didn't have to take any action concerning Janice today. "However, we are fortunate that Nate Empson has agreed to continue indefinitely as interim music director."

According to Diane the vestry had a few upcoming votes concerning the music program. Each would come in June. We had to accept Janice's resignation, and we had to post the job opening and determine how the applicants should be screened. When the Music Committee had completed the job specs, we could officially adopt and fold them into the search process. Neither today nor later did the vestry have to appoint Nate. The rector could do that on a week-to-week basis or set a designated period. Nate, of course, was free to apply for the permanent position. Diane asked for questions.

Somewhere on Route 3 Nate was driving to an afternoon gig in Cambridge. Apparently his hasty departure after the service had kindled fears he might never return. Over the last two days Nate had created quite a following, Charlie Prendergast among them.

"I have no question," he said, "but I strongly recommend the rector hire Mr. Empson to be the long-term substitute until the regular position is filled. She should offer an increase from the usual substitute's stipend, which is quite lower than Janice's salary. We can ratify the agreement at the June meeting."

Irene scribbled away. I asked if there were any objections to Charlie's preference, a question answered with a long string of compliments for Nate's work over the past two days, and I let it all go on. Fred said, "The choir sounded wonderful." It was true, and nothing like it had been spoken in a very long time. Diane said she would gladly act on Charlie's suggestion.

I had one more agenda item.

"Before we move on to the reason I think most of you have come today, I reserve the chairman's right not to recognize any speaker other than the rector and vestry members."

This was a day of easy faces to read. Fred approved. All the others did as well, except Harriet and Rachel who looked like they had given up approving of anything for the rest of their lives.

"The primary purpose of this special meeting has been met. We have appointed a junior warden. As to the rector's recent letter, any parishioner wishing to voice his or her opinions to me may do so, and I will relay them to the vestry. I will be in the conference room Wednesday night from seven to nine, this Saturday afternoon from one to three, and a week from today during the coffee hour. Any vestry members who would like to accompany me are welcome."

This idea came to me after Friday's lunch with Fred and Bill. I didn't want the likes of a public forum. The parish had one annual meeting a year. An emergency might demand a second, but this situation didn't apply.

"As always parish members may call me or anyone else on the vestry at any time. And the rector, as she wrote in her letter, will meet with persons about this or any other issue."

All that remained was to let Harriet and Rachel say what they wanted.

Harriet heard her defeat in Diane's sermon and the applause that followed. She heard more after two acolytes, a fourteen-year old girl and a younger boy whose red robe scuffed the floor, brought the collection plates to the awaiting gray-haired couple at the foot of the chancel's steps. Nate gestured for the choir to stand. He played an opening refrain to *Amazing Grace*. While the congregation dropped envelopes into the passing plates, they read along with the choir's singing. That all changed with the fifth verse and the two-hundred additional voices:

When we've been there ten thousand years, bright shining as the sun,

Cloudy Hands

We've no less days to sing God's praise than when we've first begun.

Never before had I heard a St. Joseph's congregation sing so loud.

Fred closed his folder of papers. On each was printed a paragraph from the Constitution and Canons of the Episcopal Church. It says a rector can't resign without the approval of a majority of the vestry, nor can a rector be removed by the vestry against the rector's will unless a set of proceedings are followed at the diocesan level including mediation and consultation with the parties and possibly a trial if there are charges of misconduct. The bishop makes the final decision.

Harriet never had a prayer. I invited her to speak and said Rachel's turn came next. The two peered at each other until Harriet spoke.

"I don't think it's advisable for me to say anything at this time."

Rachel said she only wanted what was best for St. Joseph's.

CHAPTER 28

I bounded down Main Street towards Fernando's Hacienda having parked my car two blocks away. Minutes earlier I dropped off Qiao-Yun and Anita. They waited outside Fernando's in the early afternoon sun while heavy weekend traffic plodded by. A parking spot in front of the restaurant opened when an SUV drove off. A red hatchback zipped into the open space. I recognized it. Diane was having a very good day.

When the vestry meeting ended, most people took their time leaving the parish hall. Harriet and Rachel fled. The gathering around Diane kept her from my view. Two angels trotted up to me. One said I did a great job. The other said I needn't worry and this was over.

Vestry members swarmed Bill and took turns pumping his hand. I tapped Olivia's shoulder. She followed me to the vacant serving counter.

"Katelyn knows Cheryl Sinclair. She called her and found out Jerry's trip was about protecting St. Joseph's."

Olivia's eyes filled up.

"And Cheryl thinks Harriet is a nut case."

Olivia brushed her cheek. "She's not the only one."

"Did you catch what Harriet said when she declined my offer to speak?"

"Something about what wasn't advisable."

"So who's advising her to shut up? Cheryl?"

Olivia had the best answer. "Just about every parishioner at St. Joseph's. And no one's missing Janice, not after what Nate has done."

Even though Harriet and Rachel and the grumpy eight didn't know it, Diane's good day was theirs too. Olivia said we had to help them understand. She was right, of course. Dwayne and his friend approached us. Dwayne introduced him as Tom and said an invitation was coming. They spoke as though I knew theirs was one of the two marriages Diane would bless. I didn't say otherwise. They thought the senior warden knew everything. Anita wheeled herself through the crowd. I invited her to Fernando's with Diane, Qiao-Yun, and me. Anita said she loved Tex-Mex, the spicier the better.

Before we left St. Joseph's, I called Luke. The Mini had just crossed the RFK. LaGuardia was coming up fast. Luke put his phone on speaker, and my family learned what happened. They cheered.

Afterwards Charlie helped me fold up Anita's wheelchair and push it into the VW's trunk.

The short drive to Fernando's passed Linnehan's and North Street. I often pass such places. Everyone must. Within the past ten months two persons I deeply loved died. A lot of other people I loved didn't. You can't tally a score. Don't try. I've been blessed with the legacies Cara and Jerry gave me. Those who live continue to bless me. Before the year ended, I moved to another house in Scrooby, the town where I wrote about George Herbert and still feel heaven-sent energy gently falling on the earth. All it needs is slow breathing and graceful discipline to make it work.

A man about my age exiting Fernando's held the door for us. Diane guided Anita's chair. Qiao-Yun and I were right behind them.

Qiao-Yun's warm hand took mine. "You must be hungry," she said.

I squeezed her palm. "*Dwayluh.*"

ABOUT THE AUTHOR

Peter Trenouth is a retired high school English teacher. He lives in Plymouth, Massachusetts, where he writes and occasionally participates in local theater productions as an actor and director. He also studies and teaches Tai Chi with his wife, Fang-Chih Lee.

CPSIA information can be obtained
at www.ICGtesting.com
Printed in the USA
LVOW04s1411260716

497713LV00044B/912/P